The Bodies at Westgrave Hall

Nick Louth is a best-selling thriller writer and an award-winning financial journalist. A 1979 graduate of the London School of Economics, he went on to become a Reuters foreign correspondent in 1987. He was for many years a *Financial Times* columnist, and a regular contributor to many other financial titles in print and online. *The Bodies at Westgrave Hall* is his seventh book in the DCI Gillard crime series, and his ninth thriller overall. Nick Louth is married and lives in Lincolnshire.

Also by Nick Louth

Trapped
Heartbreaker

DCI Craig Gillard Crime Thrillers

The Body in the Marsh
The Body on the Shore
The Body in the Mist
The Body in the Snow
The Body Under the Bridge
The Body on the Island
The Bodies at Westgrave Hall

NICK LOUTH

THE BODIES AT WESTGRAVE HALL

CANELOCRIME

First published in the United Kingdom in 2021 by

Canelo
31 Helen Road
Oxford OX2 0DF
United Kingdom

A CIP catalogue record for this book is available from the British Library.

Print ISBN 978 1 80032 324 7
Ebook ISBN 978 1 80032 170 0

Look for more great books at www.canelo.co

Printed and bound in Great Britain by Clays Ltd, Elcograf S.p.A.

For Louise, as always

Chapter One

2018, Kazakhstan, Central Asia

Russian Air Force Colonel Lev Rossivsky checked the radar screen, picked up his largest binoculars and made his way up to the roof of the control tower of Kuznetsov Air Base. It was only a single flight of stairs and led out onto a rough concrete roof. The wind was blowing from the east again, whipping up a fine sand from the endless miles of parched scrubland and leaving a rose-tinted haze that masked the distant sparkle of Lake Balkhash, eighty miles to the south. As he put the Carl Zeiss Jena lenses to his eyes, he didn't even glance at the rusting hulks of obsolete helicopters or the remains of the 1950s MiG 15 jet fighter that littered the base. He was looking for something that even in all his thirty-year air force experience he had never seen. The base was not much used since the fall of communism, but still had one great asset that came into play from time to time. It had the longest runway in Kazakhstan. Today, it might well need every inch of it.

Rossivsky peered south-west, looking high in the sky for the glint of sun on aluminium. Then he saw it, a bright silver dot. He watched the approach as the aircraft grew and grew, gradually getting lower, until he could make out the distinctive twin tail-fins and hear the approaching roar of the six giant jet engines. Sixteen pairs of landing wheels appeared underneath the giant jet's fuselage and nose. The Antonov An-225 Mriya, the world's largest cargo aircraft, 640 tonnes fully loaded, was coming in to land. With a puff of dust, and the scream of reverse thrust, the Antonov touched down, and rumbled past him right the way to the end of the runway. Bigger than a jumbo jet, the An-225 was originally designed to deliver the Buran spaceplane to the Baikonur launch site nearly 1,000 miles west, when that now-obsolete project was on the frontiers of space science.

Its cargo today was nothing to do with cutting-edge technology, Indeed, it was not a product of human ingenuity at all.

It far predated that.

Rossivsky turned his attention to the concrete apron. An olive-green articulated low-loader with military markings growled into life. Plumes of filthy diesel smoke rose from the MAZ-239 as it began to inch forward. The transporter, designed to carry six forty-tonne T72 main battle tanks, was being tested by an even heavier load. On its back, and in places wider than the vehicle itself, was a 185-foot-long object, roughly the shape of a giant dagger, wrapped in a silver tarpaulin. He had not seen beneath that covering, for all of the weeks of organisation that had been required to bring it here from the mine of Karabulak, 400 miles to the north-east.

The low-loader approached the Antonov, whose rear tail ramp had now been lowered. Four large mobile cranes were on hand to manoeuvre the object gently from the low-loader onto two specially-made motorised cradles, self-propelled undercarriages each capable of dealing with a 200-tonne weight. Once the object was safely stowed on the cradles, engineers in hard hats used handheld remote controls to drive the irregularly-shaped silver-sheeted object inch by inch into the belly of the aircraft. It took an hour to stow it.

The project was the brainchild of a reclusive British-based billionaire, a man who had the money to do anything he wanted.

Oxfordshire, UK

RAF Brize Norton was used to some unusual flights, but the arrival an hour before dawn of the An-225, the first ever British landing by this unique aircraft, created quite a stir. A sizeable media presence was there to see the unloading onto the specially-made twenty-two axle Nooteboom low-loader and the huge convoy of cranes and marshalling vehicles which were to accompany it on its hundred-mile journey via the M40, M25 and A3. Although about the same length as a wind turbine tower, the cargo was much heavier. The convoy travelled at ten miles an hour, accompanied by a five-mile tailback of frustrated drivers, until it finally left the A3 and headed into the Surrey countryside. The smaller roads to its final destination had been closed off in advance by arrangement with the police. The UK traffic management plan alone had cost half a million pounds, one of the smaller overheads of the exercise.

Onlookers lined the lanes as the lorry crawled the last three miles to Westgrave Hall. There, waiting for it, were three giant eight-wheeled cranes, their jibs already arching into the sky over a half-completed building. Teams of high-vis-jacketed construction workers, helmeted in orange, oversaw the cargo's final movement. It was a 300-yard lift from the road and into the building. That was not too far in general construction terms, but for the 240-tonne relic within, it was a monumental piece of travel. Arrangements took much of the day, and it was almost five in the afternoon when the enormous silver-jacketed cargo was finally lifted from the low-loader, and manoeuvred across into the building that had been designed to receive it.

A lad on a bicycle stopped to watch, amazed at the hundreds of people who had gathered in this normally quiet rural lane. He pointed at the now-suspended object, its huge shadow falling across the crowd in the late afternoon sunshine. 'What's in that thing?' he asked no one in particular.

'Haven't you read the papers, Steven?' replied Mary Hill, the verger of St Michael All Saints' parish church. 'It's a giant fossil, 170 million years old.'

'Is it a T-Rex?'

'No. It's a fish-eating plesiosaur, even bigger than a Tyrannosaurus.'

'Cool!'

Mrs Hill's husband Colin leaned towards the boy. 'It is, apparently, the largest one ever found. It used to swim in shallow tropical seas in what is now Central Asia.'

'Why is it coming here?' Steven replied, scratching his ear.

'You'd better ask the Russian chap who owns West-grave Hall,' Colin replied.

–

For the previous six months, a continuous stream of construction traffic had poured into the grounds of West-grave Hall. Quarry trucks rattled and roared down the

4

narrow lane, churning up the manicured grass verges, carving ruts through the carefully cultivated roadside wildflowers, spreading mud and drowning out the bird-song. Late into the night the growl of diesel engines and reversing beeps could be heard, only stopping for a few hours before beginning again at seven in the morning. Pile-driving seemed to begin at the crack of dawn, each impact a mini earthquake which rattled crockery throughout the village. Arc lights on crane jibs lit up the night sky, in mockery of the moon, confusing the birds who began singing into the small hours. On occasion the rhythmic thudding of a helicopter heralded the arrival of the estate's new owner. The villagers, curious or furious and sometimes both, regularly congregated on the rocky outcrop at the back of the churchyard, with sandwiches, scones and thermos flasks of coffee supplied by the Women's Institute, to peer across the road and over the Westgrave estate's high stone walls. It was the best vantage point in the village to give a view into what was happening. There on Buckridge Mount, where an Iron Age fort once stood, a concrete and glass building had taken shape, ready for the precious cargo from Kazakhstan. The Volkov Library was a two-storey white concrete edifice with a glass frontage more than a hundred yards long, fronted with tinted glass panels, each as big as a badminton court.

Then, in the days after the fossil's arrival, and the installation of the library roof, the noise began to diminish. The inhabitants of Steeple Risby began to look at the finer details of the transformation of the Westgrave Hall estate.

'Did you look at the final planning document, Colin?' asked Nigel Welland, chairman of the local parish council. He stood in the churchyard with Colin Hill watching workmen fixing the library's slightly pitched steel roof. Nigel was resting a hand on the lichened headstone of Edwina Fortescue (1806–59), a distant relative on his mother's side, who had gone off to become a lady in waiting in the court of Queen Victoria.

'Yes. Ignored all the tree protection orders, the archaeological excavation plan, objections from the water company, the caveats from highways who said this road was not big enough. Talked about benefits to the community, education and investment. Mary is absolutely incandescent.'

To Colin Hill, retired insurance underwriter and chairman of the local antiquarian society, living in Steeple Risby had shifted from being a retirement dream to a living nightmare. The parish council, of which he was secretary, had been molten at its impotence, having objected at every stage to the planning application, as had the district council. The Westgrave Hall redevelopment plan, prepared by a top City legal firm and award-winning architects a year ago, was rejected locally, but an immediate appeal went up to the national planning inspectorate. Before they had a chance to consider it, the minister called it in and personally approved it.

'Bloody oligarch must have greased some palms,' Welland said. 'Payment to party funds no doubt.'

Colin nodded. 'Money talks.' He knew that because he had money himself, quite a sizeable sum from working a lifetime in the City, and he reckoned he had some influence too from the friends he still had there. But it didn't take long before he realised that his resources were as nothing compared with the stranger who had arrived from Russia, a man who was destined to change his life for ever.

Chapter Two

It was more than a year after the arrival of the fossil in June that the machinery finally fell silent. The work was completed, and Colin and Mary Hill received an invitation to go up to Westgrave Hall for the opening of the Volkov Library, where they would be able to see the fossil. Mary had shown her husband the expensive envelope and thick golden card.

'I'm not going to go,' she said. 'They mess up the village, make our lives a misery and then they think they can just snap their fingers and bring us up to the hall when it suits them.' She folded her arms.

But Colin was tempted. The card described a guided tour of the new library and an explanation of the fossil from the renowned TV palaeontologist Dr Sophie Cawkwell. The press would be there too.

'Come on, Mary, don't be obstinate. If we get to speak to him, maybe we can get the footpath reopened.' He left unsaid his desire to see Dr Cawkwell, whose spectacular figure and penchant for cut-off shorts and tight T-shirts always guaranteed Channel 4 a good audience from middle-aged men, whether they liked fossils or not. They enjoyed seeing her, in cowboy hat and hiking boots, crouching in some desert in Mongolia or South Dakota, tapping away at a piece of limestone or sandstone. At least he could say hand-on-heart he was genuinely interested in what she was talking about.

Colin recalled the very first day that Alexander Volkov arrived in the village, back in August 2016. Colin was mowing the lawn at the front of the churchyard, when a shiny black Mercedes stopped and from the rear door emerged an enormous black-bearded man, wearing a sports jacket and jeans. He must have been six foot four, and he was grinning as he bounded across to the low stone wall which encircled the parish church. Colin stopped the mower and walked through the lychgate, not wanting the stranger to vault the wall and crush his carefully nurtured delphiniums. Hill prepared to offer directions, something he often did to motorists confused by the profusion of back lanes around the village.

'My name is Alexander Volkov, and I am the new owner of Westgrave Hall,' the man said in a thick accent, taking one of Colin's gardening-gloved hands in both of his. Colin took a step back, thinking the visitor was going to give him a bear hug, but discovered he was merely happy to occupy his personal space.

Colin introduced himself. 'Nice to meet you. I thought the estate was being left to the National Trust.' Both he and Mary had been lobbying for the Westgrave family to pass the estate to Britain's most loved custodian of things grand and ancient. Lady Margaret had apparently indicated on her deathbed that it was her desire, or so local gossip went. However, the four Westgrave children, not one of them under seventy, had seemingly chosen the glitter of money over a burnished posterity.

'No, I have bought it from the family. But I will be a good neighbour to all of you in Steeple Risby.' It was clear he had practised pronouncing the name of the obscure village. 'You must come to my home, soon. I have Georgian champagne and the best Altai mountain vodka, filtered through birch charcoal. It is wonderful!' With that, he bounded back to his car.

Over the next two years, the Hills had watched in consternation as Westgrave Hall was first encased in scaffolding and then shrouded in tarpaulins. No one in Steeple Risby had in fact been invited up to the house, and dog walkers using the three public footpaths which crossed the parkland found that the stiles had been blocked off with ugly metal fences and wrapped in razor wire. The parish council complained, to little effect.

Enquiries to the local county council eventually led to enforcement action, but the rights-of-way officer and besuited lawyer armed with a court order were no match for the shaven-headed heavy with a snarling guard dog leashed in each hand. The police declined to intervene, calling it a civil matter.

Mary Hill, now in her seventies, had been responsible for the maintenance of the Westgrave family chapel and necropolis at the hall, but since the arrival of the Russians had found her services no longer required. Worse still, she was unable to visit the grave of her first husband, William, who was buried on chapel grounds. The locks on the site gates had been changed, and barbed wire had been looped along the top of the parkland railings. This she considered to be ridiculous and unsightly. The cattle which grazed the parkland were still there, and the tenant farmer continued to look after the land, but the house itself was now what she termed occupied land.

Originally the seat of Lord Henry Algernon Westgrave, whose beloved only son died in the infamous Charge of the Light Brigade in Crimea in 1854, Westgrave had a rich history, of which Mary was proud to be a custodian. The family chapel recorded the Westgraves' role as defenders of the faith right back to the Siege of Acre in 1190. The honourable aristocrat, a cousin of Lord Palmerston, would have been appalled had he known that his ancestral home was now owned by the descendant of his Crimean enemies. That a Russian, an upstart social climber from what Mary termed a family of Siberian convicts, and who had come into his billions only twenty years ago, was now occupying the fifty-two-bedroom Palladian stately home would send a shiver down his spine.

–

The open day for the Volkov Library turned out to be a great success. Colin Hill had finally persuaded his wife to come with him, though it was clear from her choice of a scruffy black cardigan and fusty beige skirt from the Oxfam shop that she was determined a) not to enjoy herself, and b) to make a point. They were there together with a few members of the parish and district councils. There were also a great many journalists, not only from local papers but the nationals too.

And there was plenty to see.

Entering via double glass doors, the visitors looked up to see a cavernous library building constructed around the 240-tonne limestone slab. The rock was 185 feet long, 22 feet wide at its widest and 8 feet deep, suspended within an atrium on gigantic iron chains, each link the size of a tea-tray. These carefully restored anchor chains were from the German battleship *Tirpitz*, sunk in 1944 in a Norwegian fjord, and were suspended from a series of fifteen giant cedar beams which traversed the ceiling. Exposed granite walls on both the ground floor and the balconied mezzanine above were interspersed with glass-fronted bookcases filled with leather-bound volumes titled in Russian.

It was possible to walk right under the colossal stone and see many of the smaller ammonites and brachiopods caught within it, illuminated by carefully positioned spotlights on the ground floor. At this lowest point, a steel keel had been screwed in from end to end, which prevented the rock from falling apart when it was being moved. But it was only by ascending to the gallery and looking down across the atrium that it was possible to see the plesiosaur in all its serpentine glory, partially exposed on the upper surface of the rock. The creature's beautifully delicate neck was stretched out, as were the two desk-sized front flippers. The ribs and vertebrae were in beautiful condition, apparently undisturbed in the 170 million years since its death. Moving along the length of the fossil, after the ribs diminished and the tail bones tapered off, there were ten yards of featureless rock before the most moving sight of all. A baby plesiosaur, just six feet long, a perfect miniature version of its parent, behind which it had been swimming when they both met their untimely end.

Colin Hill was almost moved to tears by it, as he made his way along the balcony to join the crowd now gathered there for the presentation. Dr Sophie Cawkwell, elegant in a navy trouser suit, held centre stage as she described the life and times of these extraordinary creatures.

'What you see in front of you is the most perfect example of a plesiosaur fossil ever discovered. She was found, and I'm insisting on she even though we're not very good at sexing marine dinosaurs, in an opencast copper mine in the centre of Kazakhstan. The addition of the find of a juvenile, presumably her offspring, makes this a one-in-a-billion discovery. Those who are *au fait* with ancient sea creatures, and there are a few of my academic friends in the audience, will recognise the similarity to the giant southern-hemisphere elasmosaurus of the late Cretaceous. However, the extreme length of the neck and tail in this case marks them out as taxonomically distinct, and their discovery in a mid-Jurassic sediment reaffirms that.

'What I'd like you to imagine is Lebyodoushka swimming in the shallow warm seas of that period, hunting sizeable fish, and teaching her youngster the tricks of the trade. Those who would like to see more detail about how we found and moved this wonderful creature can watch my documentary, which is due to be shown on National Geographic TV in the middle of next year.'

It was only at that moment that Colin Hill spotted Alexander Volkov, who had just arrived at the other side of the gallery with an entourage of friends, and who was shaking hands with officials. Cawkwell chose that moment to turn to Volkov, microphone in hand, and say: 'I'm delighted to have been involved in this extraordinary project from the earliest stages. It is thanks to the generosity and foresight of my friend, Sasha Volkov, that we are able to display this magnificent creature in a setting that does full justice to it.'

There was a round of applause as she handed over to Volkov to continue.

The Russian, seeming slightly nervous, gave a prepared speech. In it he gave halting thanks in English to all those who were there, before switching to Russian for what seemed like a more poised and polished performance, judging by the cheers and applause it generated from the

Russians present. At this point, waiters in evening dress made their way amongst the throng handing out blinis, caviar, and shot glasses of vodka. There were then at least half a dozen toasts, of which the first was to peace and the last to Lebyodoushka, the Jurassic swan.

Mary gave Colin her shots to drink and he was soon enjoying himself, standing opposite a slender almond-eyed Russian, a glamorous forty-or-so, who seemed to have no difficulty downing the hard liquor. 'Are you enjoying our *zakuski*?' she asked him, referring to the nibbles.

'I am indeed.'

The woman, who had introduced herself as Natasha, probed him expertly about the village antiquarian society, and laughed at even his lamest jokes, at one point resting her delicate hand on his arm. 'What English wit,' she said. 'I love it.'

He asked her what she did, and she answered: 'I run a concierge firm.'

'What exactly is that?'

'When the wealthy have a dream, I make it come true.' Seeing the open-mouthed look on Colin's face, she added: 'It's a management company really. We own an art auctioneer, a florist, we own a part-share in a luxury car dealership. We arrange education for the children, parties, shopping, travel. Anything really. I once helicoptered in a champagne picnic for six to a remote Patagonian glacier at four hours' notice when one of my clients decided to spend an extra day in the mountains.'

'Astonishing.'

'Yes, people like my dear friend Sasha are not like the rest of us.' She indicated Volkov with a gesture of her glass. 'Four years ago, he bought a five-hundred-hectare estate with its own castle and watermill just half an hour's drive from Florence. It was at the time the most expensive property in Italy. To my knowledge, he has never actually visited it, although it is kept fully stocked with the finest foods and fresh flowers in case he decides to.'

'Are you responsible for this planning application?' Colin asked, indicating with his glass the building around them.

'Partly. Obviously, I farmed it out to experts.' She waved her elegant fingers, as if spreading confetti. Colin imagined that she was quite adept at greasing political palms too. He wasn't fooled by the humble bragging. *They're not like the rest of us.* He had finally recognised her. Lady Fein. He had seen photographs of her and her ennobled husband David hobnobbing with the wealthy. She was definitely one of them, despite her husband having made much of being brought up the son of a hospital porter.

They were interrupted by a couple of other guests, who steered Natasha Fein away.

After half an hour of socialising, the guests were led down the stairs to the ground floor where trestle tables had been decked with an enormous spread of Russian food, laid out on white linen tablecloths in the shadow of the creature. Georgian champagne flowed freely, and Colin had more than a few glasses. As Mary was nowhere to be seen, he made a beeline for Sophie Cawkwell. She was standing with Volkov and a male reporter from *The Times* who was interviewing him, but when Colin asked her about who found the fossil, she turned to him and smiled.

'It was the foreman at the number six pit. I only heard about it a few weeks later when I got a call from Sasha's representative in London. They were kind enough to pay my expenses to fly straight out there so I could examine it. I have to tell you, the mine at Karabulak is an extraordinary place. One of the largest opencast mines in the world, two thousand feet deep at its lowest point, nine miles wide at the rim, and more than a thousand miles from the nearest sizeable town.'

'It's such a huge piece of rock,' Colin said.

'Yes. It was Sasha's decision not to break the limestone which connected the mother to its baby. It was a philosophical as much as a sentimental decision not to sever that sedimentary umbilical, but of course added massively to the expense. Forget the pyramids or Stonehenge, this is by a factor of at least three the longest single piece of rock ever moved by man, and the heaviest object ever moved by air.'

'Fantastic,' Colin said, stealing a glance down her cleavage.

'Sasha was extraordinarily generous in funding the careful excavation required, and all of the enormous overheads in creating specialised transporters. But for him this will be a tremendous legacy.' At this point Colin noticed her hand reach across and squeeze Volkov's. It gave him a stab of envy.

Finally, when the party had thinned out, Ms Cawkwell made her excuses. Colin, dizzy with lust, watched her departure by chauffeur-driven car. Volkov was nowhere to be seen. Colin was left with just a few of the officials, security men and waiters clearing up. He'd had more than enough to drink and was just thinking about going home when Lady Fein reappeared, her almond eyes wreathed in smiles. He tried to recall her name. Nadine? Natalya? Natasha!

'Mr Hill, I hope you can now see what it is we're trying to achieve here?'

He nodded, not quite trusting himself to pronounce a non-slurred sentence. 'Rather splendid, actually.'

'We are aware of a little friction with some of you at the parish council, and hope that we can smooth things over. We are going to get the footpath diverted, right away from the hall, as you may have heard. This is essential for the security for Mr Volkov.'

'Well,' Colin said. 'I'm not sure…'

'Anyway, let's not discuss such serious matters for now.' She gestured to a waiter who was hovering nearby. 'You've not yet had your guest bag, I see.' The waiter came over and passed across a ruby-red cloth bag, edged in golden thread. Inside it were two exquisitely wrapped boxes, and what looked like a half bottle of Georgian spirits.

'Oh, that's extremely kind,' Colin said.

'Everybody has had one,' said Natasha. 'It's a bit of a random assortment, I'm afraid, but you shall probably find something in there you like.'

Colin thanked her and let her steer him towards the exit. He followed the footway, crossed the slender white stone bridge over the moat back towards the main gardens of Westgrave Hall, then followed the thoughtfully set carriage lamps, whose soft caramel glow guided him down the track which converged with the main drive.

I'm stinking drunk was his only coherent thought as he staggered down the path. *Mary is going to kill me. Best take a few minutes to sober up.* He stopped for a moment at a bench, and sat on the damp wood, sucking in the chill air and watching his breath plume into the night sky. He peered into the bag and pulled out one of the small parcels. Clumsily, he undid it. Handmade chocolates. He slid off the sleeve and popped one into his mouth. Delicious. He then worked at the next package, which was a similar size and weight. Removing the paper, he saw a satin covered jewellery-type box marked Vacheron Constantin. He lifted the lid and saw an exquisite wristwatch.

'Bloody hell,' he whispered to himself, lifting up the timepiece and inspecting it. Carefully he took off his own cheap Seiko and slipped the heavy watch onto his wrist, where it glinted beautifully. As he sauntered home, he couldn't help wondering how much this gift had cost, and what on earth his host was doing handing them out to all his guests.

–

Mary Hill awoke at five, as usual, and saw from the closed door across the landing that her husband had slipped into the spare room. He didn't emerge until nearly ten, by which time she was in a simmering rage. The argument over the breakfast table, verbal grenades tossed over the newspapers they both held up, seem to go on and on. The subject was Dr Sophie Cawkwell, and the puppyish looks of longing Colin had bestowed on her.

'For goodness' sake, I don't think she's interested in me.'

'Well, obviously she's not. But that's not the point. You shouldn't be advertising that you are interested in *her*.'

'I wasn't.'

'You *were*, Colin. Why don't you show me some respect?'

'Ah yes, my wife, the Oxfam shop catwalk model.'

'There's no need to be nasty.'

'You started it.' He held up the *Telegraph*, as if signalling the conversation was over.

Mary wasn't finished. 'I just don't understand why you stayed there so long. And mooning over that Natasha Fein half the time.'

He lowered the paper and glared at her, between bushy eyebrows and half-moon reading glasses. 'You just told me I was constantly looking at Sophie Cawkwell. Now apparently I wasn't, I was looking at somebody else.'

'Stop splitting hairs, Colin. They're both other women.'

For a few seconds he didn't reply. 'Did they give you a goody bag when you left?' he asked.

'They did, but I gave it straight back, unopened. I could see what they were trying to do.'

'Could you?' he said, reaching out for the colour supplement. His sleeve rode up as he did so and she immediately spotted the chunky new watch.

'What's that?' she asked.

'Oh this?' he said as if noticing it for the first time. 'It's the one the Bermuda underwriters' syndicate gave me when I retired.'

'I don't think I've seen that.' She held out her hand, which meant *give it to me now, I want to take a look.*

'It's not as good as it looks, I'm afraid.' He lifted a slice of toast and marmalade to his mouth and returned to the colour supplement.

–

It was only when Lucy Welland rang Mary that the truth came out. 'Nigel was given an expensive Swiss watch at the oligarch's party, did you hear?'

'No, I didn't,' Mary replied. 'Colin was terribly drunk when he came home last night. He'd got some chocolates and a bottle of firewater. I gave mine back without opening them. I'm not going to be in the pockets of those frightful people.'

'Well, I do agree. But I looked up Nigel's timepiece. Unless I'm being dim, it's worth £15,000.'

'Oh, it can't be. That's silly. Even for them.'

'No, Mary, I Googled it. Exact model number and everything. A Vacheron Constantin. On the quiet, Nigel is as pleased as punch.'

'He should give it back.'

'Well, let's not be too hasty. Don't want to be more Catholic than the Pope, do we?'

'Look, Lucy. We are considering taking legal action against them, it doesn't look too good if we've been accepting gifts, does it? Nigel being chair of the parish council and all.'

'Oh, but Nigel says there's a deal in the offing. Moving the footpath, and so forth.'

'Lucy, we weren't consulted! And what about access to the chapel? We've always had our Christmas service there. And William's grave.'

'Sorry, Mary, I don't know the details. You'd have to ask him.'

Mary said her goodbyes and then slammed the phone down. *So that's where Colin got the bloody watch. I'm not having this*, she thought to herself. *I'm going to stop it. Just because people have money doesn't mean to say they can do exactly what they want.* This was her village, her life and her country.

How dare they.

-

Matters came to a head a few months later when Colin Hill came face-to-face with Volkov's son Oleg. On a cold

19

morning early in December, Colin had been easing his aged Peugeot around the narrow lanes of Steeple Risby, when an enormous black Humvee tore round the corner at speed, and almost crashed into him. The driver was an Asian-looking young man in a white jacket, with a heavy gold chain around his neck. Colin could see angry words spilling from his face, but couldn't hear them thanks to the heavy rap music booming out of the vehicle. Having right of way, Colin gestured that the Humvee should reverse just a few yards to a passing place. Instead, a sunglassed giant in a black jacket and rollneck sweater emerged from the passenger side and shouted at him in American-accented English. He then started banging his hands on the bonnet of Colin's car. Intimidated but resolute, the retired insurance underwriter emerged from the car to remonstrate. In five seconds, he found himself face down over the front of his own vehicle, his arm pressed painfully up his back while he was frisked.

'This is outrageous behaviour,' he said. 'I shall be calling the police.'

'Call the Queen if you like, but just get out of the fucking way,' the big man said. Colin, his face held side-ways on the bonnet of the car, could see a small tattoo on the inside of his assailant's wrist. A dagger, entwined with the initials M.J.D.

Finally persuaded, Colin reluctantly reversed his Peugeot a hundred yards to another passing place to allow the larger vehicle to pass. He rang the police as soon as he returned home in the evening. A young and pretty constable named Zoe Butterfield came to see him the next day.

'I'm afraid their version of events is rather different,' she said. 'I telephoned the security manager at the house, and he said the driver of the car insists that it was in fact you that got out and banged on the bonnet of the other vehicle, and that it was you shouting and swearing.'

'That's absolutely preposterous,' Colin said. 'Utter nonsense. This simply cannot be allowed to continue.'

Having established that Colin Hill had neither taken photographs nor was in possession of a dashcam, PC Butterfield told him that there was no proof of what had happened.

'What about the tattoo I saw? Dagger plus initials.'

'Yes, I know, we're not in doubt who we're dealing with, but it doesn't prove he did what you say. Look, I know you must be very frustrated at this. I will go round and have a word with the driver. That usually does the trick.'

As soon as Colin had closed the door on the officer, Mary emerged from the kitchen.

'So, what are they going to do about it?'

'Nothing. She's going to go up and have a word with them.'

Mary folded her arms. 'Well, I'm sure that's going to have them quaking in their boots. Colin, why didn't you take a tougher line, and insist that they are prosecuted? You were assaulted after all.'

'I know, I was there. The police just won't do anything.'

'What about the tattoo?' she asked.

'Doesn't prove a thing, apparently.'

'Colin, why don't you have any backbone?'

Her husband walked away into the lounge and slammed the door.

Mary thought about her first husband, as she always did at times like this. Poor Will. Almost forty years dead. *If only he was with me now. He'd know exactly what to do.*

PC Zoe Butterfield drove her patrol car up the rear service road of Westgrave Hall and parked it in a prime place by the summer house, amongst a line of high-end four-by-fours, between the Humvee in question, and a brand-new top-of-the-range Bentley. She walked around and inspected the Hummer, whose military origins were obvious. When Colin Hill had first reported the incident, she had checked the registration plate he had given her. The vehicle was registered in Ukraine, of all places, but had incurred sixteen UK traffic and parking violations in the last four months alone, mainly in the central London congestion zone. Not one had been paid. That was at least something that could be put right. She made a mental note to check later whether a foreign-registered vehicle could be towed away from private property.

She was surprised by a noise behind her and turned to see a beefy young man emerging from the building.

'Hey, what the fuck you doing?' The young man shouted at her. The accent was American mixed with something else, and he was in absurdly tight shorts and a T-shirt which barely contained his bodybuilder limbs. He had several chunky gold chains around his neck and numerous rings.

'I'm a police officer, and you will not take that tone with me,' she said.

'That's my car,' he said, advancing until he was firmly in her personal space, arms folded, showing the enormous bulging biceps.

'Sir, I advise you to stay back.' Her hand strayed to her Taser.

Another man appeared on the steps from the main hall. In his mid-thirties, he was solidly built, but shorter and

22

with a neat goatee beard and tinted spectacles. 'Oleg, she is a cop,' he said.

Oleg, clearly unimpressed, released a verbal volley in Russian or a similar language, illustrated with copious hand movements directed towards the new man, and then to his precious vehicle. The reply was softer and more conciliatory. It was clear who was boss.

The second man turned to Zoe. 'I am Wolf. Are you PC Butter, lady I spoke to on phone?'

'Butterfield, yes.' Zoe put her hand on the Hummer's door handle. The younger man's face contorted into a proprietorial snarl.

'What is your name?' she asked Oleg. He didn't reply.

'His name is Oleg Alexandrovitch Volkov,' Wolf said.

'There are numerous unpaid penalty charge notices related to this vehicle which must be settled before I allow you to remove it. I suggest you give me the keys,' she said, holding out a hand.

'Oleg, give key, don't produce trouble,' Wolf said, then turned to Zoe. 'Come to office. I pay this money now.'

Oleg slapped the keys into Zoe's hands and stalked off, rolling his shoulders and cracking his knuckles. He made his way to a black Mitsubishi Warrior, got in and drove off down the drive at speed.

'I make apologies for him,' Wolf said, as they watched the car roar down the drive. 'Child of cracked home. Never easy, despite all lolly he has.'

'Lolly?' Zoe suppressed a giggle.

'English word for money, yes? In my country we have *Only Fool and Horse* on TV. Very funny. Lovely bubbly.'

Zoe couldn't hold back a grin at the misremembered catchphrase. 'Jubbly,' she said. 'Lovely jubbly.'

Wolf repeated the corrected phrase to himself a couple of times. She followed him into the rear entrance hall of the grand house, where a twenty-foot-tall Christmas tree reached only halfway to the teak-panelled ceiling. Zoe had years ago visited Westgrave Hall with her parents on one of its rare public open days in the height of summer. Her childhood memory was of grandiose roofs, spires, chimneys and a Victorian walled garden. The most pungent recollection was of a huge glass hothouse, within which exotic palms and ferns sweated, in what her mother had termed a jungle. She had dreamt of it for years afterwards.

'A cup of Rosie?' he asked her.

'Yes please,' she said, giggling again. 'Milk, no sugar.'

'Now we go round the Johnny Horner and up the apples and pears,' Wolf said with a wink, as he led her up a grand curving staircase, past a Christmas tree on the landing, and along a corridor hung with Christmas decorations.

'Why have you been learning Cockney rhyming slang?' she asked.

'To fit in. English people don't like Johnny Foreigner, yes? So I think if I speak local twang, I fit better in.'

She grinned at him. 'Taking comedy language off the TV or Internet doesn't make you sound English, but it will make everyone smile.'

'Well, that is good anyway.'

He took her along a passageway, and into a walnut-panelled office, in which there was yet another Christmas tree. There at a computer screen, she guided him through the online process of settling the congestion charge penalties. She watched him type an enormously complex name,

Vakhtang Ashkharmitzvili, then extract a corporate credit card. She turned away while he keyed in the number.

'Is done,' he said finally.

'How do you say your name?' she asked.

He had laughed, and said, 'Vakhtang, it means Wolf, so call me Wolf. That easy one. I am from Georgia, and my family name is...' The sound was as if he was clearing his throat of an annoying fly. 'Yes, is impossible. I always say, registrar of births he get tired typing my name, and so he fall asleep.' He mimed his head crashing forward onto the keys of an imaginary typewriter, a splatter of random letters. He gave PC Butterfield a business card, in Russian on one side, English on the other.

'Mr Hill was very upset about the incident,' she said.

'I understand,' he said, nodding. 'Oleg has hot blood, like mother. And too much lolly too easy.'

'I think we can both agree on that.'

'I will go see Mr Hill to apologise. Saying sorry is important to the English, I have learned this.'

'That would be much appreciated, I'm sure.'

Wolf gave a shrug. 'My job always to run behind horse with shovel. Here, many wild Volkov horse, only one shovel.'

Zoe laughed.

'You have nice English smile, lady constable Butter.'

'Oh, you have a way with words, Mr Wolf.' She was grinning all over her face.

'When you have day off, you want to come for evening in Fox and Hounds in village for a pint of hand-pushed bitter? That is English way, yes?'

'I'm very flattered,' she replied. 'But it wouldn't be appropriate, given that we have official dealings.'

Wolf pressed his hands to his chest. 'My intention honourable, lady Butter. Not shag. Just friendly.'

She snorted helplessly with laughter. 'I have a boyfriend, but thank you.'

As she left, she was grinning from ear to ear.

Chapter Three

It was one a.m. on Christmas morning. The Surrey Police patrol car slid down Westgrave Lane under the glare of a crane-mounted arc light, high in the sky, which seemed to be lighting up half the county.

'Feel like we're the wise men, following the star,' said Constable Paul Thorne, as he squinted into the light and guided the vehicle up the shadowed lane.

'Hope you've brought the frankincense and myrrh, then,' answered PC Zoe Butterfield.

'Yeah, gold they do not need.'

Even at this hour, parked cars lined the narrow lane for half a mile before they reached the main gates of the Palladian country house.

'Wow, look at that,' Butterfield said, as she peered through the intricate wrought-iron gates and up the half-mile drive to the honey-stoned turrets and frontages of Westgrave Hall. The place was even more magnificent now, as the entire approach to the house was coated in a thick blanket of snow, and the mature lime trees which towered over the drive were individually decked in densely packed fairy lights. From a distance it produced the effect of a sparkling frost.

'It's like something from Dr Zhivago,' she breathed.

'Bet they've had snow machines working on that all day,' PC Thorne said, always down to earth. 'Must have cost a fortune.' He looked at the vehicle dashboard, which gave a temperature of 3°C. 'Half of it will have thawed by morning, I would have thought.'

'You've got no romance in your soul, Paul.'

'Just wait until you're married. That will knock it out of you. I see parties and I think drugs, vice and illicit cash.'

'I never get invited to parties,' Zoe said wistfully.

'Parties like this are beyond us mortals,' he said. 'Let's go in and take a look.'

The drive here was blocked by a giant log. 'See the sign? You have to go in by the Oakham Gate, that's round the west side,' Zoe said.

Thorne put the patrol car back into gear and drove for two miles along the high stone walls of the estate until they came to the junction of Oakham Road. Turning right, he then drove north up the western edge of the estate. After four miles they saw Oakham Gate. The large wooden gates were open, but there was a chain across the road, decked with reflective plastic snowflakes. The snow machines had been busy here too, covering the meadows and the dense yew trees, in which were hung many flickering lanterns. Three shaven-headed and beefy security men stood by a Mitsubishi pickup. They were dressed in quilted jackets and big boots, with radio handsets and earpieces.

'Ah, there he is,' Butterfield said. 'Wolf, Volkov's head of security.' She pointed him out, the shortest and widest of the three, with tinted glasses and a goatee. He was muttering something into his radio in a foreign language. 'He's a hilarious guy, offered me a cup of Rosie Lee when I first came to talk to him.'

'Well, would you Adam and Eve it,' said Thorne. 'Who'd have thought Cockney rhyming slang would have reached Russia.'

She buzzed down the window. She could hear loud church choral music. At first she thought it was coming from the Mitsubishi, but then realised from the echo that it was over a PA system.

'Just wanted to check that everything is okay, Wolf,' she said.

'Is fine, Miss Butter,' he replied. 'Everyone is having a great time.'

'Well, not quite everyone,' she said. 'We've had complaints from the residents about the noise. You really should turn it down this late.'

'Always they complain,' Wolf said with an expansive shrug. 'Too many noise, too much traffics. We told them months ago. It's Christmas, yes?'

'Yes, I've seen the notification. But the music was supposed to be turned down at midnight.'

The shrug again. 'It is turned down.'

'You could hear this in Trafalgar Square, mate,' Thorne said, leaning across his colleague. 'Think of kids trying to sleep.'

'Children, in this village? I don't think so. They are all older than the dinosaur,' he said, jerking his thumb over his shoulder. 'They reminisce together about good old Jurassic times.' He laughed, a booming baritone.

'What about these lights, mate?' Thorne said. 'Poor bloody owls will be colliding with each other.'

Wolf turned to look. As if on cue, the lights went off, throwing the small group into a ghostly shade, lit only from below by the glow of the snow. Then the sky was torn open by a series of ear-splitting explosions and dazzling showers of red, green and golden sparks as the firework display began.

'So much for kiddies' bedtime,' Thorne said to Butterfield, thinking wistfully of his own young children, tucked up in bed in Woking. 'These people think they're untouchable.'

'That's money for you,' Butterfield responded, as she watched a blue and violet starburst almost overhead, sending spirals of glittering motes in all directions.

'Come, see display,' Wolf said. 'I will bring you to big house.'

Butterfield turned to her partner, and he said: 'Go ahead, Zoe, and see if you can speak to the boss about the racket. I'll stay here. But just make sure they don't think you're the kissogram,' he winked at her.

-

PC Butterfield followed Wolf as he led her through a maze of outbuildings at the back of the hall. Once she was beyond the Victorian walled garden and could see the house itself, it was clear the snow machines had neglected nothing. The entire structure had been decked with thick layers: roofs, battlements, terraces, even window ledges. Icicles were already beginning to dangle from the gutters, gargoyles and turrets, spattering icy drips onto the ground. It looked like something from Hans Christian Andersen. Lights blazed from within, and guests could be seen at the upper windows, gazing out.

'Tonight, over one thousand guests, fifty-three different nations,' Wolf said. 'We have nine members of royal families. Kings, princes from all the world, including the important Prince Andrew, yes. Strong industrialist, much money from Silicon Valley and China, finance kings from New York.' He turned to her. 'Hey, Ms Butter. You too late for Beyoncé.'

'He hired *Beyoncé*?' she gasped.

'Yes, she arrive by helicopter.' He mimed the clatter of rotors. 'She lower on rope ladder onto stage for two-hour set at eight p.m. Two Siberian tiger babies on stage with her.' He mimed a growl and claws. 'They have special man to control for her. Is very good.'

'My God!' Butterfield knew that Volkov had money, but this kind of cash was almost beyond imagination.

A waitress approached them, all legs and cheekbones, carrying a tray of champagne in fluted crystal glasses and a pot of caviar in a bowl of ice. Wolf gestured to the constable. 'Help yourself.'

'I can't drink when I'm on duty. But I will try a little of this,' she said, helping herself to a teaspoonful of the tiny black fish roe. 'Mmm, delicious,' she said. 'I had expected it to be more fishy.'

'The caviar is *malossol*, low in salt, meaning it is the best,' Wolf said. 'Hint of ocean, a breeze of coast, not a strong taste fishy.'

'So how did he become so rich?' she asked, through a mouthful of caviar.

Wolf's broad smile betrayed this as the most naïve of questions. 'Breaking rocks for metal in hole. But is politics, also. Right place, right time. In Russia you have to smell the opportunity.'

'I understand that Mr Volkov was getting engaged at this party?' Butterfield said.

'Yes. The beautiful Dr Sophie Cawkwell.'

'The dinosaur lady from Channel Four, well, well.' She was aware of the carefully curated appeal of Ms Cawkwell. Butterfield's own father, who had previously shown no interest whatsoever in palaeontology, had been glued to every episode of *Dig!* ever since he had watched her wading through some tropical river, apparently bra-less beneath her clinging shirt, glistening sweat on her neck as she pointed out some obscure lizard which was the nearest living relative to a dinosaur.

Sex sells.

It was only when Zoe rounded the corner to the front of the house that the true opulence of the party became apparent. There were three ranked snowy terraces, each the size of two tennis courts, leading down towards the main drive. The first and highest one was packed with waltzing couples, in full evening dress. Many of them from their poise and grace were clearly professional dancers. It made *Strictly* look like a village fete. The terrace below had been turned into an ice rink, on which dozens of skaters in glittering costumes circled around a team of four white-plumed horses, fastened to a sleigh. The sleigh itself was a seven-foot high-diamante pumpkin, as dazzling as a disco ball, its open door revealing a blood-red velvet interior. Around the edge of the rink were dozens of space heaters, each one encircled by a chest-high table, around which guests chatted.

'You know of the library and what is within?' Wolf asked, pointing to Westgrave Hall's newest building, its enormous smoked glass windows reflecting the full glory of the fireworks. Subdued lights were on inside the upper floor.

'The fossil? Yes, but I've not been inside. Will it be open to the public?'

Wolf shrugged. 'I no think so, maybe few special occasions, who knows? Mr Volkov is a very private person, very careful about security.'

'A private person!' Butterfield laughed, gesturing to the hundreds of partygoers milling about in the snow-covered surroundings, and a TV crew which seem to be interviewing someone in Russian.

Wolf smiled, and pointed her towards the graceful marble bridge, a thirty-yard swan's neck over the moat which divided the main house from the grassy promontory on which the library was built. 'You get best view of the house from there,' he said. 'I hope you will excuse, I have to organise stuff.' He turned and headed off back towards the main house.

As she crossed the bridge, a dazzling woman emerged from the library. It was Dr Sophie Cawkwell herself, resplendent in a long, tight peacock-blue dress, her hair piled up like Marie Antoinette. She shuffled her way carefully along the slushy pavement to the bridge where she greeted two other people with air-kisses, one of whom lit her a cigarette. Butterfield recognised him as Lord Fein, a former government minister well-known for his networking skills. With him was his Russian wife Natasha, a famous socialite and fixture of the celebrity magazine pages. Beyond them stood a tall ponytailed security man, all Slavic cheekbones and five o'clock shadow. He didn't even glance at the fireworks but seemed to be watching over the Feins.

A waiter came up with a silver tray of fluted glasses and offered drinks to the group. Zoe admired the skill with which the two women balanced handbags, cigarettes, canapés, phones and drinks, even as they tottered on high heels in the slush. She couldn't follow what they were talking about with all the noise, but it didn't give the impression of being very consequential. The policewoman looked out across the bridge, to a large lake behind the library, where a giant fountain in the shape of a fish squirted water a hundred feet into the air. Beyond the lake lay dark woodland, its edge silvered by the lights. The whole place was more than 4,000 acres, reaching west into Hampshire.

All eyes returned to the heavens as the firework display reached its climax, a fizzing explosion of gold and royal blue sparks. With an enormous bang, the sky seemed to shatter and billions of silver petals drifted down all over the house, grounds and lake. Soaring strings throbbed Tchaikovsky over the PA system.

Then a dozen irregular cracks echoed across the snow. Guests looked above in vain for fizzing sparks above which might have spawned the discordant coda. For a few seconds there was nothing but music, then more bangs, a dozen in quick succession, then a gap. Then more.

Butterfield just happened to be staring at the grand front of the library, and it looked to her that one of the big panes of glass upstairs had frosted. Then, right before her eyes, another bang was followed by a small shower of glass fragments, tumbling down the front of the building.

Gunshots?

There was a collective gasp from the crowd. Then a lot of things happened at once.

Dr Sophie Cawkwell broke off her conversation, looked over her shoulder, and started to run as best she could through the slush back towards the library door. The ponytailed security hunk got on his radio, yelling in Russian, his brow furrowed. PC Zoe Butterfield suddenly realised she was in the middle of a crime scene. She

34

checked that the bodycam on her tunic was working, found a pair of unused latex gloves in her tunic pocket, then radioed in to Thorne to come and join her.

'What's happening, Zoe?' Thorne asked.

'I don't know. Gunshots, possibly.'

She saw a tall dark-haired man in evening dress sprinting from the direction of the house. He vaulted a table and tore towards the bridge as if his life depended on it. Ponytail guy shouted to him as he passed: 'Got the code?'

'Yes, but it shouldn't be locked,' he yelled as he ran past Butterfield, overtook Cawkwell and reached the glass door of the library first. He leaned back and pulled the handle. The floodlit reflection of Westgrave Hall flexed in the glass, but the door remained closed. Locked.

The music from the PA suddenly ceased.

'Call it in, ambulances as a precaution, give CSI a heads-up,' Butterfield shouted to Thorne. 'We're going to need lots of uniforms for crowd control.' She slipped on the latex gloves.

'Roger that.'

'I'm going to take a look.' She set off for the library, watching the athletic man fiddle with a keypad by the double doors, while simultaneously talking on a phone clutched between neck and shoulder. He managed to open the door just as Sophie Cawkwell, the hem of her long dress gathered up in one hand, arrived by his side. 'Sasha's in there!' she shouted. 'I've got to help him.'

'No, stay here,' he said, easing himself in. He closed the door in her face, trapping the hem of her dress. A few moments later Zoe arrived as the TV presenter banged on the glass with both hands, swore vigorously and yelled, 'Sasha! Sasha!'

Ponytail man was now at the door, still on his radio. 'Wolf, come now!' He bellowed into the device.

'Get this door open!' Sophie yelled at him, trying to wrench out the fabric which trapped her leg against the door.

'Just a moment,' he said, pressing his thumb against a receptor and tapping in a code on the keypad. He still appeared to be on the phone, shouting to someone in Russian. The door didn't open, but merely flexed when he pushed it. 'Shit, yesterday's code.'

Another shot rang out. Then another.

'Open the damn thing, for Christ's sake, Sasha's being murdered!' Sophie yelled.

Ponytail guy ignored her, yelling in Russian even louder into the phone as he worked the keypad.

Peering through the smoked glass, Zoe could make out a short section of entrance hall, lined with bookshelves, and an open-plan staircase going up a half landing, then turning back on itself. The view higher into the atrium was completely blocked by the huge lump of suspended rock, the massive fossil she had heard so much about. Only a few ground floor spotlights appeared to be on, but there was more lighting on the floor above.

Four more shots rang out in quick succession, and there was a cry. Someone tumbled down the upper half of the staircase, arms and legs flailing, coming to rest face up on the half landing. It was the same man who had just entered, a huge red patch spreading on the crisp white of his shirt. A pistol slipped from his right hand and clacked and banged down two more steps.

'Oh my God, we've got to do something,' Sophie screamed, crouching down until she could get the material from her dress into her mouth. She began tearing it with her teeth. 'Fourteen thousand quid's worth, ruined,' she said, spitting out fibres as she ripped the dress.

Ponytail man tried the keypad again. No luck.

Zoe ran back towards the bridge and picked up a waist-high freestanding ashtray and offered the other end to Sophie. The TV star was now free of the door hinge, but in half a dress, ripped to the waist on one side. 'Let's give this a go,' Zoe said.

'Right,' Sophie replied.

The two women made a short run at the door and smashed the heavy ashtray at the lock. The door merely shuddered.

'Don't do that, you'll break the lock!' the ponytailed man yelled.

'That's the whole idea, you moron,' Sophie said, as they swung for another blow. Natasha Fein joined them, struggling to carry another ashtray she had found in the middle of the bridge. A group of young men from among the guests ran to help, masculinity clearly threatened by female initiative. They were joined by a half a dozen members of the security team, identifiable by their shaven heads and earpieces. Every one of them seemed to be shouting to everyone else.

Wolf could now be seen running over the bridge, gesticulating wildly. 'If you jam lock, we never get in. This glass armoured glass!' he yelled at the women, before returning to bellowing over the phone. 'Why he need code change every day? *Suka, blyat!*' he yelled, to no one in particular.

Finally, one of the security men passed across a slip of paper to Wolf, who tapped in a code. The door released, and he and Sophie were first in, running straight past the fallen body and upstairs. Butterfield squeezed in after them and then, seeing the great press of others converging on the door, slammed it shut. A satisfying clunk as the lock kicked in. This was a crime scene, and she had to do what she could.

She knelt by the man on the stairs and felt for a pulse. None. Blood no longer flowed from the hole in his shirt but was seeping from his mouth and down his chin. He was clearly dead. The only dead body she had ever seen before was in her first week as a constable, an old man of ninety who'd died on the toilet in a tower block. This was completely different. This guy had been young and fit, handsome too, with everything to live for. She took a deep breath. Mustn't think about it. Keep focused.

From upstairs she heard a great wailing cry from Sophie Cawkwell: 'No, no, no!' Wolf was shouting too, almost beside himself with panic.

Adrenaline was coursing through Zoe's veins. A hundred actions crowded into her head. Which to choose? In seven years on the force, she had never had such responsibility.

Images, images, images. Before the crime scene became too compromised. It was the best thing she could do. With her phone she took half a dozen pictures of the body on the stairs, then made her way up, taking care not to add to the trail of bloody footprints Wolf and Sophie had left behind. However, she heard the ping of metal, and realised she had probably just kicked a cartridge case.

The stairs led up to the gallery, which ran right around the edge of the two-storey atrium within which the huge blade of rock was suspended. There was a body on the walkway fifty feet from where she stood. A sizeable man, middle-aged, wearing evening dress, with long whiteish-blond hair. He was face down in a huge pool of blood.

He was clearly dead, a triangular hole in the back of his skull revealing a mauve pulpy mass beneath. It was only one of many visible wounds.

'Who's he?' Butterfield shouted to Wolf, pointing to the body in front of her. Sophie and Wolf were at the far end, almost sixty yards away, crouching by a third man. He was seated on the floor back against a wall as if tired.

'You not know? That is the famous Maxim Talin,' Wolf replied.

She took a good dozen photographs with her phone. 'What about the guy downstairs?'

'Bryn Howell. Is Sasha's bodyguard.'

'I thought you were his bodyguard, Wolf?'

'No, I'm security manager. Million jobs without trailing after boss.'

'Well I guess you won't have to do that anymore,' Zoe muttered to herself. She made her way along the balcony toward the third body. A clear trail of fresh crimson footprints, Sophie's and Wolf's, led from one recumbent victim to the other. More pictures.

'Is he still alive?' she called, although Sophie's wailing had already answered the question.

Wolf shook his head. 'Mr Volkov is dead. No pulse. No heartbeat.'

'Then this is now a crime scene, and I need you to move away. Both *please* take off your shoes, so you don't leave any more gory footprints.'

Sophie removed her high heels and placed them sideways on a bookshelf. 'Has anyone seen Yelena? She was here with Talin when I left them.'

Wolf shrugged. 'I don't know who was here.'

Zoe carefully made her way along the balcony edge towards them, avoiding the still-wet bloody footprints.

As she approached the body of Alexander Volkov, she could see at least three bullet wounds, including one in his cheek. Blood had poured from his nose and mouth down the front of his white evening jacket and shirt. She took pictures. If she stopped to think about what she was actually seeing, she was not sure she would cope.

'Wolf! Come away from the body. Take your boots off and walk around the other side of the balcony.' He just looked at her and blinked, showing no signs of complying. From somewhere came the muffled sound of banging. The crowd outside, maybe.

There was hammering on the glass downstairs and a rising chorus of shouts. In the distance the sound of sirens. And still there was the muffled banging noise, as if there was building work next door.

'I think the ambulances have arrived,' she said. Wolf was now walking round the other side of the balcony. He still had his boots on.

The banging continued.

'We have to keep everybody outside, Wolf. For just a couple more minutes, until the paramedics come. I've got to get lots of pictures before the paramedics trample through everything. Take your boots off!'

'What is noise? Is coming from inside,' Wolf said, walking back towards Volkov's body.

'Is it not downstairs?' Sophie asked.

'No. It from here I think.'

'How many rooms are there in this place?' Zoe asked.

'Two large conference room downstairs, the three toilets plus some storage and office. Up here one conference room, two office...'

Suddenly the lights went off, throwing the room into darkness except for the green glow of the emergency exit sign downstairs.

'Maybe assassin still here in building,' Wolf said, flicking on his mobile phone. It lit his face from below, giving him a devilish appearance, and throwing his shadow like a giant on the far wall.

Shit! Zoe needed help, and she needed it now. She reached for her tunic torch and turned it on. If the shooter was still in the building they were in serious trouble. Her light knifed the darkness, as she tried to isolate where the sound was coming from. She reached under her jacket and unholstered her Taser, a weapon she had never used outside of training.

Three dead already.

Now it was down to her to prevent another three dying on that blood-soaked balcony.

Chapter Four

DCI Craig Gillard was the on-call detective overnight. It was just his luck to be lumbered with the Christmas shift, which this year he'd really wanted to avoid. His wife Sam was still struggling with post-traumatic stress disorder after being kidnapped earlier in the year and had wanted him to be home with her. But unfortunately, day-to-day staffing requirements intervened. Gillard still had no boss, DCS 'Radar' Dobbs being off again with depression, and there were three other detectives off sick, including DI John Perry, who had flu. Perry had been due to take this shift.

The good news was that he'd got to 1:15 a.m. and it had so far been pretty quiet. Sam had gone to bed, and he was thinking of joining her. The only incident he'd been called out to was an altercation at a city centre pub in Redhill, in which a young man had been stabbed in the arm. Painful but not normally life-threatening.

Most Christmases you would expect a few domestic incidents, often including a murder. Families forced together, the expectations of happiness, and the pressure cooker of all sitting down at a table together caused no end of trouble. Uniforms were at the sharp end of all this of course, the late-night call-outs, the drink-driving and the pub fights. He was only involved in the very worst cases. Tonight, there had been very few of them.

Gillard was in shorts and T-shirt, squinting into the mirror. His wife had always described him as rugged, by which she meant sexily scruffy. Certainly he could do with a shave, and his short iron-grey hair was expanding into his sideboards, making him look further into his fifties than he was. His five-eleven physique too was a little out of shape, muscle definition awaiting a return to his regular swim. He was just cleaning his teeth when the control room rang his mobile. He wiped toothpaste away on the towel as he answered.

'We're getting reports of three dead in a shooting in the village of Steeple Risby,' the operator said, her wavering voice betraying a little emotion at the unexpected death toll. 'I've already called CSI, and paramedics are on their way.'

Steeple Risby was at the far western edge of Surrey, almost in Hampshire. 'Do you have any details of exactly where?' he asked.

'Westgrave Hall. Christmas party. It was called in by PC Thorne.' She passed on the postcode, which Gillard tapped into his phone. 'Happy Christmas, sir.'

'And to you,' he said.

Gillard dressed rapidly, snatched up his grab bag, which contained wellingtons, torch, booties, gloves and a fat stash of evidence bags, and headed for his unmarked Vauxhall parked on the drive. The moment he was in the car, he called PC Thorne on the hands-free phone.

'DCI Gillard here, on my way over to you. What's happened?'

'Three dead in a shooting. No further injuries reported.'

'Has CSI arrived?'

'No. But I hear sirens. That could be paramedics,' Thorne said.

'Is the crime scene secure? I heard it was a party.'

'Describing it as party, sir, is like describing the *Titanic* as a boat. We're having trouble to be honest. The good news is that the scene is self-contained, it's a library with one entrance and I'm on it. The bad news is that one of the dead is the billionaire oligarch Alexander Volkov. There is a big crowd outside, with a Russian TV crew recording the whole scene.'

'How did they get there so quickly?'

'I think they were already here to film the party.' There was a bang and some shouting, then Thorne said: 'I'm holding the door with the help of their head of security. PC Zoe Butterfield is inside the library, taking pictures. I'm told it's a mess.'

'Any ID on the other dead?'

'One just behind me is the bodyguard, British national I believe. The other guy we don't know for sure, but it may be the US businessman Maxim Talin.'

'Good grief. I've heard of him. The billionaire battery pioneer?'

'Don't know, sir.' There was a lot of background shouting, some of it in a language Gillard didn't understand. He heard Thorne, clearly rattled, telling someone to back off, before he returned to the call. 'Got to go, sir. I hope the cavalry arrive soon,' Thorne said.

Gillard hung up, and then immediately picked up another call from Chief Constable Alison Rigby. With his boss off sick, Gillard was often exposed to her workaholic scrutiny.

'Happy Christmas, Craig,' she said. 'I'm sorry that the festivities have been interrupted for you.'

'Part of the job, ma'am, particularly when you're on call.'

'Indeed. Just a heads up for you. I was awoken by a call from the Home Office about this... incident. Expect Special Branch to be poking their noses in, with the security services in tow. If I were you, I'd get every bit of evidence you want ASAP, before they pull rank. You don't want to lose control of the crime scene.'

'Yes ma'am. Did they say why they were interested?'

'No, they never do. I rang Counter Terrorism Command to see if it was in connection with that, but it seems not. At least not at this stage.'

'Russian oligarchs dying unexpectedly in the UK,' Gillard said. 'We've had a few, haven't we, ma'am?'

'Yes. Like those Russian dolls, one mystery inside another. I should think by now we've got the complete set. Work fast, Craig. Nail down everything you can as quickly as possible. I don't trust the security services. Their priorities are not always our priorities.' She hung up.

–

In the Volkov Library the lights came on again after a few seconds. Then off. On and off and on again several times, in an almost rhythmic fashion. Zoe took out her own torch and turned it on.

'*Suka, blyat!* What now?' Wolf yelled. He was back on the phone in Russian, expressing furious shrugs to whoever was on the other end.

The flashing lights continued for the next minute, but the banging stopped. 'It's Morse code,' Sophie said. 'SOS. Three short flashes, three long, three short.'

'But where is it coming from? Where are the light switches?' Zoe asked. 'Maybe the same person was making the tapping.'

'There's a panic room here,' Sophie said. 'I heard Sasha mention it.'

'Yes, behind here,' Wolf said, tapping the granite end wall. 'Six-inch thick steel door, own air supply, food, computer room, snooker table and pinball machines. All down in basement. Sasha's body is blocking door which leads to staircase.'

'Somebody must be in it, trying to get out,' Zoe said. 'Which way does the door open?'

Wolf frowned. 'Outwards. Yes, outwards.'

'So that's it,' Sophie said, leaning towards her dead fiancé. 'If we move Sasha, we can open the door.'

'Do NOT move that body,' Zoe yelled. 'This is a crime scene.'

Wolf gave an expansive shrug. 'If someone in panic room, why they no ring? There is satphone in it.' Not getting an answer, he sighed heavily, took his own phone and tapped out a number. 'I ring satphone now.'

A ringtone sounded on Volkov's body. Zoe gingerly reached inside the dead man's jacket and retrieved a larger than normal mobile phone. It was sticky with blood. 'Maybe he was trying to use the phone when the shooting started.'

'Okay, so satphone is here.' Wolf killed the call, and the ringing stopped.

Zoe's radio crackled into life. Thorne was downstairs, asking to be let in. 'CSI is on its way. I can see the first ambulance coming up the drive.'

'Hold them back for now,' she said. 'We've got three dead bodies but no injured.' She watched Wolf, finally

46

taking off his boots. He had pink socks on, with a hole in one toe.

The tapping resumed.

'Wolf, I take it there is no other way into the panic room?' Zoe's radio continued to crackle away, updating the arrival of more police resources.

He shrugged. 'Whole point of panic room is only one entrance.'

Zoe realised that whoever was inside may well have been a witness to the shooting. 'Is there any other way of communicating with the panic room?'

'Electronic shield, yes of course, like main panic room in Westgrave Hall. There is no mobile phone reception, except via satellite phone aerial. Command system has own computer, and I can send email, whoosh, over secure line. Panic rooms both have own encrypted WhatsApp addresses.'

'That's fine if you're familiar with it. But I think it must be Yelena who is in there,' Sophie said. 'She wouldn't have the passwords or anything.'

'Who is Yelena?' Zoe asked Wolf.

'Volkov's ex-wife, and now Talin's partner,' Wolf said. 'A royal pain in bum.' He shook his head.

'Okay. I've got to go and let my colleague in,' Zoe said. 'Please stay away from the bodies, don't touch anything else.' She made her way carefully downstairs, stepped over the body on the stairs, and saw a great press of police uniforms by the door.

She pressed the exit button, releasing the door lock.

–

Even blue-lighting it from home it took Gillard an hour to reach Westgrave Hall. The tiny lanes were lined with parked cars from onlookers who had presumably arrived to watch the fireworks or had heard about the shooting. Despite the sirens, it took him a few minutes to weave past the steady stream of high-end vehicles that were leaving the hall.

He made his way up the main drive, outflanking those coming the other way by driving on the bumpy snow-covered pastures. There were some very expensive-looking cars leaving the place: Bentleys, Ferraris, Aston Martins, and several more sober vehicles with diplomatic plates. Parking almost in front of the grand porticoed entrance, next to four patrol cars, he left the blues on to make it clear whose car it was, and then headed off into a mêlée of guests. Uniforms had set up a couple of trestle tables by the edge of the ice rink, to take initial details of all the guests who were present. Two hundred yards further on, beyond the alabaster bridge, a crime-scene tent had been erected around the entrance to the library. A CSI transit van had somehow made its way across the moat and reversed up to be close to the tent.

Gillard was delighted to see Yaz Quoroshi, CSI chief, directing operations. 'I understand it's a bit of a mess in there, Yaz.'

'To put it mildly. Gory footprints all over the place. PC Butterfield did a superb job getting some pictures, but it's going to be the devil's own job untangling who trod where and when. We've found two handguns and a good two dozen cartridge cases. It does seem the deceased all died from gunshot wounds.'

'I've woken Dr Delahaye up,' Gillard said. 'Not happy about being dragged out on Christmas morning. Really quite grumpy about it, which is unlike him.'

'I sympathise,' Quoroshi replied 'Who wants to be dragged out at Christmas? Not me, certainly.'

Gillard was a little surprised, knowing that Yaz was Iraqi-born and of Shia Muslim descent. The CSI chief seemed to read the expression on his face. 'It's the kids, Craig. They are nine and six. Christmas is a big thing to them, we have a big vegetarian lunch, watch some films. They expect presents just like their friends at school.'

'I can imagine the expectations,' Gillard replied.

'Looking at this lot, I don't expect I shall see them opening their gifts today. Third year in a row, unfortunately.'

The DCI thought of all the Christmases he and Sam had missed over the years. She'd been angelic about the disappointments, but there was no denying that his job made it very hard to be sure he could ever get the time off he needed.

'I'm planning to move one of the bodies immediately,' Quoroshi said. 'There seems to be someone trapped in a panic room, and the door can't be opened because of a body.'

'That's fine if you're happy with the photographic evidence. Delahaye won't be here for two or three hours and, as he reminded me, he is no ballistics expert. He said that if we want to move the bodies that's up to us.'

'Given that it's a Russian oligarch all I can say is thank God it wasn't poison,' Yaz said. 'I was dragooned into the Salisbury investigation when they ran short of CSI staff. Quite the most frustrating and difficult operation I've ever been involved in. Give me a good old-fashioned shooting any day.'

'Agreed,' Gillard said. 'At least you know right from the outset who is dead and who is alive.' The poisoning by nerve agent of former Russian spy Sergei Skripal and his daughter Yulia in March 2018 was the first known act of chemical warfare on British soil and led to the death of an innocent bystander. Russian agents had been identified as the assailants, but the Kremlin had denied all involvement. No one had been arrested. Gillard was determined that a failure like that wasn't going to be replicated on his watch.

–

Once Gillard had donned his Tyvek suit, gloves and booties, he went in to take a look. The first person he saw was PC Butterfield, sitting on a chair by a ground floor window, drinking a coffee. She looked exhausted and was staring at the floor. She wasn't wearing any shoes and had a large stack of sealed evidence bags next to her.

He crouched down. 'How are you doing, Zoe?'

She blew a huge sigh. 'Not so bad, considering. We've got three dead bodies, gunshot wounds. No other injuries and a very messy crime scene. These bags here contain the footwear of everyone who came in, but we still need to get the victims' shoes—'

'Whoa, it's okay. Take it easy. Quoroshi has already briefed me. From what I've heard, you've done a great job, and we'll take it from here.'

'There is someone trapped in the panic room.'

'Yes, I heard,' he said gently. 'The best thing you did was to keep everyone else out. That makes our job so much easier.'

'Yaz Quoroshi has got my phone. I've taken hundreds of pictures.'

'Good work.' Gillard took a quick look upstairs at the crime scene then stood aside to let CSI do their work. He shrugged his way out of his Tyvek, left it in the CSI tent, then retreated into the main house where key witnesses had been corralled in the ballroom after making their initial statements. Needless to say many of them, tired and in some cases tipsy, were not happy about it. They wanted to leave, to go home, to get away from the mayhem.

As the senior investigating officer, Gillard realised gathering evidence rapidly was his most important task. Managing the logistical complexity of doing so and ensuring that witnesses stayed around was going to be a great challenge. It was clear from the denuded car park that hundreds of guests had already left. He had however detained the four people who were closest to what had happened. Wolf, the head of security, was sitting at the grand piano in the hall, constantly on the phone. Sophie Cawkwell, wrapped in a borrowed coat, was lying full length on a golden settee in the East Lounge, her wavy blonde hair dangling over one end, her tanned and shapely legs over the other. She was wearing sunglasses and had a glass of ice held to her forehead. She looked like a film starlet from another era, right down to the two male admirers, one holding her hand, the other stroking her cheek. A rather weary Lord Fein and his effervescent wife Natasha were still giving their statements in the marquee. Waiters continued to ply their trade, offering coffee and warming borscht to the remaining guests.

The detective was just reading the statement taken from the head of security when his phone trilled. It was Yaz Quoroshi. 'We've just rescued a woman called Yelena Yalinsky from the panic room. She was in quite a state and had been trying to get out for an hour.'

'Good work. Let's get her over here to give a statement.'

'We've now found over forty cartridge cases, and six bullets embedded in walls,' Quoroshi said. 'Four shots seem to have hit windows. There are others in the bookcases and floor.'

'Sounds a bit like the gunfight at the OK Corral.'

'We've retrieved two handguns from the deceased: one on Maxim Talin and one from the bodyguard Bryn Howell.'

'Nothing on Alexander Volkov?'

'No. Nothing on the lady found in the panic room, either.'

'Did she see anything?'

'She says not. She just dived for safety when she heard shooting begin.'

'The only survivor,' Gillard said. 'She's going to be important.'

'Absolutely, but she's not coherent yet.'

'I noticed the skylight above was open. Did you do that?'

'No. I hadn't noticed it, to be honest. Thought it was cold in there.'

'It wouldn't be an easy escape route. Must be a thirty-foot sheer climb from the gallery,' Gillard said.

'None of it is easy in that place.' Quoroshi described how it had taken forty-five minutes to get the two bodies out from the upper floor. They were each put into body bags in situ and then lowered over the balcony to gurneys on the ground floor. 'We minimised the disturbance to the bloodstained hardwood floors,' he said.

It was only then that Gillard realised there was one urgent piece of work to be done outside before morning. He had already been told that the only way into or out of the high security library was through the main door. But if anyone had tried to force their way in there might well be footprints in the snow. He had to take a look before it melted. That applied to the roof, too. If the skylight was a possible exit, then there would be prints on the gently pitched roof.

Leaving a uniformed sergeant in charge of the witnesses, the detective shrugged on his coat and made his way down through the three terraces back towards the stone bridge. The high arc lights were now back on at his request. Though the snow still looked pristine, slushy footpaths were beginning to show through. It was half past three, and though not exactly warm, he reckoned the melt was progressing pretty fast. Grass would be showing through before morning. The library sat upon a knoll, surrounded by its own shallow grassy ditch, and could only be reached easily via the stone bridge. He circled the library on the embankment which encircled the moat. Though the footpath was slushy, the deep snow in the cut was largely undisturbed, only thinning where a stream ran underneath the western edge. He took plenty of photographs, and after circumnavigating the library was satisfied that no one had gone in or out except on the bridge. And for that he had four witnesses to say there was just one: the bodyguard, who entered after the shooting began.

Chapter Five

Gillard made his way back into the ballroom. Dozens of guests were standing around in groups, urgently discussing the night's events, many of them clearly in a state of shock. Others were on the phone, and at least a couple of the male guests seemed to be on two phones at once, as if they were city traders seizing some great market opportunity. A tall, pale young woman was sobbing on the shoulder of a grizzled pot-bellied man of Middle Eastern appearance, who stroked her back with one hand and texted with the other, his thumb playing a single digit concerto across the screen of his phone. Two enormous dogs, bigger and hairier even than Irish wolfhounds, stared with sad eyes at the crowd. A gaggle of young children, the boys in mini tuxedos and slicked-down hair, the girls in sparkly dresses, seemed to be playing hide-and-seek amongst the grandiose furniture, as if nothing had happened. A single cherubic toddler sat alone under a piano stool, wide-eyed at all the activity, sucking his thumb and holding a small teddy to his cheek.

The detective threaded his way through to the biggest crowd, past the TV crew where the reporter was doing a piece to camera, and into the East Lounge. At the centre of it all, Yelena Yalinsky was sharing a sofa with Sophie Cawkwell, who was now in a different dress. Black and backless, it was as if she'd packed for the possibility of death. They were surrounded by a press of well-wishers, some crouching, clearly offering kind words and condolences. The two women held each other's hands and wept. The detective eased his way through the crowd, watched as they embraced, Sophie stroking the long, dark, wavy hair of the other woman. He waited until they released each other, and then introduced himself.

Yelena was partially hidden by a silk handkerchief she was holding to her tear-streaked face, but above it her kohl-lined eyes surveyed him from beneath heavy eyebrows. She looked to be in her late forties. 'Ah, the man in charge,' she said. More petite than Sophie and barely five feet tall, she was resplendent in a red silk dress and matching shoes. Yalinsky was the daughter of the finance minister of Kazakhstan and her mother was a white Russian émigré of royal lineage going back to the Romanovs. Gillard recalled her face, which had rarely been out of the papers because of a long-running divorce case with Volkov, fought out in London's High Court. The tabloids had listed her extravagances: shoes, handbags, private jets, perfume and, most notoriously, the 500-litre tank of bottled Evian water at her Paris apartment kept constantly replenished for bathing. Things had got nasty in court. Volkov testified that she was brutal with staff. When a kitchen porter was found to have incomplete papers, she reported him to the immigration authorities in France. He was later deported back to Mali and died in prison there. Her allegations against Volkov were equally sweeping: a litany of affairs, neglect of their children, and an ingrained habit of bribery.

Gillard wasn't there to judge, but to get to the truth.

'My condolences on the death of your partner,' he said.

'I've lost everything,' she wailed, her huge brown eyes filled with tears. 'Maxim, the love of my life. And Sasha, the father of my children.'

'You're lucky to be alive,' Gillard pointed out.

She shrugged. 'Maybe it would have been better had I been killed too.' She began to sob, and she reached for a fresh handkerchief from her red velvet handbag.

Gillard knew from long experience the discomfort he would feel asking his next questions. 'I know it might seem like indecent haste, but in order to solve this crime we need to act immediately. So I was wondering if you could spare fifteen minutes for me to take a statement, Ms Yalinsky.' He indicated a rather grand door off to the left. 'We have the drawing room reserved for some privacy.'

'Can't it wait until tomorrow? I've had a terrible shock.'

'No, I'm afraid it can't.'

'I've already told Mr Quoroshi what little I saw.'

'It won't take long.' Gillard guided her through to the palatial grandness of the drawing room, decked with tapestries and with what looked like a harpsichord at its centre. Incongruously, at one edge of the room three stackable plastic chairs had been grouped around a coffee table.

Yelena sat down in a rustle of silk and wiped her eyes while Gillard got out his digital recorder and notebook.

'Perhaps you'd like to describe to me what you saw.'

Yelena blew her nose and pocketed her handkerchief. 'I don't know what there is I can tell you. The whole thing is a tragedy. I'd flown over from LA with Maxim. I was invited to the party by Sasha to seal the peace between me and him. We were married for ten years, have two kids together, but have been fighting for seven years since the marriage broke down. We have had a long-running divorce litigation here in London, which just seems to go on and on, guzzling millions and simply generating hatred. And in the last few months we had finally agreed a settlement, helped by David Fein as a go-between. Maxim came over because he wanted to be supportive to me.'

'What time did you arrive?'

'At nine, I think. You can check that with the driver. Yes, nine. I think the library was locked for most of the evening, but Sasha wanted to give us a private tour. We went in just before midnight. Sophie, Sasha, Maxim and me.'

'To see the fossil?'

'Yes, in its full glory. Utterly magnificent, but I think it should have remained in my country. We'd looked around, been shown some of the rare books, and peeked into the panic room. Sasha was always very careful after what happened to Berezovsky. He knew him well and was upset that it was ruled a suicide.'

'Understandable.' As a detective inspector at the time, Gillard had been peripherally involved in the investigation of Boris Berezovsky's death in 2013. He had always believed the killing of the oligarch was murder, but he wasn't SIO and it wasn't his decision.

'Anyway, we had just come up from being shown the panic room when the shooting began.'

'But Sophie wasn't with you, was she?'

'Sophie? No, I'm sorry, I forgot. She had gone out for a cigarette break a few minutes before, so there were just the three of us. Anyway, Maxim was first out, and was walking towards the middle of the balcony. I think that's when we heard the first shot.'

'Where did it come from?'

She hesitated for a long time, starting to say something, then stopped. 'Actually, I have no idea. Sasha helped me into the panic room and said he would follow.'

Gillard knew she was lying. It was patently obvious in the hesitation, captured in full on the recorder. 'What happened then?'

'I went into the panic room and ran down the stairs, but he didn't follow. There were more shots.'

'How many did you hear?'

'I don't know how many, sorry. The next thing I knew the door slammed shut, so I assumed Sasha was inside, but when I looked up the spiral staircase, I could see no one.'

'Did you see Mr Volkov or Talin pull a gun?'

'No. I don't think either of them had one.'

'We found one on Talin's body.'

'Really? I am surprised. I knew Maxim could shoot, but I didn't think he'd carry one in this country.'

'Had the two men fallen out, to your knowledge?'

'Well, they had been enemies for a long time.'

'Because of you?'

She inspected the ceiling, far above, her eyes still damp. 'Yes, partly. Business, too, and other things. But all that was over.' She turned her gaze on Gillard. Even in grief, this was a face that could mesmerise any man. 'You see, they had made up in the last two years, and Sasha and I had arranged a deal on the divorce, and tonight we had papers to sign. It's absurd to think they might fight now, when they were about to do some important business together. Kazakh Minerals owns considerable deposits of lithium, which is what Maxim needed for his battery technology. It's what's called a win-win situation. So the whole idea of one shooting the other is crazy.'

'What do you think happened, then?' Gillard asked.

'I don't know. I was stuck in a room. No one else came in. I didn't see the bodyguard. Maybe someone else was hiding there before we came in? What other answer is there? I didn't shoot them.'

'Wouldn't you have wanted Sasha dead?'

'Sometimes, of course, yes. In past years, but I never stopped loving him, either. Love and hate are two sides of the same coin, and in that particular currency I am very wealthy.' Gillard was just about to ask another question when the door opened and three guys in suits walked in. He recognised the first before he introduced himself: DCS Geoffrey Corrigan, the head of Surrey's Special Branch. He was a rangy and capable-looking fellow, with a stellar reputation. The second man was smaller, bespectacled, grey-haired, his suit a little on the baggy side, introduced as Haldane. The third man was built like a wall and exuded the physical poise of someone who had been in the armed forces.

'I think we've met, Craig,' Corrigan said, striding forward to shake his hand. 'These are some of my people. They're adept at handling incidents that have what you might call ramifications.'

'We'll take it from here, detective chief inspector,' said the military-looking guy, beginning to interpose himself between Gillard and his interviewee. 'You can have your witness back in a day or two.' He showed Gillard a security pass which identified him as a member of MI5. The detective gave a silent word of thanks to Alison Rigby for having tipped him off.

Gillard took Corrigan to one side, out of earshot of Ms Yalinsky. 'Look, sir, I need another half an hour, and specifically I need to be able to swab her hands and clothing for gunshot residues.'

'We can do that, don't worry,' said Haldane, who had clearly been eavesdropping. 'Let us know any questions you have, and we'll ask them as well as our own.' He had a soft voice and cultured tones which only made him sound more patronising. 'We'll need to speak to some of the other witnesses too. We'll let you know in plenty of time.'

'Don't let her leave the country,' Gillard said. 'She's got clout. If she leaves, we'll never get her back. She'll be given diplomatic immunity by Kazakhstan.'

Haldane chuckled. 'We can't stop her leaving, unless perhaps you think she's a suspect.'

'She is, obviously, as the only survivor,' Gillard said.

Haldane laughed again, and Gillard flexed his fists in frustration as he watched Yalinsky pick up her handbag and walk out with him and Corrigan. The big MI5 agent meanwhile stood staring at the detective, daring him to intervene.

'Good boy,' he said. 'Remember. This didn't happen.'

The detective watched them leave, the big guy gently closing the door behind them. He shrugged and turned to the coffee table.

His notebook and digital recorder were no longer there.

Bastards.

–

Furious that he had been so unceremoniously robbed of his evidence as well as dislodged from the case, he risked calling Alison Rigby. Waking your chief constable at gone four a.m. was not to be done lightly, even though she had already rung him at half past one. Rigby was the ultimate workaholic, her car often in the car park at Mount Browne even before the early uniform shift got in at six, and frequently there until midnight. He tried her mobile first, which was switched off. He left a message for her, and then thought about ringing her landline. Very few officers had been trusted with that number, the one which really would wake her up. His fingers hesitated over the keypad. She had already told him she couldn't do anything, hadn't she? Only the home secretary could intervene.

He decided against it and put his phone away, then marched out through the open dining room doors onto the first of the three descending terraces. He looked across the snowy meadow towards the library and the CSI tent stuck to the front of it like an unwanted blister. He could see a lot of Tyvek-suited figures standing around drinking coffee. That's odd, he thought. They've got plenty to do, why are they milling about?

He hurried down through the terraces, skirted the ice rink, which was now turning into a slush pool, and made his way across the bridge. Spotting Yaz Quoroshi, Gillard walked straight up to him and asked him what was happening.

'We've been chucked out while a Home Office team looks around,' he said, jerking a thumb over his shoulder.

'Not sure they can do anything that you couldn't.'

'Well, not quite true. I think it's Novichok and radio-active precautions, as they are all sealed up in noddy suits. I'm told we can go back in half an hour.'

Gillard shook his head. 'That's baffling.' He made his way through the CSI tent until he got to the taped-off doorway of the library. There, just inside the lobby, he saw a large figure in a green inflatable NBC suit with his own backpack supply. He looked like a cross between a Teletubby and a 1960s *Doctor Who* monster. He was waving around a handheld device.

'Geiger counter,' Quoroshi said, having followed the detective.

'This is farcical,' Gillard said. 'All this chemical and nuclear stuff is a smokescreen to keep us off the crime scene.'

'So do you think we killed them?' Quoroshi whispered.

'We?'

'Britain, the security services. Bumped off two Russian oligarchs.'

'I wasn't saying that,' Gillard said.

Quoroshi shrugged. 'Well, that's the only reason I can think of for them to keep us off the crime scene.'

--

Once back in the drawing room, Gillard sat opposite Wolf. The unpronounceable Georgian was sprawled in a chair, his head in his hands, elbows on his knees, a big mug of coffee cooling, forgotten, on an adjacent coffee table. He was rubbing his face as if he couldn't believe what had just happened.

'I know we've taken a brief statement from you already,' Gillard said. 'But as you are in such a pivotal position, I do need to ask you some more questions.'

'Yes, of course,' he said, his face still in his hands.

Gillard began by carefully writing down the man's full name. No easy task. 'When were you appointed head of security?'

Wolf sat up and rubbed his neck. 'From start, Mr Volkov arranged for me to get my British credentials when he bought the house here in 2016. I bodyguard for him for a while twelve years ago, when he in Moscow. He remember people, you know?'

'Were you responsible for security-checking the guest list?'

'Part, yes. Natasha Fein made list, and I sent list to private security fellows. We had a few come up dodgy on background checks, as you English say, so they left off invitation list. I made own checks in some cases.'

'Where were you when the shooting began?'

'In house. I just emerge from control room. In basement,' he said pointing to the floor.

'And what is controlled from the control room?'

'Everything. Light for house and garden, CCTV, remote lock. You name, it control.'

'Does that include the library?'

'Yes, normally. But Mr Volkov want library closed off during party. So two days past I set locking system for local control, which means combination of thumbprint and entry code.'

'Do you know why he wanted that change?'

Wolf shrugged. 'He give order, I follow. He no want bloke wandering in library, and I think he want show something important to Mr Talin and Ms Yalinsky. That is why internal CCTV cameras also switch off. That is also why his own bodyguard, Bryn Howell, who go him everywhere, he sent away.'

'Had you ever known him do anything like that before? Sending away his bodyguard?'

A smile slipped across Wolf's jowly face. 'When he with woman for shag, always. But otherwise, not much. I don't ask myself questions. He the boss, he give the order.'

'So from your initial statement, the first time you were aware of the shooting was when one of the security guards called you on the radio?'

'Yes. He told me Bryn already gone in, so I think under control soon. I was shock all same. I could even hear shoot over radio.'

Gillard turned off the recorder, borrowed from CSI. 'All right, thank you for your help. Please don't go anywhere in the next day or so. I'll send someone to get a tour around the control room, to see if we've missed anything.'

Wolf nodded.

'One final question: who do you think killed your boss?'

Another shrug. 'Talin, maybe. Who else?'

'You've known your employer for a dozen years. Who else had a reason to kill him?'

Wolf blew a long sigh. 'A rich Russian has more enemies than there are snowflakes in Siberia.'

Chapter Six

The Tangled Life and Death of Maxim Talin

By Michael Rensman, Russians Abroad magazine

Maxim Talin, who died in a shooting on Christmas Day, was born in November 1963 in St Petersburg to a well-connected composer father and ballerina mother. Talin was a gifted scientist and mathematician and studied at Moscow State University from 1981–1984. He was a rising star until in 1982 he sat in class next to Yelena Yalinsky, the daughter of the finance minister of Kazakhstan.

Seemingly shy, Ms Yalinsky was an ambitious, talented and beautiful woman with whom Talin was to have an intermittent and turbulent relationship for much of the rest of his life. Talin, described by friends as intense and beady-eyed, with a wild head of dark hair, fell head-over-heels for Ms Yalinsky. He flunked his finals and dropped out. She, meanwhile, got top marks at Moscow in chemistry and geology. It was fate that she met the tall and classically handsome Alexander Volkov in May 1983, in the same university course.

For several months over the summer, Yelena had an affair with Volkov, without telling Talin. Leaving Talin in her dacha outside Moscow, she secretly took Volkov with her on a so-called sabbatical back in Almaty. Talin was suspicious, and eventually discovered her duplicity in October. They had an argument on the telephone. 'You will never amount to anything,' she told him. She returned to her sumptuous flat in Moscow, overlooking Red Square. It was an apartment that was later to be owned by Kremlin chief of staff Igor Sechin.

'Maxim was an immensely passionate individual who threw everything into that relationship,' remarked one classmate of the time, now a top foreign ministry official. 'He was insane when he discovered what was going on.'

Anna Kirov, a long-time friend of Talin's, remembered what happened: 'The doorman was under instructions not to let him in, but the lovelorn Maxim would go into the Museum of the Great Patriotic War across the street, and stand staring out to the balcony of her apartment, hoping for a glimpse. He would embrace the warmth of the huge radiator that ran underneath the museum's third floor window, and watch the snow drifting down between him and the woman he loved.'

'We are now separated by a coldness. Between us is nothing but ice,' Talin wrote to Ms Yalinsky that winter. On a couple of occasions, he saw his rival Volkov on her balcony, staring back towards him.

Within a year, Talin had become active in student politics, and had poetry published in the west. He became known as a dissident, and in 1988 – thanks to the connections of his parents – was allowed to go to the United States, where he became involved in the electronics industry in Silicon Valley. Friends say his English, always good, improved dramatically. It was during the last days of the Soviet Union, in 1991, that Talin returned to Russia and sought out Yelena.

One friend recalled the fateful meeting. 'They had a meal in a private restaurant in St Petersburg, and he pleaded with her to come with him to California. He thought he had everything he needed to snare her now – the prospects, a life in the most exciting part of America – but alas, she had just got back together with Volkov, and wouldn't go.'

Talin almost went bankrupt in the tech bust of 2000 but was taken on by a small company planning to revolutionise the world of batteries. At the time, it was considered a niche area, and for a long time nothing happened.

Talin ran into Volkov at the funeral of Volkov's close friend Pavel Friedman, and after drinking heavily there was a fight. One friend recalled: 'Volkov broke Talin's nose, and from the floor, in front of dozens of witnesses, Maxim threatened to kill him.' For almost a decade the two men didn't speak.

PC Simon Woodbridge hadn't reached the end of the long obituary, but he shoved his phone back in his pocket to stop his hand getting cold. He'd read the rest later. He'd certainly drawn the short straw. Only three months on the Surrey force, and here he was at silly o'clock on Christmas morning standing outside a CSI tent, up to his ankles in slush, looking at the aftermath of the party to end all parties. He would have preferred to have been at home with his girlfriend Sally, marking their first Christmas together, planning when he was going to move in to her new flat. Instead, he was shivering in the bitter cold wind, tasked with keeping an eye out for anyone up to no good. To alleviate the boredom, he had been trying to find out what had just happened here at Westgrave Hall by Googling the news on his phone.

Because his superiors had told him sod all.

He was just a basic bloody plod. The famous thin blue line obviously referred to the state of your fingers and toes after a December night shift.

He looked around. It helped that the arc lights suspended from a crane jib for the party had been left on. Everything on the three terraces beneath the main house was still sharply illuminated. He stamped his feet to stay warm. The waterproof reflective jacket and overtrousers helped, as did the long johns beneath. He had a thin woollen balaclava beneath his regulation flat cap. And he was still freezing cold.

Simon really wanted to see the fossil. When he was a young lad he had wanted to be a palaeontologist. Even learned to spell it at the age of seven. He'd read all about the famous relic. There were two CSI officers still working inside the library, but he didn't dare ask them to show him around. There were still a few of his colleagues in the distance, by the house. But nearby there was nobody. He watched his breath plume in the light.

God. He was dying for a fag.

Not allowed on duty.

To take his mind off it, he walked backwards and forwards along the flagstoned terrace that surrounded the library on its little island. The remains of the snow still lay in drifts in the shallow grassy moat. To the left, 200 yards away, was the road and the little village of Steeple Risby, nestled among the tree-lined lanes. In the other direction, maybe quarter of a mile away, was Westgrave Lake, a mist hanging over it, and beyond that the forbidding darkness of Westgrave Woods, ancient woodland undisturbed since the time when King Richard I and his cronies used to go hunting there.

He could feel a packet of cigarettes in his breast pocket underneath his cape, right over his heart. No, mustn't think about it.

He walked up and down a bit more briskly now, stamping his feet to keep warm. Peering out over the lake again, he thought he saw movement on the shoreline on the far side. Whatever it was was obscured by the fountain, whose noisy jet shot water high into the air and created a mist downwind. But beyond the tendrils of curling vapour he saw what looked like a teenage girl, slender and ghostly, her existence proved only by a long finger of shadow cast by the arc lights onto the woods behind her. He could almost feel his heart beating, tapping against the cigarette packet.

The mist shifted, and he lost sight of her. He blinked to fix his focus but could see nothing for a minute or two. Checking furtively behind him to see if anyone else was around, he fumbled in his pocket, withdrew his cigarettes, put one to his lip and felt for a match. He cupped his hands to obscure the flare of light as he struck it. The first familiar inhalation calmed him, the burn in the throat and the lingering taste. He exhaled gradually. Once the smoke cleared, he saw her again. She was closer, making her way towards him along the edge of the lake, her gaze turned wistfully towards the water. He couldn't see her feet through the mist. He tried to banish from his mind enticing Arthurian tales of ladies in lakes.

This was certainly a real person.

She must be freezing. She didn't appear to be wearing a coat, only some kind of oversize green cardigan, and below it a thin thigh-length dress or nightdress. As he took another drag on his fag, he could see her peering out into the lake, then down to the reeds at her feet. She was still a couple of hundred yards away at least, but something about her radiated melancholy. She stared into the water, and her shoulders shook. She was crying. An enfolding premonition began to build in him. She took a first step towards the water, her face distending as if about to cry.

Oh fuck. Don't do it.

'Hey there,' he bellowed. 'Stay out of the water.'

She seemed not to hear, but slowly and deliberately shrugged off the cardigan, and stepped into the water.

'For fuck's sake,' he muttered to himself. He called into his radio, alerting on all frequencies to anyone near Westgrave Lake to assist. But he knew it would be down to him. He didn't have time to cross on the bridge, which was in the wrong direction. Instead he ran down the embankment into the snowdrift on the moat, waded across the rapidly melting snow, and clambered up the other side, using his hands on tussocks of grass to make his way up. The control room came back to him, asking for more detailed information, but he didn't have much time. 'The lake north of the library at Westgrave Hall. We might need an ambulance too.'

By the time he clambered up the slope onto the path around the outer edge of the moat he was freezing. Snow had got up the trousers and into his shoes and was melting. He set off across rough pasture towards the lake. When he got within fifty yards of the water's edge, he pulled out his torch and shone it across the vapoured surface.

No sign of her.

He sprinted along the rough track which ran around the lake towards the place he had last seen her. Clouds of mist obscured the surface and there was no sound but the taunting laughter of ducks. He called out to her, his voice sucked into the cool night air. Scouring the water's edge with the harsh LED light, he spotted fresh bare footprints in the mud. Then a few yards further on, he heard coughing, and saw her in the water, struggling in a bank of reeds, up to her waist.

He jumped in, plunged up to his thighs first in mud and then in water. He reached out and grabbed her arm. She was cold but looked at him through narrowed eyes. He scooped her up in his arms. She weighed almost nothing and was shivering. It was only five yards from the shore, but it was a struggle to keep his footing as he attempted to wade through the reed bed. She held him tight, her arms about his shoulders, her freezing face pressed to his neck.

'What on earth would you want to do something like that for?' he asked, when he finally got her ashore. She looked as miserable as a drowned dog. All she was wearing was a nightdress and underwear. He badly needed a blanket to wrap her in.

'Please, give me a cigarette,' was the first thing she said to him, as he stood her up on dry land. She had some kind of foreign accent.

'No chance,' he replied. 'You need a cuppa and some soup.' His jacket was wet, but he wrapped her in it for want of anything else. He hurried her along the path, scooped up her cardigan, and had got halfway back to Westgrave Hall when two uniformed constables arrived. One swapped his dry jacket for Woodbridge's wet one and put his arm around her. The shivering PC followed on behind, his teeth chattering. He felt he was dying, goodness knows what the girl must be feeling like.

A few minutes later he was sitting in the grand morning room of Westgrave Hall, warming up in front of a roaring log fire, with a blanket around him. The girl was being attended to in an ambulance.

–

By first light, the spooks and their three unmarked vans had melted away from Westgrave Hall's car park, along with most of the snow. Surrey Police was back in charge of the crime scene, and with fifteen officers tramping backwards and forwards, much of it had turned into quagmire. As senior investigating officer, Gillard had been keen to make sure that the evidence was secure. He had appointed Detective Sergeant Vikram Singh as evidence officer, working out of a long-wheelbase Transit van. The Sikh had already set up shelves inside the vehicle which were turned over to ballistic evidence, footwear, clothing and DNA markers.

'So where are we with this lot?' Gillard asked, peering at the footwear shelf. He picked up three hefty brown paper envelopes, which were marked as containing the footwear of PC Butterfield, Sophie Cawkwell and Wolf, the head of security.

'We've got shoes from all three victims too,' Singh said. 'We'll get the clothes once they're at the mortuary.'

'What about Yelena Yalinsky's high heels?'

'Nope. Maybe MI5 has 'em.'

Gillard sighed heavily. His own voicemail message to DCS Corrigan, asking about the whereabouts of his note-book and tape recorder, had so far gone unanswered. 'Have they asked you for anything from our evidence collection?'

'No. They wanted to know how many guns we'd found, and I told them: two. We've also located forty-six cartridge cases from the library, and located and marked nineteen bullets embedded in walls, books and so on.'

'Even they wouldn't be so stupid as to start levering bullets from walls.'

'No, and we have photographs of each of those bullet holes,' Singh said. 'Butterfield did a tremendous job. We've got excellent pictures of the footprints and we should at least be able to start figuring out who was where when shots were fired.'

'Did you get the footage from the Russian TV channel?' Gillard asked.

'Yes. They've sent us a copy which apparently captures the sound of every shot.'

'Great. Then we will be able to ascertain whether we are missing any bullets.' Gillard looked at his phone, where a message had just come through. 'Ah, the Khazi is on its way.' The mobile incident room, a notoriously cramped and ill-ventilated Portakabin mounted on the back of a truck, was brought into use whenever a complex crime scene demanded detectives remain on site.

Logistically, the next stage was going to be the most difficult. Gillard had already rung and woken up an ill-tempered duty magistrate to grant the required warrant to search Westgrave Hall. It had arrived by email an hour later. He now needed the manpower to make it happen. With fifty-five bedrooms, over a hundred other rooms, a converted stable block with twenty-six rooms, and at least twelve cottages for various employees across the 4,000-acre estate, he was going to need an army. He had been jotting down how he hoped to do it and had already emailed a request to the chief constable for at least fifty uniformed police for three days. One thing he knew for certain: he would be enduringly popular with the rank and file for the overtime they would earn.

He just hoped they managed to find something to justify the cost.

–

The day shift took over at eight a.m., led by DI Claire Mulholland. She had with her an experienced uniformed sergeant from Staines, Vince Babbage, and six of his constables to start the search. They would be based at Steeple Risby village hall, which the parish council had kindly agreed to provide as a bunkhouse. That wasn't bad for short notice on Christmas Day. But it was only a start. Gillard had just had confirmation by text that at midday a coach would arrive with fifty-eight uniformed officers, overtime-hungry volunteers from all over the county. Gillard knew this crew was guaranteed to be made up of the badly overdrawn, the gambling-addicted or the unhappily married. Anyone for whom Christmas was less important than a few hundred extra quid.

'How are you doing, Craig?' Claire asked, as she found Gillard in the hall's elegant drawing room.

'Not too bad. The crime scene is a total mess, but at least it's self-contained.' He briefed her on what had been found so far. 'I'd like you to start with the bedrooms occupied by the victims and their partners, principally Volkov and Dr Sophie Cawkwell, Maxim Talin and Yelena Yalinsky, plus of course Bryn Howell.'

'Who's he?' Claire asked, struggling to hold the myriad details in her head.

'Volkov's bodyguard. He was late into the crime scene and got shot dead for his troubles.'

No one can work twenty-four hours a day, and picking the moment to take your break is quite an art. Having passed the baton to Claire, Gillard had been planning to drive off for a couple of hours' nap at home. However, the Westgrave Hall housekeeper had a better idea. She was a thin and severe-looking woman in her sixties called Mrs Bell. 'We have a number of rooms spare that we are happy for you to make use of, to sleep in but also if you need to have interviews or store evidence.' She had a thick Scottish accent, and a face seemingly built from decades of disappointment. If she was shocked by the night's events, she didn't show it.

'That's very kind,' Gillard replied. The bunkhouse being organised at the village hall was the alternative, but it would be busy now with plods sorting out their equipment. Rigby had demanded a ten a.m. incident room meeting, so Gillard would be able to get twice as much sleep by not having to drive. 'I think we will have to remove all physical evidence to a secure location, but would certainly like to take you up on the offer to interview those witnesses whom we have persuaded to stay.'

'Would this room be suitable for interviews?' Mrs Bell asked. She showed him into the Fitzroy Room, which she described as a small ballroom. It was far from being small, with enough room to play a game of doubles tennis. The 250-year-old teak flooring still bore the imprints of high heels, and Gillard could almost imagine the gavottes and minuets that had occurred here in its heyday. With an exquisite wood-panelled ceiling, gigantic tapestries and a profusion of porcelain vases on lacquered stands, it seemed an incongruous venue for the discussion of murder.

'I can see it's not quite suitable,' she said. She then led him down by a narrow staircase into a warren of corridors adjacent to the kitchens. Finally, she showed him into a dark low-ceilinged room, lined with iron racks from which wicked-looking hooks dangled. 'The scullery, originally used for hanging meats to age. If you want something a bit more Dante-esque this fits the bill.'

Gillard looked around. The only thing missing from the place was a mediaeval rack. 'If you don't mind, I think we'll revert to the ballroom.'

Mrs Bell had just the scratch of a smile on her granite features. 'I'll show you to your bedroom now.' She led him up a grand curving staircase to the first floor. 'I'm afraid the place is a bit of a rabbit warren, and there is still a lot of work to do on the eighteenth-century annexe where you'll be sleeping. But I think it will be perfectly adequate for a doze.'

She showed him through a smaller door in wood-panelled wainscoting to a narrow panelled corridor which looked out over the interior quadrangle of the main house, a dizzying distance beneath. He was led up a metal fire escape to a narrow corridor with a low ceiling in what was clearly the attic. There were three numbered rooms; she took out a key and unlocked the first, and showed him in. The room was a dormer bedroom with a sloping and badly cracked ceiling. It smelled musty, and the ancient electric light struggled to cast more than a pale glow. The double bed was of heavy wooden construction, and there was a plain dark crucifix over it. The pink worn-out candlewick bedspread clashed with the orange nylon paisley-pattern pillowcases. The whole place was depressing, the kind of garret where Gillard could imagine some young Victorian chambermaid dying in agonising childbirth while bearing the illegitimate offspring of the landowner.

He took off his shoes and lay on the bed. It creaked alarmingly and sagged in the middle.

He picked up the telephone, an enormous black Bakelite object with a woolly cord, and heard a dialtone like a purring cat. Wondering if it worked, he put his finger in the metal dial and rang Sam, listening to the whirr as each digit unwound. She answered, her voice edged with an echo as if in another solar system. He let her know that he wouldn't be back by breakfast time as she had expected.

'The TV news is full of it,' she said. 'Multiple shooting with three dead. There's even video footage where we can hear the shooting.'

'That didn't take long to find its way into the media,' he said. 'We've only just got a copy of it ourselves.'

'So I expect you're not home for Christmas lunch,' she asked.

'No, sorry. Save me some turkey.'

'Okay. Don't work too hard.' Gillard could hear the disappointment in Sam's voice. She been making great progress with her therapy for the PTSD since the abduction, but she did have relapses when she felt anxious being left alone. Her parents were coming down on Boxing Day from the Lake District, but this would still leave her largely alone on Christmas Day.

He blew a kiss, told her he loved her, and placed the heavy receiver back on its cradle.

He could hear crying. A female voice, faint but insistent.

Gillard made his way over to the window and pulled apart the heavy dark curtains. Pale morning light was beginning to filter through. The mullioned window looked out over a steep slope of mossy slates. To the right were several other gables like his, culminating in a belfry on the roof of which a bronze lion gazed towards the horizon. Below him was a modern flat-roofed building. There was no indication where the sobbing was coming from, even when he opened the window and leaned out as far as he dared.

He could see through an open window two storeys below. Two slightly-built dark-skinned men in white kitchen uniforms were labouring at a sink under cold strip lighting.

78

They weren't crying.

He wondered about the future of the stately home and its dozens of employees, many of whom had probably never met Alexander Volkov during his period of ownership. How often might that have been true over the centuries. If you worked in the kitchen it probably didn't matter to you whether the owner was a Russian oligarch, a French aristocrat or an obscure member of the German royal family. Long hours, low pay, and little recognition.

The detective closed the window, drew the curtains, lay on the bed and fell immediately into a deep but troubled sleep.

–

Detective Inspector Claire Mulholland was standing in Westgrave Hall's grand entrance lobby with security manager Wolf, the bulky figure of Sergeant Babbage, and his half-dozen bobbies. Just a quick glance at Wolf's floor-plan showed that the stately home was as big as London's Victoria and Albert Museum, and searching it properly could take weeks.

Wolf handed a hefty bunch of keys to the big sergeant and said: 'Please. Is very important you not break, scratch or nick work of art and antique stuff here. Very valuable things. So especially not nick,' he said.

'I can assure you we will be very careful and gentle,' Babbage said. 'My lads are honest to a fault.' He then turned to his boss. 'So where do we start, ma'am?'

'On the first floor, the principal state bedrooms occupied by our murder victims,' she said. 'Here's how I want you to do it. Everyone wears latex gloves. In each room, video the room before you go in so we can put everything back as you found it. For each room you'll have a plastic sheet, four feet square, which should be set out in the middle of the room. We're looking for phones, laptops, wallets, purses, handbags. And guns, should we be so lucky.'

'Righto,' Babbage said.

'Electronic items should be labelled, bagged and brought out to Vikram Singh's evidence wagon. Non-electronic items should be photographed and placed on the plastic sheet, with the evidence tag number visible. We patently do not have enough space to store everything that might turn out to be of interest, so most items will remain in the rooms where you found them. When you finish with a room, photograph everything on the square, and detail exactly what has been removed before locking it.'

'Has CSI been through?' Babbage asked.

'No. They're up to their eyeballs just with the library. We're not doing fingerprints here at the moment. As long as we are careful about how we touch things, we might be able to do that in future if required. Likewise with DNA.'

'How thorough are we going to be?' Babbage asked. 'I mean are we lifting floorboards or what?'

'No. Desks, cupboards, drawers, wardrobes. Coat and jacket pockets, suitcases and other baggage. No need at this stage to remove bedlinen. Bathrooms should be checked for toiletries and I want toothbrushes and combs marked and brought in in case we need DNA.'

'Cistern swab for cocaine, ma'am? Bound to be lots of cokeheads among the gentry.'

She shook her head. 'We are not trawling for gener-alised evidence of criminality. I have no doubt that we could keep ourselves very busy doing just that. In the first hours we will be concentrating on the bedrooms of the murder victims and their next of kin, so we must behave with absolute respect.'

'Received and understood,' Babbage said.

Escorted by Wolf they trooped up the grand curving staircase into a wide wood-panelled corridor hung with chandeliers that would not have disgraced Versailles. As the uniforms padded along the thick carpet, Wolf pointed out four bedrooms, each one named after a British poet.

'This one for Volkov, Ms Sophie next door,' Wolf said. 'Opposite is Mr Talin and Ms Yalinsky.'

'Where is Bryn Howell's bedroom?' Claire asked.

'Third floor, above the kitchen annexe, five minutes from here.'

They set to work, and Claire left them to it.

–

PC Simon Woodbridge awoke in a sleeping bag on a camp bed in Steeple Risby village hall. It was eight o'clock. There had been plenty of noise in the bunkhouse for the last couple of hours and he was unable to sleep through it anymore. Memories of last night's soaking in Westgrave Lake came back to him. After delivering the shivering girl to the ambulance he had been wrapped in a blanket and escorted down to the bunkhouse. After a hot shower he had been given a sleeping bag by the sergeant in charge and had fallen asleep almost immediately he got in it. He wasn't on duty until nine but got up and dressed in a spare police-issue fleece and trousers and made his way towards Westgrave Hall.

Outside the Khazi he saw an overweight detective whom he recognised as DC Hoskins, eating what looked suspiciously like a bacon sandwich. Hoskins beckoned him over.

'Was it you stopped that suicide attempt last night?' he said, chewing his sandwich.

'It was. Not sure if she wanted to kill herself.'

'Well, she is Volkov's daughter. Anastasia's her name. Her dad was murdered yesterday, so she's probably not a happy bunny.'

'Did she go to hospital?'

'Nah. She's all right. Just cold, I heard. She's in her room on the second floor.'

Woodbridge thanked Hoskins and, after finding the Westgrave Hall housekeeper Mrs Bell, was directed up the grand staircase to the higher floor. He knocked gently on the door, and was told to come in.

The room felt tropically warm. Anastasia was sitting up in a grand canopy bed against a mountain of pillows, with an enormous shaggy wolfhound lying on either side of her. Her chestnut hair was tied into a ponytail, and she looked young and vulnerable. She had been playing video games but set the console aside and turned off the TV as he approached. Her eyes were bloodshot, and she had clearly been crying. Dozens of discarded tissues were scattered on the bed and floor.

'How are you doing then?' the PC asked, as the two dogs yawned noisily.

'Okay. Thank you for saving me.' She managed a wan smile. Her face had the pallid androgyny of a catwalk model. There seemed nothing to her at all, he could imagine her with any personality he wanted. The dogs, woolly mountains with big brown eyes and shrewd expressions, gazed balefully at him.

'I only did what anybody would have done.'

'Not anybody.'

'Why were you out there in the freezing cold at that time of night?' he asked.

'I thought I might as well kill myself.'

'What a terrible thing to contemplate!'

'My dad's just been murdered, in case you hadn't noticed.' Her face began to distend, and she sobbed silently.

He nodded. 'I'm really sorry for your loss, but you have to look after yourself. Even if you won't do it for yourself, think about your mother.'

'My mother! She was probably the one who killed him.' She reached out and fluffed the ears of one of the dogs, who looked up at her adoringly.

Woodbridge's eyes widened. He wondered whether the girl had given a witness statement.

'My mother hated him. She's a good shot and been scheming to get him for years.'

'Because of the divorce?' Woodbridge asked, feeling surreptitiously for some paper and finding nothing in his fleece pocket. His standard-issue notebook was drenched, still sitting in his other jacket with his useless matches.

'And other stuff.'

'Would you be prepared to tell the detectives what you know?'

'What I know? I know what every newspaper reader knows. That sooner or later my dad was going to be murdered, like all the others. Either by the Kremlin, a business rival, or my mother. And my money was always on her.' She looked at him through narrowed eyes. 'Can I have a cigarette, please?'

Woodbridge felt in his trouser pocket. Yes, the rescued packet was there. 'Are you sure you're allowed?' he asked, bringing it out.

'For God's sake, I'm eighteen in a few weeks,' she hissed, holding out her hand. She looked like the kind of girl who was used to clicking her fingers.

He made his way to the bedside, tapped the pack and passed it towards her, then fumbled in his pocket for a lighter, borrowed earlier from a colleague. The cheap disposable flared first time. She leaned towards him, and her hand rested delicately on his wrist as he held the flame. As she sucked in greedily, her narrowed grey eyes scrutinised him. 'What's your name?'

'PC Woodbridge.'

'Is that what your mother named you?' she asked, blowing a plume of smoke towards his face. 'It's a boy, I'll call him PC Wood—'

'—Simon.'

'And how old is Simon?' She sucked in another deep inhalation. The smoke drifted from her nostrils as if she was an apprentice dragon.

'Twenty-two.'

'Well, well, my knight in reflective hi-vis armour. My Lancelot.' She stroked the other dog, which rolled onto its back submissively.

Woodbridge didn't know what to say to this precocious young woman. 'I'm glad you're feeling a bit better now,' he said looking towards the door. Time to be going.

'I'm not feeling better. My life was shit before, and now it just got worse. No one cares about me, except my lovely Pyramus and Thisbe. If not for them, I might as well be dead.'

'I'm sure that's not true.' He wondered whether a family liaison officer had been requested for her. He made a mental note to ask.

Anastasia blew a cloud of smoke upwards to the silken canopy of her bed. 'You know, I actually did see my mother at the party. Not to talk to, of course, she was far too busy. Still, it was the first time I'd laid eyes on her for two years.'

'Why was that?'

'Because my upbringing has been outsourced to people who are paid to pretend to care about me, and supposedly educate me.'

'What are you studying?'

'Modern media and photography.' She rolled her eyes. 'For the last year I've been in a Swiss finishing school. To teach me how to be a fucking lady.'

Woodbridge felt like a rabbit in the headlamps of her attention.

'You must have learned a lot.'

'Simple Simon, what did I learn? I am fluently bitchy in four languages. I can tell a fake Hermès scarf or Gucci handbag at a glance. I can snort cocaine elegantly and without sneezing, and know exactly how much I should pay for it. I can ski a double-diamond black run without falling.' She raised her hands behind her head and freed her hair, before fixing him with a stare. 'And I give truly fantastic head: slow and unbearably delicate. I could make you faint with pleasure.'

Woodbridge gulped.

'And, really, I suppose that I should do that. It would be my thank-you for saving my life,' she said, kneeling up in bed, stubbing out the cigarette in an ashtray. She clicked her fingers at the dogs, who slunk off into a corner of the room, shooting hateful glares at Simon.

'I'm back on shift in an hour,' he said lamely, parading a fig leaf of duty.

'Well, I'll need all of that,' she said, patting the bed beside her. 'And I'm afraid I do need to tie you up. It works best when you're helpless, begging for release, when you can't take any more.'

The young policeman had lots to consider: she was plain and skinny, with a miserable expression. She was dangerously young. He loved Sally and they were planning to move in together in the spring. And last but not least: if this came out, getting entangled with a witness could cost him his job.

But he was twenty-two and male. And a blow job is a blow job.

PC Simon Woodbridge didn't realise he'd even made a decision, so was surprised to see his own trembling hands almost blurred with haste unbuttoning his jacket and shirt as she reached across for the belt on his trousers.

Chapter Seven

It was 9:07 a.m when PC Simon Woodbridge lurched down the corridor from her room, a smile plastered across his face that would take some shifting. She hadn't lied. It was amazing. Truly amazing. To get him out, she'd initially tried waking him up with a kiss, and when that didn't work, she'd pushed him out of bed. She'd bundled him into the huge en suite and almost thrown his clothes at him. Straight after the scalding shower, he turned on his radio, and logged in with the sergeant, saying that he was on his way.

That gave him five minutes' grace to steady himself.

Down the corridor, just a few yards down from her room he found a staff bathroom to get his breath back. It was a cramped place with two cubicles and a single washbasin. In the small mirror his face was flushed almost scarlet, his eyes bloodshot. He also had a sore throat. He remembered that at one point she had clamped her hand over his mouth, telling him to be quiet.

Woodbridge threw cold water over his face, but it did nothing to eradicate the smirk. That would be there for years.

As he emerged into the corridor, he almost collided with one of the security guys he had seen before. A rangy fellow, a good six-three, with a blond ponytail and five o'clock shadow.

'Are you lost?' the man asked, his accent vaguely Eastern European.

'No. I just came to see Anastasia, to check she was all right.'

The big man's face tightened, and his brown eyes narrowed. He ran his gaze over the constable's features. 'She's fine. I think you should get back to standing in the rain or whatever it is you do.'

Woodbridge could feel a proprietorial edge to this man's stare. There was no doubt that he was currently an intruder in enemy territory. Not welcome at all. But a young man who has just had an illicit blow job is not easily cowed. The corners of the constable's mouth were twitchy, heralding that irrepressible grin. He turned away to hide it, and walked off jauntily towards the staircase, feeling the bodyguard's eyes boring holes in his back.

–

Woodbridge grabbed a breakfast sandwich in the village hall kitchen, then checked in at the bunkhouse where Sergeant Vince Babbage looked him over. 'Hero of the hour, I see.' He stared at the young constable's face and walked slowly around him as if inspecting a statue. 'Looks like you've been awarded the bloody life-saving medal already, son.'

PC Woodbridge continued to stare straight ahead, trying to suppress his smirk as much as possible. 'Well, well, well. That takes me back a few years,' Babbage said, standing behind him. 'PC Collins, may I borrow you?'

'Yes sir,' said a young constable about the same age as Woodbridge, who was half dressed and had been shaving in a portable mirror.

'You're a young man of the world, Collins. Come and have a look at this,' Babbage said.

Woodbridge was thoroughly alarmed by this unwelcome attention. He just couldn't think. He had certainly dressed in a hurry and may well have got his collar creased.

'What is your forensic opinion of this, PC Collins?' Babbage had his finger pressed about two inches below Woodbridge's ear.

'Looks like a love bite to me, sir. And a big one.'

'A love bite, yes indeed, just what I thought. One big enough to have its own fucking postcode, I would say.' He thrust his face back in front of the constable. 'Wouldn't you say so, Woodbridge?'

'I don't know, sir, I can't see it.'

'Then you need to get yourself a pair of spectacles, don't you, constable? Get yourself down to Specsavers, because you must be going fucking blind, boy.' The sergeant clicked his fingers towards Collins, who passed across the shaving mirror. 'Take a look at that, it's as glorious as a Baywatch sunset.' He held the mirror at an angle to the PC's neck. Woodbridge had to look sharply to the right to see the mirror. Only half the love bite was visible above his shirt collar, a two-inch purple semicircle.

'Looks like you spent the night with Mick Jagger, constable. Someone with a gob big enough to do that to you.'

His throat went dry. He had no recollection of her even kissing him there. Maybe it was as she was waking him up. 'I wasn't on duty at the time, sir,' he croaked.

'Ah, yes. Not on duty. The classic get-out.' The sergeant paced around him. 'Nevertheless, constable, you are in a public place, an ambassador of Surrey Police. What kind of impression do you think it gives the great British public, if they see a member of the thin blue line looking like he's been attacked in the night by a deranged bloody vampire?'

'Not a good one, sir.'

'Indeed. Not a good one.'

PC Collins had his back turned while he finished dressing, but it was clear he was killing himself laughing.

Babbage hadn't finished with him yet. 'I hesitate to speculate, Woodbridge, but I don't suppose this was the only part of your putrid undernourished body that this particular succubus had her gob on. But those parts are, thank God, not normally waved around in public like the back of your neck is. So I shall draw a veil over further inquiries. Just make sure you get a big Elastoplast right over that abomination and start behaving professionally.'

'Yes sir, right away sir.'

Babbage had had his fun. 'All right, I've taken pity on you. PC Alison Smith is taking the all-nighter tonight. Presumably I won't see her with her throat torn out in the morning, but of course these days you never know. Anyway, gives you the chance to get some clean clothes and wipe that grin off your face. You're directing traffic in the lane today outside Steeple Risby, then back at Mount Browne tomorrow morning.'

Woodbridge was relieved to be able to escape from the village hall. A few minutes later, a dressing carefully placed on his neck, he was making his way back up the drive to Westgrave Hall to retrieve his wet police-issue jacket, when he saw DCI Gillard walking in the other direction. 'Ah, Woodbridge. I understand you rescued the lady from the lake last night.'

'Yes, sir.'

'Give you a sword, did she?'

'No, sir.' Woodbridge fought to stop the stupid grin returning to his face.

'Good work, anyway. How is she this morning? Well enough to be interviewed, would you say?'

'I should say so, sir.'

Gillard drew the young constable aside, and led him into the Victorian walled garden, away from prying eyes. They stood side-by-side looking at the watery sunlight filter amongst the bare branches of the lime trees. 'Have a cigarette if you want. I won't tell Babbage.'

Woodbridge needed no encouragement. 'Thank you, sir.' He lit up and took a deep inhalation.

'Was she really trying to commit suicide, do you think?'

Woodbridge nodded. 'I think she's very confused.'

'Yes. Not the best way to commit suicide, wading into a lake.'

'She's grieving for her father, sir. Kept crying when she mentioned him.'

'Understandable.'

'Hates her mother. Blames it all on her.'

The detective turned to look at the younger man. 'What exactly did she say?'

'She said that her mother probably killed Volkov.'

'That's very open of her, to tell you, a perfect stranger, all that.'

'I suppose so,' Woodbridge said.

'Nice girl?'

Fighting the reappearing smirk, he couldn't quite find the mental tools to articulate his opinion. 'I suppose so.'

Gillard peered at the dressing under the constable's ear. 'I sincerely hope that it wasn't her that gave you that. Daughter of the murder victim. Key witness, potentially.'

Woodbridge couldn't believe he already knew. He didn't say anything, but the smirk kept resurfacing, even though he knew he was in trouble.

'So it was her.' Gillard sighed.

'Sorry, sir.'

'Trouble is, Woodbridge, I don't think you are. That compounds your grievous error of judgement, and since you paraded it through breakfast at the village hall, everyone knows. I'm sorry, but I can't have you on the case any longer. What duty are you on today?'

'Directing traffic in the lane, sir.'

'No, much too prominent. Can't have you running into her again. I'm sending you back to your station, go and tell Babbage. And think yourself lucky you're not on a disciplinary.'

'Yes sir.' As Gillard walked off and left him, Wood-bridge's smirk finally disappeared.

–

Gillard recognised Anastasia. She was the willowy girl he had seen in the ballroom wailing in the comforting arms of a portly man. Today, when she sat down opposite Gillard in the Fitzroy Room, she looked a lot more casual: jeans, sweatshirt, ankle boots. Her hair had been neatly combed, but she retained an unnatural pallor.

'I hope you're feeling better today,' Gillard said.

She shrugged and looked out of the window.

'I am sorry about your father. We do have family liaison officers if you feel you need support.'

She nodded and stared down at her nails. This was clearly going to be hard work.

'Anastasia, you made some comments to my colleague PC Woodbridge, about your mother.'

Finally, she looked at him. Her pale grey eyes betrayed no emotion. 'You want me to accuse my mother of murder?'

'PC Woodbridge reported that you felt Ms Yalinsky may have had some responsibility for what happened last night.'

She shrugged. 'It was a private conversation. My mother hated my dad and wanted to screw every penny out of him in the courts over the divorce. So, yeah, if she had a hand in it, I wouldn't be surprised. But I'm not going to stand up in court and point the finger.'

'I'm not asking you to do that.'

'So what are you asking?'

'Did you ever witness any violent confrontations between your parents?'

'You seem to assume that because we are biologically a family we spent any time together. I was a nuisance from a young age and was farmed out like a loss-making business. Who did I grow up attached to? Nannies, private tutors, chaperones and bodyguards. In the last five years I've seen my parents within slapping distance of each other maybe three times.'

'Overall, you spent more time with your father?'

She chewed her nails absentmindedly. 'I was at boarding school here in Surrey for a few years, that was before I got expelled and sent to Switzerland. Dad was nice, and I loved him because he actually tried. He used to take me out to lunch. But he was always busy, and he didn't know what to say to me. I mean he didn't know me, or who I am. He spent half the time on the phone, while I played with my food. Then after an hour so I'd get taken round the shops by Natasha. I just pointed at things I wanted, and they got sent to me.'

'Natasha Fein?'

'Yeah. Slimy bitch. She was screwing him for years.'

Gillard tried to assimilate these insights into a ruined childhood. 'What about your brother, was it as bad for him?'

'Oleg?' she laughed. 'My mother adores him. Oh! The toddler who never outgrew the playroom, a boy who can do no wrong.' She rolled her eyes. 'Maybe he killed my dad. They didn't get on well. And before you ask, no, I never heard him threaten to kill anyone, except some guy in the village who got in the way of his Hummer.'

'I was hoping to interview your brother, but he's apparently left, even though he said he would stay.'

'Yeah, that's Oleg.'

'Do you know where he's gone?'

'Maybe to his flat in Knightsbridge. He's got a place in Italy somewhere too, near our castle. There are quite a few brain-dead gold-digger girlfriends and hangers-on he might be staying with. He could be anywhere. But one clue you might find useful. If the Hummer is still here, he'll be coming back soon.'

'Well that's good to know.' He could feel the interview sliding away into irrelevance and tried hard to get back on track. 'Can I ask you about the evening of the shooting. Where were you?'

'I was in my room some of the time. I was sick, too much drink probably. I'd been dancing earlier and watching the skaters.' A slight smile stole across her face, the only hint that she was capable of enjoyment or happiness. 'I heard the fireworks but didn't get that there was any shooting. It must've been fifteen minutes later when Uncle Dmitry told me. I couldn't believe it.'

'Had you met Maxim Talin?'

She snorted in derision. 'Yeah, once. Mum brought him over to Geneva to meet me and we went out to lunch. The love of my life, she introduced him as. "The only person I ever really loved." Well, thanks a bunch.' She rolled her eyes again. 'A sweaty toad of a man. Dyed his hair blond. I know the idea is you've got a kiss a lot of frogs to find your prince, but if you read the instruction manual it says once you discover an amphibian you move on. For some reason she decided to stay in the pond with him and raise frogspawn.'

Anastasia glanced up at the puzzled expression on Gillard's face. 'Okay, you probably don't know this. She was having fertility treatment, can you believe? Had her prehistoric eggs frozen in some clinic. She's forty-seven! It's like Frankenstein or something. And toadman had apparently been freezing his sperm for decades.' She shivered. 'Disgusting. It didn't work. Just as well. Whatever they produced would have been an abomination, fit only for a forgotten cage at the back of the circus.'

Gillard had never seen such naked hunger for love in his life. Jealous of a child yet to be conceived. The kid was mixed up and no mistake.

'Okay, thank you for your time. One final thing. We asked all guests to surrender their phones just to help us track of where people were. We were really hoping that every member of the family would comply, but neither you nor your brother have.'

'You seriously expect me to give you my phone?' She looked at him like he was mad.

'I do. It would be useful to see any messages you had exchanged with your parents recently, that might give us an insight into their state of mind in the run-up to the events of Christmas night.'

'You don't need my phone for that,' she retorted, fluffing out her hair. 'My dad was besotted with the fossil woman, and my mum only had eyes for toadman.'

'I'd still like your phone. You can have it back within an hour.'

'Get lost.' She stood up and walked out.

–

It was 9:45 a.m. when Gillard ascended the wooden staircase into the Khazi for the inaugural incident room meeting. As he pulled open the plywood door on the Portakabin and peered inside, he could see that no one had recently cleaned off the black mould which was threatening to overwhelm the institutional off-white paint. He turned on all the extractor fans, hoping that their whining noise would be less of a problem than the smell of the mould they were designed to eliminate. With ten minutes to go before the meeting was due to start, he took off his jacket, found the cleaning cupboard and started to give the most accessible surfaces a good wipe-down. The threadbare carpet, like something discarded by an East End pub in the 1950s, was beginning to fray at the edges, but there was nothing he could do about that.

He was just cleaning off the three wall-mounted whiteboards when the squeaking of the door alerted him to someone entering. DC Carrie Macintosh, universally known as Rainy, was wearing her trademark black trouser suit and white blouse. She grimaced as she took in the surroundings.

'Aye, this reminds me of my auntie's flat in the Gorbals.' Rainy was a stockily-built former junior doctor from Glasgow, who maintained she'd joined the police to get away from the fighting, blood and unsociable hours of A&E. Frying pans and fires, was the general opinion.

Watching her boss clean up, she pitched in too. She also managed to find a portable space heater, which she plugged in and set on maximum. 'Och, it's a lovely wee fire risk,' she said, holding out her hands to the warm air as the smell of scorched dust began to replace that of black mould.

Over the next few minutes, DI Claire Mulholland, Research Intelligence Officer Rob Townsend, financial specialist Shireen Corey-Williams and Detective Constable Michelle Tsu all filed in to take their seats. The last to arrive was the widest, DC Carl Hoskins, halfway through eating a sausage and bacon bap he had managed to inveigle from the Westgrave Hall kitchen.

'Don't bring that in here,' Shireen said. 'I haven't had any breakfast.'

Hoskins tore the remains of the bap in half and gave her the soggier ketchup-drenched end in a greasy napkin. 'Happy Christmas, love.'

'Thank you. I like the festive wrapping paper,' she said, holding the napkin gingerly. Shireen, of Iranian and Lebanese descent, had learned to love the British banger through her marriage to a Brummie, which also gave her a bit of the Midlands accent. Even so, her colleagues were a little surprised to see her tuck in without hesitation to the morsel Hoskins had offered her. Finally, DS Vikram Singh arrived with a neat folder and what looked like two rolls of wallpaper.

'Smart guy,' said Hoskins. 'Always a good idea to bring spare paper to the Khazi.'

Singh laughed.

Gillard called the meeting to order and set out the priorities.

'All right everybody, good to see you all here on Christmas overtime pay rates.'

'Yay,' said Rainy, giving Michelle a high five. 'I need every penny.'

'We're going to be under a lot of pressure on this one. The media camp that is building at the end of the lane will not have escaped your notice. This is by no means the first killing of a wealthy Russian oligarch on British soil, nor the first in Surrey. Conspiracy theories will abound, and you will no doubt be getting calls from your usual press contacts. Christina McCafferty will be here to brief you in more detail later on what we're saying to the press, but the short answer at the moment is nothing. Do not expand upon the terse one-liner: three shot dead, no reason to suspect any wider danger to the British public.'

'Sir, what were all the guys doing with the noddy suits last night?' asked Hoskins, still chewing the last of his bap.

'We weren't provided with the luxury of an answer,' Gillard said. 'However, no one heard any clicks on the Geiger counter, and given that the noddy-suits were all gone within an hour, I don't think we are anticipating any nasty chemicals.'

'Of course, we're just a bunch of wee guinea pigs if there is any nerve agent,' Rainy said.

'You know, I went to Salisbury once when I was a kid,' said Michelle Tsu. 'All I remember is sitting in that park, the same one the Skripals were found in, with my mum and dad, having an ice cream.'

'Novichok-ice, I expect,' Rainy said, to widespread groans from the other officers.

Gillard turned to Singh. 'Vikram, how are we doing on evidence?'

'It's coming together. However, one item seems to have gone missing. PC Butterfield retrieved Alexander Volkov's satellite phone from his inside jacket pocket. She put it on a bookshelf, as she'd run out of evidence bags. When I went in to bag it up, it had gone.'

Gillard's face tightened. 'Was that after the spooks took over?'

'Unfortunately, yes. I'd been too busy with other things previously and hadn't been able to re-enter the crime scene while CSI were examining the footprints.'

'Have you got all the other cell phones?'

'Yes.' Singh counted them off on his fingers. 'The dead bodyguard's, Maxim Talin's, and that of the unpronounceable head of security.'

'Just call him Wolf. All right, leave the issue of Volkov's phone with me,' Gillard said. 'Rob Townsend will take charge of the examination of the phones. Anything I should add, Rob?'

'Yes, sir. We've got twenty-or-so phones volunteered by witnesses who were taking video or pictures at the time of the fireworks, so we should be able to identify who was where as the shooting was taking place.'

'Okay, but concentrate on the devices of those within the library. The rest can wait.'

'Yes, sir.'

'The cartridge cases and bullets have been parcelled off for ballistics and we should get an answer by Boxing Day on some of the basic questions. Claire, how is the search going?'

'Not bad. We've not found anything unexpected. Volkov had over £10,000 in cash in his room, in various currencies. It was just lying in a drawer, admittedly a locked one. There's a safe in there too, with a combination lock. It was behind a picture, believe it or not. Wolf said that only Volkov would have had the combination.'

'Anything else?'

'Plenty of electronic devices. We'll need a Russian translator to help Rob understand what's on them.'

'I've already got a request in to the chief constable. To save time we could use Wolf on anything that seems important to begin with, and then get everything checked later.'

Claire nodded. 'Let's concentrate our resources on where we can make progress quickly.'

'Agreed,' Gillard replied, turning to the Sikh officer. 'Okay, Vikram. I understand you've put together a map?'

'Two maps, actually. I thought it would be helpful to plot exactly where all the bullets and casings were found, putting together the photographs and markers.' Across a desk he unrolled a six-foot length of decorators' lining paper. The seventy-yard-long mezzanine floor of the library had been carefully drawn to scale and was spotted with red and yellow dots. 'I have marked on here the location of every bullet in red, except those still in the bodies. Cartridge cases are in yellow, forty-six in total. We have accounted for thirty-five bullets, again not counting those that may be in the bodies. Some of the embedded ones are still in situ in shelves and walls.'

Gillard looked at the map. 'This is a very useful contribution, Vikram. What is the other one?' He glanced at the second scroll of wallpaper.

'Footprints, sir,' he unrolled the second map. An identical drawing of the mezzanine was marked with numerous coloured arrows. 'I basically tried to match up the shoes to the victims, based on the photographs and my own investigations. The red and the blue are Volkov and Talin, while the green, orange and yellow are those of the three who came in after the shooting stopped.'

'Interesting that we don't have any for Yelena,' Gillard said.

'That's right, sir,' Singh replied.

'Backs up her assertion that she was out before the bullets and the blood.' Gillard glanced at the confusing mass of colours and realised that this was going to require some serious analysis. 'It would have helped enormously if the three rescuers had minded where they put their feet.'

'To be fair, sir, PC Zoe Butterfield did,' Singh responded. 'And she told me she nagged the others about it.'

Gillard nodded. 'In any case, it's an excellent piece of initiative, as is the bullet map. I take it Yaz Quoroshi has seen them both?'

'He helped compile them.'

Gillard turned to his research intelligence officer. 'Rob, I want you to get an early look in on all the cell phone activity in this area for twenty-four hours before the shooting and four hours afterwards. I want to know who was talking to whom amongst this group.'

Rob nodded, and made some notes.

'Excuse me for being a bit dim, sir,' said Hoskins. 'But isn't this an open and shut case?'

'Let's hear it, Carl.'

'Well, correct me if I'm wrong, but it was a shootout between these two rival businessmen about the woman. This bird was previously married to one, and was having a bit on the side with the other one, so it's your basic love triangle, isn't it?'

'Did you get that startling insight from *Hello* magazine?' Michelle asked.

Hoskins grinned. His deliberately non-PC language was designed to ruffle feathers amongst female colleagues and rarely failed.

'That's one interpretation,' Gillard said.

'Maybe the woman shot them both,' Shireen interjected. 'Being understandably fed up with men.' She glared meaningfully at Hoskins.

'Nah. She was in the panic room,' Hoskins replied. 'Couldn't get out, because Volkov, who is an even bigger guy than I am, was sitting there dead with his arse against the outward-opening door.'

'So who shot the bodyguard, Bryn Howell?' DS Singh asked. 'He only went in when the shooting began and was right down the other end. Assuming he wasn't shot by his own employer, he must have been shot by Talin.'

'Or the woman,' Shireen insisted.

'Nah, she was definitely inside the panic room by then,' Hoskins said.

'Says who?' Shireen persisted.

'She did,' Gillard said. 'But that's no reason to believe her. I'm sure she's not telling me the truth, at least not the whole truth.'

He tipped several dozen photographic enlargements out of an A3 envelope onto a desk. The officers crowded around to take a look. 'CSI did a Bluestar examination of the library gallery and ground floor this morning. The place was lit up like a planetarium.'

The old method of finding bloodstains in a room was to use a substance called Luminol, but Bluestar was far superior. The reagent that CSI sprayed onto surfaces in the room did not require absolute darkness and did not produce false positives from bleach as Luminol did. Using 400 ASA film it was quite easy for CSI technicians to spot and record even the tiniest pinpricks of blood. A low-light video recording captured in a panoramic sweep how the various images connected together.

One finding already illustrated by Singh's bullet map became even clearer on the blood analysis. The shooting had divided the mezzanine floor of the Volkov Library quite neatly into two halves. The balcony adjacent to the long panoramic window on the southern edge of the building was almost entirely free of blood and footprints. The other side of the gallery was drenched. This was the side where all the bodies were found, and which backed onto the library shelves, a few back offices and the two staircases. Spatters and droplets covered the walls like measles, as well as the more obvious pools and footprints on the floor. It was like the Saint Valentine's Day massacre.

'Och, what a mess. Reminds me of my first time in theatre to do an emergency caesarean section,' said Rainy. 'I could have done with wee windscreen wipers on my specs.'

'Certainly a lot of bullets,' Hoskins said.

Gillard nodded. 'And remember, every bullet is like an encyclopaedia, packed with information. So we've got forty-odd volumes of evidence. Give me that over a single-shot marksman any day.'

'I remember the Kingston architects shooting we were involved with a few years back,' Claire Mulholland said. 'That gave us no end of trouble.'

'It certainly did. Here, I'm hoping that we can quickly gather together some crucial evidence and then stage a reconstruction of the shooting.'

Rainy's hand shot into the air. 'Hey, bags I play the baddie. Are yers planning to use live ammunition?'

'Not a re-enactment, Rainy, just a reconstruction,' Gillard said with a smile. It was clear to him that the Glaswegian enjoyed being the class joker. Her jocularity and insubordination didn't quite hide the very sharp brain that she possessed.

'Given all the embedded bullets in the bookshelves, most of the firing must've been from the window-side balcony,' Claire said. 'There were only four shots which hit the windows.'

'That's right,' Hoskins said. 'And the victims must've been on the library side almost the whole time.'

'If they'd been running around a lot, wouldn't we find bullet impacts more equally distributed?' asked Shireen.

Gillard smiled and raised both hands. 'I want to keep an open mind, but the points you've raised show we've already got contradictions here. One is the simple idea that the two men shot each other. That would be the neatest solution. But if that was so, as Claire says, one of them must have been firing from the window side for a while to get off twenty or more shots to impact on the library side. Moreover, there are at least three bullet wounds in each victim. At least one in each case also has an exit wound, and a messy one at that. It's quite a stretch to believe that so much shooting took place from the window side, and that it was only when that shooter came back over to the library side that he in turn was mortally wounded.'

Shireen was grinning as if vindicated. 'The woman in the panic room may have started the shooting, and one of the other two finished it off.'

'Where's the gun?' Hoskins asked bluntly. 'She didn't have one, according to Quoroshi. We've only found the one upstairs, plus the one on the bodyguard.'

'It's a good point. CSI insists they searched the entire place, top to bottom, including the panic room,' Gillard said. 'No gun.'

'Maybe the spooks have got it, along with your note-book and tape recorder, sir,' Rob Townsend said.

Gillard gave a wry smile. 'They must have moved quickly to locate a weapon which eluded Zoe Butterfield, Sophie Cawkwell and Volkov's head of security, who were in the library alone for more than forty minutes.'

'It's still possible,' he said.

'Yes, it is,' Gillard conceded.

'Maybe Sophie Cawkwell pocketed it?' Shireen suggested.

Gillard inclined his head in acknowledgement. 'All interesting suggestions. However, I'd like to return to the facts at this stage.' He dimmed the lights, then pressed a few buttons on his laptop. On the wall-mounted screen, a glamorous red-headed TV reporter wearing a dark fur coat and matching hat was shown against the snowy back-ground of the party. She was talking enthusiastically in what sounded like Russian, and pointing out with long scarlet nails the various activities that were taking place behind her.

'Let me move it on to the relevant section,' Gillard said.

'Spoilsport,' muttered Hoskins. The fast-forward showed her waddling rapidly down each of the snowy terraces, past dancers, the Cinderella-type carriage and skaters, towards the bridge.

'Och, she reminds me of a wee penguin heading for the sea in one of those David Attenborough documentaries,' Rainy said.

'I'd look after her egg for her,' Hoskins said. 'Balance it on me feet.'

'Aye and offer to fertilise it for her too?' she winked at him. 'In yer dreams, sunshine.'

Fireworks began on the screen, and Gillard slowed down. The woman was looking over her shoulder, somewhat redundantly pointing out the multi-coloured explosions, which drowned out her speech.

'Who made this?' Hoskins asked.

'I'll get yer a copy for your birthday, Carl,' Rainy said.

'The producer works for TV96, which is apparently a celebrity TV channel in Moscow,' Gillard said. 'The presenter is a former figure skating world champion, Irina something. Earlier footage they sent me shows her whizzing round the rink with the professionals.'

Shireen folded her arms. 'I imagine if you're stuck in a freezing flat in Siberia in the middle of winter, this is supposed to cheer you up. Remind you why they had a revolution.'

'The next thing from Netflix: Return of the Romanovs,' Michelle said.

'Tsar Turn,' Rainy suggested.

Hoskins laughed. 'Celebrity Snow Island, perhaps?'

Gillard shushed them for the tail end of the fireworks. It was quite hard to disentangle the start of the gunfire on the video from the final aerial explosions, but once the shooting really got going it was unmistakeable. They listened to it right through three times.

'I make it forty-six shots,' Claire Mulholland said.

'Forty-three, by my reckoning,' said Hoskins.

'That cannae be right, Carl, since we have recovered forty-six cartridge cases,' Rainy said.

Vikram Singh peered at the screen. 'I calculate it was shot twenty-eight which frosted the window facing us. And we got up to thirty-nine at the point when we saw the bodyguard go in.'

'That's all useful information,' Gillard said. 'It's fantastic to have a timeline backed by incontrovertible video evidence. By my reckoning, the entire incident from first shot to last took ninety-three seconds. The personal protection officer was inside at eighty-five seconds.'

'When the poor bugger had only eight seconds left to live,' Shireen said.

'The question that gets me is why he was outside at all,' Claire said. 'His job is to be with his boss, protecting him.'

'It could only be because Volkov felt completely safe in the company of Talin,' said Michelle.

'Oh, do me a favour,' Hoskins said. 'Yelena Yalinsky was in there too! What bloke ever feels safe in a confined space with his ex? Especially when they have been fighting for years about billions in a divorce settlement.'

'I'm with you on that,' Shireen said.

Hoskins warmed to his theme. 'I mean my ex would have scratched me eyes out in a heartbeat, and we were only fighting over a second-hand Ford Mondeo, a DFS leather settee with a rip down one side and her Barry Manilow CDs, which I lobbed in the skip.' The chuckles in the room were particularly marked amongst those officers who had known Hoskins a decade ago when his divorce was going through.

'Don't forget the china pug,' Claire said. 'I took an irate phone call from her about that.'

'Yeah, that bloody thing,' Hoskins muttered. The ornament had ended up in the skip too.

Gillard held his hands up. 'For whatever reason, Bryn Howell was not in the library, and it appears he laid down his life in an attempt to get back in. Motivations at this point are beyond us. Like I said, stick to the facts for now, and when we get the full range of witness interviews we might be able to shed some more light on the "why".'

'You know we've got an Appeal Court judge on our witness list?' Claire said, looking at a list of attendees 'Richard Gibbon is Lord Justice Gibbon.'

'Yes, I don't think the circumstantial side of evidence is going to be a problem,' Gillard said. 'The biggest conundrum will be what actually happened in that library in the ninety-three seconds of the shooting. That is where I hope that Neville Tufton will be able to help.'

Chapter Eight

The arrival of National Ballistics Intelligence Service expert Neville Tufton moved the debate to a higher level. Gaunt, grey-haired and resembling a superannuated geography teacher, Tufton had been the Met's lead on ballistics before being transferred to the Birmingham-based NBIS. He and Gillard greeted each other like long-lost friends. As Tufton set up his slides, he told Gillard not to expect too much.

'All but five of the bullets I examined were fired from the same weapon,' Tufton said. 'But that weapon is not in our possession, and it's not on the national database either. As far as we know it's never been used in any crime.'

'What can you tell me about it?' Gillard asked.

'It's a .38, exhibiting the most common barrel configuration with six broad grooves, narrow lands and a left-hand twist. Judging by the number of rounds we have recovered, the assailant must either have had a larger-than-normal magazine or stopped to reload a couple of times. The profusion of cartridge cases widely spread about indicates it wasn't a revolver, which retains them within the casing until a manual reload. Given more time, I may be able to narrow down the exact manufacturer and model, but the only way to be really sure is to have a candidate gun in your possession and test fire a bullet from it to compare to the others.'

'I have nae idea about guns, but it sounds a bit wild to me. Like amateurs, spraying bullets everywhere,' Rainy said.

Tufton nodded. 'Good point, well done.' He really was like a schoolteacher. 'That was my first impression on seeing the impact map. This is a world away from a professional hit job. Bullets in the ceiling, embedded in the hardwood floor on the ground level and in the book-cases. Now that doesn't necessarily mean that professionals were not involved. If a weapon jams, and an assassin is unable to get off his first shot, a surgical operation could easily deteriorate into mayhem.'

Gillard interrupted. 'We do know that Bryn Howell, the personal protection officer, had considerable firearms experience and training, because of his military back-ground. I don't know whether that was true of either Volkov or Talin.'

'What can you tell us about the two guns we do have?' Claire asked.

'The Browning found near the body of the personal protection officer I believe to be his, an unlicensed weapon. Only one bullet was missing from the magazine and we have found a matching bullet in the ceiling and cartridge case on the ground floor.'

'Witnesses do say that Howell only entered the building during the very last moments of the shooting,' Gillard said.

Tufton nodded. 'The other weapon is a Glock 9mm found in the possession of Maxim Talin, again not on the database.'

'Another illegal weapon,' Gillard said.

'Yes. Four shots were missing from the magazine, and we found three around the room. One lodged in a window frame, one embedded in a wall and another on the ground floor. That leaves one to find, assuming the magazine was full to begin with and he didn't have a chance to reload.'

'I wonder if any of Talin's bullets are in Volkov?' Shireen asked.

Tufton smiled. 'That's a critical question, and one I can't answer yet. I will be looking forward to examining them when they are retrieved.' He turned to Gillard. 'When is the post-mortem, Craig?'

'Tomorrow,' Gillard said.

'Aye, the usual way to spend Boxing Day,' Rainy Macintosh said. 'Dr Delahaye carving up the leftovers, followed by a wee few tins of lager and nodding off in front of *The Sound of Music*.' This generated some chuckles amongst the assembled detectives.

She continued. 'I may be a wee bit slow, but it seems to me the killer has got away. If we havenae got the weapon, it must have left with the killer, right?'

'I'm not really able to say, I just look at the ballistic evidence,' Tufton replied, looking to Gillard.

The detective chief inspector turned to Rainy and asked: 'How did he get out? There is no emergency exit from the library, so the only way in and out is through the main door.'

'What about the skylight?' she replied. 'It was open about a foot and a half, enough for a man to squeeze through.'

'Yes, and I haven't so far found anyone who admitted to opening it,' Gillard replied. 'It must have been opened after the snow blowers finished, which was six p.m. Otherwise there would be melted snow on the floor underneath.' He gave a sceptical shrug. 'For all that, it's a thirty-foot climb from the mezzanine floor to the skylight. All right, you can manage the first six feet clambering on a bookcase, but you'd need Spiderman to do the rest, and it only gets you out onto the roof. Less than two hours after the killing I saw myself that there were no footprints in the snow on that pitched roof, and I think if a helicopter was involved everybody would have seen and heard it.'

Rainy was not deterred. 'Sir, maybe our cunning wee assassin could have hidden in the library, in one of the teaching rooms, and only exited through the skylight after you had done your inspection of the snow.' She held up a photographic enlargement of the three-foot by four-foot skylight.

'How is it controlled?'

'There's a wee button on the wall outside the panic room. It's alternate open and close. Nothing clever.'

Gillard pursed his lips. 'CSI was already in the place, but I suppose it's possible. I still would have expected to see some footwear marks on the wall just below the skylight, even assuming he's a skilled climber. I've done a bit of free climbing, but there's no way I could do that. Besides, it still leaves the question of how he got in.'

'Way earlier, before or during the party perhaps,' Rainy said. Claire Mulholland nodded in agreement, as did a couple of the other cops.

'Ah, do me a favour,' Hoskins laughed, slapping the table. 'So our Superman is invisible, or at least not notice-able, on his way in. Leaves no footprints at the crime scene that we know of. Climbs like a cat burglar on his way out, without using his feet on the wall. Flings himself off the roof somewhere without leaving a footprint on the roof or the surrounding snow. Given all those skills, why did it take him forty-odd bullets to finish off two pissed, overweight billionaires?'

There was some laughter at this. 'What made you think they were drunk?' Michelle Tsu asked.

'Oh, come on!' Hoskins rolled his eyes. 'It's a Christmas party, the booze is free, they're male and they're Russian.'

Michelle, who had often been on the wrong end of Carl's racial stereotyping, said: 'Maxim Talin has been teetotal for five years, and vegan for ten, according to last year's *Sunday Times* profile.'

'Nah, teetotal Russians are rarer than unicorn poo.'

Keeping incident room meetings on the point was always difficult. Craig Gillard always wanted his team to explore the possibilities, and to bounce ideas off each other, but when time was pressing, as it usually was, he needed to bring them back on track to examine the evidence before their eyes. Now seemed to be a good time to teach them about their two principal victims.

Gillard started running some slides. 'Alexander Vasiliyovich Volkov, fifty-five, born in Perm in Siberia. His father was in a Siberian gulag for twenty years. His mother was a hydraulic engineer. I've not covered the details of his education, and early working life because none of that is significant until—'

'Until he laid hands on all the lolly,' Hoskins said.

'Exactly. Volkov is valued by *Forbes* magazine's rich list at $6 billion, making him the seventeenth richest person in the UK. He has a controlling interest in Kazakh Minerals, which is basically all about copper. Fell out with the Kremlin about a decade ago over the lack of tax paid on his profits but is seemingly in their good books now.'

'Or not, as the case may be,' DS Singh said.

'I'm just going by Wikipedia,' Gillard said apologetically. 'Haven't had chance to do much more as yet.' He turned back to the whiteboard. 'He's got two kids by Yelena Yalinsky: Oleg, twenty-one, a self-styled influencer and playboy, and Anastasia, seventeen, a student. Both were at the party.' He glanced around the room. 'I've interviewed her already. Spoiled brat, unsurprisingly. Plenty of emotional baggage.'

Carl Hoskins laughed. 'Maybe PC Woodbridge should have left her in the lake.'

'The second victim was Maxim Talin, a Soviet émigré and scientist who'd built his fortune in recent years on a new generation of rechargeable batteries. Talin works in Silicon Valley, and has built a $100 million home modelled on the Versailles Palace in Trousdale. He commutes by helicopter. Forbes puts his fortune at $9 billion. Talin went to university with Volkov, and as Carl has pointed out, Yalinsky was originally Talin's girlfriend at that time. Following the divorce from Volkov, she became Talin's partner once again.' Gillard capped the marker pen he been using and turned to the audience. 'You don't need to be a rocket scientist to see endless motives here. Not only are both men extremely wealthy, but they have had an overlapping love life. For most of the last twenty years they have reportedly been enemies.'

'Then of course there is the Kremlin,' DS Singh said.

Gillard nodded. 'As I said earlier, let's concentrate on the evidence and leave the motivations for later. Finally, let's not forget about the personal protection officer, Bryn Howell. We're awaiting his full military record and security clearances which should be here this afternoon. However, on the face of it, his death looks like collateral damage.'

'I hope no one is going to say that to his wife,' Michelle Tsu said.

'Obviously not,' Gillard replied. 'Family liaison officer Gabby Underwood has been asked to make the approach.' He looked at his watch. 'All right, that's all for now. Shireen, I'd like you to dig up everything about the background of these oligarchs that you can. Michelle, chase up all the witnesses and go through the statements, but your first priority is to see if we can get hold of Yelena Yalinsky before she leaves the country.' He collected his papers and put them into a folder. 'Carl, you and I are going to have to take a good look inside that panic room.'

–

When they re-emerged from the Khazi, it was raining. They made their way across to the library where the CSI tent was still in place, and one CSI van remained. Greeting the female uniform who was guarding the entrance, Gillard then peered inside the marquee structure, and recognised investigator Kirsty Mockett, even though she was in a hooded Tyvek suit and staring down at a laptop.

'Will you be much longer?' he asked the young woman. 'Or should we suit up?'

'Booties would still be appreciated so you don't drop any grot, sir. The staircases are still being examined, so if you want to inspect the balcony, please use the ground floor access and go via the aerial platform. We've got quite a few latent prints away from the bloodstained areas, thanks to the fact it was snowy outside. I'm trying to match them up to the footwear evidence. I'll be a while yet on that.'

'We need to go to the panic room.' Gillard pulled out his phone and rang Wolf, Volkov's head of security. He'd need to be here too.

'That's fine, there's duckboards just there above the bloodstains.'

'Okay.' Gillard was impressed by the progress made by Ms Mockett in the year since her qualification. She had undergone something of an ordeal by fire by stumbling across a crime scene, another snowy one, oddly enough, on the day before she was due to start at Surrey Police. She had acquitted herself well. Now the girlfriend of his research intelligence officer, Rob Townsend, she seemed like a fixture of every good CSI investigation.

Once Wolf arrived, Gillard briefed him and they all slipped on plastic overshoes and gloves then went through the tent into the building. The staircases, the first where Bryn Howell died and the second at the other end, were still sealed off with crime tape, so the group made their way along the ground floor underneath the fossil rock until they came to the wheeled platform, big enough for three. They climbed the rattly ladder three feet onto the platform, then Gillard operated the lifting console which controlled a hydraulic scissor-lift to bring them up onto the balcony twelve feet above.

'Where exactly is this panic room?' Gillard asked Wolf.

'Is concealed door there,' the Georgian said, pointing to a section of stone-clad wall. Gingerly, they made their way out of the cage, over the balcony rail and across the plastic duckboards until they were in front of the door. 'I left unlocked,' Wolf said. He pressed a finger into a cavity in the stonework at waist height, and a small metal ring handle popped out. 'We have to move plastic,' Wolf said of the duckboard immediately in front of the door. 'Otherwise door will jam.'

Hoskins unclipped the plastic tile and moved it away. Wolf pulled the door, which slid silently open. It was four-inch-thick steel.

'This is like something from *The Matrix*,' Hoskins said. The door gave onto a small landing and a spiral metal staircase descending.

The panic room was more like a home, with a lounge, shower and bathroom, and a bedroom bigger than Gillard's own, all tastefully decorated in grazed steel and glass. Picture windows gave the illusion of being in a Swiss meadow. There was even a small separate wine cellar.

'Very comfy,' Hoskins said. 'All mod cons.'

'Of course, what would you expect?' Wolf gave the detective constable a withering look. The centrepiece was an office with a safe, numerous screens and some pretty sophisticated-looking electronic gear. It seemed the kind of set-up that some stock market trader might have.

Gillard scrutinised the various controls and saw a row of rocker switches labelled in Cyrillic. 'Ah, this controls the lighting. That must have been how Ms Yalinsky was signalling she was trapped. When CSI finally removed the body of Mr Volkov and was able to open the door, she told Yaz Quoroshi that she been trying to get out for more than an hour.'

Wolf skilfully worked some switches on the control panel, and a monitor screen crackled into life. He rewound until he reached the last footage. 'See, nothing after four p.m.'

'Can you show me the other cameras?' Gillard asked.

Wolf's finger skated lightly over the keyboard until the screen divided into a three-by-three grid of CCTV images into the library. 'That is the current picture.'

'Can you go back?'

'I can, but earlier was switched off.'

'How did you know that?' Gillard asked.

'Because I was in main control room in house when Mr Volkov asked me. Most security systems here in library can be overridden from the main panic room.'

'The main panic room?' Hoskins asked incredulously. 'So he's got two?'

'Of course. There is a five-bedroom, three-bathroom flat in basement of Westgrave Hall, with own oxygen and water supply and a secret escape tunnel.'

'We'll need to see it,' Gillard said.

Hoskins shook his head in amazement. 'He must have been terrified to have all this. What was he so scared of?'

'He was rich, detective constable, and he was Russian,' Wolf answered. 'Yes, the rich always have something to fear. These are not idle fears, as I think you know.' He pointed to one of the nine images on the screen, which showed Kirsty Mockett, in Tyvek suit, crouching down on the balcony over an enormous pool of dried blood.

'Death, Mr Hoskins, that is the reality.'

–

After they had carefully exited from the library and crossed the stone bridge, Wolf led the two detectives through a walled quadrangle towards the northern side of Westgrave Hall. They descended a set of stone steps to a substantial black metal door, with a fisheye lens camera. Wolf touched a fingerprint receptor, then pressed his eye to a small lens. The door clicked, and Wolf was able to push it open.

'A lot of security you have,' Hoskins observed.

'Didn't help, did it?' Wolf said, ushering them into a long, low flagstoned corridor. Their footsteps rang as they made their way along the mediaeval passageway, following thick black cables and emergency lighting, which were the only concessions to the current century.

'This is fourteenth-century bit of hall, which predates main building. There were places of worship here in pagan times,' Wolf said. He tapped an old iron door. 'This passageway leads to what you may call a dungeon. Oliver Cromwell's men tortured Catholics here.'

'Nice,' said Gillard. The sarcasm was lost on Wolf, who gave him a peculiar stare.

A little further on on the right, a modern steel door yielded to Wolf's fingerprints, and opened out into a wood-panelled stairwell, sweeping upwards for three floors, thickly carpeted and lit by a magnificent golden chandelier high above. 'Now we have entered the sixteenth century,' Wolf said. He did not lead them up the stairs but across the stairwell, to another metal door. This required both iris sensor and fingerprints to open. Wolf showed them into a well-equipped, windowless but well-lit modern office with half a dozen workstations, a state-of-the-art CCTV monitoring system and an enormous paper shredder. A bearded young man sat at the far end of the room hunched over a laptop and exchanged brief greetings with Wolf.

'This nervous centre of Westgrave Hall,' Wolf announced.

They took it all in. There was nearly as much kit there as Gillard had seen at British Transport Police's London CCTV monitoring centre at Ebury Bridge, Victoria.

Even for a stately home as big as this, it seemed completely over the top.

'Your boss must have been a very worried man,' Hoskins murmured.

'Even the paranoid are allowed real enemies, as they say in my country.'

'So is this where Volkov worked when he was here at Westgrave?' Gillard asked.

'No, no.' Wolf found the notion amusing. 'Had big office on the second floor with grand views. Still, all communication routed through here. Do you need to see big office?'

Gillard looked at his watch. It was eleven a.m. and he still had witness interviews to conduct. 'No, not right now. I've got to leave. Perhaps you can show Carl here how it all works.'

Wolf sat Hoskins down in front of the CCTV monitors. The detective was familiar with the type of set-up, and soon found the master screen. It would take hours to check all the footage that had been recorded on the system from the time of the party through until six o'clock the following morning, but a quick run-through showed that what Wolf had said was correct.

'We've got everything right through except the internal cameras at the library,' Hoskins told Gillard. 'There are four cameras, and they were turned off from four p.m. until we ordered them switched on again at two in the morning.'

'Okay. Are there any external cameras around the library?' Gillard asked Wolf.

'Yes. Six, they give 360-degree coverage. I don't think those were turned off.' He checked on the master system. 'Yes, they were on all evening.'

'Good,' said Gillard. 'Carl, I want you to look through those from twelve hours before the attack to twelve hours afterwards. The killer must be on them somewhere.' The confident prediction sounded hollow in Gillard's own head. What if they're not? He knew this was shaping up to be the most high-profile case of his career. Everything depended on him not missing anything, even the smallest piece of evidence. A crime scene this big, there were lots of ways to screw it up.

–

By late morning on Christmas Day, most of the remaining overnight guests had left the hall after passing across their contact details to police. A few important witnesses, increasingly impatient, were demanding to be interviewed immediately so they could go home to salvage what remained of the festivities. Most of them were waiting in the drawing room. Gillard had set up the adjoining Fitzroy Room for the interviews, where he had been shown to an eighteenth-century writing desk, at which Dr Samuel Johnson had once sat to pen part of his dictionary. One of the staff had covered the large desk with a foam rubber protector and a damask tablecloth. While Gillard set it up, Claire went out to the drawing room to select an interviewee. The cosy wood-panelled room resembled the lounge of some country hotel. A fire blazed in the huge hearth, and fresh coffee and sandwiches had been laid out on the low tables which separated the many leather padded wing chairs in which the guests were seated. Family liaison officer Gabby Underwood was there, talking to Anastasia, and behind them Wolf was talking loudly on the phone to someone in Russian, illustrating his conversation with emphatic hand movements.

Dr Sophie Cawkwell was close by, Skyping her daughter on a laptop while the uniforms were upstairs searching her room. As Claire approached, she heard Sophie say: 'Sorry, darling, Mummy's got to go now. Yes, Mummy's friend has gone to heaven. I am sad, yes. Very sad. Look darling, have a happy Christmas until I get there! Be good for Daddy, and I'll see you later today. No dear, the police aren't going to put me in prison. They just want to ask me some more questions about last night. Tell Daddy I'll ring him later.'

She terminated the call and immediately burst into tears. After a minute or two she rubbed her hand over her face, shuddered and stood up to face Claire. She was dressed in jeans, a mauve pullover and trainers. 'I'd promised to be there for Christmas lunch, so Emily is disappointed of course. She's only four. I'd really wanted to watch her opening her Christmas presents.'

As a mother herself, Claire could understand the anguish of being separated from your child at such a time. She had done a little hurried research on the palae-ontologist and TV presenter, which would have given plenty of scope for celebrity gossip if that's what she was interested in. Dr Cawkwell was married at twenty-one, then widowed and wealthy at twenty-four. She had subsequently married a BBC producer, but the failure of the decade-long marriage had coincided with her rise to prominence and long overseas absences. The palaeon-tology series her independent production company had made, simply called *Dig!*, had now been sold in half a dozen nations, including Russia.

'Now, where do you want me?' Sophie asked.

Claire escorted her through into the Fitzroy Room, and the thirty-yard walk to the desk. 'We just want a little more detail on what you told us last night.' She showed Sophie to the seat opposite Gillard and explained that they would try not to take too much of her time. 'We know you must be very upset, it's just that we have to find out as much as we can while all witnesses are still present.'

Sophie nodded. 'It's been such a shock. I can't get my head around it.'

'We just want to go back to what you actually saw,' Gillard said. 'According to your initial statement you were on the bridge talking to Lord Fein and his wife Natasha.'

'Yes. I'd gone out for a cigarette break. I'd been describing Lebyodoushka—'

'That's the name of the fossil, is that right?'

'Yes, it means female swan. The baby is Molodoy, which just means kid. I've been describing how they were found to Maxim and Yelena, pointing out various features like the baby teeth on Molodoy, and the faint suggestion of fish vertebrae inside the stomach of the mother. I mean it really is an extraordinary find, enough for National Geographic to commission a documentary from me. Then Sasha turned to me and said there was something he wanted to show the two of them. I assumed it was business, or maybe something to do with the divorce settlement he'd been working on, so I said I would step outside.'

'And how long was that before the shooting began?' Gillard asked.

'I don't know, a few minutes.'

'How many cigarettes did you smoke during that time?'

'Two. God! I'm supposed to be giving up. I just had a few quick puffs on each, honestly. Still, I guess it must've been a little bit more than ten minutes.'

Gillard leaned forward. 'Dr Cawkwell, whatever they were talking about could well have been very important. You said in your initial statement that they all seem to be getting along fine.'

'Yes, that's right. It was the first time that I'd met Yelena, and she was utterly charming, I have to say. I thought there might be hostility, you know, towards me, but—'

Claire interrupted. 'But she was now with Maxim Talin.'

'Yes, but there's massive emotional baggage on all sides. I got the impression that during the worst times Sasha could only be happy when he knew that Yelena was suffering, and vice versa. It's as if the divorce case wasn't just about money but about winning, doing the other side down. *Schadenfreude*, the German word, best describes it. Delight in the misfortune of another. During the first few months when I was dating him he seemed to want to show me off to the paparazzi.'

Gillard smiled to himself. He could well imagine why a man, even a wealthy one, would want to parade a woman such as Sophie Cawkwell.

'Whereas I wanted to keep it quiet,' Sophie continued. 'You don't want to wear your heart on your sleeve. I mean I have friends on Facebook, and the moment they've met a new man my God it's all there, all the details, pictures of the food from the restaurant. It's all so bloody premature and public. Then after weeks of gushing about the guy it all goes quiet. And suddenly there's a meme, capital red letters on a black background: All Men Are Bastards, or something similar. You can see why it happens amongst eighteen-year-olds, but these women are in their forties, for God's sake.' She sniffed and shook her head. A tear was sneaking out, and she wiped it away angrily.

'Anyway, I thought Sasha was putting too much pressure on us as a couple in the early days. I thought the reason he was doing it so publicly was quite simply to enrage Yelena.'

The detective chief inspector decided to draw her back to the events of the previous night. He asked her to describe what happened when she had heard the first shot. Her account was clear and precise, and coincided pretty much exactly with that given by PC Zoe Butterfield.

'Sasha had bought me this beautiful dress, an iridescent blue,' Sophie said. 'Cost a fortune, and I had to rip it when it got trapped in the door. Poor Sasha.' She sniffed heavily, and Claire passed her a tissue.

'Were you aware of anyone else who had been in and out of the library earlier that day?' Claire asked.

Sophie shook her head. 'I was there with Anastasia around lunchtime, we were planning how to photograph the fossil for best effect. Apart from that, I have no idea. I spent the afternoon getting ready. The early part of the party was so busy. I mean there were so many guests to greet, Sasha wanted me by his side, and then the snow carriage, the dancing and the skaters and finally the Beyoncé set, which was fantastic. I didn't have a moment to go into the library.'

'So why were you in there later on?' she continued.

'Sasha asked me to give a little bit of a tour, to explain to Maxim and Yelena all about the fossil. I was a bit reluctant. I'd had a few drinks, I just wanted a chance to relax, but it was easy enough in the end. Just ten minutes.'

'What do you know about the relationship between Maxim Talin and Alexander Volkov?' Gillard asked.

'I know it goes back a long way. They were at the same university together. I think it's fair to say they hadn't always been friends.'

'Why is that?' Claire asked. 'Apart from the link with Yelena.'

'There's always been a rivalry. I don't know all the details, but Sasha made a lot of money through Yelena's connections in Kazakhstan. He benefited a lot initially from political favours, because Yelena is the daughter of the finance minister. Talin's decision to leave Russia put him on the wrong side of the Kremlin. I mean that happened to Sasha too, but it was a lot earlier in Talin's case.'

'After all that, do you have any ideas about who was behind the killing?' Gillard asked.

She blew a long sigh. 'I've thought about it almost every waking moment since. It doesn't make sense. The conspiracy theorists will always say the Kremlin, and God knows there are enough precedents for that, but from what I understand Sasha had made his peace with the powers that be, at considerable cost. They had no reason to kill him now.'

'What kind of person was Sasha?' Claire asked. They had agreed in advance to allow Sophie to vent her feelings towards the end of the interview.

'He was the most wonderful man I have ever met. So passionate, so loving. He wasn't one of these hard-nosed businessmen, always thinking about the money. He had some luck, and I suppose you could say he married well, at least financially, first time. But he wasn't Machiavellian. He worked hard and played hard, and he would have made a great father.' She stopped and her fingers strayed to her midriff. 'I don't know what I'm going to do without him.'

Gillard and Claire shared a glance. That brief and almost unnoticeable caress told them Sophie was pregnant, or at least thought she might be.

'How did you meet?' Claire asked.

'It was in 2015, when I was filming in Mongolia, which as you know is the site of many famous fossils. This particular excavation happened to be on the edge of one of the copper mines that his company owned, and he came down to see my team and me. He seemed utterly charming and was kind enough to provide us with a helicopter when we needed to move to an adjacent site. I kept in contact with him and things gradually developed. It was just a few weeks ago when he asked me to marry him...' Her face distorted and sobs convulsed her. 'I'm sorry,' she blurted out.

Gabby had her arm around Sophie's shoulders and passed her a tissue.

Chapter Nine

While Dr Sophie Cawkwell was being interviewed down-stairs, three male uniformed constables unlocked the grand state room which she had occupied upstairs. They saw a magnificent four-poster canopy bed, an enormous ornate gilt mirror, mullioned windows that looked south over the main drive, and a beautifully painted rococo ceiling. The place was untidy. The bed was spread with clothing, a selection of women's shoes was scattered on the floor, and a pink wheeled suitcase was lying open on a blanket box, a second nearby, closed. A table by the window held an array of gifts, many still partly in their wrapping paper. Sergeant Babbage had informed them that Ms Cawkwell had left the room exactly as it was and had been moved by Westgrave Hall staff into an adjacent bedroom to get a few hours' sleep.

'Right lads,' said the oldest and most experienced, PC Jim Murray. 'Remember anything you break you've bought, and most of the stuff in here will cost you your entire lifetime's salary and pension.' He quickly videoed the room from the door. His two young charges, PCs Chris Livermore and Richard Perrin, moved into the room and made straight for the ornate writing desk.

'Do you watch *Dig!*? You know, her programme about fossils?' Perrin asked Livermore. 'Quite a fit bit of totty, for forty,' he said.

'No, I don't,' said Livermore as he removed the drawers from the desk. 'Ah, I've got a purse here. Jim, what are we doing with these?'

'Stick it on me square,' Jim said, as he unfolded the white plastic sheet. He ferreted in his pocket and brought out a numbered plastic marker. The three officers worked methodically through the room. When Murray's attention was distracted, Perrin snatched a pair of skimpy lace knickers from the open suitcase. He nudged Livermore, then waved them at him, grinning, and raised his eyebrows as he mimed pocketing them. Livermore just rolled his eyes.

Murray peered at the gifts on the table. 'Okay lads, leave this to me. Wow,' he said as he raised a necklace on his latex-gloved finger. 'Look at these jewels. Emeralds, I think.'

'Blimey,' said Perrin, making his way over. The gems were each the size of a pea. 'My missus would love these.'

'Don't even think about it,' said Jim, photographing the jewellery in situ. 'It's not for the likes of us. Ratners was good enough for my old lady when we married thirty years ago.'

The two younger coppers exchanged a weary glance at the mention of the now defunct down-market jewellers.

–

The arrival of a coachload of uniformed policeman accelerated the pace of the search. They were given the same strict instructions as the original group, and very soon an array of electronic items were being carried in plastic bags to Vikram Singh's evidence van. Periodically, Gillard would go up to see whether any particular room had yielded something of interest. The most common findings were various objects that had been left behind by overnight guests at the party: toiletries, clothing, jewellery and electronics. It was mid-afternoon and Gillard was just coming back from overseeing the search of the room occupied by Lord Fein when research intelligence officer Rob Townsend buttonholed him in the corridor.

'I think you should see this, sir,' he said, holding his mobile up to the detective chief inspector's face. 'It's from Oleg Volkov's Instagram page.' Gillard glanced at the image of the son of the murdered oligarch. He was outdoors, wearing aviator shades, tight maroon leather trousers and a white leather waistcoat over his otherwise unclothed and very hirsute chest. His muscled arms were crossed, and in each hand was a pistol, one large and black, the other small and gold.

'If it was a crime to be a tosser we'd have him bang to rights,' Gillard said, shaking his head.

'There's more,' Townsend said, swiping to the other image. This one showed him standing on a landing stage by a boat, a bikini-clad model on either side kissing him on the cheek while he brandished an assault rifle.

'Did you bring me this just to annoy me?' Gillard asked. 'Examples of self-indulgence for those with unlimited money.' He was already aware that Oleg Volkov was an online influencer, a rising Russian rap star and had several million followers across his various social media platforms. He even had his own logo, a silver O over a golden V on a black background, which appeared on his signature aftershave, sunglasses and baseball caps.

'I think it's the fact he is a gun enthusiast,' Townsend said. 'There are hundreds of pictures of him toting weapons.'

'There is a snag.' Gillard picked up a thick manila folder and waved it at Townsend. 'These are all the witness statements. Oleg Volkov was seen on the balcony of his room and in the ballroom in the hour before his father was killed. I don't think we have anyone who witnessed him cross the bridge between the house and the library. So he has an alibi.'

'I still think we should investigate him.'

'Agreed. As a presumed beneficiary from his father's death, he's definitely on the list for interview, just not at the top. Keep researching, see what else you can find. Have you got anything else on the mobile phones I asked you to look at?'

'Not much,' Townsend replied. 'The service providers are a bit slow, this being Christmas Day and all. From what we've got back so far, the networks light up like a Christmas tree soon after the shootings. Thousands of calls, hundreds of phones. Obviously people spreading the news.'

'Can we narrow any down to within the library?'

'Where we have the phone, yes.'

Gillard shrugged. 'Well obviously. The phones belonging to Sophie Cawkwell, Maxim Talin and Alexander Volkov would naturally confirm they were there. I was just thinking about the GPS on any further phones. If we could find evidence that a different phone, that does not belong to any of the victims or to Ms Yalinsky, was moving around within the library at the time the shooting took place, it's almost as good as finding the gun, isn't it?'

'Yes, sir. But I'm not sure it's technically possible to start with a GPS location and find out who was in it.'

'Why is that?'

'Because the satellite transponder doesn't receive or store data from the phone, it only sends it. The phone's GPS chip picks up and stores the encoded location from the satellite signal within the device. Apps that use GPS send the data to and from the phone via the cell tower in an encrypted form, only decoded by the device at the other end, like Google Maps and so on.'

'All right, keep trying anyway,' Gillard said grumpily.

'I'm trying to get a tower dump,' Townsend said. 'It's a list of all the devices that were in the vicinity from an hour before to an hour after the shooting. That could certainly help.'

'Okay, thank you,' Gillard said. He pulled up Oleg's Instagram page on his own phone, and flicked through. There were plenty more pictures of scantily-clad women fawning over him while he was on a yacht somewhere sunny, in a nightclub in Tel Aviv, on the beach in LA. Gillard found himself increasingly irritated by this self-styled celebrity, his feelings tinged with pangs of envy. The page had music videos galore, which Gillard didn't bother looking at, plus videos of Oleg and American-accented friends using an automatic weapon at a firing range in a desert somewhere. Oleg's Hummer was in many of the pics. The golden pistol made a couple of reappearances too, once in the desert firing range, which proved it wasn't simply a replica, and another with him leaning out of the Humvee with a historic building in the background.

Gillard recognised it. Westgrave Hall.

Gotcha! So Volkov had a weapon in the UK. Gillard rubbed his hands together with satisfaction. If that weapon was not registered and licensed, he would come down on Oleg Volkov like a ton of bricks.

Assuming he was still in the country.

A phone call from Hoskins interrupted him. 'Sir, I'm still in the control room. I've been through all six external cameras like you said. I've concentrated so far on the hours after the shooting. The only people who exited the building did so through the main entrance: Dr Sophie Cawkwell, Wolf and our own PC Butterfield, and then later on the various CSI officers and ourselves. Everybody was captured on the two cameras covering the door. The other four wide-angle cameras on the corners of the building only captured one person at the far-reach of the angle in all that time, and that was you when you walked around in the small hours.'

'That's disappointing news.'

'I've only skimmed the hours leading up to the shooting on fast-forward so far. A few people, mainly staff, came in and out in the afternoon until the library was locked at six. Later, once the party began there were far more people around but apart from Volkov's private tour, at eleven p.m., no one went in.'

Gillard sighed heavily. 'I don't get it, Carl. Someone got in there, someone fired thirty-odd shots, killing three people, including a professional bodyguard, and got out again with the murder weapon. Unless he's invisible and can fly, or can burrow in from underneath, he must be on camera.'

'I wish I knew, sir. I'm planning now to go through the earlier footage from the two door cameras and count everybody in and out.'

'All right. Good work. I'm going to check out the cameras from the outside.' His worst fears were coming to pass. A killer this professional must have Kremlin paymaster stamped all over him. And based on previous

British experience, they would never get him. He'd take it very personally, if that were the case.

–

Gillard had got used to following the labyrinthine corridors in the lower part of Westgrave Hall, and soon got himself out through the main east exit, which led down through the terraces and on towards the library.

He realised he must have walked miles that day, back and forth to the library from the main house, and several trips down to the main gate, past the sizeable gaggle of reporters with their satellite vans and outside broadcast units, and across the road to the village hall where most of the police vehicles were now parked. Logistically, the operation had gone well; a good few of the guest bedrooms had now been searched, and the police operation was running like a well-oiled machine. What he desperately needed was a breakthrough: CCTV, footprints, fingerprints, DNA; he didn't care what type of evidence it was, he just needed to find out how someone had got into that library and committed these audacious murders.

By the time he got to the footpath encircling the library and its shallow ditch, he could see that the snow had almost melted away everywhere. Only in the long grass at the bottom of the moat and in the long winter shadow of the library did the white patches persist. He took his time, walking through the grey slush on the outside footpath beyond the moat, and then over the bridge to the flagstoned terrace which ran around the library. The cameras were at a good height, twelve feet off the ground, and he could see that their coverage overlapped. There were not as far as he could make out any blind spots, which was exactly as it should be. If anyone had come into or out of that building, they should have been seen. Hoskins had already carefully checked the master log on the main system, which showed that there had been no editing or substitution of footage. If Wolf were in on the killing, it might have been possible for the cameras to have been nobbled, but that still wouldn't account for the unanimity of the witness evidence and the undisturbed blanket of snow. No one had been in or out.

It just wasn't possible.

Or was it? He considered something from his exchange with Hoskins.

Burrow in from underneath. Was there a secret route into the library from the hall?

–

Having finished Sophie's room, PC Jim Murray looked down his list, and the attached map. 'Volkov kids, Anastasia and Oleg, second floor,' he said. The three officers trooped upstairs, where the corridors became a little less grandiose and somewhat narrower. They plodded along the carpet, peering out at the view over the steeply gabled rooftops.

'It's just like Dracula's castle,' Perrin said.

'Not really,' Livermore said, pernickety as always. 'And that was in Transylvania.'

Perrin groaned to himself. He really wished he had been teamed up with someone a bit more fun than Livermore. Then he could have pocketed Dr Sophie Cawkwell's undies without worrying about being dobbed in for it. It would have given him tremendous bragging rights down the pub.

'Right, this is it,' Murray said. 'Oleg Volkov.' He looked through the keys that Wolf had given him, found the label with the corresponding number and unlocked it. The door would not open.

'There's another lock, Jim, knee height,' said Livermore.

PC Murray looked down at the brass plate. 'Bugger, this is a security lock. No one told us about this.'

'There's one on the other door too,' Livermore said.

'That's the daughter's room,' Murray said.

'The door's big but pretty old,' Perrin said. 'Couple of kicks would have us in.' He was quite anxious to see inside Anastasia's room, after what had reputedly happened to Simon Woodbridge in there. If it was true. Knowing Simon, he doubted it.

'Don't you ever listen, Constable Perrin?' Murray said. 'No damage to be inflicted.'

'Better ring up that head of security,' Livermore said.

'No, it's all right,' Murray said. 'Bryn Howell's room is just down here. We probably should have done that first anyway.'

Murray led them on round a dog-leg in the corridor, and through a fire door into a much smaller passageway. There was lino on the floor and the walls were lined with faded woodchip wallpaper.

'This is a bit grotty,' Perrin said.

'Yeah, you would do well to remember that if you ever leave the force to join private security,' Murray said. 'You may be there to take a bullet for the boss, but the conditions are often crap. My brother-in-law told me all about it. He's a personal protection officer for a former Northern Ireland secretary, so he's all right, but a lot of his mates aren't.'

He found the key and unlocked the room. It was a dreary garret with a sloping ceiling and only a small window at knee height.

'Former member of the SAS, Howell was,' Murray said, looking at the dark and miserable room with its faded green walls, tidy single bed and MFI self-assembly furniture. There was a washbasin, a small mirror above and no apparent en suite. An ironing board stood in the middle of the room, a steam iron upright but unplugged on the heatpad, two pairs of formal trousers neatly pressed and folded nearby. 'Tours of duty in Iraq and Afghanistan. Top of the class in pistol marksmanship, according to my brother-in-law. He was shocked to hear of his death.'

'And he lived like this,' Livermore said.

'Yeah. Wife and two kids back in Wales, that he hardly ever saw. Poor bastard.'

They all stood staring into the room for a moment or two before Perrin walked in and up to the washbasin. 'This must be the family, then,' he said picking a framed photograph from the wall. It was a smiling selfie of the craggy-jawed Howell with a pretty, dark-haired woman and two grinning children, all squeezed together in a giant embrace.

'Oi, Perrin, we're supposed to video this first,' Murray said.

Perrin replaced the photograph, then said, 'Hello, hello, what's this then?' He picked up a metal waste bin and offered it to his colleagues.

'What have you got there?' Murray asked.

'Letters, piles of 'em, all ripped up.' He picked up a sheaf of fragments and started reading. 'Listen to this.' He read it out in a little sing-song voice. '"My darling Bryn, I will love you for ever. What we have is special. Don't have doubts about us". There's loads of little hearts scribbled over it, and a big lipstick kiss.' He waved the bin under Murray's nose.

'You'd make a good tabloid journalist,' Murray said, and his expression showed he didn't mean it as a compliment.

'You're appalling,' Livermore said to Perrin. 'The guy died trying to save the life of his employer.'

Perrin's face creased in puzzlement. 'Look, guys. This is a murder investigation, right?'

'He was a victim, dimbo, not the perpetrator,' Livermore said.

'So? Bryn Howell was married,' Perrin said.

'Maybe they're from his wife,' Livermore said.

'Nah, I'm married, mate, you're not. Wives don't send love letters like this. Not after the first year, anyway.'

'Cynic,' muttered Murray. He was twenty years married, but secretly agreed with every word.

'He obviously had something going on here,' Perrin said. 'His room's only just round the corner from Volkov's daughter.'

'You cannot possibly be suggesting…' Livermore said, shaking his head.

'Motives, right? Conflict of interest. Who knows?' Perrin replied.

'Right,' said Murray. 'Put that bin back, Perrin, and get out here so I can do the video.'

Perrin complied, and watched as Murray used his camera to take a panoramic view of the room.

'Are you going to bag the letters then, Jim?' Perrin asked.

'The man is *dead*. Why put his wife through that pain?' Murray said. 'I don't want to log it.'

'It's up to Gillard, though. He's SIO. You've got to let him know.'

Murray held up his hands 'All right. I'll have a word. Stick them in an evidence bag. I don't want it on the evidence computer. You can't control who gets to see them. It's not fair on his memory.'

–

Vikram Singh was quite pleased with the job he had done organising the evidence in the long-wheelbase Transit van. He had rigged up eight rows of shelves running the entire length of the vehicle, and had bagged up shoes, clothing, bullets and cartridge cases from the library, as well as the more interesting of the thousands of items which had been photographed in the main Westgrave Hall building. Hundreds of phones and electronic items had been logged and the most important few dozen sent out for analysis. He concentrated most of his time on what had been found in the library building where the shooting took place. Almost everything that had been found there fitted neatly into the various categories he had set up. Maxim Talin's spectacles, for example, had broken and fallen to the ground floor, although not necessarily in that order. There were a few cigarette ends, again from the ground floor, parcelled up individually and sent away for DNA analysis. There were also a few oddments, basically sweepings from the ground floor, which he was keeping in a tray until he figured out what to do with them. These included a Russian branded chewing gum wrapper, a pencil, a brooch of an owl with tiny yellow gems for eyes, and some fragments of thin grey plastic, including one with a tiny metal bolt and retaining screw through it. There was also a human tooth.

The arrival of Detective Constable Carl Hoskins broke his reverie.

'How's it going, Vikram?' Though Singh was senior to Hoskins, the two had enjoyed a good friendship ever since attending the same forensic training course in Manchester. They had spent every evening down the pub, it being a revelation to Hoskins that Punjabi Sikhs were often enthusiastic drinkers. Hoskins reckoned Singh must be the only Sikh chair of a regional branch of the Campaign for Real Ale.

'Not so bad.'

'Fancy an early tea?' Hoskins looked at his watch; it was nearly five p.m. 'Tatiana in the kitchen is cooking up a big pheasant stew, if you're interested.'

'You didn't waste any time there, did you?' Singh said.

Hoskins laughed. 'She enjoys feeding me up.'

'That makes two of you, then.' He offered Hoskins the tray of evidential oddments. 'What do you reckon to this lot?'

'Is that a tooth?' Hoskins said, donning a latex glove so he could give it a prod. 'Where was it found?'

'This lot was found on the ground floor. The brooch is intriguing.'

'Maybe it came off Yelena's coat. Looks valuable enough.'

'Any idea about the bits of plastic?' Singh held up one of the thin fragments to him.

'It's obviously been smashed, whatever it is. Maybe something Talin or Volkov were holding, or maybe something on the bookshelves. Knocked off in the chaos and dropped down onto the ground floor.'

'Okay, but where's the rest of it? Put these bits together, and you get something about the size of my thumb, and there's still bits missing. If it didn't have that tiny bolt, I'd say it was one of those little plastic ice cream spoons you get for tubs in the cinema.'

Hoskins shrugged. 'Dunno, mate. You coming for that stew or not?' Singh locked up the van, checked there was a uniformed officer nearby to keep an eye on it, and followed Hoskins towards the main house. The detective constable led him to a narrow set of stone steps at the side of the house, which descended to a basement door which Hoskins opened. Singh was then led along a narrow and musty corridor, past various storerooms.

'This place is a warren, Carl. But you seem to know your way around.'

'I can always find food, me.'

After several turnings, and the crossing of an internal courtyard, they arrived in a large but antiquated kitchen in which half a dozen mainly Asian staff toiled over pots and pans on an old-fashioned range.

A sizeable middle-aged matron greeted Hoskins by kissing him on both cheeks, and pulled him into a bear hug. She had winged glasses and auburn hair tied back in a ponytail under her chef's cap. 'Is this your friend?' she asked Hoskins.

'Tatiana, this is Detective Sergeant Vikram Singh, my friend and drinking buddy.'

She kissed Singh on both cheeks too, before showing them both to a table in an adjacent low-ceilinged room, a cosy place with photographs hung on the wall, and a small Eastern Orthodox shrine in an alcove. Tatiana then brought in big bowls of delicious-smelling casserole.

'Dead birds from the estate, shot and prepared by myself,' she announced. 'An old Ukrainian recipe. Enjoy!'

'Thank you,' said Singh.

'Have you discovered who killed Sasha?' she asked.

'No, not yet,' Hoskins replied.

'I think it was his bodyguard. Bryn Howell. Not a very nice man.'

'What makes you say that?' Hoskins asked.

'Every time I bring in food for Sasha, he looked in the pot, or even tried a sample. He also searched my kitchen just before mealtimes, getting in the way.'

'That's probably part of his job,' Singh said. 'Looking for poison.'

'You're crazy,' Tatiana said. 'Food poisoning? I am a good cook! Besides, whoever heard of a Russian being poisoned?'

The two detectives shared a glance.

'The man was a nuisance and a racist,' Tatiana continued. 'Once, I found him in my room, going through my things.'

'Again, that's probably part of his job,' Hoskins said.

The cook wasn't convinced. 'He did bad things, not just to me. Last summer, when Anastasia was here, I over-heard Sasha furious with him about something, shouting and swearing in Russian. When the bodyguard left the room, his face was red and he was very angry. I think Bryn had a reason to kill his boss.' She tapped her nose and winked.

'The shooting started before the bodyguard went in, you know,' Singh said.

Hoskins shook his head at his colleague. *Don't hand out that kind of detail.*

'So Tatiana,' Hoskins called as he began to eat. 'Did old Volkov treat you okay?'

She walked back into the room wiping her hands on a tea towel. 'Yes. He was a lovely, lovely man, it so, so sad.' Tears filled her eyes, and she wiped them away with a sleeve. 'He was away a lot, but he made a point of coming down to see us below-stairs-people when he came back. He was terribly lonely, you know.'

'Really?' Hoskins said.

'This is delicious,' Singh said. 'Really tasty.'

'Yes. He never wanted to leave Russia, but he was frightened. Always frightened. He had money, but money makes you lonely, makes you sad.'

'Does it?' Singh asked.

'Of course. Money is a wall. It was the wall between Sasha and the world. Every woman he met, every new friend, he thought: "Does she like me, or does she just want the cash?" For me it is simple. I have no money, so my friends like me for me. I can trust them.'

'Maybe they just like you for your cooking.' Hoskins said, as he lifted another spoonful of stew to his mouth.

Tatiana beamed, and pinched Hoskins' cheek. 'Ooh, you are a very naughty little boy,' she said, attempting to ruffle the sparse stubble that inhabited Hoskins's scalp. It was like trying to caress sandpaper. 'You know, Sasha liked to eat his meals here, at the place you are sitting. He had grand luxury dining room upstairs. Magnificent! Beautiful!' She gestured with her arms, her eyes mapping out a huge imagined space. 'But often he would come here, sometimes in the middle of the night, and wake me up. Get out the vodka and tell me stories of his childhood until dawn. Then I would tell him my stories of a broken heart. He would always listen, even though I am just an ordinary person. Sometimes, with too much vodka, he would weep. Often he would say: "Tatiana, you are the only one I love. You and Mother Russia." Then I would make him a big Russian breakfast, and he would go back to his room. It is so wrong he is gone, I am so sad.' She began to sob. Tears rolled down her cheeks.

Hoskins gave her a brief hug and stroked her hair. 'Come on, you'll get over it.'

'No. It's terrible, terrible. I will never get over it. All the staff loved him.' She sniffed and took a deep breath. 'One story, he would tell me. When they came for his father in dead of night.'

'Who came?' Hoskins asked.

'KGB, who else comes in the night, silly boy? It was the middle of the night, and he was only four years old. His father was taken away to the gulag for writing anti-Soviet leaflets. Sasha and his mother wept and pleaded and begged, but the big green van drove away through the snow, leaving only tyre tracks and heartbreak. You know, I don't think Sasha ever recovered.'

'How awful,' Singh said.

'When his father was eventually released, Sasha was in his twenties. The father they returned to him was a pale shadow of the man he had lost. An old man, a broken man. Thin, confused, and very soon confined to an asylum.'

'Got any more of this lovely stew?' Hoskins asked, scraping up the dregs with his spoon. As Tatiana rolled her eyes and headed back into the kitchen, Singh gave him a withering look.

'What?' Hoskins asked.

'You know something, Carl? You're the kind of bloke that farts in the middle of *Swan Lake*.'

Gillard had promised Sam that he would make it home sometime that evening. He was determined not to spend another night at Westgrave Hall. But something was bugging him. He sat in the Khazi, at a computer terminal on HOLMES, the Home Office complex enquiry system, flicking through the latest evidence reports and finding nothing of use. He picked up his phone and rang DC Shireen Corey-Williams, who had been working from home since midday.

'Hi, Shireen,' he said. 'Any luck getting the plans of the library from the architects?'

'Well, it is Christmas Day. But I have left a message.'

'I think we need to try a bit harder than that. Otherwise they won't get back to us until the new year.'

'Aren't there any plans at Westgrave Hall? Volkov would have had a copy?'

Gillard sighed. 'Wolf said there are physical copies in the safe, but we can't get into that. Rob Townsend has got Volkov's iPad, but again it's quite secure.'

'Why the hurry, sir?'

'I think there might be a tunnel from the hall into the library. Wolf is adamant that there isn't anything, but it seems to me the only possibility for how someone got in and out of the library without being seen. Can you see if there's any resources like ground-penetrating radar we could have access to?'

Corey-Williams said nothing for a moment. 'I'll have a look, but at Christmas—'

'Will you stop reminding me what day it is, detective constable? This is urgent. Get onto it, will you?' He hung up.

Gillard tracked Wolf down in the control room. He was sitting at the master screen, giggling to himself and eating an entire family-sized Christmas pudding from a foil dish. '*Only Fool and Horse* Christmas Special 1991. Very funny,' Wolf said, gesturing at the screen with his spoon.

'You know you're supposed to eat them warm,' Gillard said, indicating the pudding.

'Yes, Tatiana, she also say this. She call me inbred Georgian peasant for eating figgy pudding from fridge, so I bring here where no insult. Still nice when cold.' Wolf raised a glass of some ruby-coloured liquid to his lips. 'Tawny port. Very good year. I don't think Mr Volkov miss it now,' he said with a grin. 'Wolf, he inbred peasant perhaps, but he know nice drink.'

'About this underground passage, Wolf,' Gillard asked.

'From main panic room, yes. An old tunnel goes north to the woods, but not in good condition and very wet. But like I say, nowhere near library.'

'Are there any plans of Westgrave Hall which show it?'

Wolf blew a sigh and put his pudding aside. 'No peace even at Christmas. Goodwill to all men, but Wolf still he works. Phew, Wolf, he must be plonker.' He shook his head in exasperation and got up.

He led Gillard upstairs to a storeroom which contained piles of documents. 'This is all stuff from the Westgrave family,' Wolf said. After a few minutes' search, he found a series of aged A3-size documents and brought them out onto a table with more light. 'No, this quite clear. The old tunnel just goes north. In any case, the main panic room has security doors which block off tunnel. Only if you are in panic room can you open door. Mr Volkov, he had idea to restore tunnel which is centuries old, but that work never priority.'

Gillard couldn't quite make sense of the plans, but accepted Wolf's assurances.

'I can take you down tunnel tonight if you want. See for yourself. Just let me finish *Only Fool and Horse* first.'

The detective chief inspector looked at the time. It was already nearly eight o'clock. He dearly wanted to spend a few hours at home before going off to do a couple of witness interviews in London the following morning.

'One more thing,' Wolf said, pulling a data stick from his pocket. 'Is this yours?'

Gillard took the proffered object and examined it. 'I don't think so, where did you find it?'

'In rear USB port on the master terminal here. A place not easy to see.'

'Have you looked to see what's on there?' Gillard asked.

'Not yet. I thought: "Okay, Surrey Police has warrant and maybe copying evidence." So I leave alone. I do notice that it has antenna, which means could be transmitting data by wireless.'

'That's all a bit sophisticated for Surrey Police.'

Wolf shrugged extravagantly. 'It wasn't there yesterday, and the only people who have been in here apart from me and my assistant are Surrey Police. So that's you, Mr Hoskins, and those guys with the suits who came in this morning.'

'What?'

'Yes, big man from Special Branch and the quiet fellow in the bad suit. They asked me to let them see the place at seven a.m.'

'I knew nothing about this,' Gillard said.

'Ah, so these people is not police?' Wolf's face tightened.

'Corrigan is from the police, yes.'

'But they did not tell you? Left hand not know who right hand what doing?'

Gillard apologised. 'I have to look into this, would you excuse me?'

Chapter Ten

Boxing Day morning

Gillard had agreed to drive in to meet Lord Fein at nine a.m. at his London office, which turned out to be in one of the 1980s tower blocks on Leadenhall Street in the almost-deserted City. Shown up into the financier's twenty-third storey office, Gillard was soon looking out with his interviewee over the changing streets. 'When I first took the lease, the outlook here was tremendous,' Fein said. 'But first came the Gherkin at St Mary's Axe, then a whole load of other glass monstrosities. For half the day in the summer, we're in shade thanks to this.' He stabbed his finger out towards a tall but rather unimaginative glassy block on the other side of the street.

'What's that one called?' Gillard asked.

'Oh, I don't think it's got a name,' Fein replied with a sigh. 'Just the address, number one. Russian money in there, too.'

Gillard cleared his throat. He'd agreed to come in because Fein had to catch a flight to New York at lunchtime and would be unavailable for face-to-face interview for two weeks afterwards.

'Thank you very much for your flexibility, Craig. Hope I've not interrupted the festivities too much.'

'Happy to oblige,' Gillard said, knowing that the noble lord was probably wholly uninterested in the wreckage of his home life. 'At least on Boxing Day the traffic is light.'

'A silver lining, Craig, I suppose.' Fein had a habit of referring to everyone by their first name, even when, as in this case, he had never met them before. When he was trade minister, some years earlier, he had been interviewed by the combative John Humphrys on the *Today* programme on Radio 4. Finding himself in a corner over the issue of his expenses, Fein had tried to silkily ease his way out by using the interviewer's name as if they were old pals. It hadn't worked then, and it wasn't working now. Gillard found it patronising.

'I've got just over an hour before I need to leave. Americans are such uncivilised people, don't you think, Craig? Wall Street is open on Boxing Day, for goodness' sake, and I have a meeting there this afternoon. I have to be over there from time to time, and I often spend Hanukkah in New York, but I could never live there.' He gave a brief shudder.

David Fein was a great political fixer, slipping almost effortlessly between the two main British political parties. His flexible ideology was considered suspicious by many party stalwarts on both sides, but few could doubt his contacts among the press barons, his skills as a negotiator – particularly in trade and the EU – or his apparent background role in the Good Friday Agreement to end the Troubles in Northern Ireland.

For a man in his late fifties, Fein exuded youthfulness. Dapper and well-dressed, he had an astonishingly bouffant head of silver hair, with the thickness and luxuriance that one would normally associate with a Hollywood A-lister. Though he would often play with it, running his hands through it in TV interviews, it never seemed dishevelled. When he was being doorstepped by the press during the Parliamentary expenses scandal, Fein was never caught by the cameras taking out the rubbish in his dressing gown, as a few of his colleagues had been. He would emerge from his tastefully decorated home in Virginia Water, fully dressed in suit and silk tie before eight o'clock in the morning, smooth and unflappable. On several occasions he and his glamorous wife Natasha had dispensed mugs of tea and coffee, and a large tray of bacon and tomato sandwiches on his home-made sourdough bread, for the gentlemen of the press, as he called them. Fein had also been known to offer interviews while on his morning run, for any journalist who could keep up with him.

'Lord Fein,' Gillard began. 'We already have a brief statement from you on what you actually saw last night. But I want to ask you about the wider context, and your connections with Mr Volkov.'

'That's absolutely fine. Look, I've known Sasha for over twenty years, and Maxim for, oh, eight years, so I'd regard them as good, close friends. Both astute businessmen, absolutely. Of course I'm shocked by what happened yesterday. An awful occurrence.'

'Did they get on, in recent years?'

'Well. I wouldn't exactly say that. What I would say is that differences had been buried, as a matter of expediency.'

'Expediency?'

'Yes. There was a big contract in the offing, between the two of them, and the final settlement of the divorce deal with Yelena was being undertaken simultaneously. It was all to be tied up over Christmas.'

'What kind of deal?'

'I'm not really at liberty to say, but I'm not giving away much when I say that minerals were at the heart of it. Sasha had them and Maxim needed them. It was confidential, obviously, and there are other parties to consider. Speak to Sasha's lawyer, Belshin. He might be able to shed some light.'

'And linked to a final settlement to the divorce?'

He held up his hands. 'Now there, Craig, I really can't disclose anything.'

'Were you assisting them in those negotiations?'

Fein's mouth adopted a slight moue of satisfaction. 'Well, my role was more facilitator than anything. I was definitely in the background.'

'You were at the Christmas party, so presumably you could say whether either or both of these apparently linked deals were signed by the time of the shooting?'

'I'm afraid I couldn't, actually.'

'It could be that someone wanted them not to sign this deal, that's what I'm saying.'

'Well, that would seem a little far-fetched.' Fein ran his hands through his hair.

'You seem to be skirting the issue, if I may say so.'

'My hands are tied,' Fein said, with an expressive shrug which proved that in literal terms they were not.

Gillard tried another tack. 'All right, a yes-or-no question: do you think one might have tried to kill the other?'

Fein's eyes narrowed and he ran his fingers through his hair. 'Well, there *was* a time, of course. But I'm absolutely convinced they would have seen the bigger picture by now.'

'You dealt with them both in business, and sometimes together, is that true?'

'Well, individually many times. Together…' He sucked his teeth ruminatively. 'Craig, I'll be honest with you. I'm not sure there were more than two or three times when I was right there in the same room with them both. Excluding big social gatherings, naturally.'

'Naturally,' Gillard said, feeling he was lost in a swamp of nuance. 'Did you ever witness arguments between them?'

Fein searched the ceiling as if the answer might have been written there. 'I can't say I did, to be perfectly frank.' He smiled. 'But what I would say is that the ingredients for conflict were certainly in place. Now, Craig. Perhaps I could ask you a question? My sources tell me that you don't possess the murder weapon. Is that really true?'

'I couldn't possibly comment.' *Two can play at that game, mate.* 'Lord Fein, you would best help this inquiry by answering *my* questions. A bit of history, perhaps. Tell me a bit more about when that enmity began. Beyond the issue with Yelena Yalinsky.'

Fein permitted himself a small laugh, which showed a perfect arc of small white teeth. 'Well, I think we have to go back to Hookergate, as it became known. Do you know about that?'

'No.'

'All right. Well, in Russia there is a great tradition of digging up *kompromat*, compromising material which allows an individual to be blackmailed. It was always the cornerstone of the KGB's recruitment attempts. It makes for very loyal spies. But of course it has other uses. Now in 2013, Sasha lost several billion in a Zimbabwean platinum deal, for which he blamed Talin. It's all very complicated and clever, but it basically revolved around the fact that Sasha had got too many debts and, because of the impending divorce, struggled to service them. Anyway,' he dismissed the complexities with a wave of his hand. 'A year-or-so later, Talin happened to be in Sochi, you know, the Black Sea resort, and decided to have a party in his room involving two ladies of the night.' He rolled his eyes as if such shenanigans were beneath contempt.

'And this was filmed, I presume?' asked Gillard.

'Yes. I'm surprised that Talin didn't sweep the room, because he's normally very careful like that, but in any case, there was a camera behind the main mirror which perfectly captured what was going on.'

'Was Talin married at the time?'

'He was, to an American woman, though that wasn't the issue. Somebody leaked the tape to a TV station owned by one of Sasha's allies, and it played on a loop for months and months until everyone was sick of it.

'Does Russian TV allow erotic content to be shown like that?'

Fein laughed. 'No. And it wasn't erotic at all, Craig, that is what was so damaging. It was rather pathetic.' The expression on the financier's face showed no obvious sympathy for the victim.

'So Talin reckoned Volkov was responsible?'

'He said as much. He threatened to have him killed.'

'And was he responsible?'

Fein held up his hands. 'I couldn't possibly say. But as the old saying goes, if the cap fits wear it.'

'You spoke to them both at the party, I presume?'

'Yes. I sat in the same table as Sasha and Sophie, and then had quite a long conversation with Maxim during which Sasha came up to talk to him. I remember Sasha putting his hand on his old friend's shoulder. Honestly, I think they were getting on fine, at that point. But who knows, perhaps something was said when they were in the library.'

'Did Mr Volkov carry a gun, generally?'

Fein looked shocked. 'Good heavens, no. I don't think he even knew how to shoot. He did his conscription like everybody else, but because of his geology experience he was sent to the corps of engineers. His links to the Komsomol, the communist youth group, meant he became an officer almost immediately. Some things don't change, you see. The only shots experienced by the engineers are the endless rounds of vodka that they down. The unit is mostly famed for its ability to throw lavish parties.'

'Another thing that doesn't change,' Gillard said. 'Did he ever mention to you about being worried about being killed?'

Fein blew a sigh. 'Many times. When Berezovsky was killed, and Perepilichny, after the Skripal attacks too. We talked about it often. But the person he mentioned most often was her.'

'His wife?'

'During the divorce, yes. "Yelena Yakolina Yalinsky. Three Ys. Why, why, why did I marry her?" He said it many times, it was his little play on words. Of course, there were two sides to this marriage. She and Natasha are very close. We heard her side of it too. Yelena was mistreated, undeniably.'

Gillard waited for more details, but none were forthcoming.

'If you want chapter and verse, speak to Natasha. She knows everything.'

'I will, but can I first ask your assessment: is Yelena capable of murder?'

'Capable? Certainly. Unlike Sasha, she enjoys hunting. She is a very good horsewoman, and a first-class shot. She's very smart and well-connected. An incredible amount of the British export business to Kazakhstan came our way because of our connections to Yelena.' When he said 'our', his eyebrows twitched, indicating that the word in question was actually 'my'. My connections. Gillard could see exactly how the noble lord had come to be an indispensable tool for British economic diplomacy.

'But as far as threats were concerned, he made no mention of any in the last few weeks or months?' Gillard persisted.

Fein pursed his lips. 'No. If anything, he seemed much more relaxed. That was the strange thing. At times in the past Sasha had genuinely become paranoid. But just recently, he had relaxed and become more normal.' He shook his head. 'It's quite ironic isn't it, given what subsequently happened?'

–

After Fein had made his excuses and left, Gillard drove his unmarked Vauxhall back along the damp and quiet City streets. His hands-free buzzed; the number indicated was the chief constable's. He answered, with his usual sense of foreboding. 'Yes, ma'am,' he said.

'Craig, I've made some progress with the security services. I've got Volkov's satellite phone and have passed it on to Rob Townsend for analysis. MI5 claim no knowledge of your notebook or tape recorder. Ms Yalinsky is in Switzerland, apparently, on a skiing trip—'

'Really? It's a weird time to go skiing, just after both husband and lover have been murdered.'

'Indeed. Be that as it may, she is only there until Sunday, when she plans to head back to Moscow. I think it's important that we speak to her, so I'd like you to go to Geneva tonight.'

So much for getting any time with Sam. 'All right. I still have to speak to Natasha Fein today. I'm on my way to her home now.'

'How is the forensic side going?'

'We've got lots of information but no conclusions. The most obvious explanation would be that the two businessmen shot each other, but that doesn't accord with the ballistics, which shows the vast majority of the shots were fired by a weapon that we don't have.'

'I asked MI5 about the missing gun, and they gave a kind of collective shrug.'

'They don't have it?'

'So they say. The good news is that no suspicious contaminants or radioactivity were detected.'

'Nice of them to tell us so many hours after we would have been exposed to them.'

Rigby laughed. 'I hope you'll enjoy speaking to the outgoing Mrs Fein.'

'What are you trying to tell me, ma'am?'

She laughed still more loudly. The detective suspected he was the subject of some kind of in-joke. 'Seriously, Craig. Be careful with her. Be circumspect. Use your judgement.'

–

Virginia Water is one of the most exclusive districts in Surrey's millionaire belt. Sandwiched between the Wentworth golf course and the famous lake and gardens which give the area its name, the heavily wooded neighbourhood is both opulent and discreet. Gillard twice missed the Feins' home, which was reached on a narrow and unmarked laurel-lined track between two large houses. The track only became an asphalt drive a good hundred yards from the road and opened out into manicured parkland dotted with horse chestnut trees. The house itself was a 1930s mock-Tudor mansion with extensive outbuildings and converted stables. Gillard self-consciously straightened his tie and brushed the shoulders of his jacket as he approached the front door. A teenage girl in riding hat and jodhpurs was just emerging.

'Are you looking for Mum? She's in the pool, over there.' She pointed to the stable block. Gillard made his way across. The stable door was, as the saying goes, wide open, but the characteristic chlorine smell and echo of a swimming pool made it clear he was in the right place. The detective walked down the tiled corridor towards the sound of splashing and emerged into an enormous glass-domed room with an Olympic-sized pool as its centrepiece. Someone was ploughing up and down at an impressive rate, streamlined front crawl lengths that would certainly not shame any member of a competitive swimming club. Gillard took in the potted palms and ferns which lined the place and gave it the feel of a colonial dining room. There was no one else around.

It was only when the swimmer diverted from her lengths to cross the pool obliquely to him that Gillard realised she was entirely naked. A head of dark hair broke the surface as she reached for the ladder at his feet.

'Detective chief inspector, so good to see you.'

'And you, Mrs Fein.' She began to climb out, and he backed away, partially to avoid getting wet. He tried hard to keep his eyes on her face and away from her perfectly sculpted body. But he was male. He failed, and she knew it. The smug feline expression said it all.

'Want to join me? There's heaps of towels and, if you need one, spare costumes.' Her arm movement, like a little bit of backstroke, spattered droplets all the way up his trousers and shirt. 'Sorry.'

He smiled. 'If you don't mind, I'm quite pushed for time. I was told you were joining your husband in New York tomorrow morning.' He gazed around the edge of the pool, looking for the towels she had alluded to. She padded along to a parasoled table, and picked up a large bath towel, which she slung over one shoulder.

'Follow me.' He did so at a distance, watching the well-oiled swing of her hips. 'You British are so uptight,' she said over her shoulder. 'Nakedness is such a privilege, if you have the space, the warmth and the seclusion. There's nothing quite like it for swimming, to feel water caressing every part of your body.'

Gillard could now see exactly the nature of Alison Rigby's warning. The woman was clearly an exhibitionist. Naturally, it helps if what you have is worth seeing.

'I'll stay out here until you're ready,' he said.

'No need. I don't mind.' He made no move to follow her into the changing room, where she left the door open. 'Yelena said some very interesting things to me at the party. About the divorce,' she shouted out. Gillard stood by the open door, not looking inside, but he could hear the shower going, its thunderous roar drowning out whatever it was she was saying.

'I can't hear you,' he called out. The reply was loud, but obscure. He waited a minute, still unable to discern the words, but determined not to be lured into the changing room. Her husband's mention of *kompromat* was still fresh in his mind, and he wouldn't be at all surprised if there were cameras here. He couldn't immediately think why she would want to put him in a compromising position, but he didn't want to take any chances.

It must have been a good fifteen minutes later when Natasha Fein emerged, wearing a loosely tied bathrobe. 'Anyway, I think that could have some bearing on the case, don't you?'

'I think I'd like you to repeat it somewhere where I can take notes.'

She shrugged and pointed to a poolside table. He got out his digital recorder and notebook, and she sat opposite him.

'Lady Fein, can you clarify your role at Westgrave Hall?'

'Yes. As you probably know, I run a concierge company. I'm effectively a freelance facilitator. I helped organise the passage of the fossil from RAF Brize Norton to here. I helped organise the party, and generally made things happen in the way that Sasha would like. But I was also a friend.'

'To both Mr Volkov and his former wife, I understand?'

'Yes, and their children. Even after they fell out, I worked hard to keep the line of communication open between them. I'm a bit like the red hotline telephone used in the Cold War.'

'I see. And what was it you were saying to me, from the changing room?'

'Just that Yelena wanted to settle the divorce case. A final judgement on the case was due early in the new year, but there was a big snag. And this, detective chief inspector, is absolutely confidential. Yelena wanted to have a child with Maxim Talin, and being quite far-sighted, had frozen her remaining eggs in liquid nitrogen some years ago when the marriage to Sasha was failing. She used a Swiss clinic to store them for her, but last year, when Sasha discovered it, he spent over three billion Swiss francs buying the entire pharmaceutical company that owned the clinic. And then he used various legal barriers to bar her from access to her own eggs.'

'That's rather spiteful.'

'Indeed. She was furious, and began a legal retaliation. That's when I got involved as a go-between. I could see that this wasn't going to be good for anybody. It took months, and Sasha was driving a hard deal, getting Yelena to relinquish part of her stake in the minerals company. She was willing to do it to get the eggs back. Then, in the final few days, there was a disaster. There was a power failure at the clinic, and all the freezers failed. Everything was lost.'

'Was it Volkov?'

'Yelena thought so, but he denied it, swearing so on the lives of his children, and I believe him. He's not a good liar. But Yelena, well, she's never got over it. Some things no amount of money can replace.'

'And the divorce deal?'

'It got rejigged. She now insisted she was keeping all her stake in the mining firm rather than just half of it, and Sasha, who it has to be said was riven with guilt, agreed. So we had a deal, just a week before Christmas. There was plenty of distrust, naturally, but all the paperwork was ready to sign after the party.'

'I've already asked your husband, but perhaps you can tell me if Volkov expressed any worries about his personal security in the period running up to this party?'

'He was worried about lots of things: the quality of the caviar, about nailing down the contract for our star attraction Ms Beyoncé Knowles, and the immigration technicalities for the bloody circus performers—'

'—but no worries about his own safety?'

'Not that he mentioned. Of course he had years ago, before the rapprochement with the Kremlin. But he felt safe, and from everything I hear from my own contacts back in Moscow, he *was* safe.'

'Obviously not, in the end.'

She paused. 'Horrible, just horrible. I thought I'd never be in this situation again, after Boris.'

'I'm sorry?'

'Boris Berezovsky. I did a similar job for him as I did for Sasha. They say he committed suicide, but I never believed it. Never. Unlike Sasha, he kept needling the Kremlin. It was very foolhardy.'

Gillard wondered whether she would be considered a bad omen. To lose one employer is unfortunate, but two… 'From what I've heard you worked more closely with Mr Volkov than anyone else.'

'I suppose that's true.'

'And how would you describe his state of mind in the weeks before his death?'

'He was excited, overall. He'd fallen head-over-heels in love with Sophie, quite understandably. And had finally stopped being maudlin.'

'Why maudlin?'

'Oh, he was terribly homesick. I don't think he really got Britain, as such. Surrey was always a useful bolthole, but I didn't think he would ever love the place. He missed the open spaces, the forests, the warmth of good friends. Britain is so crowded, and the people are so grey, they always limit themselves. In some ways Sasha was terribly sentimental, terribly nostalgic.'

'With money you can recreate many things.'

'Absolutely. I organised the planting of the spruce and birch woods at the back of the hall. It's only eight hundred acres, unfortunately, but one day it might look like a small slice of Siberian forest. The hall he ultimately wanted to become full-on Romanov, but even he hasn't got enough money to make all that happen. Even my most optimistic plan for the estate would need twenty years. But he wanted it yesterday. I mean, he wanted to plant hundred-year-old birch trees on the estate, and had located some in Russia that he planned to fly in. He wouldn't accept the professional advice, which is that moving such mature trees would kill them. His child-ishness could be charming, but also terribly wearing. I worked to get him to understand that not everything can be solved by money. Sometimes you just need time. With trees, especially. You plant saplings and wait. But he wouldn't wait.'

'What was it that forced him to leave Russia in the first place?' Gillard asked.

'I think the final straw was the death from cancer of his great friend, Pavel Friedman. He had relied on Pavel for so many years. He was the brains behind their wealth. He was the last of Sasha's allies, and the engine of their mining business. I think he decided to remove himself from the day-to-day running of the business, that's all.'

Gillard looked at his notes, which were a little damp from the droplets flung out whenever Natasha emphasised her points. 'Thank you, Lady Fein.'

'You're very welcome,' she said. 'Feel free to come for an off-duty swim, whenever you want. David is very understanding.'

Gillard blinked at the brazen juxtaposition of those two comments but decided to ignore them. It was time to head back to Westgrave Hall and look in a bit more detail at some of the events in the history of Volkov and Talin.

As he left he tried and failed to eradicate the image of a naked, tanned Lady Fein from his mind.

–

After a distracted drive from Virginia Water, Gillard slipped the unmarked Vauxhall into a parking space near the Westgrave Hall portico. PC Zoe Butterfield was standing with her back to him, just a few yards away, chatting with Wolf. They seemed to be laughing and joking like old friends, and clearly hadn't noticed him. At one point the Georgian security man rested a hand on her shoulder.

Gillard emerged from the car and slammed the door. They both jumped, and she dropped her clipboard onto the gravel. Wolf stepped back guiltily from her personal space.

'Returning to the scene of the crime, Zoe?'

'You made me jump, sir,' she said, scooping up her clipboard. Wolf gave a cheery wave and made his way back into the main house.

'Sorry about that. So, what has Wolf got to say for himself?'

'Not much. He's worried about losing his job. His residency status in the UK depends on it.'

'He's a funny guy, isn't he?'

'Absolutely hilarious,' she said, with a grin.

'Think he's the murderer?'

'Of course not!' She looked outraged.

He'd proved his point, at least to himself. 'Don't get too close, constable. Don't do a PC Woodbridge.'

'Sir, what *do* you think of me?' she said, straightening her hat, as if she'd been insulted.

'It's all right, Zoe, I trust your maturity and common sense, which is aided by the lack of testosterone in your half of the human race.'

She grinned again, and then turned, embarrassed, back to the task of cleaning the mud off the clipboard.

Gillard didn't have long before catching his flight, but headed back to the Khazi, where he sat at his terminal and logged on. Lord Fein had, as promised, sent a web link to the *kompromat* humiliation of Maxim Talin. The link took him through to a satirical website in Russian, seemingly dedicated to great fails, with the relevant video near the top of the list. The view was from almost ceiling level of a large double bed in a hotel bedroom. An overweight naked male was lolling in bed, his dark hair all over the place, while one beautiful girl in erotic lingerie gamely tried to give him an erection, while another sat watching the TV and yawning. There was sound in Russian, which of course Gillard didn't understand, but there were helpful subtitles in English. Talin certainly looked out for the count, probably on alcohol, and as portrayed here was no woman's dream lover. The punchline came when the girl on the bed stopped bobbing her head up and down on Talin's groin, looked at the unappetising morsel between her fingers and muttered to the other, 'I'm wasting my time here'. It was the fact that the women were so obviously bored witless that made it so tawdry and humiliating.

With a homing instinct for filth that Gillard had long admired, Hoskins burst into the Khazi before the video had finished. The DCI felt the need to explain why he was apparently watching cheap porn, but he knew that the overweight detective wouldn't judge him, at least so long as he got to see it too.

'Oh, that is so bad,' Hoskins said shaking his head. 'Imagine getting two gorgeous girls in your room and not being able to get it up.'

'And it being on film for all the world to see,' Gillard said.

'And that's Talin, is it?'

'Yep, ten years ago, before he dyed his hair blond. All set up by Volkov, apparently.'

'I'm surprised they could ever be friends again after that,' Hoskins said.

'Maybe they weren't.'

Hoskins shrugged and pulled his notebook out. 'There's a freelance journalist who wants to speak to you, name of Daniel Levin, coming to Redhill police station at four this afternoon.'

Gillard groaned. 'I'm flying to Geneva at six thirty, and I've got to go home first for luggage and passport.'

'That's why Michelle booked him for you at Redhill. Just a quick half hour before your Gatwick flight, just down the road. He'll only speak to you.'

'Carl, I simply don't have time to speak to the press, you know that.'

'You might find time for this one, sir. Claims he knows who killed Volkov.'

Chapter Eleven

Gillard arrived five minutes early at Redhill police station, having grabbed his luggage and passport from home. That left no time for more than a cursory Google search on Daniel Levin. It showed that he had been a writer at an independent news magazine in Moscow before coming to live in the UK. In high-profile cases there are always time wasters, and he was trusting Carl Hoskins' judgement that this wasn't going to be one of them.

Gillard just happened to be peering between the slats of the interview room blinds when a bent man, wearing a trilby and using two walking sticks, emerged from a small camper van in the disabled parking space and made his way slowly up the ramp to the front door of the station. The desk sergeant came to open the door and help him in. Luckily, Gillard had been offered the comforts of the rape suite, the only ground floor interview room and just a few steps from the front desk. The duty sergeant offered his help, but the man shook his head. Gillard opened the door and watched the man laboriously manoeuvre himself in. Daniel Levin took more than a minute to travel the five yards into the rape suite, and his twisted face and frequent moans of pain showed that every step exacted a price. Only when he was seated, on the only hard chair in the room, and had doffed his hat did Gillard see that this emaciated man was probably younger than he was.

The thinning white hair and pallid complexion spoke of a difficult life.

'Mr Gillard,' Levin began in firm but accented English. 'Thank you for agreeing to see me at such short notice. I have unique information which I think will be helpful.'

'I hope so. First, can you tell me a little bit about yourself?'

'Of course. I worked for Ria Novosti in my youth, and then joined Pavel Friedman's independent TV station Kal21 in 2008. I was a business correspondent and covered the rise in the fortunes of Alexander Volkov during those years. His was a gilded career, aided by an alliance with my employer, and his marriage to Yelena Yalinsky.' His dark watchful eyes flicked up. 'I'm sure I've no need to tell you anything about her.'

'She was there when the shooting took place.'

'Of course she was. Understand her, and you understand everything.' His thin lips twisted into a semblance of a smile. 'But she did not kill him.'

'Who did, then?'

He looked around as if he could be overheard, and then looked accusingly at the big old-fashioned police tape recorder. 'Let me explain. To you, I'm sure, people like Volkov and Talin are just rich Russians, with more money than sense. But it is not that simple. When the Soviet Union collapsed, Boris Yeltsin allowed whole industries to fall into the hands of a few favoured allies. These oligarchs, people like Mikhail Khodorkovsky, Roman Abramovich and of course my friend Boris Berezovsky, were the first wave of Russian plutocrats, from the late 1990s. They benefited from patronage, cheap loans, and in some cases the subversion of the privatisation process. After the fall of Yeltsin in 1999, the KGB effectively took over the

Kremlin. You know who I'm talking about. These well-connected intelligence officers were jealous of the wealth that the young upstarts had illicitly amassed. The KGB, its successor the FSB, and the military intelligence people at GRU, had everything they needed to take back what had been stolen from the Russian people. After all, these were experts who had cut their teeth in the Cold War; with blackmail, extortion, disinformation and the subversion of Western democracies.'

Levin felt in his pocket and pulled out a hip flask. 'Do you mind? It is the most effective painkiller known to man. I should know, I have tried them all.' He unscrewed the top and took a quick swig, wiping his mouth with the back of his hand.

'How does this fit in with Volkov and the killing?' Gillard glanced at his watch, thinking about his approaching flight check-in time.

'Patience, please, you need the context. To understand Volkov's life you need to understand his best childhood friend. It is him I'm going to tell you about.'

'If he so significant, perhaps I should interview him myself,' Gillard said.

'Are you planning a séance?'

'I'm sorry?'

'Pavel Friedman is dead.'

'Ah yes, he died of cancer in 2008.' He'd remembered that Natasha Fein had mentioned him.

'Yes, he did. But he was murdered.' Levin stared hard at Gillard.

'I don't see how cancer could—'

'Patience, please. Now, the Kremlin could see how much Russian wealth was flowing abroad. To Zürich, to Vienna, to Cyprus and of course to London. They needed to act to show these oligarchs that money alone is not power, at least not a power to match the state. They made an example of Khodorkovsky, jailing him for failing to pay taxes, *pour encourager les autres*, as the French say. Abramovich was clever and saw which way the wind was blowing. He made sure he stayed on the right side of the Kremlin. But Boris Berezovsky, ah Boris. He came to London and thought he was safe.' Levin shook his head.

'Yes, I know the background.' He glanced at his watch again.

'Volkov, Talin and Pavel Friedman were part of the second wave of oligarchs. They drew their power from *within* the intelligence structure. Volkov and Friedman grew up in Perm, in Siberia, which I assure you is the most windswept, nondescript middle-of-nowhere place you have never heard of. Friedman, the third of five children, grew up in poverty and spent his childhood selling apples grown on his father's smallholding to passing traffic. He quickly realised that he could make more money by buying apples from remote cottages and storing them to sell in the winter when prices were higher. By the age of twelve he had learned which varieties would store well and had offloaded the selling to his younger siblings. He didn't make much money, but he had learned a valuable lesson in economics.'

Gillard was getting quite fidgety now, but Levin was just getting going.

'You see, these two Russian boys understood early on what you had to do. Friedman because he was a genius and Jewish, which meant he was an outsider, and Volkov because his father spent twenty years in the gulag for publishing a critical pamphlet about Brezhnev. Latch on to power, and ride with it. And if you were born in Perm in 1964, then you joined the Komsomol, which is the youth league of the Communist Party. That way, when they went to Moscow to university, they already had a powerbase.' Levin pulled a blister pack of pills from his pocket and popped two, washing them down with liquor from his hip flask.

'Volkov studied geology at Moscow State University, while Friedman, a Jew like me, was not allowed to apply. He went instead to the Mendeleev University of Chemical Technology, also in Moscow, but they stayed good friends and met up for drinks and meals. It was at one of those meals when Volkov first spotted Yelena. She was already being courted by Maxim Talin, one of Volkov's classmates. Volkov was captivated by her beauty, but it was Friedman who pointed out how wealthy she must be, as the daughter of the finance minister of Kazakhstan, which of course was then part of the Soviet Union.'

Levin laughed. 'Friedman pointed out that Kazakhstan was the Klondike of copper. "Just you wait and see. You need roads, and you need money, but there is huge potential. She could be your key to unlock it. Go for her!" That is how far-sighted he was. Decades ahead of the game.'

'If so, how did Friedman come to be murdered?'

'He was too successful. With Volkov's marriage to Yelena, their company, Kazakh Metals, was able to get a licence to expand and modernise the copper mines at Karabulak. The attraction wasn't just new deposits, but the hundred million tonnes of tailings heaped up during the mine's first expansion in the 1880s.'

'You mean slag heaps?'

'Not exactly. The process to extract copper in the 1880s was pretty rudimentary and left lots of ore still in the rock. Friedman had developed a technique to use ammonium chloride solution to get an additional six per cent yield of copper. It worked particularly well on alkaline deposits, like those at Karabulak. What you must understand is that it's much cheaper and faster to reprocess existing deposits than to dig new ones. Your resource is already lying in front of you.'

'So that's how they made the money?'

'Yes. From there, Friedman drove an international expansion, setting up a bank in Cyprus which purchased refined copper from Kazakh Metals at the subsidised domestic price which was used to sell to Russian industry, and then selling it abroad at the international dollar price, which was three times as high and earned precious foreign exchange. The mining company made very little at these prices, but the bank made a fortune. The mine paid taxes to Kazakhstan on what little it earned, while the bank didn't have to pay any meaningful tax in Cyprus. That sleight of hand ensured that Friedman and Volkov became billionaires.'

'You're saying Friedman was the brains behind the operation?'

'Yes. He really only needed Volkov for the connection with Yelena. Of course, she had a substantial shareholding in the mineral part of the business, from broking the deal to buy the deposits, which meant she was earning a lot too, though she was in effect a sleeping partner. Anyway, that's where Volkov's money came from. He rode to riches on the coattails of Friedman's insight.'

'Where did it go wrong?'

Levin shrugged. 'They got on the wrong side of a very powerful man within the Kremlin. A very clever man, who wanted to own Kazakh Minerals for himself. From about 2005, Pavel Friedman knew his life was in danger. New forces in the Kremlin were rising, and they were jealous. Look at Litvinenko, poisoned with radioactive polonium in 2007. Perepilichny, assassinated in 2012, found with poisonous gelsemium leaves in his stomach just a couple of days after meeting a glamorous Ukrainian model in Paris. A cover-up by Surrey Police, yes, you guys. They didn't even interview her. Then of course my good friend Boris Berezovsky, supposedly hung himself in his own bathroom in 2013. Two of his close associates had already died. Then there were three British fixers who aided Russian oligarchs to get their money abroad, including Scot Young, fifty-two, thrown to his death and impaled on railings in 2014. Not one of them older than sixty, and all dead in a series of mysterious accidents. Two of the favourite methods are heart attacks, brought on by untraceable poisons, or a fall from a high balcony.'

He stopped and wiped his forehead with a filthy cotton handkerchief. It was not hot in the room, but he was sweating. 'I can tell you, I stopped meeting contacts at restaurants or bars years ago. Anyway, Friedman had two very good Israeli bodyguards and an ex-Mossad intelligence officer who swept the bank's headquarters in Cyprus for electronic bugs. But they all missed something.'

Levin shook his head at the recollection. 'Pavel started to get these terrible headaches. Like the worst migraines, that forced him to lie down for hours and hours. Once when he came to St Petersburg I had arranged to interview him at his hotel suite. I was shown into a darkened room, where he was lying down on a sofa. I had to try to remember my questions and rely on the tape recorder to pick them up. His voice was slurred and he clearly wasn't at the top of his game. Eventually he was given an MRI scan and they discovered an enormous tumour in the back of his head. Completely inoperable.'

'I thought you said he was murdered,' Gillard said.

'He was. Three years previously, in the bank's headquarters in Limassol, Cyprus, Friedman's head of security had picked up a listening device, hidden in a desk. So Friedman decreed that all the office furniture would be changed. Everything was bought from new, direct from the factory. He got himself a brand-new leather-covered designer chair. Everything was X-rayed before installation. Nothing was left to chance. Or so he thought.'

Levin took another swig from his hip flask and waved it in the air. 'There is only so much you can do, yes? Well, when Friedman was taken into hospital, the security chief had an idea. He borrowed a Geiger counter and swept Friedman's office. There was a faint radioactive source from the chair. It turned out that a small part of the polyurethane stuffing in the head cushion had been soaked in a radioactive source, the kind of thing you might find in a hospital. For a passing exposure it would have been no problem, less radioactivity than you would get from a single X-ray. But hour after hour after hour is something else. For three years, it had been irradiating the back of Friedman's head.'

'That is scarily clever. To have the reach to get that in at manufacture.'

'That is the murderer the Kremlin employed, the person I'm here to tell you about,' Levin said. 'He killed Friedman, and I think he killed Volkov too. He has been trained to dispense death.'

Finally, we get to the point, Gillard thought. 'What's his name?'

Levin closed his eyes and his mouth tightened as if he was plucking up courage. 'They call him the Ghost. He leaves no trace. He can get anywhere, he can kill anyone.'

'What is his real name?'

'I don't know. But I have seen him with my own eyes.'

Gillard watched Levin's tears welling up.

'Mr Gillard, can you believe that only five years ago I was able to run a marathon? I raised thousands of euros for Chernobyl cancer victims.'

The detective's eyes widened. 'What happened to you?'

Levin turned away, screwing up his face against some horrible memory. He lifted a fist to his mouth to mask his trembling lips, but there was a shaking in his shoulders.

'It was August 2016. I had arranged to meet a good source of mine who had flown over from Moscow to Amsterdam. I was working on an article for the *New York Times* about corruption in the mining industry. The source was a senior official in the Russian Ministry of Mines. We met in the Hotel Okura, in the south of the city. When I got back to my own hotel, a charming little gabled place on Rembrandtplein, someone was waiting for me in my room. I have no idea how he got in because I had picked the place specially. It was small, with only a single staircase, five bedrooms, and the staff had seen nothing. But he was there, anyway, waiting for me. I am not a big man. He overpowered me, held me face down and gave me an injection which stopped me struggling. He said, "I have come with some sad news. To announce the suicide of Daniel Levin. He had been feeling quite down for some time, so it isn't a surprise".'

Levin looked up at Gillard. A single tear tracked down his lined face. 'He threw me off the balcony. There were cast-iron railings three storeys below, lots of bicycles chained there. He missed, and I landed on a car roof. I broke my spine. The ambulance was there very quickly and saved my life. For two weeks I was in a coma, and when I awoke I couldn't remember anything that had happened. My blood was found dosed with antidepressants and alcohol.'

'What did the police say?'

'Of course, they assumed I had thrown myself off. For the first two weeks that's what I thought too. It was only when I was offered a hypnotism course to recover lost memories that I remembered what had happened to me.'

'Hypnotherapy worked?'

'Not exactly. I was on my way to the appointment when I suddenly remembered what happened.' He barked a short ironic laugh. 'Naturally, they were reluctant to believe my story. There were no footprints of anyone but me in the apartment. No fingerprints, nothing.'

Hairs lifted on the back of Gillard's neck: No footprints, no fingerprints. The parallels were ominous. 'What did this man look like, do you remember?'

Levin lifted a slim leather briefcase to the table and unbuckled the two straps. He slid out a thin manila folder and opened it. He showed Gillard a single piece of paper, a photocopy. 'This is the Ghost. It's an artist's impression I had made soon after the hypnotherapy.'

The image was arresting in its intensity. If provoking fear had been the objective, the artist had done a remarkable job. The buzz-cut white hair, small angular ears and sharp cheekbones combined with dark, deep-set eyes to give a kind of ethereal presence.

'Do you recognise him?' Levin asked.

'I'm not sure.' One of Volkov's security men had a slight resemblance, the guy with the ponytail. But the hair was completely different. 'So what is the current status of the investigation by the Dutch police?'

'Buried, is the best description. Dead and buried.' Levin looked up. 'But not for the Ghost. For him, I'm unfinished business, Mr Gillard. I am in fear for my life.'

Chapter Twelve

Daniel Levin took several minutes to prepare himself for the short trip back to his car. Gillard looked through the details of the journalist's statement and saw that the desk sergeant hadn't made a note of his address or contact details. 'Where are you staying, Mr Levin?'

'Not at home,' he replied. 'My wife and children are abroad. I dare not go back to my London home. I have friends who help me. Part of the Russian diaspora.' He gave a thin smile. 'I am reluctant to endanger them, so quite often I sleep in my van.'

'That can't do your back any good.'

Levin shrugged. 'The vehicle is adapted for my disability. It allows me to be in a different place every night.'

Gillard nodded, and looked down. 'Can you at least give me a phone number or an email address? We want to help protect you.'

Levin gave a bitter laugh. 'You can't protect me. My death certificate is written, but not yet delivered. If I have anything more to say I will let you know.'

-

Once Levin had gone, Gillard checked his watch. He had less than ninety minutes before the flight to Switzerland. As he hurried to his car, he rang the Khazi, hoping that somebody would be in the mobile incident room. DI Claire Mulholland picked up. He summarised what he had heard from Levin. 'He's convinced it's some Kremlin-directed assassin called the Ghost, who doesn't leave fingerprints or footprints.'

'But if this Ghost is a real person, as Levin says, it still doesn't explain how he can get in, kill Volkov and Talin and get out again without leaving any forensic evidence apart from bullets and cartridge cases.'

'No, it doesn't. I've asked Redhill to scan the drawing, so you should get a copy by email soon. I have to confess though, the security guy the drawing resembles, the one with the ponytail, was outside the library throughout the shooting.' Gillard sighed, and checked his watch. 'So still no footprints?'

'No. We found one cartridge case actually on the fossil, a good five feet in from the edge. That makes it look like the assailant was actually standing on the rock.'

'Ejected cases can travel quite a few feet, even from a pistol. That's what Neville Tufton said,' Gillard said.

'Yes, and that's probably what happened, because we couldn't find any footprints on the fossil, and if there were any, we certainly would have found them.'

'The Ghost supposedly threw Levin out of a third-floor window in Amsterdam.'

'Poor guy!'

'He lived, but is severely disabled. If you'd heard him tell the story you wouldn't doubt it. Someone has put the fear of God into him.' Gillard got to the car, got in and started the engine. 'I've got to go now.'

'Good luck in Geneva,' Claire said, then added, 'One last thing: Delahaye has finished the post-mortems of the three dead. Reports to follow, but the headline is what you'd expect: deaths caused by bullet wounds, loss of blood, trauma and shock. We've got five bullets retrieved from the corpses, sent off to Neville Tufton for analysis.'

'Thank you, Claire.' He realised that however much progress was made in unearthing the histories of those who died, without real forensic progress it was simply circumstantial. Someone had been in that library and fired roughly four dozen shots, without leaving any evidence of who they were. It just didn't make sense.

'One other thing you should know, Craig. Someone tried to break into the Khazi,' she said. 'I'm not sure when it was, but there's been an attempt to lever off the ventilator cover. I only noticed it this afternoon. There were some wooden chips on the carpet, and when I went up to the roof, I could see damage from where a crowbar had been jammed in.'

This wouldn't be the first time. Gillard remembered the Khazi's generator being stolen overnight during a murder case five years ago. It was eventually found in a caravan park and scrap metal yard near Reading. 'What's the CCTV coverage like?' he asked.

'Not bad. The Khazi itself is out of view but there is a camera which covers the path leading across the side of the hall. At the moment we've still got a uniform on the door of the library, and a patrol car twenty-four seven at the entrance to keep the press away. I really don't want to have to ask for yet another uniform to stand outside the Khazi getting wet and cold.'

'All right. We don't need a fresh body, just reallocate a nightshift detective from Mount Browne to Westgrave Hall. Whoever it is can work from the Khazi. We might even pick up some fresh leads. Who would that be tonight?'

'Hoskins,' Claire replied with a laugh.

Gillard chuckled too. 'It will do him good to be out of his comfort zone. Set him some tasks to stop him falling asleep.'

—

By seven p.m on that Boxing Day evening, Claire Mulholland was sitting with an untidy pile of witness statements in the splendour of the Fitzroy Room, at the desk made famous by Dr Samuel Johnson. She and a team of uniformed officers led by Sergeant Vince Babbage had pieced together as best they could what had been seen and when, around the time that the shooting began two days before. The final detailed statements, from the housekeeper Mrs Bell, the cook Tatiana and the two Bangladeshi kitchen porters, had now been taken. Like any jigsaw, there were pieces missing; particularly any contribution from Yelena Yalinsky, former wife of the dead oligarch, and their son Oleg, but it was already clear that the fundamentals of the mystery remained intact: how could someone in the library have gunned down Volkov, Talin and Bryn Howell and escaped the building without being seen?

As she flicked through, making notes on the most significant contributions, Claire was aware of the approach of the substantial figure of Babbage, followed at some distance by an elderly woman in a grey cardigan, a mauve gilet and dowdy mid-calf skirt.

'Sorry to disturb, ma'am. This lady has apparently been waiting to speak to you for several hours.'

'Is she a witness?'

The expression on Babbage's face was nuanced scepticism. 'Not exactly. She apparently phoned in something suspicious earlier but hasn't heard anything back.'

Claire nodded and beckoned her to come forward and sit opposite her.

'I do apologise if you've been kept waiting. This is a very complex logistical inquiry.'

'My name is Mary Hill.' She then trotted out her address, telephone number and the incident number she had been given over the phone. Claire had a quick flick through her index of evidence and could find no mention of the woman.

'You say you've given a statement?'

'Twice now, actually. One's expectations of the police have naturally enough sagged over the years, but I have to say I am appalled at the slipshod fashion in which this inquiry seems to be run. Every year the precept for Surrey Police seems to go up and up, and we get less and less for it.'

Claire propped her head up on her hand. She knew Mary's type of old. 'Perhaps we can home in on what it is you actually witnessed.'

'Certainly. At exactly 6:37 a.m. this morning, I was walking with Oswald along the public footpath on the north side of Westgrave Lake when I saw someone in a rowing boat—'

'And Oswald is?'

'My spaniel.'

'Wasn't it dark? Sunrise isn't until eight o'clock.'

'Yes. Oswald has a red glow collar, and I have an LED pen light so I can see where he's done his business.'

'Can I ask how you came to be there at such a time on Boxing Day morning? I understood the footpaths were closed for maintenance.' This is what Wolf had mentioned, when Gillard had asked about the chance of journalists getting into the estate.

A touch of steel tightened the woman's face. 'Detective inspector, there is no legal right to close a public footpath without county council approval. Even for a diversion, due notice and proper signage must be used, after having gone through the appropriate process. Mr Volkov and his gangland cronies have in recent years attempted to interfere with the centuries-old right of access, have padlocked gates and looped razor wire between the trees—'

Claire held up her hands in surrender. 'So you saw someone on the lake. Can I ask how you manage to see them, given that it was dark?'

'Well, those bloody arc lights are still on, so it wasn't hard to see the silhouette. But I also saw a light from a torch. Quite a powerful one, and a fishing rod. It was about a hundred yards away, close to the southern shore.'

'So was this just a fisherman?'

'Not a legitimate one. All the angling licences were rescinded in June 2014, shortly after the Moscow takeover, and before they built that atrociously tasteless fountain in the middle. Besides, no fishing was taking place. I just saw a pair of binoculars, and a torch being shone into the water.'

She had Claire's interest now. 'Across the water, or into it?'

'Into it, for part of the time. I was at least a hundred yards away on the north shore. But I think you would agree it's pretty odd to go out in a boat at that time on Boxing Day morning.'

And it's pretty odd to walk your dog at that time too. Claire decided to keep that thought to herself.

'Can you describe this person?'

'Big, broad shoulders, though I thought I saw a pony-tail. Of course, these days that doesn't mean anything, does it? Men wear hair like girls and vice versa.'

'Height?'

'No idea of the height as he was sitting, but wearing a woolly hat and scarf as well as a bulky coat. He kept leaning over the back of the boat, sticking his torch into the water.'

'As if he was looking for something?'

'Yes.'

'How long did you watch for?'

'Maybe five minutes. It was a bit cold to hang about.'

'And did he see you?'

'I don't think so. I hid behind a tree and muffled the dog's snout with my hand.'

Claire sat back and rolled a pen between her fingers. 'I see.'

'You know, when I heard about the killings, I thought good riddance, frankly.'

'I understand that Mr Volkov was not at all popular in the village.'

'That's putting it mildly.' She began to document some of the affronts she and her husband had suffered, but Claire raised her hand. 'Can I just ask you how regularly you visit the grounds around Westgrave Hall?'

'I have walked my dogs there every day for twenty-six years, except for a short period when Volkov first blocked the paths in 2017.'

'How did you get in if, as you say, Volkov draped barbed wire everywhere?'

'My father escaped from a German POW camp in 1944,' she said, light glinting from her spectacles. 'I know how to use wire cutters and then tape where the cut has been made.'

'And is that why you go so early in the day? To avoid being caught?'

'Precisely. In actual fact, these days I have a bit of an understanding with that funny little man Wolf. He's got cameras near to the house, and a pack of dobermans kennelled behind the stables would you believe, so I don't go there. But he doesn't seem to mind me using the public bridleways, or going through Westgrave Woods.'

Claire stroked her chin thoughtfully. 'Have you been into the library to see the fossil?'

'Yes. Overrated, frankly. If you want to see some real bones, I could take you to the ossuary.'

'The what?'

'The ossuary. It's a crypt beneath the Westgrave family chapel, going back to the Crusades. There are plague victims in there too. I'd love to go back to the chapel. I'm the verger, and the chapel is in my bailiwick, though I haven't been able to go inside for years now, because they keep it locked. I'm hoping that if Volkov and his lot go, I might be able to get back in. I'd happily give you a tour if you can arrange access with Wolf.'

'I'd certainly be interested in that, thank you. Perhaps tomorrow, if you're available?'

'Yes, that's fine. I'll ring you when I have a time.' Hill nodded, turned away and walked out.

Claire couldn't imagine quite what somebody would be looking for in Westgrave Lake before dawn on Boxing Day morning. Perhaps there was some kind of unusual wildlife, and despite Mary Hill's protestations to the contrary, Claire felt it would probably be fishing. She made a mental note to ask Wolf. If Volkov had stocked the lake with some kind of exotic species, that could easily explain a little bit of poaching.

But the ponytail was intriguing. What might the body-guard have been doing on the lake on Boxing Day morning?

-

The easyJet flight to Geneva left on time, and Gillard had only just made it. He was travelling light, carry-on luggage with just a change of clothes, two digital recorders and plenty of spare batteries. He was in the middle seat, squashed between a male ski fanatic from Worthing who regaled him with stories of the black runs that he had conquered around the world, and an elderly woman who was going out to see her daughter for the New Year. Given that it was Boxing Day, he wasn't surprised to see no one else on the flight wearing a suit. He'd chosen his newest, a nicely tailored charcoal grey with a silk tie. Sam had pouted when she saw her husband getting dressed, knowing that he was planning to interview one of the world's wealthiest women at Geneva's luxury Mandarin Oriental hotel instead of spending any of Christmas with her.

Geneva Airport was busy with skiers clutching huge bags of equipment and carrying plastic ski boots. Gillard managed to snare a taxi, whose meter gobbled up his euros at a breathtaking rate even while they were queueing to leave the pickup zone. The cost of getting to the hotel was enough to repay the debts of a small African country.

Gillard walked into the imposing lobby of the hotel and scanned the huge opulent lounge. Ms Yalinsky had said she would be waiting here. In his peripheral vision he noticed a large smartly dressed man scrutinising him. He had a neat beard that did not quite disguise the tell-tale spiral wire coming from his ear and into his shirt collar. Gillard turned to him as he approached. 'Detective Chief Inspector Gillard, the lady is waiting.' He carefully checked Gillard's identity and led him to a lift.

They emerged on a silent floor, thickly carpeted and lined with expensive panelling. The detective was led to an anonymous and unnumbered door. The security man tapped lightly, and the door was opened from the inside by another bodyguard. The suite was huge and had a ten-yard long balcony giving a view over the river. Yelena was sitting on a sofa near a roaring fake-log fireplace. She looked up at Gillard's approach. 'Good to see you again,' she said, offering him an adjacent chair. 'I'm so sorry I had to rush off before.'

Gillard sat. There were two other men on an adjacent settee. They were older and had the self-confident glaze of lawyers or accountants.

'I'm glad I was able to catch you, Ms Yalinsky. We have one or two areas on your witness statement that we need to clear up.'

'Okay, then ask away.'

Gillard carefully set up the digital recorder and got out his notebook, setting them on the coffee table but out of reach of the lawyers. 'You said that you never saw who it was firing?'

'That's right. I heard several shots, and Maxim said I should rush to the panic room and he would follow me.'

Gillard looked puzzled. 'Previously you said that Volkov had pushed you back into the panic room and would follow.'

'Actually, I don't think I said that.' The look she gave him made it clear that she knew he didn't have any record of what she had said before. 'It was Maxim who told me to get in the panic room. Both he and Sasha were going to join me. To be honest I don't think it matters.'

'Everything matters. We need to try and build up a second-by-second picture of what happened in those crucial ninety seconds between the start of the firing and its cessation.'

'I was in the panic room for almost all that time,' she said.

'Do you know how to use a gun?' Gillard asked.

'Yes. A rifle, because I've been a hunter in the past. It's a tradition in my country. I have been taught how to use a handgun, though I have had no practice. I rely on my bodyguards to protect me.'

'You don't possess a handgun?'

'I'm sure there is one somewhere in my home, back in Nur-Sultan. But in Europe, no. It's not legal to have an unlicensed weapon, is it?'

'No, in Britain at least it's not.'

'Have you found a gun that you cannot account for?' She smiled at him.

'I'm not able to share that information with you at this stage.' Gillard knew that she wouldn't be fooled by this evasive and bureaucratic answer. He still felt he wasn't getting the truth.

'I'm not a suspect, am I?'

'Not necessarily. But I think that seeing as you are the only witness to any part of the shooting, the only survivor, you can't be surprised that we are extremely careful to check everything that you tell us.'

One of the grey-haired men on the sofa opposite raised his hand. 'Ms Yalinsky is very happy to co-operate, but you must understand that if you make any accusation of her complicity, things may get a little more difficult for you.'

'Are you threatening me, Mr...'

'Crowley. Gregory Crowley. I'm a partner at Harries Chase Kilmore.' Gillard had vaguely heard of the London legal firm, one of the so-called magic circle. 'I'm merely pointing out the reality of the situation. Ms Yalinsky has kindly made herself available to you at short notice in order to aid the inquiry. She didn't have to do that.'

'She's under a legal obligation to assist us—'

'One that has practical jurisdiction limitations, I think you'll agree. As she says, she is happy to help.'

Gillard got the message loud and clear: get tough with her and she'll vanish to a place the British legal system cannot reach.

–

Back in the Khazi, DI Claire Mulholland and DCs Rainy Macintosh and Michelle Tsu were crowded round a terminal, flicking through hundreds of photographs of bloody footprints taken on the balcony. They were trying as best they could to separate out the movements of the protagonists in the gunfight from the later contamination from the rescuers. A simple idea, but practically impossible to do.

'Och, this is like a Dulux nightmare,' Rainy exclaimed, as they carefully flicked through the images. 'Having hurriedly decorated the wall, we're now trying to extract the undercoat.'

While they had labelled the images within each photograph with the shoe types, it was still confusing. Maxim Talin seemed to have moved very little, at least once he had stepped in his own blood, but the larger tread from Alexander Volkov, who only had blood on the right shoe, showed that he had raced from the middle of the balcony to the end where the panic room was. There, he made several steps in different directions, as if dithering, before falling over and producing a large pool of his own blood.

'Talin stood and fought, which matches the fact he had a gun,' Michelle said.

'Whereas Volkov looked to be running for safety,' Claire said, pointing a pencil at the widely spaced bloodstains from the oligarch's right shoe. 'That's a three-foot gap at least.'

'If he had blood on the sole of his other foot, we've lost it in the mayhem of the subsequent contamination.' They had labels in place for Wolf's boots and Sophie Cawkwell's fashionable Manolo Blahniks. Hers were easy to trace for the most part – firstly because the roughly triangular sole of the high heel shoes was so different from the male footwear, and secondly because hers were the last prints. Helpfully, there was a tiny paper label stuck on her right sole which acted as an absorbent stencil, stamping out her path in blood across the balcony and the landing by the panic room.

They finished the first slideshow of 178 pictures taken by PC Zoe Butterfield and moved on to the even larger number taken by CSI. 'We could be here until the wee hours and still make no sense of it,' Rainy said.

The plywood door of the Khazi squealed and crime scene technician Kirsty Mockett walked in, shaking the rain off her overcoat. 'Ah, good to see you Kirsty,' said Claire.

'A late entrant to the girls-who-missed-Christmas club,' said Rainy. Her son Ewan was being looked after by Claire's plasterer husband Barry, who had incorporated him into an impromptu family Christmas at the Mulholland home in Staines. From Christmas morning onwards, Claire had fielded calls from Baz about cooking turkey, making bread sauce, thickening gravy and even the procedure for preparing instant stuffing mix. Two of her boys were there too, but despite her best attempts, none of the male members of the household could cook.

'I've got something here which may help on the footprints,' Kirsty said.

'Well we could certainly do with that,' said Claire. 'We've got Raj's map on a roll of wallpaper and loads of confusing photographs. That's about it.'

'Ah well, this is some imaging software from the University of Groningen in the Netherlands,' Kirsty said. 'It allows you to specify footprints, and then visually remove them from the photograph. In theory it should show you what was underneath but masked. Of course, what it really does is to replicate the specified print, but it should give a better idea of an individual's path.'

The four officers took the next hour to set up the software, until they were able to strip away the contaminating footprints applied after the shooting had finished. The first to be removed were Wolf's big outdoor boots, and then Sophie's shoes. They then passed each of Zoe's images through the filter to see what else they could glean.

'Yes, it's clear Volkov was running, but instead of jumping into the panic room after Yelena, he seemed to turn round,' said Michelle.

'That accords with the ballistics evidence,' said Claire. 'There were exit wounds both in his back and his chest, so he was shot from both sides.'

'So it was right here that he was shot,' Kirsty said.

'And then sat or fell down, against the panic room door, poor wee bugger,' Rainy said.

'Not so wee,' said Kirsty. 'It took four of us to shift his body into the hoist.'

Michelle had moved the screen on to CSI's own images of the bloodstains, which were close-ups, each covering a smaller area. 'What's this?' she said. She was pointing to a small triangular print surrounded by a large U-shaped pool of smeared blood.

Kirsty looked at the number and referenced the index sheet. 'I think that's where Volkov had been sitting. It's right next to the panic room door.'

'You think Sophie Cawkwell managed to move him?' Michelle asked.

'I don't think so. He was a big guy,' Kirsty said.

'Then how come she got her feet underneath where he was sitting?' Michelle asked. 'They must have tried to lift him.'

'Just to be clear,' Claire asked Kirsty. 'When Volkov's body was removed, there was no one around but CSI, right?'

'Correct. Certainly no one wearing high heels.'

'So if Sophie couldn't have moved Volkov, and there was no blood for her to step in when she was previously in the library, how did this footprint come to be here?' Claire shifted the focus to look more closely at the images. 'Here's another odd thing.'

'What have you seen?' Kirsty asked.

'The little label isn't visible in this one.' Claire looked up at the puzzled faces of the women around her. 'Sophie Cawkwell had a little label on her right sole.'

'Let's get the shoes in here,' Rainy said. She headed off to Raj's carefully organised evidence van, which was parked outside, and came back a few minutes later with a large paper evidence bag. 'Right, let's have a wee look.' While the women all donned evidence gloves, she undid the seal strip, and pulled out two kingfisher blue Manolo Blahniks.

'Gorgeous,' breathed Kirsty.

'No change out of seven hundred quid,' Rainy said. 'And they'll still bugger your toes and ankles eventually, and that's even if you don't fall off them while pissed.'

'Rainy, you are such a little ray of sunshine,' Michelle said.

'Don't get me wrong, hen, I'd still love to own a pair.'

'Amazing workmanship,' said Claire, turning over the right shoe. The instep carried the continental size and the stencil 'handmade in Italy'. There was no tread on the sole, just flat leather and a small label, originally white but now dark brown. The remains of the bloodstains looked like a little map of Ireland on the sole.

Michelle looked at the image on the screen and the sole of the shoe. 'It doesn't match this stain. Nor does this,' she said picking up the other shoe. 'It isn't just the absence of the label, but the shape of the bloodstain.' She pointed to the image. 'If the footprint doesn't belong to Sophie, it must belong to Yelena Yalinsky.'

'Well, that makes sense, because she was on her way into the panic room,' Claire said. 'That print is literally one foot away from the door.'

Michelle shook her head. 'She claimed that she headed in the moment the shooting started. Would there have been any blood to step in at that time?'

'No,' said Claire. 'Trouble is, we don't have any footprints for her to check against.'

'And we don't have the shoes either,' Rainy added.

The women all looked at each other. 'What time is it in Geneva?' Michelle asked.

Claire checked her phone. 'It's an hour ahead, so it's just coming up to ten.'

'What time is Gillard seeing Yalinsky?' Rainy asked.

'Nine, so with any luck he might still be there.' Claire punched out her boss's number.

He answered immediately.

'Craig, it's Claire. Are you still with her?' The other women looked up expectantly. They saw her face contract and the excitement leach out of it. After a minute-or-so she hung up.

'He's in a taxi on his way back to the airport. The interview's over. He's going to try to ring her, but she's been pretty evasive so far.' There were a few groans of disappointment among the assembled officers. 'He's got one other suggestion. To prove it is Yalinsky, we should look for bloodstains inside the panic room.'

'We did that,' Kirsty Mockett said.

'With Bluestar?' Claire asked.

'No, we only did the main room with Bluestar,' she conceded.

'Come on, let's go and take the panic room apart,' Claire said.

The four officers changed into Tyvek coveralls and booties, filled rucksacks with the tools they expected to need, and trooped out of the Khazi. They made their way through the Boxing Day darkness, past the shadowed portals of Westgrave Hall, and the flagpoles flying at half-mast, the flags of Russia, the UK and the US. They trudged across the alabaster bridge to the library. A uniformed officer, his face red with cold, greeted them and undid the enormous police-issue padlock which secured the doors. They stepped inside, flicked on all the lights and shuffled their way along the ground floor under the enormous bulk of the great primaeval rock, until they reached the scissor lift. Claire operated the lifting console. At the top, she turned to the lighting console rigged up on the edge of the scaffolding and flipped on the arc lights. The bloodstains, partially covered by CSI duckboards, were still shocking to look at. The profusion of yellow and white markers indicated the location of bullet holes and cartridge cases respectively. Above her, the skylight had been closed to prevent rain getting in.

Carefully, Claire led her team from the platform over the balcony rail and onto the duckboards. She braced and gradually pulled open the heavy panic room door by its stainless steel handle. She flipped on the lights and stared at the top step of the metal staircase. No blood was visible on any of the steps. The four women made their way down gradually. At the bottom she allocated tasks.

'Kirsty, could you Bluestar the panic room staircase? Michelle, I want you to search again for ballistic residues. Rainy, I want you to take the bathroom apart. I want that gun found.'

'Aye, I always get the shitty jobs,' Rainy muttered to herself as she wandered into the luxury bathroom. A huge gold framed mirror threw back her Tyveked reflection, like some kind of bespectacled jelly baby. There was a neat pile of monogrammed linen hand towels, just like she'd seen at the poshest hotels, and a choice of different liquid soaps. The two large cubicles had no visible cisterns, so she began by using a screwdriver to pry off the brass caps on top of the screws which held in the ceramic panels. It took five minutes to reach each cistern, and she was able to verify that there was no weapon hidden within either. She then took a hacksaw to the plastic soil pipe and cut out a melon-shaped slice. She hoped that in such a new building that the fittings would be pristine and there wouldn't be any nasty residue inside the pipe.

She was right.

From her rucksack she took out a reel of cable with a small device on the end. This was the inspection camera, which she intended to use to find out what was in the cesspit. She fed out the cable gradually for about forty feet and then connected her mobile phone to a terminal at the reel end and activated the camera and light.

Opening the app, she saw a chamber about a yard across that was a foot deep in water. Floating half on the edge of this was what looked like a piece of towelling, and just a few soggy lumps of toilet paper. The water was relatively clear and when she dipped the camera in, it showed that there was no weapon.

After twenty minutes Claire called them back in. Kirsty was already there. 'Bluestar shows there's been an attempt to clean blood off the staircase,' she said.

'Nothing in the bedroom, no obvious storage places located,' Michelle said. 'I didn't pick up any ballistics residues.'

'The cludgie was a damn sight cleaner than my local municipal swimming baths,' Rainy said. 'Not a single piece of shite. But I think I found the hand towels that may have been used to clean blood off the stairs. The canny wee bugger must have flushed them away. Expensive towels as well.'

'That's very good, team,' Claire said. 'Shame there was no gun.'

'Are we now thinking that Ms Yalinsky is the murderer?' Michelle asked.

'It's got to be a possibility,' Claire said. 'She was out there long enough to get blood on her shoes. She clearly didn't want that to be known, otherwise why would she clean the stairs and flush away the towels?'

'But how did she manage to get Volkov to trap her in here?' Rainy asked.

'It's a good question,' Claire replied. 'Carl Hoskins is on the night shift. I think it's time we borrowed him.'

-

By the time they got back to the Khazi it was nearly eleven, and the light filtering from the Portakabin almost made it look welcoming. Carl Hoskins was already there, making his way through an enormous pile of turkey leftovers from an aluminium foil parcel.

'Do they not feed you at home?' Rainy asked.

Hoskins nodded, and licked his fingers. 'This lot has just been delivered by a nice lady at the Westgrave Hall kitchen. Got some leftovers from the party too, in that parcel,' he said, pointing to another turkey-sized aluminium clad parcel.

'Leave that for now,' Claire said. 'Come with me everyone. Carl, you'll need to suit up.'

A few minutes later the entire entourage trooped back again, under the fossil and via the lifting platform back to where they had been an hour previously. 'Michelle, you're about as petite as Yelena Yalinsky. I'd like you to move into the panic room and wait at the top of the spiral stairs.'

Michelle heaved open the heavy steel door and stepped inside.

'We're going to shut you in. In exactly one minute I want you to try to push the door open.'

'Okay.'

'Now, Carl, shut her in, and sit down against the door.' He gradually eased the door closed and sat back against it. 'Sorry to ask a personal question, Carl, but how much do you weigh?' Claire asked.

'About seventeen stone, give or take. The original two-hundred–pound gorilla.'

'He's a wee black hole of Christmas pud, and I cannae escape his gravity,' Rainy said, leaning towards him as if helpless.

'You're a fine one to talk,' said Hoskins.

'Och, that's no way to speak to a lady.'

'No, it wouldn't be.' He chuckled.

'Quiet everyone,' Claire asked. 'Okay, Michelle, push!' she shouted. Everyone looked at the door for signs of movement. Nothing.

'I can feel a pressure on my back, but nothing that would shift me,' Hoskins said. Soon afterwards they could hear tapping.

'Okay, let her out.'

Hoskins stood up and pulled the heavy steel door open. Michelle Tsu emerged. 'I couldn't make any progress. It was impossible.'

Hoskins gave a guilty shrug. 'Too many chips for too many years.'

'Volkov, being a few inches taller, probably weighed even more than Carl. I think we can conclude that it would have been pretty difficult for Yelena to shoot him fatally, and then get inside the panic room,' Claire concluded.

'But not impossible,' Michelle said. 'If he didn't collapse for a few seconds afterwards.'

'There could be some other possibilities,' Hoskins said. 'If she fired the gun first, then passed it to her boyfriend—'

'But we don't have the gun!' Rainy exclaimed. 'None of this gets us anywhere. Somewhere in this place there must be another gun.'

'It could have been chucked out through the skylight,' Michelle said.

Hoskins peered up. 'That would be a hell of a throw, and even if it was hard enough to reach there, you'd probably just hit the glass the first half dozen times. I didn't find nothing when I was up there yesterday. I searched all the gutters.'

'It looks a bit unlikely,' Claire said. 'Okay, team, well done for today, we'll meet up tomorrow morning, when Gillard gets back. I'm getting a tour round the ossuary first. Carl, are you staying in the Khazi?'

'Yeah. Might catch up with some reading first,' he said, indicating the array of books in the library.

'Shireen has sent through what we know about Volkov's will. You might want to start with that.'

'All right.' The one unvoiced thought in Hoskins' head was the promise of a big fry-up for tomorrow's breakfast. One benefit from having chatted up Tatiana, the chef, a Ukrainian woman with a golden tooth and ample bosom.

PC Simon Woodbridge was relaxing at his one-bedroom flat in Reigate, just outside London's orbital M25 motorway. It was Boxing Day evening, he had a couple of cans in and there was a Bond film on the TV. He'd just got off the phone with his girlfriend, Sally, and had arranged to meet her at her parents' house in Bracknell for lunch on Saturday. Sally's eager questioning of him about the juicy murder at Westgrave Hall made him feel guilty about what had happened to him there, and he told her he wasn't allowed to say anything. That hadn't stopped him giving his mates Steve and Geoff a blow-by-blow account of his entanglement with Anastasia. In fact, it was almost the first thing he had done when coming off duty that morning.

The call on his mobile took him by surprise. It was a withheld number.

'Hello simple Simon,' came the husky voice. 'It's Anastasia.'

'Oh hi, how are you?' He was shocked. He didn't think he'd given her his number.

'I'm taking you to dinner,' she announced. 'Unless you have already eaten.'

Simon considered the pre-Christmas leftover curry lurking in the back of his fridge. 'No, I haven't, not yet.' His heart rate suddenly climbed, getting rather ahead of the evening's events.

'I'll give you directions. Whereabouts are you?' he asked.

'Waiting right outside your flat.'

He leaned out of the window and looked down the three floors to the street. Right outside, gleaming under the streetlamps, was a shiny blue sports car. Beside it, standing waving up at him, was Anastasia.

'Oh my God,' he said, and rushed into the bathroom. He washed his face in cold water, slapped on some after-shave, and combed his hair. He sniffed his armpits, felt they were just about acceptable, and grabbed a shirt from the wardrobe. Luckily, he had an ironed white cotton shirt to hand. His hands were trembling doing up the buttons almost as much as they had been the last time he was in her presence. Then, of course, buttons were being undone. He grabbed his wallet, keys and phone and raced down the stairs.

Emerging onto the pavement, he saw her leaning on the bonnet of an Aston Martin Vantage roadster. It was easily the most gorgeous car he had ever seen. She looked the part too, wearing a thigh-length white wool coat, a silk scarf and black leather high heel boots. He had no idea why he had *ever* thought that she was plain. Made up the way she was, her hair thick and lustrous and those amazingly long shapely legs, she looked amazing.

'Don't just stand there staring, get into the car,' she said.

Simon pulled open the passenger door and sank into the plush leather seat. 'Is this really your car?'

She laughed. 'No, I borrowed this. I wrapped my Maserati round a tree last month. I did consider getting my Porsche flown in from Switzerland, but Natasha said she'd get the other one repaired in a week or so.'

Anastasia fired up the engine, a throaty roar settling to a purr, then pulled out from the kerb. He stared at her open mouthed. 'How did you know where I lived?'

'You told me, the other day. You gave me your phone number, don't you remember?'

He really couldn't remember. He knew that he'd fallen asleep immediately afterwards. Like a dead thing, in fact. Maybe she had gone through his wallet. He dismissed the thought. His address certainly wasn't anywhere in his wallet.

'Say something, simple Simon,' she said, as she accelerated hard onto the main road.

'Oh, watch this junction. There's a speed camera. Thirty. *Thirty!*' He pointed ahead and glanced at the speedo, which was flicking up to fifty.

She hit the accelerator so hard, he was sucked back into the seat. They shot through the junction at nearly eighty. She laughed uproariously at the look of horror on his face.

'Did you see the camera flash?'

'Of course.'

'That'll be a hefty fine, you know.'

'So?' she turned to glance at him.

'Slow down, you're crazy,' he shouted. 'You'll kill somebody.'

'Maybe us!' she grinned, overtaking a Peugeot at a zebra crossing. In the space of a minute, she failed to give way at a roundabout, shot a set of pedestrian lights and overtook a van on the inside. Then she reached the M25 and really put her foot down. The Aston Martin touched 140 miles per hour as she raced past a procession of lorries.

'I'm a fast lady, aren't I?' She was looking at him now, but his eyes were glued to the road ahead, feet pressing imaginary brake and clutch as if he had the power to somehow safely guide the vehicle back from danger.

'Anastasia, please please please slow down,' he implored. 'I'm a policeman. That was an ANPR camera. This vehicle will be noticed, there'll be somebody on our tail in no time. I could lose my job.' His whining was unbecoming, and he hated to do it when he so wanted to impress her. Finally, she did slow down. Eighty still wasn't exactly a legal speed, but it felt like crawling compared to what they were doing before.

'If you're still seventeen, you must have passed your test right after your birthday,' he said.

'I'm driving on my forged international licence.' She just looked at him and winked.

He clasped his hands to his face and groaned. 'Oh God. That means no insurance. Please tell me this isn't happening.'

She roared with laughter and banged the steering wheel with her hand.

'Where are we going?' he asked.

'The Dorchester. My father has a table there.'

'What, permanently—?' He interrupted himself to point out another speed camera. But instead of slowing down she accelerated, ton-up as the Gatso flashed. Then another camera a hundred yards further on, another flash.

'What did you do that for? You could get banned, assuming you even have a licence, just for the offences you've committed tonight.'

'Stop moaning! I love to spend money.'

'It's not just money, Anastasia. You'll be banned even before you've got the chance to legally drive.'

'Simon says this, Simon says that,' she muttered to herself.

Eventually the heavy traffic on the way to central London frustrated Anastasia's attempts at speeding, firing her impatience. She banged the horn and shouted at other vehicles as they wound their way up the A23 through Coulsdon, Streatham, Brixton and on into central London. Eventually they arrived at the Park Lane entrance to the hotel. The forecourt was full, and there seemed no place to park, so Anastasia simply stopped in the road, double parked, blocking one lane of Park Lane. There was an immediate cacophony of horns.

'You can't stop here,' Simon said. He watched open-mouthed as she got out, slung her handbag over her shoulder, closed the door and beckoned him to follow.

'You really can't just…' he said. She shrugged and made her way to the pavement, stopping only to blow a kiss into the gale of honking traffic behind. After five seconds he realised she really wasn't coming back, so he leapt out of the car, miming abject apologies to the angry drivers behind, and followed her, snaking his way through the parked vehicles across the pavement, into the forecourt and up into the Dorchester. A doorman in green coat and black top hat opened the door for her. She passed him the car keys and pointed to the car. The moment they entered the sumptuous reception area, the hush of luxury replaced the cacophony of traffic. She waved to the reception desk, and one of the male staff came round to greet her, bowing slightly.

'This is Simon,' she said. 'We'd like my father's table.'

'Yes of course, madam, follow me.'

As they entered the lift, Anastasia said to him. 'You see, Simon, that I have been educated for how to live. And it is rather fun, would you not agree?'

'What about the car?' he said. He had fallen in love with the car.

'My father had a special arrangement for valet parking.'

The head waiter greeted her in exactly the same way as had the man at reception. Anastasia and he had a brief but obviously fluent conversation in French. The waiter seated them at a secluded table, not visible to other diners.

White linen and polished silver. He surveyed the menu, which was entirely in French.

'You've got to have the negronis here, they are fantastic,' she said.

He didn't know what a negroni was, but assumed it was some kind of cocktail. He deferred to her, and she ordered one for each of them, and a bottle of some wine of a particular year. The approving nod from the sommelier showed that she knew what she was doing.

'You're amazing, you're absolutely amazing,' he said. And he meant it. He'd never felt so alive as during that insane drive from Reigate.

'But I'm crazy too, aren't I? That's what you think, right?'

'I suppose so. I mean why did you deliberately break the speed limit? Are you trying to get in trouble?'

She laughed. 'That car belongs to my brother, Oleg, the most annoying idiot in the world. I am trying to get them to take his licence away, to punish him for his transgressions.'

'But he'll just point out he wasn't driving.'

She shook her head emphatically 'No, Oleg has so much coke up his nose most of the time he has no idea whether he's driving or flying, let alone where. He will pay to get poor Wolf to take the points for him, like last time. But Wolf told me his own licence will be forfeit with another big speeding ticket, so he will refuse. Oleg will then try to get another member of staff to take the points, and I have already bribed them that I will double whatever he offers them, if they refuse. They all despise Oleg anyway, so it's easy.'

The food was fabulous and the wine superb. He hadn't any great experience in wine and had never been anywhere remotely as posh as this in his life. It began to dawn on him that Anastasia had offered to 'take him' to dinner, but that didn't necessarily mean she was paying. He certainly hoped she was, because he couldn't begin to imagine how much this would cost. The menu he had been given had no prices on it. He was pretty sure that it would max out his credit card. But aware that he had been whining and complaining his way through the evening, he was now going to show a bit of class.

He sat and listened as Anastasia chattered about the people she knew and the places she'd been. Only when she went to the bathroom did he dare look at his mobile, and the text he had received from Sally asking him where he was. Knowing he was off duty, she'd come round to his flat with a Christmas gift to surprise him but had could get no reply to the doorbell. A wave of guilt passed over him.

On Anastasia's return, a sumptuous dessert was brought, and after a cognac the bill finally arrived in a thick leather ledger. 'Shall we go halves?' Anastasia asked, offering it to him. The bill was well over two thousand pounds, of which three quarters was for the wine. The look of panic that flashed across his face amused her enormously, and she rested a delicate hand on his sleeve as her gurgles of laughter continued for some time. She called over the waiter and asked for it to be put on the family account.

'Simon, I brought you here because the account will probably be closed soon, since my poor father is dead.' She looked sad again, momentarily. 'So I have to use it while I can.'

'Phew,' he said. 'I've had about five heart attacks in one night.'

'My father has a suite here. Would you like number six?' she asked, raising a beautifully shaped eyebrow. 'Follow me, naughty boy.'

PC Simon Woodbridge tried very hard to restrain the smirk but failed. They took the lift to the ninth floor, and she led him to a grand suite. In fact it was more like a three-bedroom apartment. He oohed and aahed over the décor and furnishings, as she led him towards one of the bedrooms.

'Now, I want you to look at me.' She then took off her scarf and pulled her dress over her head, so she was standing only in her underwear.

What he saw was not what he expected.

Chapter Thirteen

Her slender pale neck was circled in thick purple bruises, and the signs of some kind of rope. Her upper arms too showed that she had been gripped, hard.

'Who did this to you?' Simon asked.

'My bodyguard and ex-boyfriend Jason. He knows about us, and he was punishing me.'

'The blond guy with the ponytail?' Woodbridge recalled the lantern-jawed six-footer he had run into outside her room. He was handsome, with the build of a personal trainer.

'Yes. He's always been jealous and possessive, and he has a nasty temper. He used to be a jujutsu instructor. You're lucky you're a cop. He would kill you otherwise.' She smiled cruelly. 'I had my own reasons for getting you out of the room by nine yesterday, before he came on duty. If he had found you, he would have murdered you on the spot, and probably killed me as well.'

Protective male pride blossomed. He pulled her into his arms and kissed her. 'I'll look after you, Anastasia. No one needs to put up with violence and possessiveness. You can report this and we can have him arrested. First thing tomorrow. I promise I'll look after you. The British police take this kind of thing quite seriously these days, believe me.'

She kissed him hard on the mouth and ran her hands through his hair. 'Simon, I'm so glad I met you. I've been afraid for so long, and with my father dying I'm in even more danger.' She kissed him again, and then looked into his eyes. 'You are so brave. I trust you.'

'I wouldn't let you down,' Simon said, his hand straying to her buttocks. She did not resist.

While Anastasia went into the bathroom, he undressed and lay naked on the enormous bed, a giant smirk spreading across his face as he thought about what would come next. Then he remembered Sally. He reached for his phone to see if she had messaged him again. She had, but there was also an email from someone he didn't know, headed: *Look at this IMMEDIATELY*. From the header it was clear it had also been copied to Anastasia's email.

The message was short and to the point. *Watch, then wait for the call.* There was an attached video, and as he opened it his blood ran cold. The view was from above, in Anastasia's bedroom in Westgrave Hall. The canopied bed was distinctive, but it was the sound, the moans of ecstasy, the begging and pleading for sexual release, which dominated.

His voice.

His body, naked, spreadeagled and bound, his sleeve of Celtic tattoos more distinctive than his partially obscured face. Anastasia, still in her bathrobe, worked on him expertly, teasingly, with hand and mouth. One of the dogs looked on, fascinated by what his mistress seemed to be eating, and she kept having to push his snout away. Simon's limbs were trembling, his hands and feet flexing in their bonds. Every time she lifted her face away, he was on display for the world to see, his manhood pointing directly at the camera.

There was a scream from the bathroom, and an explosion of tears.

She must be looking at the video too.

Anastasia burst out and threw herself into Simon's arms. 'It's Jason, the bastard has rigged up my room!'

'Oh my God, this is terrible,' he said.

'We should go to the police, yes?' she asked.

His throat was dry. 'Let's not rush into anything at this point.'

'But you said they would take this seriously...'

'Yes, but Anastasia, this would ruin me. I'd be sacked for what we did.'

'Simon, it's only your job. For me it's my reputation: all over the newspapers, the spoiled sex-mad daughter of a billionaire!'

'Does Jason have copies?'

'Of course! Of course he'll have copies, simple Simon, he's not stupid!'

Anastasia's phone rang, and she answered tremblingly, her eyes wide and resting on Simon in a look of total trust. 'Jason, of course. Yes, we've both seen it.' She listened, interjecting the word okay a few times, then handed the phone to Simon. 'He wants to speak with you.'

Simon picked up the phone.

'Well, well, not smirking now, are you PC Woodbridge?' The accented voice was Jason's, the one he had heard in their brief conversation in the Westgrave Hall corridor.

'What are you going to do?'

'The papers would love this, yes? Your nice British tabloids. And the police, ha, you'd be fired, wouldn't you?'

'Yes.'

'I've told her what I want from her, and this is what I want from you.'

Ice seemed to run down Simon's spine as he listened to Jason.

'I couldn't,' he muttered. 'It's wrong.'

'Yes, you can, and you will do it tonight. I'll text you the exact details shortly. If you try contacting the police, then you know exactly what will happen.' He cut the call. Simon handed the phone back to Anastasia, and they stared at each other in shock.

Simon spoke first. 'Does he just want you to take him back?'

'Yes, but he wants money too, of course. He always wanted money.'

'How much?'

'Enough to set him up in a security consultancy, now that this gig working for my father is coming to an end. Ten million.'

'Ten *million* pounds!'

'Meh, it's not so much.' She waved it away. 'That is easy. I'm more worried about his brutality, against me and you. What did he want you to do, Simon?'

'Oh God! I can't tell you, Anastasia. I really can't.' He squeezed his eyes shut and reached for her hand as if he was drowning. He had never felt so helpless, his entire life circling in a whirlpool of shit. He could refuse to do what Jason asked, but this video. Oh God! If this ever came out Sally would hate him for ever. Her parents, who had been so kind, and had lent him money when he was broke, would never speak to him again. Even his own mum and dad. He'd be fired from the police.

What if he did what Jason wanted? If it was ever discovered, he'd be jailed for years, decades even. Either way, he'd be unemployable for any position of trust. He could see himself in twenty years' time, some middling provincial burglar alarm salesman, with only memories of a few fantastic hours to hold on to.

He really couldn't do what Jason had told him to.

But he had to. There was no choice. He'd just have to make sure no one ever found out.

–

Gillard had left a message for Yelena Yalinsky, and he was just about to board his flight back to Gatwick when she returned the call. After pleasantries were exchanged, he said: 'We have evidence that you did not disappear into the panic room the moment the shooting started. You may have tried to clear it up, but there is blood still detectable on the spiral staircase leading down. And that would not have been there had you not walked it in.'

There was no reply.

'Do you hear what I'm saying, Ms Yalinsky? You had to be out there long enough to tread in the blood.'

She took a deep breath. 'Okay, bear with me, I'm just going out on the balcony where I can't be overheard.' The click and squeal of the sliding door, and the roar of traffic beyond came through to Gillard.

'Ms Yalinsky, I need to know what you saw,' he persisted.

She said nothing. All he heard was the rumble of traffic.

'I cannot solve this case without you. Do you not want justice for Maxim?'

'Of course I do.'

'Then please tell me what you saw.'

'Look, I only had a glimpse of him, it was nothing really. Just a reflection of muzzle flash, coming from the window side.'

'And who was he?'

'A masked man, dressed in black, with a handgun.'

'Tall, short, stocky, slim?'

'Average height at a guess, but definitely slim and athletic. He disappeared in a second or two. And below the mask, I saw signs of a beard.'

Now we're finally getting somewhere, Gillard thought. 'Why didn't you tell me before?'

She hesitated, then said: 'I can't be identified as a witness. I need to protect my children.'

'Ms Yalinsky, if the shooter saw you, you're a witness whether you say anything or not. If you need protection, it can be provided. However, if you just got the glimpse that you described, the assailant would hardly be worried.' Gillard's gut told him strongly that she had seen more than she was letting on.

For a few long seconds all he heard was the drone of traffic in the Geneva streets. 'Have you mentioned this to the Home Office interviewers?' He was reluctant to identify them precisely as British spies.

'No. They were more interested in my former husband's business deals. I think they may have been trying to work out if he was a spy.'

'I see. When are you next back in Britain?'

'For New Year. I'm due to attend David and Natasha Fein's New Year's Eve party. However, I'd be grateful if you'd keep that to yourself, I don't want my movements being too widely known, given what's happened.'

'Okay. We'll need to speak to you again, I'm afraid.'

She let out a heavy sigh. 'I'll co-operate, of course.'

It was midnight. DC Carl Hoskins sat in the Khazi monitoring the flow of evidence onto the HOLMES computer system used for large and complex inquiries. The other detectives had left half an hour ago. Dribs and drabs of ballistic evidence had been emerging all evening, though nothing that appeared to be of great significance until the final email from ballistics, which had been copied into the inquiry's collective email address. This identified the bullets which had been extracted from the victims. The big news was that whoever had wielded the missing weapon was responsible for all three deaths. In some ways that was no surprise, but it did disprove one theory that had done the rounds: that Talin had shot Volkov. The three bullets missing from the Glock's clip had been found in neither Volkov nor in Bryn Howell. Talin was either a poor shot or had been aiming at someone else.

Hoskins rubbed his chin. It was a blow to his original open-and-shut love triangle theory. While it wasn't impossible that the love triangle was the motivation for the slaying, there would have to be a more complex explanation. The arrival of Gillard's email, mentioning Yelena seeing a 'dark figure', further undercut the love triangle idea.

He wasn't sure that he would trust anything Yelena said.

There was a tapping at the door. Hoskins, who had been forewarned by Claire about the possibility of intruders, opened the squeaky plywood fixture and stared out at a bulky figure silhouetted in the drizzle against a newly rigged-up arc light.

'Mr Hosky?' Wolf asked, in his tortured English. 'You call me?'

'Yeah, can I come to the control room? Someone attempted to break in to our mobile incident room,' Hoskins said. 'Mind if I take a look on your CCTV?'

'Help yourself,' Wolf said. He led Hoskins back into the main hall and along the labyrinthine route to the control room. Wolf's iris scan and thumbprint got them in. Hoskins sat himself at the main console, went back to the start of the day, and set the analysis program for movement detection to take him to the first object that tripped the sensor.

There was a surprisingly large number of movements, almost all of them uniformed police or detectives. Wolf himself figured on the record a few times, as did a few of the kitchen staff ferrying food, and Jason, Anastasia's ponytailed bodyguard. Hoskins couldn't see anyone who appeared to be carrying a crowbar or similar object. Wolf identified the few people that Hoskins didn't recognise. 'I think he is reporter,' Wolf said, pointing to a young man in a puffa jacket with a small rucksack. 'We try to keep by the gate, but with public footpaths and so many rural access, is impossible hundred percent.'

'Yeah, tell me about it,' Hoskins replied. 'What will happen to the place now the boss is dead?'

Wolf shrugged. 'Is very good question. Someone must untangle finances, not me thank God. There's the will. All that stuff. From past occurrences…'

'Past occurrences?' Hoskins asked.

Wolf gestured expansively with his hands. 'You know, the other dead oligarchs. Berezovsky, and so on. Judging by them, everyone will get fired by the family and all assets sold. The more money at stake, the more family will fight.' He imitated a boxing match with his large hairy fists.

Hoskins realised he wouldn't like to fight this man, whose big shoulders moved easily under his jacket.

'It's always the family, isn't it?' Hoskins said. 'Fighting like ferrets in a sack.'

'What is ferrets?' Wolf asked.

'Big weasels with nasty teeth.'

'Ah, ferrets, yes.' He stroked his chin. 'I will use that saying. Very good.'

'People in Yorkshire put them down their trousers.'

'Eh?' Wolf pointed to his groin, his eyes wide. 'You make big joke out of me?'

'No, it's true. I'll send you a couple of YouTube links.'

'Yorkshires are very tough people, yes? Britain's Chechens perhaps.' He put an arm around Hoskins' shoulder and gripped him affectionately. 'Are you a York-shire?'

'No. South London. Croydon boy, me.'

'You know *Only Fool and Horse*? We see it in my country. Very funny. Plonker and lovely bubbly.'

Hoskins chuckled. 'It's lovely *jubbly*. The programme is about Peckham, which is way north of my manor.'

'Come, let us go to library. Something I show for you.'

Wolf led the way out of the control room, up one flight of stairs and out through the main entrance of the hall. Hoskins couldn't help noticing that most of the lights were still on, even though the state rooms were apparently unoccupied. Volkov had constructed an organisation that never had to worry about paying a bill, indifferent even to the concept of economy. They emerged into heavy rain, blown on a stiff breeze. Wolf helped himself to three golfing-sized umbrellas from a stand by the door and gave one to Hoskins. Unfurled, the umbrellas showed a coat of arms, which Hoskins took to be Volkov's. They braced against the wind and made their way across towards the library. The Georgian was still chuckling away about his favourite British comedies as he led the detective across the bridge towards the door. The uniformed officer standing there was wearing a police-issue cape, but still appeared to be cold and wet. Wolf passed across the third umbrella to him. 'Sorry. Shutting stable door after horse buggered off, yes?'

'Thank you anyway,' he replied. 'And thank you for the tea earlier, that was most welcome.'

'You are guest. We have to look after. Is important.'

After further thanks, the officer undid the padlock securing the library, and let them in.

Wolf led him into the ground floor in the shadow of the immense suspended rock, then switched into full tourist guide mode, describing the laborious process of getting the fossil from where it was carved out of the earth in Central Asia to here in England's Home Counties.

'Forever now this place associate with murder,' Wolf said. 'The fossil, she will be forgotten.'

Wolf made his way to the scissor lift and clambered onto the platform. 'Come with me,' he said.

'I don't think we should be wandering about on the balcony,' Hoskins said. 'That's still a crime scene.'

'No walk on balcony. But you want to see clue, yes?' Wolf set the console and withdrew the anchors which stabilised the platform on the floor. He then drove it across to the window side of the library and turned to take it halfway along the southern walkway. He gestured for Hoskins to join him, and the detective did so, clambering onto the platform. Wolf pressed a button, and the scissors expanded, lifting the platform so it was almost level with the balcony. The rock was at its widest at this point, and there was very little clearance between it and the guardrail. He then threw out an empty rubbish bag onto the walkway and made his way gingerly over the guardrail until he was standing on the bag. At this point they were opposite a ten-foot-wide section of wall, the only break between the windows on this side. There were two narrow bookcases filled with leather-backed volumes, and between them a gilt-framed painting, four-foot-by-three, on an otherwise blank slab of stone wall. Hoskins was no expert on art, and this mountain scene, all dark shades and roiling clouds, did nothing for him.

'Where's the clue then, Wolf?'

Wolf was groping about amongst the books, his hand pressed on the underside of one of the shelves. An individual spotlight came on from high on the ceiling, highlighting the painting. There followed a whirring sound, and the painting within the frame slid upwards. At first glance, all Hoskins could see revealed was some uneven stone on the wall.

'What is this?' he said, looking more closely. There were filigree marks all around it, and at the centre what looked like the bones of a squashed chicken, stuck in cement.

Wolf grinned at him his eyes wide. 'This is best-preserved archaeopteryx in the world. The world's first feathered flying creature,' he said, indicating the delicate fan-shaped impressions.

'Did he dig that up in Central Asia too?' Hoskins asked.

'No. Bought from a museum in Germany. For Sophie as wedding gift. Unique.'

'You are saying this is why Volkov was killed?'

'No, no. I think he asked Sophie to leave so that he could show it to Talin and Yalinsky in secret. Mr Volkov, he like to boast.'

'And that's why he ordered the CCTV turned off?'

'That is what I think.'

'How come you knew about this new fossil?' Hoskins pointed at the wall.

Wolf gave a big shrug. 'I have to be involved in most things. This had to have specially constructed recess.'

Hoskins nodded. 'So how much is this worth?'

'It's priceless, of course. I don't know what he paid. Millions, for sure. Everything he buys costs millions. Except me. Loyal Wolf, he come cheap.' He shrugged. 'Now Wolf, maybe no job, yes?'

–

Wolf led Hoskins back into the main Westgrave Hall building and out again, down into the kitchens where Tatiana was busy at the old-fashioned range. 'So, you have come for late-night snacks I suppose?' she asked them.

'I am inbred Georgian peasant and always hungry,' Wolf said, rubbing his stomach.

'I wouldn't mind a bite if you've got something,' Hoskins said.

She shrugged and spread her large arms. 'This place you treat like Kentucky fried drive-in. Open twenty-four hours.' She turned away and started busying herself. 'Ten years ago, I study computing at night school, thinking I can get good job, but now here doing exact same career as my poor dead grandma.'

'Was she a chef?' Hoskins asked.

'No, she fed pigs.' Angrily, she flung a ladle across the room where it clanged against a saucepan. 'Sometimes, you two are as bad as Oleg.'

Both men proffered apologies.

'She no like Oleg,' Wolf whispered to Hoskins. 'He treat her like dirt. "Come bring food to bedroom, on hurry-up," he say, which long walk up the apples and pears, and then when she get there, he having shag with two girls.' He whispered even closer in Hoskins' ear. 'One girl she laugh and say "come join us, babushka". Poor Tatiana very upset. She get drunk then lug very heavy French eighteenth-century dinner service up five flights apples and pears to belfry and chuck off roof, one plate at a time.'

'Whoa!' Hoskins muttered, turning his eyes back to the cook in a mixture of fear and admiration.

'Very strict Mrs Bell, housekeeper, want to fire Tatiana for that, but Mr Volkov, he say no, it Oleg fault not her,' Wolf said.

'Another thing,' Tatiana said, gesturing with her now recovered ladle. 'Oleg asked me to take traffic speed ticket for him, twice!' she said. 'But when it was raining, he wouldn't give me a lift to Southampton. So I had to catch a bus. He's as bad as his mother,' Tatiana muttered, her back to the men as she ladled some food from a bubbling pot onto two plates.

Wolf conspiratorially rolled his eyes, with a finger pressed to his lips.

Tatiana was just getting into her stride. 'For six months I worked for her in Paris as sous chef. When the main chef was on holiday I looked after her alone. I was keen to make an impression so I researched favourite Kazakh food for her, no expense spared, ingredients flown in. *Sorpa*, which is horsemeat sausage, and *shubat*, sour camel milk. I also made very difficult *ulpershek* which is from the aorta and fat of a steppe pony. Took two days preparation, and when I served it to her she fed it to her dogs, right in front of me. "This is peasant food," she said. "You think I am a serf from the steppes, do you? You will never cook for me again." She called me the daughter of a whore and fired me and my assistant Ibrahim on the spot. Her guards threw us both out on the street. We slept in a park for two days, until my uncle in Kiev sent me some cash. Poor Ibrahim was picked up by the police and deported.'

Tatiana set two big plates of meatballs with dumplings in front of them.

'You poor thing,' Hoskins said, as he reached for his spoon.

She smiled at him and caressed the side of his head. 'When Sasha heard how his ex-wife had treated me, he hired me for Westgrave Hall, on double the salary just to annoy her, I think. So a happy ending for me.' She looked affectionately at Carl. 'Ahh, I like a man who knows how to eat. But that woman eats only hatred, and drinks bitterness. One day she will vanish, like smoke – poof! – up her own *zad*. On that day I will be happy.'

Hoskins turned to Wolf, who was grinning at him.

'So, tomorrow we have grilled perch, yes?' Tatiana said. 'From Westgrave Lake.'

'Sounds fantastic,' Hoskins said.

–

Daniel Levin had become the lightest of sleepers and when his eyelids flicked open the VW's digital clock showed 4:14 a.m. He had parked the camper van in the

Wilmington Woods car park, not far from Worthing. The woods, famed for summer visits by nightingales, were owned by the Sussex Wildlife Trust and were reached along a muddy gravel track. There was only room for six vehicles on the hardstanding and in the depths of a still and clear midwinter night Levin was not surprised he had it to himself.

Until those soft footsteps.

There was no light, but the sound was coming closer. He lay rigid in his sleeping bag, his woolly hat pulled down close around his ears. The curtains were tight across all the windows, so he was confident he couldn't be seen.

The footsteps approached, still not a hint of any light. Levin held his breath, praying that whoever it was would move on. At the outer reaches of his hearing, he was sure he could detect breathing. It certainly wasn't his own.

'Daniel, I know you're in there.' The voice came soft as a whisper, but with an edge of steel.

Levin could feel the drumbeat of his own heart and fought to restrain a whimper of fear. He knew that voice.

The Ghost.

–

The Geneva flight was late into Gatwick, and it was gone eleven by the time Gillard was sitting in the back of the airport bus and was really able to give his full attention to the post-mortem findings on the three murder victims. Squinting at his phone, he could see Delahaye had already summarised the causes of death in an earlier email, and there was little extra to add beyond the fact that significant alcohol had been found in Volkov, not surprising given he was at his own Christmas party. Maxim Talin hadn't been drinking but tested positive for cocaine. Bodyguard Bryn Howell was given a clean bill of health, apart from being ventilated with several bullet holes. His body had been released to his widow, but the two oligarchs were being retained for toxicology tests. The only real surprise was actually nothing to do with the dead bodies at all. Delahaye referred to being copied in on a ballistics report, and a subsequent commercial lab test.

Gillard didn't recall seeing this, so he flicked back through his email inbox until he found the relevant message. One particular bullet, embedded within a book-shelf, had been recovered with what looked like animal fibres. The Birmingham ballistics centre, qualified to examine only bullets, had sent off the sample for analysis, and it had just come back.

Weasel.

The detective scratched his head. Although the bullet's forensic item number, nineteen, was given on the email he didn't have the bullet map to be able to establish its location. That would have to wait. He rang Claire Mulholland at home. She hadn't quite gone to bed.

'Sorry to disturb you at this hour, Claire. Could you crank up your laptop and pull open the bullet map for me?'

She sighed. 'Of course.' Gillard listened to her talking to husband Baz, and the sound of footsteps. It was a couple of minutes before she was able to respond.

'Bullet nineteen, you say.' She paused. 'That's about halfway along the north edge of the balcony, much closer to the body of Maxim Talin than to Volkov's.'

'That's very interesting,' Gillard said, and then mentioned the discovery of weasel fibres.

'Weasel! Are you kidding me?'

'I had two thoughts,' he said. 'My first was gloves. Whoever reloaded the weapon had picked up some fibres and transferred them to the bullets. Maybe it was a hunter, something like that. But then I realised these fibres would have been burnt up when the weapon was fired.'

'So what was thought number two?'

'Well, the DNA analysis is probably fairly approximate when not examining our own species. Something in the weasel family, but not actually a weasel.'

'Ferret or a stoat?'

'Mink. I think this bullet passed through a fur coat before burying itself in a wooden bookshelf.'

'Ah, of course. It can only be Yelena's.'

'Exactly. If so, she was standing right by Maxim when the bullet was fired – that's more than thirty yards from the panic room. Her claim to have only had a glimpse of the assailant must be false. She would have had to run for safety.'

'There's only one snag to this,' Claire said. 'I don't have it to hand, but the photograph Zoe Butterfield took of Yelena when she first emerged from the panic room showed she was wearing a red dress, not a fur coat. I can check tomorrow, but that's my recollection.'

'Okay, so maybe I'm wrong. I'm just about all-in for tonight.' Gillard could see that the bus was at the stop near his car park. 'We can deal with the rest in the morning. Good night.' He hung up, then rang Sam to say he'd be home in forty minutes.

–

Sam met her husband at the door and gave him a huge embrace. 'I've really missed you,' she said. Gillard made

224

his way in and greeted Sam's parents John and Carol, who had come down to be with her while he was deluged with unseasonal work. He was impressed that they had stayed up beyond midnight to greet him.

'So good to see you, Craig,' Carol said. She was a bubbly woman in her early sixties, with wavy grey hair and glasses. John, a retired accountant with twinkly grey eyes, passed him a glass with a good shot of smoky liquid in it.

'Glenfiddich. Happy Christmas,' he said, clinking his own glass against Gillard's. Sam's parents' dog Boris, now quite elderly, wagged his tail from the basket by the fire. Gillard ruffled the animal's ears.

He had barely sat down when his mobile rang. The caller ID showed it was Alison Rigby. 'I'm sorry, I have to take this. It's the chief constable.'

There were indulgent looks from Sam's parents. Gillard went out into the hall to take the call.

'Yes, ma'am.'

'How did it go in Geneva?'

'I had a late breakthrough. Ms Yalinsky admitted that she had seen the shooter, who was on the far side of the balcony, with his back to the windows.'

'That's quite a discovery. I wonder why she didn't admit it before.'

'I still don't think we've got the full story by a long chalk. When she was with her lawyers and officials she stuck to her previous version.'

'So no murder weapon, no fingerprints, footprints or DNA from the killer?'

'No ma'am, I'm afraid not. I'm particularly puzzled by the lack of footprints. Of course, we do have latent prints from the three witnesses: Westgrave Hall's head of security, Sophie Cawkwell and our own PC Butterfield. It's possible they have covered over earlier latent prints from the killer. Butterfield was quite adamant, however, that no one apart from Wolf, the head of security, had been on the window-side balcony from which most shots appear to have been fired.'

'So is it not possible that the Russians killed each other?'

'It doesn't accord with the ballistics evidence: neither in terms of direction of shooting, nor the absence of the weapon from which most shots were fired. Volkov was not killed by bullets from Talin's gun. If Talin was killed by Volkov, then Volkov also shot himself or somehow gave his weapon to a third party to do it. And someone somehow managed to spirit the weapon away.'

'It's a bit of a Gordian knot,' Rigby observed.

'Yes. Ms Yalinsky's admission helps in some ways, but still leaves us with unanswered questions.'

'Well, help may be at hand. The reason I am ringing is to tell you is that MI5 is willing to brief you, tomorrow at ten o'clock.' She gave him the address of hotel just off the M25. 'Corrigan will be with them too.'

'I'm surprised they haven't briefed you directly.'

'Are you? I'm afraid it's all above even my paygrade.'

–

Next morning, Friday, was two days after Christmas day. It felt like a month. Gillard was up before seven, attended to the dog, and got the kettle on. The garden showed a hard frost, the first hint of Christmassy weather this year that he'd seen outside of Westgrave Hall. Boris followed him inquisitively as he tiptoed into his home office and picked up scissors, sticky tape and some gift wrapping that he had hidden in with his cycle gear. The dog bounded beside him as he made his way downstairs to the garage and from an old kit bag dug out the Christmas gifts for Sam that he had bought back in September. Every year he tried to be ready at least three months early, knowing that fate had a way of landing him with a huge case in the run-up to the festive season. It was an old canard in CID that detectives would end up rooting about in petrol stations late on Christmas Eve in a frantic attempt to buy something for loved ones. His old boss Paddy Kincaid had once admitted to buying his own daughter a road atlas of the British Isles, a compass and a woolly hat. The girl was only four years old at the time.

Gillard had bought Sam a voucher for a day-long pampering at a posh spa and a white-water kayaking course in North Wales for them both. After her kidnap ordeal in March, he felt that those two gifts covered both the pessimistic and optimistic ends of her mental recovery trajectory. The more immediate gifts were a bottle of her favourite liqueur and an expensive Italian coffee machine. The labrador always became excited when wrapping paper was being used, and his unhelpful interventions at the garage table ended up with him getting sticky tape on his ears. As a result, Gillard hadn't quite finished wrapping the coffee machine when his mobile rang. It was not yet eight o'clock.

It was Claire Mulholland, calling from home.

'Craig, some good news. I got Vikram Singh to dig up the picture of Yelena in the red dress. There are actually some narrow fur cuffs on it.'

'So that could be the origin of the mink fibres. I'd like to get a look at that, but I suppose it's with her in Geneva.'

'But she's definitely been lying to us,' Claire said.

'Not for the first time. In her revised testimony she claims to have had only a glimpse of the shooter, but that can't be true. The bullet map shows shot nineteen was embedded in a bookshelf in roughly the middle of the north balcony, nearly thirty yards from the panic room.'

'So she must have made quite a dash for it once the shooting started, to have got inside there in time, without being hit,' Claire said.

'Except the shot through the cuff, which presumably missed her wrist.'

'There's something else,' Claire said. 'Yelena ran to save her life, rather than pick up and use the gun that Maxim Talin had. Even though she's a good shot, she abandoned him, supposedly the only man she ever loved, in a huge gory puddle.'

'That's an interesting point. But here's a cold hard fact. If she was so far from the panic room when the shooting started, how come there is only one bloody footprint from her shoes, the one by the panic room door?'

'Maybe it was Volkov's blood, acquired as she got there?'

'No. The lab tests show unequivocally that the blood from that female footprint is Talin's, not Volkov's. The significance of that was lost on me, up until now.'

'So, if she was with Talin at the time he was shot, as bullet nineteen seems to show, and trod in his blood there, why isn't there a trail of it across the balcony as she fled to safety? It doesn't add up,' Claire said.

'Correct. It's almost as if she flew from his body to the end of the balcony,' Gillard said. 'It's nearly thirty yards.' For a few seconds neither of them said anything. Still puzzled, he thanked her, ended the call and made his way back from the garage into the kitchen. In this mental reconstruction of the shooting, he knew he was missing something, but what?

–

The early morning sun glinted off the spires and gables of Westgrave Hall as DI Claire Mulholland drove down the winding lane through Steeple Risby. It was just after 8:45, and she and DC Rainy Macintosh had cooked up a plan to round off the search by midday, tackling storerooms, garages and vehicles. She hoped most of the volunteer uniforms could be home before the weekend.

'It's surprising not to have found anything of significance,' Claire said. 'Forty-five bedrooms done so far, and the stable block.'

'Let's face it, ma'am, if someone wanted to hide a key piece of evidence, a gun for example, we wouldnae find it.' Rainy stared out of the window as the unmarked Ford negotiated the icy and un-gritted side road. There was a thick hoarfrost in the shadows of the hedgerows, and motes of light glistened on the higher twigs, the ice already caressed to melting by the first rays of sunshine.

Claire turned right into the main drive of Westgrave Hall, a better-quality road than the public lane they had just left, and drove up the avenue of immense lime trees towards the grand columned frontage of the hall. 'We've still got twenty officers at the bunkhouse in the village hall, so perhaps you'd like to get to grips with searching the vehicles first. They are the most likely pieces of evidence we may lose control of. Then the garages, the workshops, greenhouses and tool sheds. I'll come and join you later, once I've finished my trip into the crypt.' She grinned.

'Make sure you take some bulbs of garlic and a crucifix with yer.'

'Oh, there she is,' Claire said. Mary Hill was standing on the steps of the hall, dressed in quilted jacket, grey slacks and wellingtons. As she spotted the approaching car, Mary sternly lifted her wrist to check the time.

'Och, five minutes late, you'll be in detention,' Rainy said as Claire slid the vehicle into a parking space.

'Do you know she originally wanted to meet at six a.m.?' Claire whispered. 'Six o'clock in the bloody morning!'

'Stands to reason. She has to be safely hanging upside down in the belfry before first light.'

Suppressing a smirk, Claire emerged from the car to greet Mary. The elderly lady looked even frostier than the surrounding countryside, and wordlessly led the detective inspector at a brisk pace to the left, across the frontage of the hall, and then turned right to head north along its western side. Claire had to hurry to keep up with the woman's pace as she went through a gate into a walled garden, and threaded her way past largely bare flowerbeds, through another gate and across the staff car park towards a squat flint-built church.

'That building you see ahead of you is the Westgrave chapel. This is effectively the new chapel, Norman design, built in 1016 A.D. by John de Westgrave. It replaced one damaged by fire in 943, although there is considerable evidence of a much earlier place of worship on the site. The remains of wooden corner posts have been dated to 315 A.D.' Mary continued in tour guide mode, producing a fat bunch of borrowed keys from her pocket. Claire followed her into the chapel porch, and waited while she dealt with the padlock. Once it was unlocked, Mary put her shoulder to the heavy wooden door, and it creaked open. She then began to describe various architectural features, until Claire stopped her.

'I'm sure this is very interesting, but I really just need to see the tunnel.'

'St John's Easement,' she corrected. 'We're not sure of the date of construction, though it probably connected many rather older vaults. You see, many of the great houses of England had escape tunnels built during Elizabethan times. This one is much more extensive than most, and clearly includes a number of priest holes for the clergy to hide from royal persecution.'

'Fascinating,' Claire said.

Mary Hill looked at Claire for signs of sarcasm. She didn't find any. 'All right, follow me. It's below the western edge of the transept.' She led the detective along the worn flagstone floor past a collection of box pews, and through a curtained-off passageway, which was barely head height. 'The old sacristy was on this side, but it was moved in 1714 and is now behind the rood screen.' Mary reached into an alcove and flicked a heavy switch. It remained gloomy.

'You see, this is the problem when I've not been allowed in to do my job. The bulb has given up the ghost, and someone's moved the spare!' She made it sound as momentous as the collapse of Western civilisation. Claire used her phone to illuminate the passageway, while Mary found a large candle on a grimy saucer and lit it from a box of matches. She then knelt by an ornate round grating in the floor.

'We need to get this off,' she said, easing her fingers under a flange on one side. Claire knelt to grip the other side. The metal was cold and worn smooth, and cast into an ornate design of devilish heads, the finger gaps being mouths.

'French, fourteenth century, quite rare. Cast in Rheims, attributed to Robert de Adelour, or possibly his son,' Mary announced.

The two women heaved off the heavy grating and slid it across the flagstones. Claire's light showed the shaft was barely two feet wide. A rusty iron ladder led down a good fifteen feet into the abyss. Drippings and gurgling could be heard from beneath.

'I take it you're not claustrophobic?' Mary asked. 'Or is that not one of the tests for new officers?'

'I'm okay,' Claire said, feeling anything but. She took some pictures, anything to delay the prospect of descending into that pit. She'd been afraid of the dark since she was a little girl. 'But I'm beginning to doubt that anyone could have got into the library if it meant negotiating this passageway. It doesn't look like this grating has been moved for a long time.'

'Agreed. But best be sure. That's what my CO used to say.' Mary Hill began to descend the ladder one-handed, the other grasping her candle.

'Were you in the forces?'

'Nine years in the WRAC. Mainly in Northern Ireland during the Troubles. Searching female shoppers, mainly in Belfast. Are you coming along, or should I just do it myself?'

Stung by the retort, Claire followed, grasping her phone in her left hand. At the bottom, the shaft broadened out to a rough whitewashed stone passageway that split into three. Mary held up the candle and gestured with it. 'This one is just sixty yards and heads south-east, emerging into what is now the kitchen area of Westgrave Hall. In the other direction, this leads about two hundred yards into the woods where charcoal pits were identified in the 1870s. They were extensively used in the Middle Ages but are now overgrown.' She then turned to the lowest of the three passageways, less than five feet high, with a flagstone floor six feet wide and cambered towards a central gully. A cold breeze moaned from it. 'This is St John's Easement. I'm afraid you're going to have to crouch. It's damp and, I warn you, there are rats.'

The two women shuffled along into the darkness, Mary with a guttering candle in hand and Claire grasping her mobile phone, photographing as she went. Water dripped on their heads from above, and scurrying could be heard from many tiny fissures in the walls on either side. When Claire swivelled her phone towards the sound she momentarily caught the reflection of tiny eyes.

'Don't worry, they won't come near you. Not unless we get trapped down here,' Mary said with a chuckle. 'I'm not sure what it is they *do* eat. Not much flesh left on the plague victims, I should say.' After about thirty yards the passageway expanded into a vaulted chamber with a higher roof. To either side were what looked like stone tombs, with a layer of rubble on top.

'Behold, the ossuary,' Mary said. It was only when she held the candle over the layer of rubble that Claire realised what she was looking at were bones. Thousands of bone fragments, and plenty of entire skulls.

'Who were these people?' she asked.

'Plague victims from the deserted mediaeval village, mostly. Some of the Iron Age bodies uncovered when the fort was first excavated in the early eighteenth century are here too. Frankly it is something of a mess, but old

Lady Westgrave, the mother of the last one, was a bit superstitious and wouldn't have archaeologists down here.'

'Why not?'

'Her eldest son Oliver died down here as an eight-year-old while playing hide and seek.'

'How?'

'Not exactly sure. Supposedly head injuries, but the only documents I could find from 1934 about the post-mortem make no mention. Hypothermia was given as the cause of death on the death certificate.'

'Well, that's too cold a case even for us.'

'Very droll.' Mary lifted something into the light. It was a skull, minus jawbone. 'This is an interesting one. Possibly from the hill fort. Ceremonial death. See the neat hole in the back?'

Claire retreated from the hideous object, which still had strands of pale, wiry hair attached.

'Oh, come on, it won't bite. Not unless I put his teeth back in.' She gestured to the shelf from which she'd found it, and then carefully replaced the skull.

Claire gazed at the ongoing tunnel, from which a ghostly keening emanated. It was even lower than the passage they had previously negotiated, and blackened with grime. It would be like entering a fireplace. 'How far away are we from the hill fort at this point?'

'Still several hundred yards, obviously. The village antiquarian society has a leaflet from the 1920s from Dr Hilding, who was I suppose what you would call an enthusiastic amateur archaeologist. He claimed to have found evidence of an escape tunnel from the hill fort, leading west north-west towards the hall. However, subsequent digs have failed to find any evidence of it. If it did exist, it would connect to this passageway about a hundred yards further on.' She gestured into the darkness.

'Have you been down there?' Claire asked.

'Yes, but not for twenty years. I'm not so supple as I used to be, since the bomb.'

'Were you caught in a bomb blast?'

'Yes. May 13th 1982, my third wedding anniversary. While off duty to celebrate with my first husband, near Newry. He was a captain in the Royal Engineers. A fine man.' She paused for only a couple of seconds. 'Now, it's a wet and muddy crawl for the last thirty yards, through what was a medieval midden, and then ends in a padlocked door, installed in Victorian days. I'm game if you are.'

Claire found herself having to recalibrate her opinion of this unflappable woman. 'I think we could do it a different way. We have an inspection camera on a cable that would do the trick. We already used it to explore the septic tank in the library panic room.'

'As you wish.'

The two women carefully retraced their steps back to the shaft and climbed the ladder. Once they were back inside the chapel, Claire indulged Mary for a ten-minute tour of the various Westgrave luminaries who were buried in the grounds. Mary rounded off her talk from a position by a rather well-tended grave, almost the only one without lichen or algae on the stone. It was marked with fresh red roses in a vase, which Mary casually rearranged. The name on the grave was Captain William Douglas of the Royal Engineers, 1949–82.

-

Mary Hill wasn't in a good mood as she strode back down the main drive of Westgrave Hall and across the road up to her own cottage. She'd soon realised that the DI Mulholland wasn't really interested in anything she had to tell her. She had watched her eyes glaze over during much of the historical background. She was used to that kind of treatment from the public when she'd been a volunteer for the National Trust, but it still rankled. She had been more surprised that the young woman wasn't prepared to get her hands dirty by crawling up the passageway, instead proposing to get some technological fix using a camera on a cable.

If even police officers have no backbone, then no wonder the country was going to the dogs.

The moment Mary had pulled her wellingtons off and got inside the kitchen Oswald appeared. He was always quick to sense her arrival and the click of his claws on the kitchen tiles was one of the loveliest sounds in her life. When you're a dog, hope always triumphs over experience. 'Hello, you silly boy,' she said, rubbing the dog's ears. 'After more biscuits are we?' Now she'd said the word 'biscuits' she would have to give him some.

She popped the kettle on then sat down at the kitchen table. She rolled up the leg of her slacks and unbuckled the plastic artificial leg at the knee. The NHS leg looked as worn and as false as a Victorian doll, but having bedded in over decades she preferred to keep it rather than wear the more modern prosthetic she had been offered through Help for Heroes.

As she rubbed cream into the stump, she considered the sacrifices she had made for her country. Her hearing and this leg, both damaged beyond repair. Forgotten. Unlike the man who planted the culvert bomb, an IRA bigwig whose name was quite well-known to the security forces. He had been treated as a hero in his community.

Immune from prosecution under the Good Friday Agreement, now breeding horses at a farm in Fermanagh and hobnobbing with politicians on both sides of the border. He'd had the sheer audacity to make a claim against the Northern Ireland government for a compensation payment for injuries sustained while he was planting a bomb, one that went off prematurely. There was uproar about it, but it might yet be paid. It would undoubtedly exceed the pittance she had been awarded for her own injuries.

There's no justice in this world, she thought.

—

There was no shortage of police volunteers to search the many sports cars and other top-of-the-range vehicles parked in Westgrave Hall's showroom-sized garage. These included a Rolls-Royce, a Bentley, a Mercedes stretch limo, a Ferrari, a Porsche and a Maserati, and no less than six identical Mitsubishi four-wheel-drives. Claire Mulholland had already locked the keys away in the evidence van on day one, and with Wolf's help in matching them to the correct vehicle, DC Rainy Macintosh passed them out to the uniformed officers.

'Och, I feel like a childminder looking after the bairns' toybox,' Rainy confided in DC Michelle Tsu, as they watched no fewer than three overweight male coppers scrambling around an orange Ferrari roadster. The largest of the officers squeezed himself into the driving seat, and after a perfunctory feel along the ceiling, moved the gearbox through the gears and held the steering wheel.

'The only thing missing is the brum-brum noises,' Michelle replied.

'I'm sure he hears it in his wee head, the poor hen.' Rainy turned her head to see Wolf looking nervously across the fleet.

'What car do you drive, Wolf?' she asked him.

'Second-hand Nissan estate. But I would like three-wheel Reliant from *Fool and Horse* TV show.' He looked at the amusement scribbled on her face and felt the need to explain. 'I don't like fast car. It give me technicolor yawn. Never drive with Oleg, never. Maniac.'

'I notice there is a Humvee parked around the back in the garage with the quad bikes, but you haven't given me the key,' she said.

Wolf shrugged. 'Sometimes I have, sometimes not. This is Oleg's most loved possession, maybe after his penis. He doesn't like anyone else to play with it, especially his sister.'

Rainy fought the incestuous image the Georgian had inadvertently planted in her head. Leaving the uniformed officers in their playpen, she picked up the keys and headed off up to the second floor to Oleg's suite, which had been marked as searched yesterday. She had the full evidence list on her iPad, supposedly organised by room and category, but she wanted to see it with her own eyes.

She unlocked it and went in.

Oleg had three large rooms, gutted and modernised at some cost to their original grace. One wall of the lounge had mounted on it probably the biggest TV screen she ever seen outside the Glasgow Odeon Luxe. The place was otherwise untidy, with plenty of evidence that the last time he'd been here he had shared the place with a girl-friend. The plastic square in the middle of the bedroom floor contained a pair of polished shoes, hightop trainers, and a bundle of hundred-dollar bills in a billfold. There was a video camera, which had been marked as checked and downloaded, an Xbox console, and various other bits of video paraphernalia. There was also a bunch of keys.

She checked on the iPad and saw that they had been marked as house keys, although the largest key on it was clearly for a vehicle; it had a remote locking fob and a keyring with the not-very-subtle Humvee logo on a leather tag. Cackling to herself, Rainy left the room, relocked the door and hurried down to the workshop. There she found a couple of disconsolate uniforms, working their way around the three quad bikes and a jet ski on a trailer.

'Hello boys, look what I've found!' She dangled the keys at them, and they gathered round her like labradors at dinnertime.

—

The Premier Inn where MI5 had chosen to brief Gillard was a low-slung concrete-fronted slab, tucked behind a slip road from a petrol station near the junction of the A3 and the M25. Gillard slid the unmarked Vauxhall into a parking space near the entrance and, as he was leaving the car, noticed a flash of headlights from a black BMW parked opposite. He made his way over and saw DCS Geoffrey Corrigan behind the wheel. Corrigan leaned across and pushed open the passenger-side door. As Gillard slipped inside, he was aware of someone else lurking in the back. Probably Haldane.

'Morning, Craig,' Corrigan began. 'How are you getting on?'

'Not too bad. Would have been better had you not pinched my notebook and digital recorder.'

There was a slight chuckle from the back of the car. 'That's a terrible accusation to make detective chief inspector. Terrible.' Haldane's voice was soft, and slightly sibilant, a trace of a speech impediment.

'So what can you tell me, gentleman, to aid the cause of justice?' Gillard said.

'Justice? Now that's an *interesting* concept,' said Haldane.

'Yes, it's what I do for a living. Bringing bad guys to justice. I hope you're going to help me. We're missing a murder weapon and a culprit as well as the other items.'

'I'm sorry, I don't think we've got any of those things,' Haldane said.

'You took my witness, Ms Yalinsky. I want to know what she told you.'

Corrigan spoke. 'Come on Craig, you got to speak to her yourself in Geneva just last night. I'm sure she answered your questions with the same truthfulness as she answered ours.'

'Quite.' *With no truthfulness at all.* 'I don't know what your interest in her is, and I don't expect you to tell me, but it's important that we get a result in this investigation.'

'We know your reputation, Craig, and we don't want to get under your feet,' Corrigan said. 'But we are entirely satisfied that Ms Yalinsky was not present during the shooting and did not witness a significant portion of it.'

'Right.' Gillard tried to keep the surprise out of his voice.

'So you'll have to look elsewhere for clues,' Haldane said softly.

Gillard had assumed that MI5 would have had access to the evidence now on the HOLMES computer, if not directly then at least through Corrigan as head of

Special Branch. The bloody footprint from a woman's shoe immediately in front of the panic room door and the fibres from the mink caught by a bullet halfway along the balcony completely destroyed Yelena's initial assertion of not having witnessed the killing. Of course, the significance of those two findings would only be apparent to those who had seen the evidence map and cross-referenced the findings from HOLMES. There were two possibilities. One was that MI5 had other fish to fry, more important than the murder. The other, of course, was that they were lying to him and were perfectly aware that Yelena had witnessed the killing. Either way, it seemed they were trying to protect her, and he didn't know why.

'Who do you think fired the fatal shots?' Gillard asked.

'Oh, that's for you to establish, and we wouldn't dream of interfering,' said Haldane.

'You already have. For example, can I ask you if it was you who planted a USB stick on the computer in Wolf's secure office—'

Corrigan interrupted. '—Actually, we do have our own suspicions. There is a person of interest we have been monitoring for some time who is employed at Westgrave Hall.'

'Who is that?'

A sheaf of photographs was passed forward from the back seat. They were close-up telephoto surveillance shots of a handsome, craggy-jawed man with a blond ponytail. In one, he was wearing evening dress and opening a car door for somebody, his gaze elsewhere and a spiral wire visible going up to an earpiece. In another he was dressed down in a puffa jacket and woolly hat, walking along an urban street. In a third, he was in a business suit escorting a pale young woman into a central London hotel. The man had poise and style and the pictures would not have disgraced *GQ* magazine.

'I recognise him. He's one of the Westgrave security men.' Gillard pulled out his notebook and riffled through, looking for the name.

'I'll save you the trouble,' Haldane said. 'His name is Jason Lefsky. Polish, aged thirty-eight, employed as a personal protection officer, currently assigned to Volkov's daughter Anastasia.'

'Ah, that's her going into the hotel,' Gillard said, indicating the pale woman.

'Yes. It's a good cover; the daughter is the heiress to billions and an obvious target for kidnapping. Lefsky isn't actually Polish. He's a Russian agent, son of a retired Russian military intelligence head. The father is no longer supposedly working for the GRU, but the Kremlin still has uses for him. Chasing down enemies—'

'Before we go any further, Craig,' Corrigan said. 'I'd just like to remind you that we have a copy of your signature on the Official Secrets Act. Nothing we tell you here will be repeated. Not even to your colleagues.'

Gillard nodded. He remembered being required to sign the Act several years previously when he was shown the confidential toxicology report into the death of Boris Berezovsky. It hadn't been his case, but he had done some of the interviewing of witnesses.

'My lips are sealed,' Gillard said. 'However, as far as this guy is concerned, he couldn't have been involved in the Volkov shooting, because we have video evidence showing him outside the library at the time it took place.'

Corrigan nodded. 'We know. That's why we are leaning towards the conclusion that the Kremlin was not involved in this one. If they were, Lefsky would have been the man to do the job, and it would have been done far more neatly than this, and surely not at a party with all those other people present.'

'In which case, if he is unconnected with the murder of Volkov and Talin, this whole thing must be unwelcome attention for him.'

'Well, yes and no,' Haldane said. 'It may have been his own good fortune that the video of a Russian TV crew and the witness statements of half a dozen other people, including a British Appeal Court judge, put him clearly outside the library at the crucial moment. It's a good alibi. On the other hand he will be aware that a lot of digging will be done, and other things may get uncovered by accident.'

'Digging by Surrey Police, you mean, as well as by you?'

'Indeed,' Corrigan said. 'That is why we are sharing rather more information with you than would normally be the case. I want you to keep your eyes open for any evidence that may implicate him, not so much in this killing, as in any others.'

'What others?'

This time it was Haldane. 'Lefsky has a hit-list. It's the usual suspects from the Kremlin's point of view. Loud-mouth émigré businessmen, exiled journalists, dissidents. Many of these people are amazingly brave.'

'I agree. One of them has already been to visit me.'

'Yes, plucky Daniel Levin. We fear for him,' Haldane said.

'Can't you protect him?'

There was a heavy sigh from the back seat. 'We'd obviously love to protect everyone who has chosen Britain as their refuge from tyrants, bullies and autocrats. But there is a resource issue.' Gillard could almost hear the washing of hands. 'We have occasionally fed Levin information that might keep him safe.'

'The poor guy is living in his car!' Gillard said. 'He's terrified of this man, the Ghost. Is that him? Is Jason the Ghost?'

There was a soft chuckle from the back seat. 'We don't believe in ghosts.'

By the time Gillard got back to his vehicle, the spooks had driven off. He watched their BMW X5 drive off on a small service road he hadn't previously noticed behind the filling station. It was clever. They didn't trust him not to check ANPR to see where they were heading or where they had come from. By not arriving from the M25 or returning to it they were making that task harder for him.

He felt profoundly dissatisfied by the meeting. MI5 could clearly see everything he was doing, probably through access to HOLMES. They were undoubtedly in a position to help the inquiry, yet didn't deign to do so. They were certainly protecting Yelena Yalinsky, though he didn't know why. In fact, he had only the vaguest idea of what their objectives were, beyond tracking Jason Lefsky. He strongly suspected they were using Daniel Levin as bait, to entrap their quarry. If so, it was cruel and heartless. The one thing they had told him, right at the end of the interview, was that Jason had now disappeared. The fact they knew that meant they must have their own eyes and ears on the ground at Westgrave Hall. The comings and goings of minor witnesses would not have been recorded on the police computer.

Making his way back to Surrey on the A3, he got a call from DC Rainy Macintosh.

'Sir, you are going to be so excited when you hear what we've discovered.'

'Go on.'

'It's a gun. One of the uniforms found it in the driver-side door pocket of Oleg Volkov's Humvee.'

'Great work. What you need to do now is send—'

'—it to ballistics? Aye, it's being couriered there as we speak. I made a note of all the technical details before I did so and rang our wee genius Neville Tufton. He says that the make of the gun is compatible with the marks on the bullets we found in the library. But he says he'll need to fire a test shot or two and compare the marks on those bullets with the ones we have to be sure.'

'I'm very impressed, Rainy. That's quick work.'

'Och, thank you, sir. But it doesnae solve our main problem. The wee bampot Oleg may well have been choking to slaughter his parents. But he was seen in Westgrave Hall on his balcony taking pictures of the fireworks at the time of the shooting.'

'If it was his gun, we're halfway there,' Gillard said. 'He's got access to enough money to get someone else, perhaps a professional, to do the dirty deed. I agree that we are still trying to figure out exactly how it was done. But once I've got Oleg Volkov sitting in our grimmest basement interview room, I'll be able to ask him.'

'Aye. But it's still pretty odd if you hire a professional assassin and have to lend him your own gun.'

Gillard chuckled. 'That's a good point. I'll bear it in mind.' He cut the call and rang Claire Mulholland. When she answered he could hear traffic noise.

'Hi Craig, I'm on my way to Knightsbridge to interview Oleg Volkov. The surveillance team says he finally showed up at his apartment.'

The Metropolitan Police had at Gillard's request been staking out the young man's flat for the last two days. They were pretty sure he had not left the country.

'Would you like to come? I'd appreciate your company.'

'More than happy to,' Gillard said. Volkov's errant son, already known to the police for a whole series of traffic infringements, now looked like being a more major element in the inquiry following the discovery of the gun.

'The Met have gone in. He's agreed to stay there while we talk to him. I gather his lawyer will be there too.'

'Surprise, surprise.'

Half an hour later, the two detectives met at Acton Town tube station to complete the journey by public transport. As they waited for the Piccadilly Line train, they each checked their phones for messages, hoping that the NBIS had received its precious golden gun and had found the time to fire it. Nothing so far. Still, they had enough to pull Oleg Volkov in anyway.

–

Oleg Volkov lived in a serviced apartment four storeys above Topshop, and within sight of Harrods, London's premier department store. The two Surrey police detectives rendezvoused with a car full of uniformed Met officers at the entrance of the building. One of the uniforms went with them and the rest waited for the agreed signal to come and search the flat. The lift was poky and old-fashioned, and the landing fairly small. Gillard rang the bell and the apartment's front door was opened by Oleg's imposing bodyguard Marcus Dolan, a good six-foot-six, like a scaled-up version of the young Kris Kristofferson. The two detectives introduced themselves and were shown into a palatial space, with floor-to-ceiling windows on both sides. Claire had looked the apartment up on Rightmove on the tube journey and discovered it had been last sold for £8 million, four years previously. The sale included a rare reserved space in the Harrods underground car park. 'He's twenty-two now, so that would have made it an eighteenth birthday present,' she had told Gillard.

Oleg Volkov was sitting on an enormous gold-striped five-seater settee, with his feet up on an onyx coffee table in front of him. He was dressed like a rap star, with gold chains around his neck and rings on both hands, as well as copious tattoos. He was wearing reflector sunglasses, which made him in Gillard's mind resemble a large and eminently swattable bluebottle.

A very small dark-suited individual sat on an adjacent chair with a hefty briefcase beside him: the lawyer. The only other aspects of the apartment that stood out were two enormous but very thin speakers, and a mixing desk at the far end. Otherwise the place looked like it had been furnished from a catalogue for just occasional use. Gillard detected the influence of Natasha Fein, concierge to the stars.

'I already made a statement on the night,' Oleg said. 'I don't get why you guys are here now.'

'Because you didn't answer any of the calls we left for you, and slipped away from Westgrave Hall without telling us where you were going, and without leaving us your phone as you'd promised to do.'

'I was upset. I needed to get away.' The mirror shades concealed all expression.

'We're very sorry for your loss,' Gillard said. 'But it's important we find out everything we can so that we can catch whoever it was that killed your father.'

Oleg took off his shades to reveal brown eyes. 'We all feared it would happen one day. Success is always taken away. He was the man, and he was taken down.' The partial American accent sounded strained. Russian vowels intruded. If he was bereaved, it didn't show.

'It would help us if we could just put all the pieces of the jigsaw together during the night of the party,' Claire said. 'So can you describe where you were for most of the evening?'

'I have a private apartment within Westgrave Hall, and I was there with a couple of girlfriends until ten o'clock.' He made sure his eyes lingered on Claire so she got the full meaning. 'We had food sent up, but I came down to watch the arrival of the sleigh with my dad's fiancée. That was pretty cool. I hung out with a few of the guys after that and watched the fireworks from my balcony.'

'Did you hear gunfire?'

'Sure, I must have done. But I guess I thought it was fireworks until we saw people screaming and running around.'

Gillard was momentarily distracted by the movement of male heads, both uniformed cop and bodyguard. He spotted the source of the activity. A slim young woman, dressed only in a smallish towel, darted out from the bathroom and into a bedroom. The door slammed behind her.

'Had you been in the library anytime that day?' Gillard said.

He shook his head. 'Fossils ain't my thing.'

'But guns are,' Gillard said. 'Your Instagram pages are full of shots of you posing with weapons, and videos of you at shooting ranges.'

Oleg's face dissolved into frustration. 'This is branding for the clothes, the shades and so on. I'm just projecting a kind of cool lifestyle. Maybe you don't understand.'

'I understand this.' Gillard showed Oleg his iPad, which had displayed on it the image of him with the golden pistol standing with Westgrave Hall in the background. 'This is your weapon? A Kahr Industries P380?'

'Yeah, sure.'

'This weapon is not registered in the UK.'

'Sure, but it's not in the UK.'

Gillard waved the iPad. 'This image is of Westgrave Hall, agreed? You are standing displaying a functional and illegal firearm in front of it. On British soil.'

Oleg Volkov said nothing for a moment, and his eyes stole momentarily across to the lawyer, who was returning his gaze as if telepathically beaming an answer.

'I Photoshopped the background,' Oleg blurted out. 'The picture was taken in the States.' A thin smile played across the features of the lawyer, but he said nothing.

Gillard rolled his eyes. 'Well, Oleg. It doesn't matter, because we have found the gun. It was in your car, the Humvee, at Westgrave Hall. And for your information, that is in Britain.'

'You're crazy. It wasn't there.' Oleg looked at his lawyer, again wordlessly appealing for assistance.

'It was in the driver–side door pocket,' Gillard said. 'It wasn't even hidden.'

The young man's jaw hung open. 'I know enough about weapons not to leave it there. It must have been planted.'

Claire actually laughed at that. 'You think Surrey Police has a ready supply of golden handguns, just ready to be planted in your car?'

The lawyer spoke for the first time. 'My client maintains that the weapon found in his car is not his. He does not possess a gun in this country because he knows it is against the law.'

'He'll have plenty of opportunity to convince a judge of that,' Gillard said. 'Oleg Volkov, I'm arresting you for a breach of the Firearms Licensing Act 2016.' He then went on to read him his rights. The detective went to the front door of the flat and opened it to let in four more uniformed Met Police officers.

As the cops dispersed around the flat, Oleg stood up and asked, 'Hey, what the hell is going on?'

'We have a search warrant for this address, which I can show you,' Gillard said. 'You'll need to go with these officers to a police station, and after you've been booked in I am minded not to oppose police bail on two conditions. One, that you surrender your passport, and two, that you remain at a known address.'

Oleg slumped forwards, head in hands. 'I can't believe this. I haven't done anything wrong.'

'If you possess any other firearms or ammunition you had better let me know now,' Gillard said. 'I shall be interviewing you again this afternoon.'

Once the young man had been taken away in a police patrol car, the two detectives made their way back to Acton Town tube station to pick up their own cars for the return trip to Surrey. All the while, Gillard kept refreshing his screen to see if the NBIS had finished with Oleg's golden gun. Even though the Met had the young billionaire's British passport, Gillard was convinced Oleg was a flight risk. As a dual national, like his father, he would have the resources to slip away abroad using another passport. It was just when he and Claire Mulholland reached their cars that a text came through from Neville Tufton.

It was simple and to the point.

> The P380 I was sent is the weapon that killed Volkov, Talin and Bryn Howell.

Chapter Fourteen

Two and a half days after the killings, things were finally beginning to make some sense. The discovery and identification of the murder weapon and the arrest of Oleg Volkov had given the investigation some focus. Gillard had called ahead to Rainy Macintosh and asked her to set up an incident meeting in the Khazi for two p.m. He and Claire got there in quick succession, to find a grand spread of food had been laid out in the Portakabin.

'What's all this then?'

'Courtesy of Tatiana in the kitchen,' Carl Hoskins said. 'She's been ferrying it here for half an hour.'

'Carl has been working on Tatiana doggedly since day one,' Rainy said. 'He's hoping for an in-depth undercover investigation at any time.'

'No gratuities or favours, Carl,' Gillard warned. 'Remember Constable Woodbridge.'

'So, no love bites either,' said DS Vikram Singh, wagging a finger at Hoskins.

'We are doing her a favour,' Hoskins said. 'She said she's running down the freezers after the party, so it makes sense to use what they've got rather than chuck it away. And I thought we could do with a bit of a celebration seeing as we got the murder weapon. There's caviar and truffles over there.'

'Aye, that makes for a fine wee Friday feed,' Rainy said, rubbing her hands together.

Gillard called the meeting to order. Including Michelle Tsu, DC Rob Townsend, DC Shireen Corey-Williams and Claire, there were eight detectives, enough to make the place feel very crowded. Before examining the implications of the murder weapon find, he asked Shireen to tell them about what she had learned from Volkov's lawyer.

'I spent the best part of three hours with Hiram Belshin, who best fits the bill of being Volkov's personal attorney. However, there are at least four other law firms involved in various parts of the business empire. Belshin was reasonably co-operative but it's clear that the complexity of the asset structures underpinning the Volkov companies would take months or even years to unwind.'

'So when we ask who inherits, you don't have a clear answer, is that it?' Hoskins asked.

'Well, yes and no. There are at least fourteen versions of Alexander Volkov's will floating around.'

'Fourteen!' Claire exclaimed.

'Yes. Belshin was able to explain it. Each time Volkov broke up with Yelena, he cut her out of his inheritance, and when they got back together again, she was back in. There were some changes made as a result of the court fight at the divorce, too. When he had a substantial new relationship, the woman tended to be added in after about six months.'

'Isn't it just a question of taking the latest will?' Gillard asked.

'That's what I had assumed, but there are complexities. The most recent was signed in Ulaanbaatar and—'

'Sorry, where?' Hoskins asked.

'The capital of Mongolia. And hasn't yet been re-signed here, according to Belshin. It may be open to legal challenge, because of Sophie's inclusion. Belshin said there was yet another will, in draft form, that Lord Fein has in his possession, which was under current negotiation. It was going to be signed over Christmas when the final details of the divorce deal were fixed.'

'Go on, tell us how much Sophie is in line for,' Hoskins asked.

'I couldn't tell you exactly, but it's clearly in the hundreds of millions,' Shireen replied.

'There's a motive,' said Claire.

'She was outside when the shooting took place,' Vikram reminded her. 'And Yelena identified the shooter as a bearded man.'

'They could have been working together,' Claire said.

'What about the kids?' Gillard asked Shireen.

'Yes, his kids would get billions, but much of it is already in trust to them. As for motive, they're already drowning in money, so it's hard to imagine what urgent benefit they would derive from gaining more. What would change, particularly for Oleg as the eldest, would be a great weight of decision-making about the various assets. He'd have a lot of work to do just to administer his extra wealth.'

'Imagine that,' Michelle Tsu said wistfully. 'Drowning in money.'

Gillard smiled. 'If you think about it, it's obvious that a sudden massive increase in wealth doesn't remove your troubles, you just get different ones.'

'That takes a lifetime to learn, sir,' Shireen said. 'And some people never do.'

'There might be financial motives amongst the staff,' Claire said. 'The opportunity to help yourself to life-changing amounts of money which to Volkov would simply have been loose change down the back of the sofa.'

The detective chief inspector shook his head in disagreement. 'My impression is this is a pretty slack organisation anyway. There are plenty of opportunities for lining your own pockets without having to kill the boss. Besides, it only brings greater scrutiny of what led up to the murder. My gut feeling is that the gigantic sums here have hypnotised us. The motive may be something completely different.'

Hoskins folded his arms and nodded. 'Your basic love triangle, end of story,' he said.

'Okay, enough speculation,' Gillard said. 'Shireen, thank you.' He then asked Rob Townsend to brief them on what he had discovered from the various phones and electronic devices.

Rob's expression was troubled. 'We've got weeks more work to do, and we don't have all of the phones that we need, and a lot of what we have got is in Russian and needs translating. Having said all that, the communications in the hours before and after the shooting are just what you would have expected. Contact between family members, lots of short texts sent immediately after the crime occurred.'

'What about Volkov's sat phone?' Gillard said. He was aware it had been seized first by MI5.

'There were no outgoing calls logged in the previous four days and the only incoming call was the attempt by Wolf shortly after the shooting,' Townsend said.

'What about Oleg Volkov's phone?'

'I can't tell you too much as I've only just got it. He certainly made quite a few calls during the hours before and after the shooting which show up on the cell tower dump, but it's what you would expect,' Townsend said. 'As for your question about finding a GPS trace for an additional phone within the library, I've had confirmed it's impossible unless you know which app was being used.' Seeing the look of disappointment on Gillard's face, Rob added: 'Sir, I really don't think electronics is going to provide the confirmation you are looking for.'

Gillard thanked him and asked one further question. 'Assuming Oleg Volkov's phone has GPS on it, we should at least be able to interrogate the app and find out whether the phone, like his gun, happened to be in the library when the shooting took place or whether, like its owner, it has an alibi.'

There was silence for a moment, until Rainy Macintosh lifted her hand to ask a question. 'Assuming Oleg's alibi stands up, then someone else was using his gun. Yelena's description seems to be of somebody else.'

'His bodyguard maybe?' Rob asked.

'Doesn't sound like him. The big guy we met at Knightsbridge is an Irish-American by the name of Marcus Dolan,' Gillard said. 'But according to Oleg, he was on leave over Christmas at an address in Liverpool. Shireen, can you check that?'

'Okay.'

'He'd have big feet. But the killer left no footprints,' Carl Hoskins said.

Claire Mulholland interrupted. 'There are several forensic reasons why a person may not leave footprints that we can detect. For example, while most of those in the building had walked in from the snow and had melting slush on their feet, this person may have had dry footwear if he had been waiting in the building for some time.'

'But how long was he waiting?' Hoskins asked. 'I've checked all the CCTV from the two cameras at the entrance of the library for the previous twenty-four hours, and every single person who walked in walked out again, except for our three murder victims, Yelena Yalinsky, and the three witnesses who went in afterwards.'

'Then it's impossible,' Michelle said.

'It happened, so it's not impossible,' Hoskins said emphatically.

'What about the tunnel idea?' Shireen asked.

'I explored that idea with the redoubtable Mrs Mary Hill,' Claire said. 'St John's Easement probably does not reach as far as the library, and it is a sufficiently narrow and awkward route that it would not lend itself to somebody nipping in and out for a killing. While I can't prove that until we get the remote camera along the narrowest passageway, I would be very surprised if it was even possible. Rob and I are going to take a look this afternoon.'

'I've got the architect's plans here,' Shireen said, swiping through images on her iPad. 'There is no basement level for the library, and the whole thing is built on a four-foot-thick slab of concrete which goes from end to end, except for the panic room which goes down another fifteen feet in its own concrete-lined pit. Even the septic tank is within that concrete shell.'

'I can verify that,' Rainy said. 'I've personally examined and tapped at every square inch of the floor of the library including the panic room, and there is nothing underneath it.'

'All right, school outing,' said Gillard. 'CSI is completely finished with the library now, so let's go over there and see if we can brainstorm any possible way in which our killer could have got in and out without being seen. DS Singh has an idea of his own, which I have to say intrigued me.'

'What's your hunch, Vikram?' Rainy asked.

'Did you ever see the film *The Thomas Crown Affair*?' Singh replied. 'Not the first one, but the remake, 1999.'

'Och, now he's made it into a quiz,' she muttered to Carl Hoskins.

–

The entire detective team trooped over from the Khazi to the library. A female PC was standing in front guarding it, blowing on her hands to keep them warm. 'Good afternoon, constable,' Gillard said. 'Have you seen any activity in the lake?'

She looked baffled. 'No, sir. I've only been here since eight. Pretty quiet actually.'

Realising she hadn't been briefed about PC Woodbridge's experience, Gillard said no more and led his team into the ground floor of the library. He turned on all the lights and led them into the first of two ground floor teaching rooms. Desks and chairs had been stacked at one end and the shelves were largely empty of books; there were just a couple of tables in the middle of the room. Rainy described to them how she had tapped on every wall and along the floor. 'This really left nowhere else to look,' she said. Then she led Gillard and a team through the disabled toilets and a couple of storage rooms which were similarly short of possibilities for hiding anything. 'So that's it,' she said.

Gillard was still smiling and led his team out into the main atrium so that they stood right under the giant dagger of rock, the length of three cricket pitches. He pointed up five feet above his outstretched arm to the steel keel which was bolted into the limestone along its full length. There were several hundred fist-sized bolts that held the metal spine in place. 'Over to you, Vikram.'

The tall Sikh stood under the rock and stretched out his arms. 'In the Thomas Crown remake, a huge sculpture of a horse is delivered to an art gallery and stowed inside. During the night, thieves emerge from within the hollow statue and steal a painting.'

'Ah, the old tale of the siege of Troy,' Rob Townsend said.

This was an 'aah' moment for several of the detectives. 'They'd still have to be in there, though, wouldn't they, Vikram?' Hoskins said, pointing at the rock. 'Whoever killed Volkov and his mate haven't had a chance to get out of the building.'

'Well, that's true.'

Townsend walked the entire length of the under-side of the exhibit, then returned shaking his head sceptically. 'If you put a secret compartment in there, you can't afford to have these massive great bolts. And once it had been opened a couple of times, whatever methods had been used to conceal the cracks around the door would become more obvious.'

There were several nods from the assembled group.

'If the exit were underneath, there would inevitably have been some ground floor debris,' Gillard said. 'Bits of limestone dust, extra footprints even. All we've got are some bits of plastic and some chewing gum, right?'

Singh nodded. 'A bit of broken spectacles frame as well, I think.'

'Well, we've got to crack it,' Gillard said. 'We can't charge Oleg Volkov with murder when everybody saw him at the party. It's a non-starter.' He cut the crime tape at the bottom of the first staircase and led the team up to the window-side balcony. He asked them to spread themselves along and look down on the fossil.

'I cannae see there being anything inside this rock except the bones of the wee creatures,' Rainy said. 'The lighting up here is very good, we'd definitely see something.'

Claire, who was down towards the head end of the creature, was leaning over the balcony squinting at something. 'I can see something.' She pointed and Gillard hurried along past his colleagues until he was standing next to her.

'I think it's a fragment of plastic, dark grey, in the hollow.'

Gillard followed the line of her outstretched finger and saw it too. A less than fingernail-sized piece. Vikram Singh had joined them and recognised what they were looking at. 'I got a couple of bits of that already, landed on the ground floor underneath here. Think it might be a light fitting, hit by a bullet.'

Three cops looked fifteen feet above them to the recessed lighting in the ceiling. It was hard to see with the light still on and dazzling them, but there was no obvious sign of damage. 'I'll get a stepladder and have a closer look,' Singh said.

A little further along the balcony there was another discussion taking place. Two of the female officers were asking Carl Hoskins questions.

'What about luggage, Carl?' Shireen asked. 'You said you counted them all in and out again on the CCTV. But did somebody go in with a big heavy suitcase and leave without it?'

'Or even leave with it, but empty,' Claire said.

'I don't remember everyone who came in over the previous two days, I'd have to go back and take a look,' Hoskins said. 'But what I am sure of is that in the short time-window after the shots, and before CSI got here, no one went out with any kind of luggage. Certainly not anything big enough to contain a person. Sophie Cawkwell went in there with some photographic kit in the morning, followed by Anastasia and Wolf, but they were out by three. We had kitchen staff bringing in food in the morning for them and clearing away the leftovers by two p.m.'

The team fell silent for a moment. In that void, the vibration of Gillard's phone seemed quite loud. Claire watched the puzzled look on his face as he looked at the caller ID before answering. She could tell immediately that something momentous had occurred, because his jaw began to sag, until his mouth was open. 'Thank you,' he said quietly to whoever the caller was.

He looked up.

'Daniel Levin is dead.'

Chapter Fifteen

Gillard was grim-faced as he addressed his colleagues: 'That was the Sussex Police control room. Levin's camper van was found in a beauty spot in Sussex with a hose from the exhaust pipe into the vehicle,' he said.

'Sounds like suicide,' said Michelle Tsu.

'Yeah, as it's meant to,' said Carl Hoskins.

'Levin was convinced he was going to be killed by the Russian government,' Gillard said, then looked at his watch. Just after three p.m. 'We really could do without this. Claire, I need you to go down and take a look, and make sure Sussex Police are treating it as a crime scene. Ring them first, ensure nobody touches anything.'

'Okay,' she said, as she began to make her way out of the library. 'Rob,' she called back, 'looks like you'll have to deal with Mary Hill alone. She's due in five minutes at the chapel, so you best be on time. She's quite a stickler for punctuality.'

There was some laughter as the young research officer rolled his eyes and left to meet the elderly verger.

Gillard thought back to his conversation that morning with the spooks. 'Carl, one of the Volkov family body-guards is called Jason Lefsky. I believe he is no longer at Westgrave Hall, and I want him traced.' After what they had told him, Gillard was far from sure that they'd ever find Lefsky. From Gillard's fleeting recollection, he didn't quite match the artist's impression of the Ghost that Levin had shown him, but at this stage it was the best that he had to go on.

'I'll speak to Wolf, he'll know where he is,' Hoskins replied.

The officers made their way hurriedly out of the library back towards the mobile incident room. The Khazi greeted them with its characteristic bad odour and droning fan. Gillard started by returning the call to Corrigan. The Special Branch officer owed him one on this. If Lefsky had killed Levin there was a good chance he was implicated in the murders of Volkov and Talin too. The spooks really should be sharing information with him. Fat chance. The call went to voicemail and he left a message. After he put the phone down, he blew a heavy sigh.

DC Rainy Macintosh was watching him. 'Och, this wee investigation is busier than a Glasgow pub giving away free beer,' she said.

Gillard nodded. 'Well, in theory Levin's death isn't on our patch, but we've got to look for clues wherever we can find them. Let's face it, we're not making much progress here, are we? Despite having the murder weapon, every reasonable suspect seems to have an alibi, including Lefsky.' He taped a copy of the artist's impression of the Ghost plus a picture of the bodyguard to one of the whiteboards, and below listed everything that they knew about him. He was careful to leave off the background, which the spooks had reminded him was covered by the Official Secrets Act. Gillard was pretty sure that Corrigan and his friends at MI5 would already have a trace on Lefsky's phone, and if they couldn't catch him that way there was little chance of Surrey Police being able to. He spent the next half an hour consolidating his ever-expanding list of tasks.

His phone rang. It was DC Rob Townsend. 'Sir, I'm standing in the chapel with Mary Hill.'

'Ah yes, our redoubtable verger.'

'I've just got out of the tunnel underneath. I've had the remote camera in on a two-hundred-metre cable, and I can confirm that the end is blocked by rubble behind a large grating. I think it's impossible that anyone could have been using this passageway to get in and out to the library.'

'All right, Rob, it was a long shot, but glad to have closed that possibility down,' Gillard said. 'The ground-penetrating radar kit is due to arrive on Monday, so that we can examine any evidence of tunnels from the library end. Perhaps I can ask you to take charge of it.'

'I've already downloaded the manuals. It just seems to be a lawnmower-sized scanner on wheels that you push along the ground.'

'I have every faith in you. But don't forget your main task is still ploughing through all that electronic data on the various phones and laptops we seized. I need a result.'

'Oleg Volkov's archives alone are dozens of terabytes, sir. There are hundreds of hours of video. With the four specialist officers working full-time it's still months of work, and so much of it is in Russian, and has to go through the translation app.'

'Okay, Rob. Concentrate on Oleg. Forget the promo videos and stuff for his brand. I'm after messages that might show who he lent his gun to, or any motive for involvement in killing his father. See what you can get me by Monday.'

–

Oleg Volkov was ferried by Met Police van to Staines police station and booked in by the desk sergeant. He was already waiting with his solicitor in the station's most intimidating basement interview room when Gillard arrived with DC Michelle Tsu at five o'clock. On the CCTV behind the sergeant's desk they could see him fidgeting nervously on the chair next to his solicitor, biting his nails and running his hands through his hair.

The moment Gillard walked into the room Oleg leapt to his feet. 'I was told I'd be released, so why are you holding me?'

'There have been certain developments since your arrest,' Gillard said. 'However, you will be released on police bail once we've finished having a chat.'

Michelle prepared the official tape recorder, and the two officers sat opposite Oleg and his brief.

'I just want to run through some of the things that we discussed earlier,' Gillard began, asking for confirmation of address, nationality, occupation and the other formalities. Gillard passed across an eight-by-ten blow-up of the golden gun. 'Now, is this your weapon?'

Oleg picked up the photo and nodded.

'Can you please speak for the benefit of the tape,' Michelle asked.

'Yes, it's mine.'

'How did it come to be in Britain?' Gillard asked.

'It seems it was inadvertently shipped over with a load of my other stuff.'

'You say inadvertently, did you pack it yourself?'

Oleg looked at Gillard as if he were mad. 'No. I have staff to do stuff like that.'

'You have professional weapons handlers?'

'No, I mean it must've been in one of my bags that was loaded for some of the concierge staff when I came over from the States last time.'

'You claim to be ignorant of its arrival, Mr Volkov, yet we have here a photograph of you posing with the same weapon in front of Westgrave Hall.' Gillard passed across a glossy enlargement.

'Like I said, that was Photoshopped. I've never touched the gun since it's been in the UK.'

Gillard shrugged, and shuffled some papers. 'Okay. Let's talk about your Humvee. Would you say that vehicle is one of your favourites?'

'I suppose so.'

'Where do you keep your keys?'

'With me, most of the time.'

'And the spares?'

'In my apartment at Westgrave Hall.'

'And that is normally locked?'

'Yes.'

'According to Wolf, he keeps most of the vehicle keys in his office. The Humvee is the one vehicle whose keys he rarely has. He says you don't like anybody else to drive it.'

He shrugged. 'Answer for the tape please,' Michelle said.

'That's true, I suppose.'

'The gun was found in the door compartment of your Humvee. Can you tell me how it came to be there?'

'I have no idea.'

'Did you leave it there?'

'No.'

'Do you have any idea how it got there?'

'Somebody planted it.'

266

'Yet as you have admitted, no one has access to the keys to the vehicle except you.'

'If I may interrupt,' the solicitor said smoothly. 'Can we put it on record that Surrey Police managed to access the vehicle, using the keys.'

'By all means,' Gillard replied. 'Those keys were found in the interviewee's bedroom.'

'Then to say that no one has access but him is not factually true,' the brief continued.

'I'm talking about in the normal course of events,' Gillard said, then turned back to Oleg. 'Earlier today, we had fresh news about your gun. Ballistics tests by specialist police investigators have determined that this weapon was used to kill your own father, your mother's partner Maxim Talin, and your father's bodyguard Bryn Howell.'

Oleg looked stunned and turned to glare at his solicitor. If the brief was managing to beam any neat replies telepathically, Oleg certainly didn't pick them up.

'What do you have to say to this?'

'On my life, it wasn't me,' he whispered. Asked for a louder repetition he shouted: 'I didn't do it!'

'Then who did it?'

'Someone who wants to frame me.'

'Mr Volkov, you ask us to believe that your gun, which nobody knew was in the UK, was used by someone else to commit a crime and then slipped back into your locked car.'

'Yes, that's exactly what I want you to believe.'

'Then who would you say this person is?'

'My sister.'

'Anastasia?'

'Yes, she hates me. Or maybe her boyfriend, Jason.'

'You mean Jason Lefsky, the bodyguard?'

'Yes. A complete scumbag.'

Gillard exchanged a glance with Michelle, then said: 'Both Anastasia and the bodyguard you refer to were outside the library when the shooting took place. We have several witness statements to that effect.'

Oleg stabbed his finger towards Gillard. 'Yeah, and those same witnesses saw me outside too, but that doesn't stop you accusing me of the crime.'

It was five p.m. by the time PC Simon Woodbridge returned to the Dorchester. As he emerged from Marble Arch tube station into the post-Christmas sale crowds, he felt his pulse racing. She had said she would be waiting for him there, in her late father's suite. Woodbridge was in civvies, his uniform packed in a suitcase should he need it again that night. He felt awful about what he had been forced to do last night, but Jason had a hold over them both. The stories that Anastasia had told him about his violence and brutality turned his blood to ice. That Anastasia felt he could be her saviour was both flattering and terrifying.

'If you can't report him to the police, you have to kill him, Simon, for both our sakes.' That's what Anastasia had told Simon over the phone. And he was coming back tonight to hear what her plan was for doing it.

Just the thought of tackling the man turned his guts to water. Jason was a trained bodyguard. Anastasia said he was a crack shot left- or right-handed, a jujutsu instructor, and an Ironman veteran. Simon, by contrast, had taken two attempts to pass his police fitness test. His only physical qualifications were a Duckling swimming certificate gained at the age of five and the Duke of Edinburgh Award he took as a seventeen-year-old in Wales, during which a twelve-year-old girl helped rescue him from under his capsized canoe.

What were the alternatives? He had compromised his professionalism entirely. Not only with his entanglement with Anastasia, but by using his pass to get into an unmanned police station late last night. Following the text from Jason, Simon had used the ANPR system to locate a vehicle and had made a request for a mobile number cell tower trace from a service provider. He had made up an incident in case he was ever asked to justify the requests, but it wouldn't survive detailed scrutiny.

His life was wired up with explosives, just waiting to be demolished.

Above all, he needed to get that video of him in Anastasia's bedroom deleted. And the only way was either money, or murder.

Simon trundled his suitcase down Park Lane and made his way through the grand entrance of the Dorchester Hotel. The moment he arrived at the reception desk and said who he was, he was treated like royalty. A bellboy whisked his suitcase from him and led him to the lift. Arriving at the door of Anastasia's suite, Simon pressed a 50p piece into the hand of the porter. A momentary sneer was followed by: 'Thank you *so* much, sir.'

She opened the door to his quiet knock. She was casually dressed in jeans, pullover and ankle boots, but with her hair done up and eye make-up, she looked fabulous. Once the door was closed, she kissed him passionately, her tongue hot inside his mouth.

'Did you do what he asked?' she whispered.

'Yes.'

'So we're safe for now.' She blew a huge sigh of relief.

'The mobile phone data was patchy, so I hope it's enough. Who is it Jason is trying to track down?'

'I don't know. He doesn't share his plans.'

'It must have been Jason who killed your father and his colleague,' Simon said.

Anastasia shrugged. 'I have thought about this many times. I spoke to Natasha, who was standing right outside the library on the bridge when it happened. She said Jason was with them when the shooting began. But I do know he despised my father and detested Bryn.'

'Jason said he might need more information from me. Only then will he delete the video,' Simon said. 'But I don't see how we can ever be sure he will do what he says.'

She kissed him again. 'Simon, I have a plan. He'll come back to me at some point, that's when we have to do it.'

'Does he know you're here?'

'He knows I'm in a hotel, but not which one. He'll soon figure it out. Did you bring your gun? It's the only safe way to bring him down.'

'What gun? British police aren't armed.'

Her face distorted in disbelief. It was the first real piece of animation he'd ever seen on it. 'I don't believe it. Okay, I understand you don't carry them around everywhere, but you must be able to *get* one.' She folded her arms and the expression on her lips was akin to the one he had seen on the bellboy. She clearly felt short-changed in her choice of saviour. 'Fine. I think Oleg has a gun back at the hall, some silly golden thing. If we can find it, I take it you at least *do* know how to use one?'

He shook his head. 'It's not something we're trained on, except officers from the specialist firearms units.'

She threw herself down on a chaise longue and shouted in frustration as she punched a cushion. 'Idiot! Simple Simon, you're going to have to learn. There is no other way out of it.'

–

Gillard sat staring disconsolately at the enormous records of evidence now accumulating on the HOLMES computer. It was nearly seven on a dismal Friday evening and the rain was hammering on the Khazi roof. He'd sent most of his colleagues home for the night, asking for them to return for an incident room meeting tomorrow at noon. Many of them were clearly exhausted. He'd particularly taken pity on Rainy Macintosh, whose fourteen-year-old son Ewan had been staying with Claire's family in Staines. She'd barely seen the boy over Christmas, and for a single mum that separation was agony. Michelle Tsu and Vikram Singh likewise deserved a bit of time with their families. Only Hoskins, emotionally bulletproof, was still around. He was probably with Wolf or in the kitchens with Tatiana, apparently his new sweetheart.

The one other exception was the research intelligence officer, Rob Townsend, who was now back with a team of specialist officers at Mount Browne. They had a ton of work to do looking through all the electronic items that had been seized.

Events were conspiring against Gillard. Wolf had confirmed to Carl that Jason Lefsky had left in one of the Mitsubishi pickups on Boxing Day morning, destination unknown. Corrigan at Special Branch hadn't returned his call. The one person who had called him was

Chief Constable Alison Rigby, who was clearly feeling the heat from higher up. The press coverage, slow to start because of the Christmas break, was now relentless. 'Yet another Kremlin slaying,' according to the *Daily Mirror*. He explained to Rigby that despite finding the murder weapon, none of the obvious suspects could have pulled the trigger. Her response was brisk: 'Craig, guns do not fire themselves. I need a result, fast. There's a Cobra committee meeting on Monday at nine a.m. The Prime Minister, Home Secretary, heads of MI5 and MI6, Corrigan too. They'll all be there. Don't leave me empty-handed. I don't enjoy looking a fool.'

She had then hung up on him.

There were small saving graces. He had some idea of the whereabouts of the remaining Volkov family, thanks to the long-suffering Wolf. He was certain Anastasia was in central London, because a gigantic bill on the Volkov account had just come through from the Dorchester. Wolf had also been notified that Yelena Yalinsky was returning to London, after hearing of her son's arrest, and wanted a room prepared. The Met Police, which was keeping an eye on Oleg's Knightsbridge flat, had rung Gillard to let him know the young Russian had returned to it after being released from custody. So far he was keeping strictly to the terms of his bail.

Claire had arrived at the crime scene in Sussex and confirmed to him that Sussex Police were treating Levin's body and the camper van with an appropriate level of circumspection. However, there was no possibility of a post-mortem before Monday morning.

With a Monday deadline, the same conundrum kept returning to Gillard with greater urgency. How had

Volkov, Talin and Bryn Howell been shot if no one had got into or out of the building?

Mulling this thought, he shrugged on his overcoat, grabbed an umbrella from a coat peg and walked out of the Khazi into the pouring rain. He greeted the rather damp duty PC, who was guarding the incident room. 'Are you signing out for tonight, sir?' the PC asked, brandishing a clipboard in a clear plastic bag, fogged with condensation.

'Not yet, unfortunately.' The DCI opened the umbrella and made his way onto the main drive. He stared up at the huge edifice of Westgrave Hall, its mullioned windows now mostly darkened, the brooding towers and belfry silhouetted against the sky. The only sounds were cawing rooks and the spattering of overflowing gutters. He turned south, looking down the drive, through the long avenue of limes, their leafless limbs reaching for the darkling sky.

The press encampment was smaller than the day before, just a couple of satellite trucks still there at the gates. Further away, in the village, he could make out the lights of the bunkhouse. Probably only half a dozen officers would stay overnight, now that the search had been finished. He made his way down to the gate where a couple of male uniforms kept guard, miserable as drowned rats. On seeing him, one of the cops picked up a bin bag from the ground.

'Ah sir, I was just going to come and see you. A courier from the National Ballistics Intelligence Service brought this a few minutes ago.' He opened the bag and passed across a shoebox-sized package.

Gillard guessed what it was and, after thanking the PC, headed back to the Khazi. Once inside he undid the package and removed a plastic bag containing the golden gun, somewhat tarnished and grimy, the gold paint flaking off in a few places. He had not actually seen the weapon close up, and he was surprised that it was so small and light. With a normal six shot magazine, it would fit into the palm of his hand. But it didn't have one. Instead, separately bagged, was an enlarged fifty round magazine a foot long, and in another plastic sleeve were four test bullets fired by NBIS, and the two sent as comparators from the crime scene.

The detective slid on latex gloves, unbagged the gun and fitted bullets and magazine. He squinted down the sight, training it at the furthest objects in the room. He held it up under an LED reading lamp to get a good close look. There was a white sticky substance on the grip, which he immediately recognised as residue from gaffer tape or something similar. He ejected the magazine and reinserted it, hearing it click soundly into place. The spring was good, and correctly seated, so there would have been no need to tape it closed.

A little puzzled, he logged on and re-read the detailed overview of the weapon that the NBIS had emailed him. Almost all of it concerned the ballistic identification of test bullets compared with those found at the crime scene. There had been no forensic examination of the weapon, except fingerprints and DNA, which had come back negative. The fact that someone had used tape on it was unremarked. There was just a single line that referred to its condition: *Evidence of superficial internal water corrosion.*

Something about this just wasn't right, and he couldn't work out what it was.

A gun can't fire itself. That's what Rigby had said.

But who had fired it? And how had it got wet?

There was a knock on the door and the duty PC put his head through. 'You've had a message, sir.'

'Who is it?'

'Lady Fein. She sent one of the staff to ask if you are free to come up to the hall for coffee.'

Gillard looked at his watch. It was nearly eight p.m. Time he took a break. The prospect of a conversation with Natasha Fein was an alluring one at any time of the day. The detective grabbed his raincoat and an umbrella and made his way out into the pouring rain and up to the house.

She was waiting for him in a chair in front of a roaring log fire. Anastasia's two huge Borzoi wolfhounds, Pyramus and Thisbe, lolled at her feet. Their soft brown eyes followed him as he shrugged off his coat on the doorstep, shook out the brolly, and made his way over. Gillard recalled that the last time he had seen her she was swimming. Naked. The clinging white woollen dress she was wearing now did little to disguise that superb figure. And she had made a pass at him, or so he thought.

'Take a seat, detective chief inspector,' she said, tapping a wing chair next to her. 'You must be exhausted. Would you like coffee, or something stronger?'

'Coffee is fine, thank you.'

Natasha swiped on her phone and tapped the screen. 'This is one of our little innovations for Westgrave Hall. It pretty much keeps track of all the staff. Summoning them, giving orders and so forth is straightforward. Coffee and biscuits are on their way.'

Gillard nodded. 'Does the app save a history of staff movements?'

'Ah, now that is a question for Tatiana, I'm afraid. I suppose you want it to find out where everyone was during the party?'

'Yes, every little thing is helpful.'

'I'll get her to message you with any records that we have.' She watched him closely, her feline eyes unblinking.

'May I ask what are you doing here on this rainy and windswept evening?' he asked.

She smiled. 'The Volkov organisation does not run itself, especially when the head has been cut off. Wolf does his best, but at a time like this there is a bit more multi-tasking required than any one person can manage. This is where our concierge services come into their own. It's pretty much an organised wind-down until the various wills are sorted out.'

Coffee arrived in a large silver pot on a silver tray, with a delicate golden jug of milk and a hand-blown glass dish containing glistening dark crystalline sugar. She poured, then looked up at him. 'I have a question of my own, if I may.'

'Fire away,' he said.

'I understand that Oleg Volkov's gun was the one used to kill his father and the others.'

'We have arrested him, yes, but we haven't released any further details.'

She gave a little laugh. 'I can see from your expression that you are surprised I'm so well-informed. Oleg's solicitor is a family friend, so I do get to hear the inside story.'

'I hope anything you hear you will keep to yourself.'

'Naturally. Have you heard about Sophie?'

'Ms Cawkwell? We took a statement from her shortly after the shooting.'

'She's in a bad way, unfortunately. She was so excited about marrying Sasha, now she seems to spend every day crying, which isn't like her at all.'

'It must've been a terrible shock,' Gillard said. 'Especially as she found his body.'

Natasha nodded. 'She is halfway through making a documentary about the fossil, commissioned by National Geographic TV. But I fear she is in no state to work on it, so I'm not sure it'll get done at all, even with Anastasia's help. There was marvellous footage taken inside the library, which showed Lebyodoushka and Molodoy in all their fossilised glory.'

'I hope she makes a rapid recovery.'

'Well it's been a blow, obviously. But she is very resourceful. The death of her first husband left her a widow while she was still in her twenties, and she seemed to cope with that. Poor Sophie, she's had more than her fair share of bad luck.'

'So it seems,' Gillard said, standing up to take his leave. He thanked Natasha for her help and returned through the rain to the Khazi, which with all the comings and goings was now an island in a sea of mud. He took one look inside the damp mobile incident room and decided he couldn't bear to stay in it a minute longer. It was time he went home.

As he bade good night to the duty officer and headed to the grey Vauxhall he thought about Sophie Cawkwell. Bad luck? Or something else. He'd really like to know what her inheritance would be.

—

Sam Gillard was surprised and delighted to see her husband walk through the door. It was just gone nine thirty.

'I thought you were staying at the bunkhouse tonight,' she said, throwing her arms around his neck and kissing him.

'I thought better of sharing a dormitory with Carl Hoskins. Need to get away from the case for a while.'

Sam's parents, John and Carol, came out to greet him. 'How's it going, Craig?' John asked, eagerly. 'The news seems to be full of nothing else but dead Russians killed by the Kremlin.'

'We've made a lot of progress. It's certainly one of the largest crime scenes I've ever been involved with, and simply co-ordinating all of the statements and evidence has been quite a headache.'

Sam knew that her father was looking for more than those generalities, but Craig was skilled at only sharing tidbits that were already in the public domain. Finding out he hadn't eaten anything but a couple of biscuits, Sam busied herself in the kitchen to see if there were any leftovers that she could reheat. Turkey, obviously. When she re-emerged with a plate of hot food, Craig was sitting on the settee next to Carol and they were watching the latest TV coverage of the murders.

'So the murder weapon's been found?' Carol asked.

'A golden gun apparently,' John said, looking up at Sam. 'It's a bit like James Bond, isn't it?'

'So much for our news blackout,' Craig said glumly.

'Tell you what,' John said, leaning forward to Craig conspiratorially. '*Dig!* is on Channel Four. It's the Mongolia episode that I missed first time round.'

Carol laughed. 'He only wants to see Dr Sophie Cawk-well's long tanned legs.'

'Nonsense, I'd not even noticed them,' he retorted, pressing the remote.

The programme had only just begun, and featured Sophie wearing an outback hat and a tight white T-shirt driving some big off-road vehicle down a steep rocky embankment, with the cameraman in the passenger seat. The pickup pitched back and forth, and Sam couldn't help noticing how this amply demonstrated that the presenter wasn't wearing a bra. Sophie gestured at the rocky layers they were passing as they descended, counting them back in time from Cretaceous to Jurassic, then Triassic and Permian. Craig, unusually, seemed to be as fascinated by the programme as her father was. But unlike John, he seemed more focused on the aerial view of the fossil site than on the presenter. At one point, there was an impressive 360-degree panorama of the mountains from high above, before it dived down to about fifty feet above the rock bed, until it inevitably closed in on Sophie. She was on hands and knees, her bottom curved winsomely for the camera in tight cut-off denim shorts, as she tapped with a small hammer on an outcrop.

'How did they get a helicopter down there, then?' Carol asked.

'That'll be drone footage,' John said. 'They use them all the time now. All these wildlife programmes are done like that now. Hundreds of aerial shots.'

'Oh, Sophie, you've really slipped under the radar, haven't you?' Craig muttered, wagging his finger at the screen. He suddenly stood up, excused himself and left the room. Sam followed him out into the hallway.

'What is it, Craig?'

'I suddenly figured out something about the case.'

'You don't have to go back in to work now, do you?' She had barely got used to the idea of him being home tonight and desperately wanted him to herself.

'No, love. I can do what I need to from here.' He started to head upstairs to his home office.

'Sophie Cawkwell was at Westgrave Hall at the time of the shooting, wasn't she?' Sam asked.

'Yes. And she was immediately on the crime scene, and she stands to inherit hundreds of millions.' He smiled at Sam and hurried upstairs.

She went back into the lounge.

'Everything all right?' her father asked her.

Sam forced a laugh. 'He gets case ideas at the strangest times.'

'John always gets ideas when he is looking at Sophie Cawkwell,' Carol muttered.

'No, I don't.' He looked up, all feigned innocence. Both women laughed.

As they watched, a news bulletin flashed up on the bottom of the TV.

Blast reported outside Buckingham Palace

'Good grief,' Carol said, seizing the remote from her husband and switching to the BBC's rolling news channel. It showed a scene of chaos amid crowds outside the palace, and the tone of the voice-over made it clear something significant had happened: *There is no official word on casualties as yet, but a Metropolitan Police spokesman said that anti-terrorist officers were on the scene.*

Dozens of police cars and ambulances were there, lights flashing, and crowd control railings were already in place, cordoning off a large area from the crowds. Rolling headlines beneath indicated an explosion. A number of vehicles were caught within the cordon, and one of them appeared to be almost destroyed, its roof ripped open like a can of sardines, smoke still issuing from the blackened interior.

The blast seems to have taken place close to the pedestrian lights at the Victoria Memorial, just a few yards from the gates. Hundreds of officers now appear to be at the scene.

'The damaged car is a stretched limo or something similar,' John said. 'Could it be royalty?'

Carol shook her head. 'Not the Queen. The flag above the palace isn't flying, so she's probably not in residence.'

'Craig!' Sam shouted, 'Come down and look at this.'

The voice-over continued: *A source for the palace has told the BBC that the Queen and the Duke of Edinburgh are currently in Balmoral, and no member of the immediate royal family is thought to be in London at the present time.*

Sam heard Craig thundering down the stairs, as the voice-over again repeated the bare details: that an explosion had been witnessed outside the palace, that it seemed to involve a number of vehicles, and that there was no information on casualties. She went online on her phone and found a Press Association report which mentioned two fatalities, one male inside the car and one a female bystander, plus a number of injured.

'*Channel Four News* has three dead and many injured,' John said, looking up from his phone.

'Do you have to go in, Craig?' Carol asked.

'Thankfully not,' he replied. 'Met Police's Counter Terrorism Command will look after it.'

'Can you find out what's going on?' John asked.

He sighed. 'I probably could, but the last thing that my contacts in the Met want is a whole load of rubbernecking by members of other forces who don't need to know.'

A text signal beeped on Gillard's phone, and he stared at it. 'Hmm. Having said that, it seems one of my junior colleagues has already been digging. There's at least one dead male from inside the car, and another seriously injured. Others may have been blown from the car. No word on victim IDs yet.'

'It's got to be somebody important,' John said, looking to Gillard for confirmation. 'That's definitely a limo.'

Sam and her husband exchanged a look. Her father had long viewed Craig as an inside source to be used whenever he felt like it.

'Well, I've just got a bit of research to do on my own case,' he told John and Carol. 'I may not be finished before you go to bed, so I'll say good night.'

Sam followed him out to the stairs and shut the living room door behind her. They embraced, and he stroked her hair. 'I'm so sorry I've missed most of Christmas, Sam. I will make it up to you.'

'Let's take a holiday in the new year,' she said.

'Yes, good idea. When this lot is finally put to bed. Rigby wants a culprit identified by Monday, ready when she goes to the Cobra meeting.'

'That's a tall order,' Sam said.

Craig shrugged. 'If my hunch is right, I might just be able to manage it.'

–

Gillard made his way upstairs and shut himself into his home office. It was just gone ten p.m. So much for a quiet Friday night. Seeing Sophie Cawkwell's TV programme had reminded him what Natasha had said about her making a documentary on Volkov's giant fossil for National Geographic. He'd quite like to see any raw footage and was minded to contact Sophie to ask for it.

Before he got a chance, his mobile rang. It was DCS Geoffrey Corrigan at Special Branch.

'Evening, Craig. Just a quick heads-up. You'll no doubt have seen the news.'

'Yes.'

'We've just identified the vehicle. A Mercedes-Benz Pullman limousine registered at Westgrave Hall to the late Alexander Volkov. Any idea who might have been in it?'

For a moment Gillard was speechless. 'I'll speak to Volkov's head of security, sir, he might know. Can I ask, was this a bomb?'

'Sorry, can't share any confidential information at the moment. I'll be sending a team down to Westgrave Hall, so I'd like you to be there to work with them.' Corrigan cut the call.

'Bastard,' Gillard muttered. This was just the kind of thing that retarded co-operation between different branches of the police and security services.

Fifteen minutes later, after numerous heartfelt apologies to Sam, Gillard was back on the road heading for Westgrave Hall. On the hands-free, he called his team. He'd already alerted them by group text, but some would be there before him and there was no time to lose. The most important person to have aboard at this stage was DC Carl Hoskins.

'Carl, are you at Westgrave Hall or in the bunkhouse?' he asked when the detective picked up.

'At the hall, sir. I'm in the kitchen.'

With Tatiana no doubt, Gillard thought. 'Look, Carl, there is a contingent of spooks on their way down, I need you to make sure the evidence van is secure. I don't trust them to leave things alone.'

'Is this connected to the bomb blast outside Buckingham Palace?'

'Very perceptive, Carl. Yes, it is.'

'I can't take any credit for the insight. Wolf left here some hours ago driving the limo and I've not been able to reach him on his mobile.'

Gillard didn't want to jump to conclusions, but this was sounding worse and worse. 'Where was he going?'

'I don't think anybody knows. Maybe to fetch Anastasia, because she was in central London, wasn't she? Tatiana thinks she's staying at the Dorchester.'

Gillard thanked him and cut the call. He rang the Met to ask about Oleg Volkov. The call handler left him on hold for ten minutes, and then she said, 'He's no longer at his designated address.'

'Shit! Can you find out when he left?' Oleg was breaking the terms of his bail by leaving the Knightsbridge flat, but that was the least of his problems if he had been in the limo.

'Hold while I check, sir.'

It was another couple of minutes before she replied. 'We don't currently possess that information.'

'Isn't he under surveillance?' Gillard said, trying to keep the irritation from his voice. He didn't want to shoot the messenger, who was only doing her job.

'I don't have that information, but I imagine we're stretched for resources given the Buckingham Palace incident.'

Gillard apologised, thanked her and cut the call. Either Oleg or Anastasia could be in that limo. Possibly both. His head spun with the possibilities. Finding himself in heavy traffic on the A3, he hit the blue lights and put his foot down.

And he hadn't even had chance to investigate his hunch about Sophie.

–

Gillard arrived at Westgrave Hall just after eleven p.m. to find two police patrol cars and two unmarked black BMWs already there. He sat in the car and used his phone to find the latest news, which now said that a female bystander and a male inside the car had been killed. The driver was in intensive care, with life-changing injuries.

Poor Wolf, if that's who it was.

Gillard peered out of the windscreen. A number of suited spooks, heavy with lanyards, were emerging onto the steps from the grand main hall. A bespectacled uniformed chief superintendent was conversing with a small man with a baggy suit. Haldane. Gillard sighed, and got out of the Vauxhall. Seeing him approach, the MI5 officer greeted him, before turning to his colleague.

'May I introduce you to one of your country cousins?' Haldane said. 'This is Detective Chief Inspector Craig Gillard of the Surrey force.'

'Clive Basford, anti-terrorism.'

'I know you by reputation, sir,' Gillard said.

'You're no slouch in that department yourself,' Basford said. 'I take it you have been briefed on the bomb?'

'No one's told me anything, sir. I've had to rely on the TV,' he said, looking pointedly at Haldane.

'All right,' Basford said. 'Our best guess is that it was a couple of pounds of plastic explosive or something similar, under the centre of the passenger compartment. It will take weeks for us to reconstruct from fragments.'

'Anything about the victims, sir?'

'The driver is alive, but critically ill. We're not sure if there were one or two passengers. One is male. It's a pretty grisly scene. I take it you took DNA samples from everyone in the Volkov family, because we're going to need them to cross check.'

'Those were my instructions,' Gillard said. 'Of course, as each of them was verified to be outside the library at the time of the shooting, we have been concentrating on other areas. Speaking of which,' he said turning to the spook. 'How are you doing tracking down Jason Lefsky?'

'I'll let you know when we have him,' Haldane said.

'So you don't have him yet?'

'As I say—'

'Daniel Levin was quite possibly murdered,' Gillard said. 'He was a useful witness in my case. It would be nice if you would co-operate with me as I have co-operated with you.'

'My hands are tied, Craig,' Haldane said. 'Nothing would give me greater pleasure than letting you see everything that we know, but this business here, even the bombing, is only a small part of a very big picture which I'm not allowed to share with you.'

Basford rolled his eyes at Gillard in conspiratorial sympathy.

'We're going to need a look at some of the evidence you've accumulated,' Haldane said. 'But someone appears to have moved the evidence van from outside your mobile incident room. I trust it hasn't been stolen?'

'We have operational reasons to keep evidence secure.'
Gillard didn't actually know, but he hoped that it was
Hoskins who had moved the van.

'Well, let's start with the CCTV then, shall we?'
Haldane said.

—

Gillard walked with Haldane to the Westgrave Hall
control room, and was surprised to find that it was already
occupied by three of Basford's anti-terrorism officers, two
of whom were making themselves at home in front of the
CCTV monitoring station. He had recalled that entry was
controlled by an iris scanner, but then remembered that
Wolf had discovered some spyware in the rear USB ports
of the main computer there. This may well have explained
why the officers were able to get in.

One of the officers turned around to Basford. 'Sir, from
the footage we've seen so far, the limousine seems to have
been parked in the garage for at least a couple of weeks,
which dramatically restricts the number of people who
could have had access. We're looking through the internal
CCTV records now, but there's certainly nothing in the
preceding three or four days that arouses suspicion.'

'Perhaps the bomb was planted when the limo was
away from here,' Gillard said.

'That's the direction we are leaning in,' Basford said.
'The satnav device in the vehicle was destroyed, but we
should be able to get access to the satnav's GPS data from
the server to find where else the car had been. We will
be in a better position once GCHQ has taken a look. If
anything can be retrieved, they can do it,' he said.

Basford excused himself to take a phone call. He then
called Haldane over and took him out of earshot of

Gillard. Just looking at their faces showed it was something momentous, so he concentrated on reading lips as best he could. It was a skill he'd been taught by a female machinist while working in a noisy factory in his late teens, and he still practised it when using public transport or in busy pubs.

Haldane was shaking his head. All he caught of the conversation was Basford saying: 'The DNA matches.' That was a good start. Lip-reading is all about context, and then hanging missed words between known syllables to produce a kind of predictive text. Big words were a great help.

'But witnesses said it was a bystander,' Haldane replied.

'I don't think so. Most of her was blown out of the car,' Basford whispered. 'That's why they thought that.'

'And the male passenger?'

'Bodyguard, possibly. We've recovered parts of what might be an earpiece, and a radio receiver.'

'Geneva didn't tell us she was coming back,' Haldane hissed, shaking his head ruefully.

'Well, with her precious son under arrest, are you surprised?' Basford said.

Gillard now knew who they were talking about. Yelena Yalinsky.

He called across to them. 'Is Yelena dead, then?'

Neither replied, but the look on Basford's face was a complete giveaway. He'd never make a spook.

'Is she dead or not?' Gillard said, as he approached.

'Yes, Craig. She was in the car,' Haldane said. 'Happy now?'

'Far from it. She's my only witness, the only one who actually saw what happened in the library.'

Haldane looked at Basford. 'Yes, it is really quite inconvenient all round.'

'The logical deduction is that whoever blew up the car is the gunman, who wanted her silenced,' Gillard said.

Haldane just looked at him, his blank countenance neither confirming nor denying. Gillard turned to the less opaque visage of Basford.

'That sounds reasonable, Craig,' Basford said. 'But there could be other reasons.'

'Such as?'

The question hung in the air like smoke before dissipating.

'We'll keep you in the loop, where we can,' Haldane said, turning away and bringing Basford with him.

–

Within an hour, MI5 and its minions had gone. In the small hours of Saturday morning, Westgrave Hall was in the hands of grim-faced junior staff, many of whom were clearly distraught about the news on Wolf. They locked up all but the essential rooms, and turned off many of the lights, leaving just a collection of candles lit in the biggest fireplace, in front of the biggest Christmas tree. Some of the chambermaids and kitchen staff were gathered there. Some, including Mrs Bell and Tatiana, planned to maintain a vigil through the night.

Gillard was the only member of the detective team present, though four police constables were still dotted about the exterior of the hall. One of those was guarding the capacious Westgrave Hall garage, where the evidence van had been parked amongst the sleek Ferraris and Maseratis. Carl Hoskins, who had stayed as long as the kitchen was open, had let Gillard know about the van as he signed off an hour ago. Hoskins was presumably asleep in the village hall bunkhouse.

After spending far more hours than he cared to count sitting in the damp, smelly Khazi, it was two a.m. before Gillard got the chance to put aside the minutiae of the case and reinvestigate his hunch. Natasha's remarks had reminded him of something. Sophie Cawkwell's first husband, an art collector called Monty Moore, had died a dozen years ago, at the age of fifty-eight, just two years into the marriage. It had been mentioned in passing in one of the articles he'd read about the Westgrave murders. He searched online for more detail and found it in an obituary in *The Times* in April 2007. Moore, it seemed, was a wealthy art collector more than twice the age of his bride. She had inherited the bulk of his art collection, although his family had contested the will, and a partial compromise was ultimately made.

Fascinating. It seemed Sophie was already rich. The one thing not mentioned was how Monty died. That answer he found in a smaller *Daily Mail* piece. He had apparently taken his own life. A collection of prescription medicines was found at his bedside alongside a suicide note. Moore had a history of depression. Sophie was abroad at the time and returned to find his body.

Just as she had found the body of her beloved fiancé Sasha.

Interesting.

Arranging the suicide of her first husband would be complex enough, but for the killings at the library, she would have needed an accomplice, someone to pull the actual trigger, who was inside when she was out. The bearded man in the dark clothing that Yelena Yalinsky had identified. And there was still no explanation of how this person, whoever he was, had managed to get in or out.

Gillard had requested a criminal record check on all of those who were key witnesses but had relied on his subordinates to notify him of anything worth looking at. Sophie Cawkwell's record hadn't been notified to him, so he assumed she didn't have one.

That wasn't quite true.

Once he made his own checks, it was quite interesting. Formally, his underlings were correct. She had no convictions, bar speeding. But in 2005 she was prosecuted for assault, then cleared, at a magistrate's hearing. That it never went to Crown Court implied it wasn't a serious assault, but still. There was no detail on who was supposedly assaulted. Could it have been Monty Moore? It had all happened several years before she became well-known. Googling her in greater detail, he learned several more intriguing facts: Ms Cawkwell had spent several postgraduate years in Russia and Kazakhstan. One of the interviews mentioned her impressive command of Russian.

Useful, of course, if you spend a lot of time digging up fossils in the former Soviet Union. And for other things too.

He emailed Claire Mulholland and asked her to visit the TV presenter first thing tomorrow. Perhaps then they would get some answers.

-

Just before three a.m. Gillard got a text from Rob Townsend, and a whole trove of new and damning evidence about Oleg Volkov. It was tempting to think of the young Russian as no more than a spoilt brat, with his sports cars and scantily-clad hangers-on. Certainly, the photographs that Townsend had uploaded to the evidence database showed an ego well out of control. As the research intelligence officer had hinted, looking through this lot was going to take months. As well as the public Instagram account, they had access to Oleg's private hard drive, and Townsend had pre-labelled various sections to examine in a more detailed search. One section covered cars, helicopters, speedboats and various boys' toys, excluding those showing a gun, which Townsend had put in a separate folder. Most of the rest was simply labelled 'home-made porn'. Gillard permitted himself a brief glimpse, and found that Oleg fancied himself a bit of a stud, particularly with amateur student-age women, who were filmed receiving handfuls of banknotes as a prelude to stripping off, and usually a whole lot more. Not necessarily illegal if permissions had been obtained and depending on which jurisdiction the filming took place in, but nasty and exploitative all the same. The detective switched instead into the weaponry section. Most of it was shooting range footage, which from the accents of the instructors looked to be set in the United States. Lots of pistol training, automatic weapons. There was even one rather alarming escapade with a flamethrower, in which Oleg blew up some oil drums and an old van. Some of the voice-overs were English, but mostly it was conversation with Russian-speaking friends. Turning back to the boys' toys section, there was one labelled 'jet skis plus miscellaneous' which Rob Townsend had marked as yet to be viewed.

Gillard casually watched a few seconds of each of these generally tedious clips, mainly show-off stunts of Oleg racing round the Black Sea coast on a jet ski with some bikini-clad babe on the back. After six trips into the manic ego of the boy-king Oleg, Gillard gave up. His eyes were drooping and he was yawning almost continuously.

Somehow, he just didn't seem to be thinking straight. All this work of Townsend's was a waste of time. It didn't matter how much of a gun enthusiast Oleg was, it didn't matter how many times he posed with weapons or played at firing ranges or even that he had the motive of inheritance, or perhaps hating one of the victims. None of that mattered. Unless it could be shown that he had paid or instructed somebody to conduct the killing, there was no reasonable chance of securing a conviction. The Crown Prosecution Service would just throw it all back in his face.

With Sophie Cawkwell it was even more difficult. She had been standing in conversation with Lord and Lady Fein up until the time of the shootings. The Russian TV footage had shown her clearly. She had stepped away to check her phone, around the time the shooting started, perhaps giving someone the order, but it was circumstantial without the smoking gun. Given that the murder weapon belonged to Oleg, it was even more of a stretch to see how Sophie Cawkwell could have managed to get it without his permission and then pop it back into his car.

So who else could have got access to Oleg's gun? His own bodyguard, certainly. Anastasia, possibly. She certainly may have known of its existence, and it wasn't hard to believe she hated him. Who wouldn't? But she had been caught on the same Russian TV video, on her own balcony, next door to her brother's, during the early part of the firework display.

Another cast-iron alibi.

A wave of sleep passed over him, and he felt himself flying, hovering over the great slab of fossil rock that lay at the heart of the case. Something hit his forehead and he realised he had been dreaming. He lifted his head off the desk and stared again at the screen, which had reverted to its screensaver. He looked at his watch. Must have been asleep ten minutes. Rubbing his eyes, he realised he was being stupid even considering anyone in the family. Whoever had gunned down three people in the library at Westgrave Hall was also implicated in the car bomb, which had just killed the only surviving witness. Basford had hinted at other motives, but eliminating Yelena was surely no coincidence.

These were both sophisticated attacks, which would indicate a professional. The Kremlin was never far from consideration. After all, that's what most of the newspaper coverage seemed to be implying, even before the car bombing. From what MI5 were hinting, the Kremlin's instrument was none other than Jason Lefsky. Despite his appearance outside the library at the time of the shootings inside, he was still the best candidate for involvement. Perhaps an assassin had been brought in too. Levin's feared Ghost, maybe. Maybe even Marcus Dolan, Oleg's giant bodyguard.

There was only one other person with the right kind of pedigree to have pulled this off. The unpronounceable Wolf had a security background, access to all parts of the building and the electronic systems. He was the sole person who could have remotely turned off the library's internal CCTV. There was only his word that it was ordered by Volkov. Like everyone else, he was outside when the library shooting took place, but he had unique qualifications to be involved.

Except for one thing.

It was almost certainly him driving the limo. If Wolf was the assassin in the library, he couldn't have known about the bomb. That didn't make it impossible. After all, it would be clever of the Kremlin to dispose of the killer and the only witness with a single bomb.

—

Gillard awoke at seven a.m. to a ringing phone. It took him a moment to recall what day it was. Saturday. He lifted his head from the desk, grappled with the landline, then briefly dropped the receiver. He tried to speak, but the inside of his mouth felt as hygienic as a Portaloo at the end of a rock festival.

'You sound quite groggy, Craig,' the chief constable said. 'I hope you're getting plenty of sleep, you need to be rested.'

'I'm doing my best, ma'am.'

'As I was saying, that's one less variable to worry about. I suppose you could call it good news, though it hardly makes this case any less mysterious.'

Gillard clearly had missed whatever it was she had initially told him. 'I'm sorry, ma'am, could you just repeat what you said at the beginning?'

'The dead male in the limousine. He met Yelena Yalinsky from the plane at London City Airport and was caught on CCTV escorting her across to the waiting vehicle. So I think that MI5 are completely baffled, because it drives a coach and horses through their main theory about who was behind the killing.'

'Right.' *But who was it?* He didn't dare ask again.

'So, Craig, hopefully you'll be able to get me a result before the Cobra meeting.'

'Yes, ma'am.'

'Monday, Craig. Don't disappoint me.' She hung up.

What had he missed? He scrolled through his phone, checking texts or emails that had arrived while he was asleep. There was nothing from Corrigan, but he was CC'd into one email from Chief Superintendent Clive Basford from the anti-terrorism branch, which gave him the name of the dead man inside the limousine.

Jason Lefsky. The ponytailed bodyguard. ID found on the body, and the DNA checked out.

Shit.

That really threw a spanner in the works. Lefsky was Gillard's number-one suspect for actually planting the bomb, but now he was a victim. The email also mentioned that Wolf was confirmed as the limousine driver. He was expected to live but remained in intensive care.

Attached to the email were dozens of graphic photographs of the crime scene which showed just how severe the damage had been. Fortunately, none of the bystanders had died, despite initial reports to the contrary. Most of the blast had been channelled upwards and injuries were largely the result of broken glass.

Feeling fairly bilious at seeing all this on an empty stomach, Gillard pulled himself upright, stretched and yawned, then lurched to his feet. He decided to seek out the bunkhouse, where breakfast might be available. Once there, he found Carl Hoskins doing what he loved best, eating. With him were a couple of uniforms, one of whom he recognised as last night's custodian of the Khazi.

'Hope you don't mind me saying, sir, but you look terrible,' Hoskins said to the suppressed amusement of his colleagues.

'I only got a couple of hours sleep,' Gillard said, rubbing his jaw, where a sandpaper-like growth of five o'clock shadow was making itself felt.

'Seems like all the suspects are killing each other off,' Hoskins said.

'Yeah, when there is only one left, we'll certainly know who to charge,' said one of the uniforms.

'Yes, it's so very simple isn't it?' Gillard said, as he walked up to the counter and ordered a full English.

–

He was making his way up the drive back towards the Khazi when Claire Mulholland rang him.

'Morning, Craig. Busy night, by all accounts.'

'Tell me about it!'

'I'm on my way to Sophie's, as requested. I've read your list of questions, though I don't quite get what you're driving at.'

'Well, it's just a hunch at the moment—'

'Oh, before I forget, Sussex Police has made progress. Lots of evidence has emerged around Daniel Levin's camper van. Footprints, and some tyre marks. There were indentations on his wrists, which might indicate he was tied up.'

'Tied up, then drugged and left to die by asphyxiation in the exhaust fumes. It was an old diesel, so he had no chance.'

'That's what I'm thinking,' she said. 'But we'll never get the chance to ask Jason Lefsky about it.'

'Nor about the shootings in the library.' He made his apologies, then rang off to take a call from DC Rob Townsend. The research intelligence officer had already texted him to say he had found something exciting.

'Hi Rob, what have you got for me?'

'Something I hope will be very useful,' he replied. 'It's a text. I've been working with the anti-terrorism guys, and I suggested that we try to find any phones that were in the exact location outside Buckingham Palace when the bomb went off. We have that timing to almost the second.'

'There must have been hundreds of phones,' Gillard said.

'Yes, of course. But we were able to use some new software from GCHQ which analyses tower data to separate out all the phones which stopped giving out their location at the exact moment of detonation.'

'You mean any phones that were destroyed?'

'That's essentially what it tells us, yes. In theory, any bystander phones that were just turned off at that moment would be caught too. But at a moment like that, phones are turned on, not off. Anyway, we traced two pay-as-you-go phones, one which we think from its history belonged to Lefsky, and the other which was bought at Geneva Airport on Boxing Day.'

'Whose was it?'

'The text we found gives it away, even though it's unsigned. It was sent to Oleg the same day the phone was bought, and almost immediately deleted on his phone. It's in Russian, but I've appended a translation.'

Gillard held the phone in the crook of his neck while he opened his iPad, and checked emails. It was there.

Я видел пистолет, Юрий. Я знаю, что это ты. Ради бога, почему?

I saw the gun, Oleg. I know it's you. For God's sake, why?

Chapter Sixteen

'Yelena knew it was his gun,' Townsend said. 'Presumably the fact it was golden.'

Gillard thought for a moment. 'Rob, there is something really strange about that. To me it indicates that Oleg wasn't holding the gun, because she would have talked about recognising *him*, not recognising the weapon.'

'Unless he was in disguise. The mask, and the beard she mentioned.'

'I don't buy that. Any mother would probably recognise her own son, even if he had a false beard. She must've been on the balcony across from the shooter for a good half-minute.'

'I suppose so.'

'Likewise, she would have identified the big bodyguard, had it been him,' Gillard said. 'Dolan has been with Oleg for a couple of years. Rob, let's suppose you're right and she didn't recognise the assailant. If someone comes for you with a gun, right, even if you don't know him, your first thought is that *he* is the murderer, not whoever owns the weapon. Wouldn't you agree?'

Townsend was silent for a moment. 'I imagine so.'

'Don't you think that's a really odd thing to say?'

'Maybe.' Townsend said. 'She had already rung Oleg's Knightsbridge landline. The call was connected for two seconds, not long enough either to talk, or leave a message.'

'I remember seeing that logged before, but I can now see its significance,' Gillard said.

'Can you?'

'Yes. Look at it this way: Oleg and his mother were close, by all accounts. There was a huge volume of calls between their mobiles logged in the days running up to her arrival for the party, as you might expect. Far more than there were between her and Anastasia. There were quite a few calls from Oleg to his mother in the days after, but none going the other way.'

'MI5 had her phone for most of a day, that's probably why. And she hadn't yet bought this burner.'

'Okay, but his were short calls, probably messages left and not returned.'

'Not returned initially because of what she'd seen?' Townsend asked.

'She was clearly upset, but maybe didn't want to tackle him about it initially. Particularly by mobile phone, because she feared she would create evidence implicating him. She didn't want to do that.'

'But he tried to kill her – or at least she thought so.'

'Did he? If so, why was everybody killed but her? She didn't even have a scratch.'

'She'd still be pissed off. That's why she didn't return the calls.'

'Initially, okay. But you can see from the text how baffled she is.'

'Okay, sir, but as we know Oleg wasn't in there.'

Gillard sighed. The same roadblock, once again. 'Yes I know, Rob, thanks for pointing it out.' He thanked him and hung up. Every time he thought he was getting somewhere, the same inconvenient truth kept raising its ugly head. He had less than two days to find the culprit before the chief constable was put on the spot in front of the prime minister at the Cobra committee meeting.

-

Simon Woodbridge was sitting at home in Redhill, watching the TV, and his smirk had returned with a vengeance.

He'd only got back first thing this morning after staying the Friday night at the Dorchester with Anastasia. She had been glued to the coverage of the Buckingham Palace bomb, and until late that night had been texting and phoning people all over to try to find out more. She had watched with her hands covering her mouth as the drip, drip of news gradually emerged. At four in the morning she had asked him whether he had got a text from Jason. He hadn't. Nor had she. So she rang him. There was no reply, and Jason's message mailbox was full, she told him. A gradual smile crept over her face her eyes wide with excitement. 'Omigod, I think he was in the car,' she said. 'Our problems are solved.'

In celebration, she had once again used her unique talents to take him to heaven.

When he woke up, she offered him a job as a bodyguard, to replace Jason.

Exhausted but happy, he had made his way home to be ready for his midday shift start at Redhill police station. There was a lot to think about.

It was only when he was eating breakfast that he saw the news flash. *Yelena Yalinsky, wife of Alexander Volkov, confirmed dead in Buckingham Palace blast along with bodyguard.*

Anastasia's mother! Simon knew he had to ring her and offer his commiserations. Even though she had admitted they were not on the best terms he couldn't think of anything worse than losing both parents in just a few days.

He rang her mobile and left a message. Then he rang the Dorchester, and was told that she had checked out that morning. Of course! With Jason dead she would finally feel safe to go back to Westgrave Hall.

–

To try to clear his head, Gillard decided to walk through Westgrave Woods. A path ran directly north past the chapel, through pastures full of grazing sheep, and into the trees. The rain from the previous two days had turned the path into quagmire. His wellingtons skidded as he turned off the main path and onto a winding track that led between hawthorn and blackthorn bushes, the latter still bearing wrinkled blue sloes. He entered a clearing, where the stumps of a few trees felled years ago were rotting. One dead tree seemed to have been used for some kind of target practice. When he went up to examine the holes, he could see that this was not shotgun fire, but something more substantial. The tree had been hit from several sides. He dug around in the undergrowth and eventually picked up a couple of cartridge cases. Superficially, they looked similar to those from Oleg's golden gun. The tree had staples in it too, holding fragments of soggy card. Perhaps targets had been pinned there.

It was increasingly clear that Oleg had lied to them, and had been practising shooting at Westgrave Hall, just as he had done in the gun ranges of the United States.

Where on earth was he now?

At the sound of movement Gillard looked up. He could hear panting noises, animals approaching at speed. Two giant wolfhounds were galloping towards him. He stepped behind the dead tree and the two Borzoi dogs raced past, looping round in a big circuit. In the distance he could hear a woman's voice, calling in Russian.

Anastasia.

Eventually she came into view. She seemed shocked to see the detective there, peering from behind the bullet-riddled tree.

'Are you playing hide and seek with me?' she asked.

'With your dogs, yes. They were running straight at me.'

She waved away his explanation. 'Pyramus and Thisbe wouldn't harm a fly.' She approached him, her face pallid, her expression sullen.

'I'm very sorry to hear about your mother,' he said.

Her gaze flicked up briefly to him, before turning out towards the lake, whose lambent light seeped in through the dark silhouette of the trees. 'Mr Gillard, there is nothing good in this world. Pain and suffering, there is nothing to look forward to.'

That is probably because it all came too easy, he thought.

They walked in silence back towards the northern shoreline, with the mansard roofs and belfry of Westgrave Hall looming in the distance.

'Do you have any idea who planted the bomb?' she asked.

'No. The investigation is being handled by the Metropolitan Police. I'm sure they will announce it as soon as they know. But I'm afraid I can't discuss it with you.'

'Do they suspect my brother?'

'Well, as you know he has been questioned about the shooting. And he's been charged with possession of an unlicensed weapon.'

'Ah, the famous golden gun. He loves to show it off.'

'Do you think he killed your parents?'

'I have thought about it very much. But I don't think so. I think it was Jason.'

'Why him?'

'Because the Kremlin was paying him, and because he was a bitter and jealous individual.'

'Really? In what way?'

She sighed. 'He blackmailed and abused me. He discovered I had been having a relationship with Bryn and threatened to tell my father.'

'You had a relationship with your father's bodyguard?'

'I was in love with Bryn. It started when he was my personal bodyguard in Switzerland, and I was still underage. We worked very hard to keep it secret and never messaged each other or took pictures, but Jason obviously suspected.' She pointed back to the hall. 'He had rigged my room here with video and caught me and Bryn together.'

'The good old Soviet *kompromat*.'

'Exactly. I told Bryn, and he wanted to kill Jason, but he was too clever. Jason said the video was ready to go off to various websites and my father's email at the touch of a keyboard. Bryn was worried that his wife would find out and that he'd lose his job and his marriage too. Something must have happened though, because my father swapped Bryn and Jason, so that Bryn became his personal body-guard here, and Jason came out to Geneva as mine. I didn't like Jason, but he made it clear he wanted me. I was young and I didn't know what to do. I had no alternative but to agree to sleep with him.'

'You must have felt used.'

'I did, and I do.'

Gillard said nothing. This unexpected confession completely explained the young woman's state of mind, and her unhappiness. Everything in her life seemed to be transactional. She'd lost her father and her lover in the same shooting, her mother and abuser in a bomb.

They were almost back at the hall now. Gillard had to get ready for the noon incident room meeting in just over half an hour, and before that there was more electronic evidence from Oleg's hard drive to be examined. So after confirming with Anastasia that she would still be at Westgrave Hall throughout the weekend he arranged to interview her again later that afternoon, after he got back from re-interviewing Oleg at Staines police station. It was going to be another frantic day.

'And I'd still like to examine your phone,' he added.

'I'm sorry. I have had my privacy violated enough for a lifetime. I don't need more. Besides, the video is on there. Ironically it's my only picture of lovely Bryn.'

Gillard knew he could get a warrant, but it might be easier to find the same evidence on Jason Lefsky's phone. Though the device was destroyed, there would be copies on various external provider servers, especially if he'd sent them to her to force her submission.

The world is full of bastards. It's the solid truth.

–

Gillard had only been back a few minutes when there was a firm knock on the Khazi door. It opened with a gust of cold damp air. The duty constable leaned in. 'Someone to see you, sir, says it's important.'

'Okay, just a mo.' Gillard threw a dustsheet over the whiteboards which detailed the investigation and stood aside as Mary Hill made her way up the wooden steps and into the mobile incident room. She was dressed in an old grey anorak with green wellingtons and was carrying an ancient canvas tool bag.

'What can I do for you, Mrs Hill?'

'I need to talk to you, confidentially.'

Gillard nodded at the constable that he could leave them alone. When the door was closed, Mary placed the tool bag gently onto the desk where Gillard was sitting.

'I've come to confess to the killings.'

His jaw dropped.

'I was just fed up with them, the whole lot of them parading their money and their entitlement—'

'I'm sorry, you said you killed them?' Gillard was tired, exhausted even, but now he was hearing things.

'Yes, I planted that car bomb,' she said simply. 'It was shortly after that appalling son of theirs—'

'Mrs Hill, sit down and just tell me exactly what you did.' Gillard reached for his notebook, and when he turned back was looking down the barrel of a revolver, snatched from the toolbag. His throat went dry. She was holding it correctly, right arm straight, left hand braced on the grip, over her right, both thumbs forward. Her aim was steady and the safety catch appeared to be off. This woman knew what she was doing. She'd been trained.

'I could just finish it now, couldn't I? Shoot you, then myself. Then it would be over.'

'Calm down, Mrs Hill.' The detective moved his legs slowly from under the desk, hoping to be able to lunge for the weapon, but she stepped back, into a position where she could cover him and see the external door too. 'Don't try anything. I may be seventy-three, but you'll find I have quite quick reflexes. I wouldn't want to be responsible for another death.'

'Put the gun down, please.'

She sighed heavily. 'I've struggled with this, really I have. I never expected it would work. When nothing happened for a few days I was secretly relieved. But now this, and outside Buckingham Palace of all places.' She closed her eyes briefly, as if uttering a silent prayer. 'I've not decided what to do, but if you try to disarm me, I'll shoot.'

'I'm not going to do anything, Mrs Hill, so long as you stop pointing that thing at me. But please do tell me exactly what you did.'

Mary Hill lowered the gun. 'I built a bomb.'

'How?'

'I have all the requisite knowledge.'

'But where did you get the explosives?'

At the mention of the word, she again lifted the weapon and pointed it at him. 'I've had the explosives for many years. And some of the other components. My husband, my first husband William, that is, served in the army in Northern Ireland, in the Royal Engineers. He uncovered a bomb factory near Newry in 1981, and secretly brought back things from it that he thought might be useful one day. Seven or eight pounds of Semtex, some lead azide detonators, that sort of thing.'

'What on earth was he intending to do with them?'

She laughed softly. 'He used to joke that they would come in useful in case Anthony Wedgwood Benn ever became prime minister. I don't think he ever *really* intended to use them.' She stopped and her eyes grew unfocused. 'A year later our car was blown up by a culvert bomb in South Armagh. He was killed, and I lost part of a leg. For years I fantasised that I should like to use the IRA's weapons against them.'

'And you assembled this bomb on your own?'

'Don't be so patronising—'

'I'm not talking about your capabilities, Mrs Hill, I'm asking if you had an accomplice.'

'No. You know, when I was in the WRAC I went on several bomb disposal courses. I came top every time, but of course they would never use women on the frontline in those days, except to search female shoppers in Belfast. I have a degree in electrical and chemical engineering, and William used to show me some of the devices he'd defused. I found it all fascinating.'

'Is your current husband involved?'

'Colin?' she scoffed, with a brief peal of laughter. 'No, Colin doesn't know anything about this. He'd be shocked.'

'Mrs Hill, *I'm* shocked. Anybody would be. You've confessed to committing an act of terrorism which has killed at least two people and changed the lives of many others.'

'I know. It's disgraceful. I regretted it weeks ago.'

'I'm sorry, weeks ago? I don't follow.'

She rolled her eyes as if talking to a particularly stupid child. 'As I said at the beginning, it was after that road rage incident, in which Colin was assaulted.'

'Sorry, when was that?' Gillard had a vague memory.

'Colin was assaulted by Oleg Volkov's big security man on December 4th.'

'Ah, yes. That would be Marcus Dolan.' He remembered now. He'd seen the case report written by PC Zoe Butterfield. Insufficient evidence for prosecution.

'The police just never do anything, do they?'

'We most certainly do, when we have enough evidence.'

'Nonsense. I just felt so frustrated! Your lot weren't going to take it any further, and Colin has been completely spineless since he received that damn watch.'

'I'm sorry, what watch?'

'They bought him off! Just like Volkov bought off the minister over that appalling planning application, like they were some Mafia cabal. I mean, these foreigners, nothing more than ill-bred chavs with tainted billions to launder, just come over here and think they can buy anything. For heaven's sake, this is Surrey, not Sicily. And some of us. Will. Not. Be. Bought.' She slammed her free hand down on the desk between them.

'How did you get access to the car?' Gillard asked, watching carefully for an opportunity to seize the gun.

'It took me two days to prepare everything, December 6th. I went out very early with the dog. It was still completely dark, and I cut through from the public footpath which runs along the edge of the Victorian walled garden. It's pretty much hidden from view and takes me straight to the rear car park. There are always lots of vehicles parked there, and I was looking for that armoured car thing.'

'Oleg's Humvee.'

'That's it. I wanted to attach the bomb to that. Anyway, all I could find, apart from the more ordinary vehicles used by staff, was a whole lot of big pickup trucks, and the limousine. So I thought, if I get the limo I might get the whole dratted family.'

Gillard was beginning to understand. 'Oleg's Humvee is usually parked inside the big garage, which I think is alarmed.'

'Well, it wasn't outside, but the limousine was. I crouched down beside the car, and attached the device carefully.'

'There's not much ground clearance,' Gillard said.

'No, indeed. It was quite a stretch, but I'd used powerful magnets so it would stick easily. It was pretty much an exact replica of the one the IRA used to kill poor Airey Neave in 1973. Obviously I didn't want it to go off anywhere round here.'

'Did you use a timer?'

'No need. The bomb used to kill Airey used a tilt mechanism designed to set it off on the gradient of the House of Commons car park. That wouldn't have worked for me. I had no idea where that Russian family would be taking their car, so needed something else, something triggered by the type of traffic conditions that you might get in central London, but probably not around here.'

'Like a sharp application of the brakes?'

'Exactly. I used a modified version of an airbag trigger, a steel ball bearing within a tube, restrained by a relatively weak magnet behind it. Any severe braking would project the bearing forwards, overcoming the restraint of the magnet, and complete the electric circuit. The detonator was simply a small lamp bulb filled with lead azide, which ignites easily on electrical contact.'

Gillard reassessed this woman, who he had first written off as a local busybody. Now he was as impressed by her engineering skills as he was intimidated by her weapons training. MI5, GCHQ and the Met's anti-terrorism unit SO15 seemed to be making the same mistakes as their US counterparts. Mesmerised by threat of Islamic terrorism, mainly knife and vehicle-on-pedestrian attacks, they failed to notice the rather more skilled capabilities of domestic groups. But then who would suspect this upright Church of England verger? Who would have seen her as anything other than a law-abiding pillar of the community?

One burning question remained. 'Was it you in the library, shooting Volkov and Talin?'

She laughed. 'I wished it was. But no. Not me.' The weapon wavered momentarily, as she spread her arms. Gillard lunged across the desk, seizing the gun by the barrel and twisting it upwards. She was strong for her age, but no match for Gillard, who with his other hand and superior weight pulled her gradually, face down, across the desk, pinioning her arms behind her back.

'Constable!' he bellowed 'I need you in here right away with the handcuffs.'

Mary Hill began to sob.

–

An hour later, Gillard and two members of the Met's anti-terrorism unit were crouching in Mary Hill's garden shed, levering up floorboards. She had not been lying. The apparatus of terrorism was there in full measure in a steel box: plastic explosives, detonators, tape, fuse wire, pliers. From the first formal interrogation of her, he was convinced that this was not a false confession.

The garden overlooked the lane and at the sound of engines they looked up. A custody van containing Mrs Hill and two accompanying female constables pulled away from Westgrave Hall, escorted by a patrol car, destination Paddington Green police station in London. She was now the Met's responsibility, and no doubt DCS Clive Basford would be in charge of the case. Gillard's job here was done. He surrendered control of the garden of Mary and Colin Hill's cottage to the anti-terrorism police and headed back to the Khazi. The Met Police's own mobile incident room, a rather grander version of the lorry-mounted Portakabin, was reportedly on its way.

A terrorist bomb outside Buckingham Palace had already stolen the headlines from the murders in the library at Westgrave Hall. When news emerged that a devout Anglican official in her seventies had confessed to the outrage, that would undoubtedly turn it into a media bombshell. Many would assume that the entire case had been solved.

It was quite the reverse.

Mary Hill's confession complicated the case enormously. She'd killed the only witness, and one of the main suspects, without becoming a tenable one herself. CCTV on the night of the shooting showed that she hadn't entered or left the library. She claimed she was at home with her husband, her grown-up children and grandchildren, watching Christmas TV. Colin Hill had confirmed that. In Gillard's view, her alibi would probably prove even stronger than that of any of the partygoers.

Mary Hill could not have fired Oleg Volkov's gun. The big question remained: who did?

–

The incident room meeting had been postponed until three p.m. and with only an hour to go, Gillard frantically reviewed the huge mass of evidence that they had obtained. Over a million items on HOLMES, and most of it, he had to admit, useless. Statements from every butler, gardener, security man and chambermaid at Westgrave Hall, from every casual guest at the party. More than 100,000 photographs across all the searched rooms, and another 10,000 of the crime scene, thousands of finger-print and DNA checks. Haystack upon haystack, and no needle to sew it all together.

He sat in his chair and leaned back with his eyes closed. Going back to detective basics meant examining once again the three key elements: means, motive and opportunity. The means was clear. Ballistics had proven that Oleg Volkov's gun was used to kill Alexander Volkov, Maxim Talin, and Bryn Howell. Testimony from the late Yelena Yalinsky, the only person to witness the shooting, said that a bearded man in dark clothing had fired the weapon. A message on Yelena's phone indicated that she suspected her son Oleg was behind it, which made sense if she had seen the golden pistol she knew to be his. In a sense that skein of evidence tied together quite well. The trouble was it did not accord with anything recorded by the CCTV.

Oleg had been on his bedroom balcony, with a couple of girlfriends. Marcus Dolan, his bodyguard, was in Liver-pool over Christmas and had been seen in a pub there. DC Shireen Corey-Williams had just tracked down the CCTV which proved it. Jason Lefsky, now dead, would have been a great candidate for the killer, having been long suspected as a Russian agent by MI5. He had apparently been blackmailing and abusing Anastasia. There was just the small matter that every witness statement – and the Russian TV footage – had Jason standing outside on the bridge when the shooting began.

Wolf, Oleg, Sophie, Anastasia. Every member of the family, every guest, every member of the staff had the same alibi. As did Mary Hill. They'd all been seen by unimpeachable witnesses outside or away from the library at the same time as the shooting was taking place inside.

Examining motives would not help. Billionaires aren't ever short of enemies, and not even their closest friends can really be trusted when so much money is at stake. Even the immediate family was fractured, divided by geography, divorce, jealousy and intrigue. Above it all loomed the shadow of the Kremlin, seemingly omnipotent and beyond punishment. He feared that in the end this case would join the others: Litvinenko, Peripilichny, Berezovsky, the lucky-to-be-alive Skripals, and many other lesser-known cases that could be laid at Moscow's door.

Gillard paced among the whiteboards, marker pen in hand, connecting arrows between suspects. He could certainly accept that Oleg had both means and motive. If he had an accomplice that would make for opportunity too. But going right back to the crime scene evidence, the bearded man in the dark clothing would have needed to be invisible, to possess the climbing ability of Spiderman, and be wearing a jet pack to leave so few clues. He would have had to have lain hidden and undetected in the library for some time and, after the shooting, escaped the crime scene leaving neither a single footprint on the balcony nor on the snowy roof.

Five minutes to go. He could hear all the members of the team chatting on the wooden steps outside. Going back to basics hadn't helped.

Now, maybe time for something wild.

He had a hare-brained hunch, which had been swirling in his head since yesterday afternoon. It seemed insane, but maybe he should bounce it off the team. There were some good detective heads there. If there was a flaw in his idea, they'd find it.

–

Rob Townsend was the first in, obviously tired but his voice abuzz with excitement. 'Sir, I've got something that may help. Passed across by the Met this morning. It's a message from the answer machine on Oleg's landline in Knightsbridge. I've got it recorded on my phone.'

'Okay, we'll have it as the first item,' Gillard said.

The detectives filed in: Rainy Macintosh, Michelle Tsu, Shireen Corey-Williams, Carl Hoskins and Vikram Singh, all of them holding big mugs of coffee and plates loaded down with doughnuts, danish pastries and fruit tarts.

'Where did you get that lot from?' Gillard asked.

'Liberated them from the anti-terrorism mobile canteen,' Hoskins said, stuffing an iced doughnut into his mouth. 'Just arrived half an hour ago.'

'Seems like the Met need crime tape just to keep you lot off their supplies,' he said.

The team looked brighter and more rested than he felt, and the buzz of conversation about Mary Hill dominated. The smell of fresh coffee was tormenting him.

'There you are, sir,' Michelle said, handing him a pastry on a proper china plate, and a coffee in a mug emblazoned with the SO15 logo. 'Belated Happy Christmas, sir,' she said.

Gillard thanked her and called the meeting to order.

'Where's DI Mulholland?' Michelle asked.

'At Sophie Cawkwell's home in west London.'

'Sir, why didn't you ask me?' Hoskins asked. 'I've been interested in dinosaurs since I was a kid.'

'We dinnae need the answer to that wee question,' Rainy muttered, sinking her teeth into a doughnut.

Gillard held up his hands. 'All right, let's listen to Rob's new bit of evidence while we eat.'

Townsend highlighted the sound file, set his phone mic on maximum and held it up so all could hear.

> 'Oleg? It's Michael. Please pick up if you are there and delete this after listening to it. Oleg, I was very concerned about what you are proposing to do. As your solicitor, my advice is that you are in a good place and cannot be convicted. The course of action you propose, however understandable, will only demonstrate that there is a way in which these murders... Oh, I just got your text. Look. I'll be there in thirty minutes. I counsel you to keep your silence. Call me ASAP if you have the chance.'

'That's Michael Houghton,' Townsend said. 'From the timing on the device, the message was left yesterday while Oleg was on his way to be interviewed at Staines police station.'

'That is very dim,' Michelle said, a frosting of icing sugar around her mouth. 'To leave a message.'

'He was trying to avert a bigger problem, by the sound of it,' Gillard said.

'And a landline is often better than a mobile,' Singh said. 'You can be pretty sure that any electronic message these days is going to be intercepted once a guy has been arrested. I presume he thought that the Met had finished the search of his home and wouldn't be going back in to check the answer machine.'

'Let's forget about the circumstantial,' Gillard said. 'Oleg clearly knows that he could be accused of the killing. That's what Houghton is referring to. We need to know the how-done-it.'

'I've been working my way through his Instagram account,' Townsend said, but then stopped when a radio crackled into life.

> Assistance required! PC Butterfield, West-grave staff car park. HELP!

Then there was a scream, cut off by a buzz. Then nothing. The meeting was abandoned and they all scrambled out, racing down the steps.

Chapter Seventeen

PC Zoe Butterfield was standing in the formal garden which bordered Westgrave Hall's staff car park, sipping a coffee. DC Carl Hoskins had been kind enough to give her a mug full of freshly brewed coffee when she'd finished her turn as sentry for the mobile incident room. There weren't many staff about, so the slow approach of a black Mitsubishi Warrior pickup from the northern track drew her eye. She made her way to a gap in the high and carefully trimmed box hedge for a better and concealed view. She watched the vehicle reverse up to one of the storage rooms in the stable block. Oleg's huge bodyguard, Marcus Dolan, emerged from the Mitsubishi. She had taken a statement from him over the road rage incident in which Colin Hill claimed to have been pinioned on the bonnet of his own car.

She didn't like Dolan.

She didn't like anyone who thought themselves above the law.

Dolan peered around in a way that invited suspicion, and as he passed out of her view she heard what sounded like the rattle of a padlock. Many of these storerooms had been locked, but some had not yet been fully searched. Christmas staffing difficulties, as usual. But each of them carried a hefty Surrey Police padlock. She heard soft cursing as Dolan discovered this. He returned to the Mitsubishi and came back with a metal toolbox. He was clearly up to no good. She felt like calling it in, but suspected it would be several minutes before anyone could arrive and the crackle of her radio would alert Dolan to her presence.

The splintering sound of wood signalled that Dolan was breaking in. Butterfield approached and confronted him just as he was carrying a photographer's hefty silver case to the open rear of the pickup truck.

'Excuse me, have you just broken into a police-secured storage unit?' she asked.

He gave her a grin, the same impervious look he'd worn when she had tackled him about the attack on Colin Hill.

'Don't worry, baby, it belongs to the Volkovs,' Dolan said. 'I'm just getting rid of some junk for them, don't bother yourself about it.' He pushed the box onto the flatbed and went back into the storeroom.

'Sir, I'm telling you to stop.' She advanced, and watched him inside the garage-sized unit, picking up a long wooden crate from among a pile of boxes.

While his back was turned, she walked to the open driver's door and pocketed the keys from the ignition.

'What the fuck are you doing?' he said, having slid the second box onto the flatbed.

'I'm arresting you,' she said, and clicked on her radio to make an all-points call. She had hardly begun to speak when he ran at her. She shielded herself with the open truck door, then darted around the front of the vehicle to the passenger side, still calling for help on the radio. He slammed the driver's door and went after her. What she hadn't expected was his athleticism. The big man put one hand on the bonnet and pivoted on it, leaping across the truck at her. The scissor kick aimed at her head only missed because she ducked, but smashed into her arm and knocked the radio from her hand.

She tried to run. But he was on her in a second and pulled her effortlessly off the ground. She managed a piercing scream, cut short as a giant fist crashed into her midriff. She doubled up in breathless agony. Dolan slung her onto the bonnet of the Mitsubishi as if she weighed nothing, holding her with one hand while he searched her for the keys. She tossed them as far away as she could, hoping that they would slip down the nearby grating. The big man swore and threw her off the truck bonnet. She landed a dozen feet away and scrambled to her feet in front of the pickup as he scooped up the keys.

She felt at her waist for the Taser, snug in its holster and buried under her hi-vis jacket. It wasn't a great location for a quick draw. Dolan had jumped into the Mitsubishi and gunned the engine before she could take proper aim. The vehicle was moving, forcing her to jump aside. As she fired, the Taser's wired darts bounced off the vehicle without apparent effect. The pickup slid past; she dodged the shoulder-height wing mirror then lunged in over the back. She was only five foot four, and just managed to grab at the longer crate, a few feet in from the open tailgate before she rolled off onto the gravel. The box had moved, but only a third of it overhung the flatbed. Dolan sped away, leaving her sitting on the ground, winded, silently cursing her luck.

A quarter of a mile ahead, as the Mitsubishi bounced over a cattle grid, she saw the box fall. If Dolan noticed, there was no sign. Sirens indicated that perhaps he had bigger things to worry about. Two patrol cars sped past, in hot pursuit.

–

Half a dozen detectives stood in a circle in the storage room Dolan had broken into, watching Gillard crouching by the now-retrieved crate. PC Zoe Butterfield had given a breathless account of what happened.

'Dolan will be caught in a little while, but I think we may already have our answers here,' Gillard said.

'Let's open it,' Hoskins said. The box looked military, with white stencilled markings in a language they didn't understand.

'Sir, we should get the anti-terror laddies to take a wee look first,' said Rainy Macintosh. 'We dinnae want it to blow up in our faces.'

'Don't worry,' Gillard said. 'If it didn't blow up after falling off the back of the truck, I think we're safe.'

'Dolan didn't handle it as if it were dangerous,' Zoe added.

Gillard flicked open the catches and lifted the lid.

'There's an AK47 automatic rifle, and some ammunition,' he said. Looking in more closely, he said: 'Aha! There's a lot of sticky white marks on the barrel, just like on the golden gun.'

'What is the significance of that?' Michelle asked.

'It's gaffer tape, and now I think I know what it was used for,' Gillard said.

'Any idea what was in the other box, sir?' Zoe asked.

'Yes,' Gillard said, with a smile. 'Let's get back to our meeting, and I'll share my thoughts. Vikram, can you retrieve those little bits of plastic you found at the crime scene?'

'It might take me a few minutes to find them in the van, sir,' he said.

Gillard led all but Singh back into the Khazi, then announced: 'I think I've cracked it. The method, at least.'

'Go on then, sir,' said Carl Hoskins.

'Maxim Talin, Alexander Volkov and Bryn Howell were, as we know, shot by the golden pistol. But no human hand fired it.'

'What?' asked Michelle. 'Someone's got to pull the trigger.'

'No. Oleg's gun was taped to a hobbyist drone.'

'What, one those wee four-rotor jobbies?' Rainy asked.

'Yes.' There was a stunned silence, so he continued. 'It was set up so it could be remotely fired from a wireless console.'

'So we've been wasting our time scouring CCTV looking for the killer entering or leaving the library,' Hoskins said.

'That's right,' Gillard said. 'Using the drone, which would have an onboard TV camera to guide it, meant that the killer didn't even have to enter the library.'

Chapter Eighteen

Michelle Tsu was shaking her head. 'Sir, maybe I'm being dim, but I still don't see how it's possible. How do you pull the trigger?'

'The same way a camera attached to a drone is operated. You just need a solenoid to turn electricity via magnetism into a mechanical action, something like that. You don't need much force, and with lightweight components it's not difficult these days.'

The assembled detectives shared an 'aah' moment.

Rob Townsend nodded. 'There are lots of military drones about, quite small ones. The Israeli army special forces have been using one little bigger than a hobbyist's device to blow up Syrian anti-aircraft missile sites from a mile or two away.'

'Aye, so it was the Kremlin after all,' Rainy said.

'Not so fast,' Gillard said. 'With the miniaturisation of electronics, yesterday's military muscle is today's hobbyist indulgence. Not cheap, but well within the budget of anyone in the Volkov family. I think I can show you.' He sat down at a terminal and called up the database that Townsend had put together of Oleg Volkov's hobbies. 'I think I glimpsed something, just when I was dozing off,' he said. 'Let's see if I can find it. Yes, here it is.'

It was a video set in some desert hills, clearly not the UK. A big pickup truck was in the foreground, with Oleg dressed in sunglasses, T-shirt and camouflage trousers. He was talking in Russian at the camera, as he assembled a drone about three feet across, with four rotors, one at each corner. Gillard was no expert, but the device resembled many of the hobbyist devices he had seen. However, one of the components fixed to the underneath of the drone was a slim metal cylinder about as long as a toothbrush, which he attached with some screws, all the time continuing to talk to the camera held by his friend.

'This is the last bit I remember – it's the worst possible moment to fall asleep,' Gillard said. 'But I have a hunch what comes next.'

'A gun,' Townsend said.

'Exactly.'

Oleg pointed out the handheld console to control it, and there was one word that Gillard finally understood: 'PlayStation.' The console controlling the drone was from a gaming device.

The young Russian then attached a kind of plastic cradle to the belly of the drone, and then picked up something off camera.

The golden gun.

He slid the pistol into the cradle on its side. He spoke on camera in Russian, but from his hand movements it was clear the gun needed to be attached sideways, so that when the extended magazine was fitted it didn't interfere with the drone's landing gear. He then fixed it in place with gaffer tape and attached the cylinder to the weapon's trigger with a retaining hook. The drone took off under Oleg's control, and after hovering briefly set off at speed towards the first target. The crack of gunfire elicited great enthusiasm from Oleg and his cameraman colleague, and after a half dozen shots they rushed forward to examine the targets.

It was a pretty so-so performance, perhaps not surprising given the weapon's recoil, which jerked the quadcopter sharply backwards.

'It explains the lack of footprints,' Michelle said.

'So the wee drone in question is in the other box that Dolan nicked from the storeroom?' Rainy asked.

'That's what I'm thinking. The drone was probably set up in the library long before the party, perhaps on a high bookshelf. After shooting everyone up, it probably flew out through the open skylight.'

'That would be a very precise piece of flying,' Townsend said.

'Yeah, that gap was pretty snug,' Hoskins said. 'I'm not sure that the big drone in the video would fit through.'

'Maybe they used a smaller one. But it does explain why there were no footprints on the roof,' Gillard said.

'And no marks on the wall on the way up,' Michelle added.

'The skylight is on the far side of the pitched roof and not visible from Westgrave Hall, especially with everyone's eyes on the fireworks,' Gillard continued.

Vikram Singh, who just walked in with an evidence bag in his hand, said, 'Oleg must have retrieved the drone, in order to get his gun back.'

Gillard nodded. 'Do you remember Mary Hill saying that she saw someone looking in the lake in the small hours of Christmas Day morning?'

There was a collective 'aah' from the assembled detectives. 'So that was Oleg looking for his drone?' Singh said.

'Hang on a minute,' Hoskins said. 'If it was flown with enough skill to get it out of the skylight, why did it crash in the lake?'

Gillard turned to the sergeant. 'Perhaps you'd care to show us the evidence I asked for, Vikram?'

Singh donned latex gloves and opened the small paper evidence bag. He poured out into his hand the small fragments of grey translucent plastic.

'Rotor fragments,' Gillard said. 'I had been wondering for a long time where these fragments came from, and about the inaccuracy of the shooting.'

'Maybe firing from a drone isn't that easy,' Michelle said.

'Yes, bullets everywhere, including a couple in the ceiling. This perhaps isn't surprising if an amateur like Talin was firing, or the drone itself, but one of them embedded in the ceiling came from Bryn Howell's gun, and his military record shows he is a marksman.'

'Ah! I get it now,' Rob Townsend said. 'Howell was shooting at the drone, above him.'

'And he hit it,' Gillard said, pointing to the fragments of plastic in Singh's hand. 'These are parts of a quadcopter rotor. The drone had three other rotors and was patently not badly enough damaged to crash immediately, so it still managed to get out of the skylight. However, it may have been losing fuel or damaged in some other way, which might explain why it fell into the lake.'

'Och, why didn't he leave it there? What was the point of Oleg retrieving the wreckage and the gun, and then being dim enough to stow the weapon in his own Humvee?' Rainy said.

Gillard smiled again. 'There's a simple reason for that. He didn't.'

'What?' said Singh.

'I don't think Oleg is our killer.'

The room went absolutely silent.

Hoskins scratched his head. 'Sir, I'm not with you. You just spent five minutes showing us Oleg practising with an armed drone, showing how it could be done, and now you say it's not him.'

'I'm with Carl on that,' Michelle said, exchanging a glance with Hoskins before turning back to her boss. 'How on earth did you come to that conclusion, sir?'

Gillard smiled at the puzzled faces of his investigative team. 'Firstly, because the gun was actually planted in Oleg's car. He was right about that. Nobody with the ingenuity to pull this stunt off would have been stupid enough to leave the gun in their own car.'

Several of the detectives nodded in agreement.

'The second reason was the various glimpses we got into the conversations between Oleg and his mother, Yelena,' he said. 'I'd fleetingly thought about drones a day or so ago, when I first noticed gaffer tape residue on the handle of the golden gun. It had clearly been attached to something. The only other reason for using tape, to retain the extended magazine, didn't seem to apply as the magazine fitted perfectly. However, I kept thinking back to Yelena's witness statement, where she said she saw a bearded man in black with the gun.'

Rainy Macintosh's brow furrowed 'Aye, but she had changed her tune, hadn't she? At first she claimed to see nothing, because she was in the panic room so quickly.'

'Yes, but there is a certain motherly consistency, even amidst the lies,' Gillard said. 'Every false statement was made to protect her son, even though she obviously saw the drone and, knowing his interest in them, believed it was him that triggered the gun.'

'Protect him? When he killed Talin, whom she described as the only man she ever really loved?' Shireen said.

'Aye, I'd have dropped the wee sewer rat in it,' Rainy said. 'Spoiled egotistical gun-toting bastard.'

'Really?' Gillard asked. 'If your son killed your ex, would you do that?'

'Och, if Ewan had killed *him*, no. In fact I'd mint the laddie a wee medal.' She waited until the laughter died down. 'But if it was someone I still loved, well, I don't know.'

'Yelena would have been furious and bereft, devastated, but blood is still thicker than water,' Gillard said.

'Was it the text message on the phone that alerted you?' Townsend asked.

'Yes – despite clearly being angry with Oleg, and not replying to his messages, she was still baffled by his motives. Like we said before, using a burner phone and not signing off the message was designed to prevent us realising it was her. She didn't want to tip us off.'

'If our killer isn't Oleg, it could be any of the guests at the party, if they were controlling the drone remotely,' said Vikram Singh.

Gillard nodded. 'It invalidates almost every alibi. In fact our suspects should still include all those who are now dead. Except perhaps Yelena herself.'

'So the late Jason Lefsky is back in the frame,' said Hoskins. 'Mary Hill said it was a man in the boat, and may have had a ponytail. It if it wasn't Oleg, then it was either Lefsky or Wolf.'

'Who is it, sir? Don't keep us in suspense,' Michelle said.

'I'm not sure, but I do know that Sophie Cawkwell was using a drone inside that very library just a few days before the killing. For her documentary, according to Natasha Fein.'

'The papers obviously suspect she was behind the killing,' said Rainy. 'There's a big exposé in the *Daily Mirror* about how much she might inherit.'

'That's so unfair,' Hoskins said softly.

Rainy pinched his cheek. 'Aww, have yer got a crush on our lovely palaeontologist, you poor wee bairn?'

There were some barely-suppressed sniggers. 'Bugger off,' he muttered.

'I thought your heart was pledged to Tatiana, Carl?' Gillard said. Hoskins hadn't been far from the Westgrave Hall kitchens since the case began.

'Och, no sir, that's only Carl's stomach pledged to her, not his heart,' Rainy said, looking at Hoskins' pronounced paunch. 'Though it's clearly the more substantial commitment.'

Gillard held up his hands. 'We'll soon know if I'm right about Dr Cawkwell. Claire is interviewing her this afternoon.'

–

It was just after three that afternoon when Detective Inspector Claire Mulholland arrived at Sophie Cawkwell's home, in the swanky London borough of Richmond upon Thames. Sophie lived in a beautiful whitewashed four-bedroom villa on a quiet side street, less than a hundred yards from the river. The door was opened by a good-looking dark-haired man in his thirties, wearing an apron. He introduced himself as Paul, Sophie's ex-partner. He showed Claire in and offered her a coffee. A young child sat in the lounge playing with upmarket soft toys, while rainforest sounds played on a voice-controlled Alexa unit.

Claire was shown into the dining room, where Sophie was wearing a headset and speaking into a microphone attached to a laptop on the table. She looked up and turned off the mic.

'Deadlines wait for no one, sadly,' she said.

'I'm surprised you feel like doing anything, given what's happened.'

'In times of crisis, I always throw myself into work. Ask Paul.' She indicated her ex with a thumb over her shoulder.

'Is that the National Geographic documentary on the Westgrave fossil you're working on?' Claire asked.

'Yes,' she said, closing the lid on her laptop.

'Actually, could you show me?' Claire asked.

'Certainly.' Sophie restored it, enlarged the screen to full size, and hit play. The footage began on the ground floor of the library in the shadows underneath the giant dagger-shaped rock. As spotlights were turned on, swelling strings could be heard as details of the discovery were intoned on voice-over. The viewpoint lifted from the ground, and the entire keel of the rock was surveyed as if by a submarine floating beneath.

'How do you do that?' Claire asked.

'It's all drone footage these days. We use them for everything.'

'Even inside the building?'

She nodded, and Claire watched as the viewpoint lifted gently in the gap between the edge of the rock and the balcony, until the full glory of the fossil could be seen. Still the viewpoint ascended, then traversed the full length.

'Isn't there a danger of bumping into things?'

'Oh yes, there would be if you did it cold. But you prepare what's called a point cloud, an electronic map of the building. You can slowly traverse that space, and when you're happy with the route, it can be saved to memory. Some big warehouses are already doing stock-takes by drone.'

'Is that all on GPS?'

'No, GPS works poorly inside. It's a different system.'

'That's very clever. I've seen you controlling a drone with a smartphone on TV, is that what you use?'

'I thought you wanted to talk about my witness statement?' Sophie asked, looking puzzled.

'Just indulge me,' Claire said.

She shrugged. 'Smartphone control is certainly coming. I mean, you can already activate a pre-loaded flight plan with a smartphone, but to really do some exploring you need a specialist console. You can use something as simple as a PlayStation, because that has all the joysticks and so on. If you need to know more, I can put you in touch with a real technical wizard.'

'Ms Cawkwell, may I see the drone you were using for this video?'

'Of course. I've got a spare in the garage.'

'No, I mean the actual one,' Claire said.

Sophie frowned. 'I don't have it. It was damaged in prep for the shoot.'

'Were you using a drone at the time of the shooting at the party on Christmas Day?' Claire's tone had become much more formal.

'No, of course not.' Her faced searched Claire's for understanding. 'It was my engagement party to Sasha, it was supposed to be one of the happiest days of my life. Why on earth would I be working?' Her eyes had filled with tears.

'I'm not suggesting you were working.'

'You think I killed him, don't you?' Tears rolled freely down her cheeks.

'You stand to inherit a lot of money.'

Sophie's face distorted and she began to sob. 'For God's sake, I don't care about the sodding money. Everyone says it's all about the money, in the press, all those pointing fingers. I didn't want the money, I wanted the man. Can't you understand that?'

Paul had walked in wearing an apron, with flour on his fingers. He winced at her last statement. 'Please don't upset her, detective inspector. She is in a delicate enough state as it is.'

Claire looked at him and wondered at the loyalty of this man: spurned for a wealthy oligarch yet happy to stay around, prepare food, mind the child and help pick up the pieces of the woman he adored. It's a special kind of love that still smoulders when unrequited.

'Just a couple more questions and then I'll go,' Claire said to him. 'Ms Cawkwell, do you know how to use a gun?'

'No.'

'Really? Wasn't there a documentary which showed you with a rifle slung over your shoulder in Central America?'

She sighed. 'You're referring to *The Hunt for the Moctezuma Basilisk*, aren't you? It was the local guide's gun. The producer suggested I wear it, as he did with that absurd hunting knife. It was simply a prop. It's all about the Indiana Jones look. I've never fired a gun in my life.' She looked up at Paul and rolled her eyes. He turned on Claire with barely-concealed rage.

'Are you for real?' he demanded. 'Coming in here, making ridiculous accusations, based solely on what you've seen on TV? She's just been bereaved!'

'All right,' Claire said, turning back to Sophie. 'Maybe you'll understand why I'm asking these questions. We believe a home-made armed drone was used to kill your fiancé, along with Maxim Talin and Bryn Howell. That drone was very precisely flown, escaping through the open skylight, almost certainly using a flight plan that you created, and was controlled from some distance outside the library.'

Sophie started crying again, huge sobs that shook her slim shoulders.

'No, it can't be. That must be wrong.'

'We're pretty certain, actually. We have video of the party from a Russian TV channel which shows you with your phone in hand as the gunfire began.'

'It wasn't me, I promise you it wasn't me! I loved Sasha, I still do.' She broke down completely, and in the other room, the child started crying too, calling for her mum. The cacophony was pitiful, and Claire felt embarrassed. Maybe she had gone in too hard. But from what Gillard had said, this was the woman with the expertise, the woman who could have set up the killing.

Paul intervened, raising his voice above the stereo wailing. 'Look, detective inspector, I think you had better

334

go, and come back when we've got a solicitor here. Next time give us a bit more notice, if you don't mind.'

Claire nodded, pocketed her notebook and pen, gathered her bag and stood up.

Sophie Cawkwell's grief was convincing. Maybe Gillard's hunch was wrong. Either that or she was a terrific liar. Paul ushered Claire to the door. Just as she was on the doorstep, he called out to her and said, 'You know this is completely unwarranted, don't you? Sophie's in a terrible state, on medication. We have press on the doorstep most days, and the things that are said about her in the newspapers, you wouldn't believe them.' He shook his head.

'I didn't want to upset her, but we have to follow the evidence.'

'What evidence? The drones that she uses are completely innocent, designed specifically for TV work. If you don't believe me, ask Volkov's daughter. She worked with her on the bloody documentary. She's the navigational genius.'

'Is she?'

'Yes.'

Claire's jaw fell open.

Chapter Nineteen

Gillard was still in the middle of the delayed incident room meeting when Clare rang him. Based on what she told him, he wound up proceedings rapidly. Hurrying across to Westgrave Hall as dusk gathered, he looked in vain for a member of staff. Anastasia wasn't answering her phone, and he had a funny feeling that she might do a runner. He ran up the deeply carpeted stairs from the main hall around the landing and then up to the second floor towards her bedroom. The corridor was quiet and when he knocked on her door there was no reply. He rang the police post at Westgrave Hall's gate, still tasked with keeping the press at bay.

'Gillard here, are you aware whether Anastasia Volkov has left?'

'No one's driven away in the hour since I got on duty, sir,' an officer replied. 'But let me check the log. What's her car reg?'

'She could be driving any of the Volkov cars. Perhaps you could check up as a matter of urgency and get back to me. Thanks.' He ended the call, and made his way to the garage, where another uniformed officer was sitting inside a green Maserati, one of a dozen high-end vehicles in the large showroom-sized space. He jumped out the moment he saw the detective arrive.

'Constable, have you seen Volkov's daughter this afternoon?'

'You mean the skinny girl, sir? Not since late this morning.'

'What was she doing then?'

'She took a Volkswagen people carrier, loaded it with loads of stuff, including those massive dogs. Said she was taking them to the vets for some jabs. I've not seen her come back.'

'She's supposed to be staying here! Did nobody think to tell me?'

'Nobody told us. Sorry, sir.'

Gillard looked heavenwards. 'Did she say when she'd be back? Did anyone think to ask her?' He looked back to the PC and saw the look of bewilderment on his face. 'No, of course you bloody didn't. Right, get me the registration number and phone it in, all points, get the damn car traced and stopped.'

Without waiting for a response, Gillard dug out his phone, rang his contact at the Border Force at Heathrow and left a message. 'Hi John, Craig Gillard here, I've got an urgent stop. Anastasia Alexandrovna Volkov, Russian national. Don't let her board an aircraft, any aircraft, going anywhere at all. Can you spread the word to your opposite numbers at Gatwick, Stansted and City Airport? I don't have the passport number or the car reg to hand, but I'll get them to you within five minutes.'

He then ran back to the incident room. Rob Townsend was there, squinting at the screen at something he had found in the huge evidence backlog.

'These are all the files that Anastasia has shared with Sophie Cawkwell and vice versa in the weeks running up to Christmas. They'd not been looked at.'

The original warrant had allowed the police to scour the phones of all guests at the Christmas party. Unsurprisingly there were hundreds of thousands of messages, texts, photographs and videos, the vast majority of which were sitting in a huge archive on the Surrey Police computer and had still not been examined. Less than one per cent of the material had so far been checked as relevant and then logged onto the HOLMES computer.

'What have we got?' Gillard asked.

'It seems that Anastasia did all the grunt work of setting up the basic flight plan to get the drone to move smoothly around the fossil,' Rob said.

'It makes sense for her to be involved in the documentary, seeing as she's studying media and photography.'

'There is a lot of backwards and forwards about technicalities on the messages between the women. I've looked at a few of the videos which were transferred via a file-sharing service. Let me show you one or two,' Townsend said.

The first one was an almost comically haphazard training flight within the library, which from the drone's own camera showed Anastasia with some kind of handheld console attempting to direct the device. The camera swung wildly. There were a few glimpses of Sophie too, and plenty of laughter.

'I recognise that console. It's a PlayStation 3,' Townsend said, turning towards his boss.

'Aha, evidence of a misspent youth,' Gillard replied.

Townsend stopped that video and activated another. This was a short clip showing the device moving very slowly, with a metal rod protruding below the camera.

'Watch carefully,' Townsend said. The drone approached a wall, the viewpoint getting more and more restricted as it climbed slowly until a small metal plate with a button set in it came into view. The drone then manoeuvred until the rod hit the button, triggering a low mechanical hum.

'That's the button to control the skylight!' Gillard said. 'So that's how she did it.'

'Finally, there is this,' Townsend said. This final video was utterly polished and in high definition. The drone began high above Westgrave Hall, showing its many beautiful cupolas and towers, the seventeenth-century crenellations and the mansard roofs. A voice-over by Sophie Cawkwell set the scene for the arrival of an unforgettable long-dead creature from another age. The drone turned and dived gently towards the library building, heading towards the open skylight. There was not much space, but the drone slid through effortlessly, descending gently into the atrium, then over the fossil in all its glory. It moved smoothly above and below the huge blade of rock, showing off its sheer size.

'Right,' said Gillard. 'No doubt Anastasia took this flight plan and adapted it for her own ends by running it in reverse. Starting in the library, going above the fossil for the shooting, and then escaping via the skylight.'

'The actual flight plan used would be stored within the drone's processor. If we had the drone's unique number we could perhaps extract it from a server somewhere,' Townsend said.

'All we need to do is get hold of Anastasia,' Gillard muttered. 'It's all beginning to fall into place.' He held up an evidence bag that had just been given him by DS Singh.

'What's that?' Townsend asked.

'Love letters, from Anastasia to Bryn Howell. They've never been logged properly and Vikram only found them this morning.'

'Sorry, I don't get it.'

'She'd been having an affair with the bodyguard for many months and the correspondence makes clear that he broke it off in December and she was furious about it.'

'Sorry, am I being dim?'

Gillard smiled. 'Right from the beginning, I was baffled by why it was that the bodyguard had so many bullets in him.'

'Ah, hell hath no fury.'

'Exactly.' He looked at his watch. 'Anyway, let's hope we catch her. There are dozens of ANPR cameras around every airport, so we'll get a heads-up as she approaches.'

–

For the next two hours there was frenetic activity in the mobile incident room. Gillard directed most of his team to comb through the stored electronic evidence to find what else they could of Anastasia's communications with others during the days leading up to the party.

Carl Hoskins got to work on ANPR, to see if they could trace the Volkswagen.

It was six o'clock on a Saturday evening, and there was not a single ANPR hit so far, which indicated she wasn't fleeing to an airport. Every airport in the country was ringed with traffic cameras.

Gillard relaxed a little and returned to the Russian TV Christmas party video footage. He looked carefully through it to the point where the fireworks began. It showed Oleg Volkov and Anastasia in the distance on their respective second-floor balconies in the main Westgrave Hall building. Oleg and his girlfriends remained there looking out at the fireworks, for almost the entire time. He had a mobile phone in hand, held up as if photographing the display. That was not the act of a man about to implement a carefully planned murder.

Anastasia, by contrast, seemed unsettled. She only glanced at the fireworks, instead examining her phone before returning to her room. She did not emerge at all during the latter half of the firework display. It wasn't possible to see what exactly was happening when the shots began because the Russian camera had turned away from Westgrave Hall, towards the library.

'Sir, sir,' interrupted Shireen Corey-Williams, pointing at her screen. 'We've got a transaction from Anastasia's credit card.'

'Where?'

'Airport parking at Farnborough.'

'When was that?' Gillard demanded. 'And why was there no ANPR?'

'The parking is for a different vehicle than the one she left in,' Shireen said, then looked it up. 'Ford Focus, 2017.'

'Ah, she's clever,' Gillard muttered, feeling outfoxed. Farnborough Airport, of course. A billionairess doesn't need to go to Heathrow or Gatwick. Private jets are easy if you have the money.

'She paid it four hours ago, I'm afraid,' Shireen said.

'She'll be away then,' Gillard said with a sigh. 'Get me the details of the flight.'

A few minutes later Shireen said: 'I've found the transaction with the airline, on her father's account. He was copied into the email, which says it was due to depart at 14:45, destination Moscow.'

'Damn, she's got away.' Gillard banged the table in frustration.

Shireen looked up from her terminal. 'That Ford Focus is registered to PC Woodbridge. And the manifest shows he's on the flight with her.'

Chapter Twenty

Former police constable Simon Woodbridge had never been on a private jet before. He couldn't believe there was so much space. Just him and her, sitting side-by-side on fat white leather seats looking out of the large porthole as the Hampshire countryside receded beneath them. Once the flight had levelled out, a steward served them chilled champagne and caviar. Anastasia's dogs lay together on a sofa, yawning as if this was how they always travelled.

She had rung him before ten that morning and asked that he come to pick her up in a village a few miles up the road from Steeple Risby. She had parked the VW there, and asked Simon to drive her to Farnborough in his car.

'Why are you leaving in such a hurry?' he had asked when they were on the road.

'Things are about to get heavy at Westgrave Hall. I need time away. I'll tell you later. Have you thought about the job? I really need an answer now.'

'Yes. I'd like to take it. I've brought my passport, as you suggested.' He'd started by calling in sick for his noon shift, and even as he was getting an ear-bashing from the sergeant for such late notice, his decision to resign had crystallised. It was in the end an easy choice. Even if he got to chief inspector, he'd never earn even a tenth of the salary Anastasia had offered him.

Now to consider that exciting future. As her head of security, he'd have lots to learn, foreign languages for a start, and he'd have to get properly fit. She'd explained that he was to be based in Liechtenstein, a place he'd barely heard of, but he'd get a free flat, medical insurance, time off, one-to-one language tuition, all sorts of benefits. Basic income tax there was 1.2 per cent. Brilliant!

The thing he was least sure about was his status with her. Was he Anastasia's boyfriend, or simply an employee? She hadn't clarified that.

As they climbed to a cruising altitude, Simon turned and looked at Anastasia's expressionless face, pressed close to the window. In some lights she did look hauntingly beautiful, but he found her pallor and sullen countenance hard to warm to. Could he learn to love her? He thought so. He obviously adored the hour-long treats she had bestowed upon him, four times now, always with him bound tightly to the bed frame, her in utter control. The hints and suggestions dropped into the conversation about when the next one might be kept him in a permanent state of excitement. He just wondered how long it would be before she agreed to actually make love with him, so he could give something back to her. When he had tried to touch her in the hotel, to give her pleasure, she had shied away. The most troubling aspect was the way she looked at him. No smile, no shine in her eyes.

Nothing. Almost a void.

Perhaps it was the trauma that she had suffered. The bullying and the abuse by Jason. Simon hoped that, with his affection and adoration, she would gradually thaw and they could enjoy a life together, away from all the murder and mayhem. He'd been amazed as she'd told him the choice of homes she'd be able to use: the huge apartments in Moscow and Nur-Sultan, the dacha near St Petersburg, the ski chalet in Switzerland, the castle in Italy, the hunting lodge in Botswana and the private estate near Bordeaux. Given what had happened, the three Volkov homes in Britain and the flats in San Francisco and New York would probably be off limits, at least until things cooled down a bit.

If it worked out, it was going to be fantastic.

If not, there was always the money. He would squirrel away every penny, just in case.

On Simon Woodbridge's face there was just the semblance of a smirk.

–

Several hours later, when they were somewhere above Northern Europe, Simon reached for Anastasia's hand. 'I want to ask you a question,' he said.

'Oh yes?' she replied, continuing to flick through a magazine.

'Now that Jason's gone, are we more than just employer and employee?'

'What has Jason got to do with it?' She was clearly amused.

'He abused you, and your statement says that he raped you, because he knew about you and Bryn Howell.' Simon had struggled with the apparent complexity of this young woman's love life, if love wasn't a redundant word.

'I lied, Simon.' She flicked the page of the magazine.

'About what?'

'Lots of things. I needed to make it seem like Jason forced me to get you involved in digging up the details about Daniel Levin. In fact it was my idea.'

'So he didn't rape you?'

'Simon, Jason was gay.' She was smirking now. 'He never even kissed me. We were friends. I helped him, and he helped me. After he'd got Levin, the plan was to go our own separate ways.'

'Gay? I don't understand. And what about the blackmail? The video that he had. I've seen it, with both of us on it.'

'Yes, but he never had that video. It was me that made it, me that sent it to you. I sent the threatening texts from a burner phone, signing myself off as Jason.' She reached for her Hermès bag, pulled out a phone, and showed him the texts she'd sent. 'See? The last of them I sent when I was in the bathroom at the Dorchester. Jason then spoke to you on my phone, just to give it added authenticity. The video was all my own work, and has now been deleted. I needed it to force you to help him, just as he helped me.'

'You've been deliberately manipulating me!'

'Oh, poor simple Simon, of course I have. Men are so easy.' She looked him up and down. 'You are like the little toy soldiers we used to have in Russia, put a kopek in the slot, and they march to your tune.'

'What did he do for you, in exchange for the details about Daniel Levin?'

She chuckled. 'A little bit of a break-in in Switzerland.'

'Burglary?'

'No, he never took anything, except perhaps some twisted dreams. He simply turned off the electricity to a couple of machines. He'd never have been caught. His Kremlin nickname is Ghost. He's extremely meticulous.'

Simon's frown was getting deeper and deeper, his lips more twisted as he tried to understand.

'What about all the bruises you showed me?'

She looked at him with an expression bordering on pity. 'Simon, I made them. I squeezed my own arms and neck, tied a rope around my own neck.'

He looked at her incredulously.

'Simon, I needed you to be scared of him. I needed everyone to think I was the victim of blackmail, just in case you opened your mouth to the clever Mr Gillard.'

Simon shook his head. 'Right, that's it. I've changed my mind about the job.'

'Think of all the money you won't earn.' She slid the magazine back in a rack, and stared out through the window, over the snowy trees of Scandinavia.

'Ah, but if there's no video, you can't blackmail me anymore.'

'Simon, you are not thinking clearly.'

'Why?'

'Can I ask you, Simon, as you know all about the British police, what would happen to an officer who illegally used police resources to supply the information that allowed a man to be murdered?'

Simon knew the answer – a lengthy term of imprisonment – but didn't dare say the words. 'Yes, obviously, but no one knows about what I did,' he muttered.

She giggled and tapped her chest. 'I know about it. Jason obviously knew about it, and I'm pretty sure that his bosses in the Kremlin got to hear about it. In fact, if the clever Mr Gillard knows his stuff, he will already have checked who it was that typed Daniel Levin's car number plate into the police database, and who it was who searched for the location of his phone. It will come back to you, won't it?'

'I was blackmailed into it!'

'Really? Where's the evidence?' she said, in mock bewilderment. 'Oh, it's been deleted. Silly me.'

She was absolutely right. 'So now you are definitely blackmailing me.'

'No, Simon, don't look at it like that. You work for me, and I need to know that you will be loyal, because I have testing times ahead.'

He stared at her with fresh eyes. 'Did you kill them in the library?'

'No.'

'You're lying!'

'Simon, you know I wasn't there. It's impossible.'

She was obviously lying, but he didn't know what to do. She'd outwitted him at every turn.

'So, Simon, as you've seen my phone, I need to see yours.' He hesitated, until she clicked her fingers and said: 'It's a condition of your employment, actually.'

He passed it over then watched helplessly as she, pretending to be him, dumped his girlfriend Sally by text and then blocked her number. She went on to delete the numbers of all his friends, one after another.

'I am your future. You have no past,' Anastasia said.

Simon stared out of the window. Below, through gaps in the cloud, he could see an endless white wilderness, dotted with trees. A tundra of bleak, friendless isolation, where he was utterly dependent on a woman who thought nothing of murder.

His future.

–

Anastasia had cleared her bedroom at Westgrave Hall of almost everything incriminating. When Gillard and the other detectives broke down the locked door that evening, they found no phones, laptops or computers. No purse or credit cards. Even the dogs' bowls and grooming kit were missing. What she had left behind were wardrobes full of clothes, enough jewellery for a branch of Tiffany and bins full of rubbish.

Breaking remotely into Anastasia's absent phone took another day but produced some interesting results. Townsend did manage to track down and restore a copy of a video from a server on the service provider's site, one that had been deleted on the phone itself.

Seeing how it began, he called Gillard over to look at it.

A camera apparently concealed in the top of Anastasia's canopy bed caught her performing oral sex on someone bound naked to the bed frame. They had both expected the recipient to be Bryn Howell, the *kompromat* video Anastasia had mentioned that Lefsky was using to black-mail her.

'Can't see the face, but he's clearly having a great time,' Townsend said.

'He's too pale to be Howell,' Gillard said. 'It's probably Simon Woodbridge.'

'So Lefsky was blackmailing him too,' Townsend said.

Gillard shook his head. He'd been going through some of the recovered texts between Anastasia and a burner phone which seemed to be owned by Jason Lefsky. 'I think this was more like a joint operation. She compromised Simon, so he would dig up the details on Daniel Levin's location.'

'That's terrible,' Townsend said.

'Why else would he flee the country with her?'

'A daily blow job might be part of the answer,' Townsend muttered.

Gillard grinned at the younger officer's envy. 'Maybe. And her billions, of course. We've got it confirmed from the ANPR database that it was Woodbridge who checked for Levin's camper van registration. I'm sure he was the cop who rang Vodafone for Levin's cell tower trace that evening too, though he used a false name. These are quite incriminating too.' Gillard showed Townsend his own computer screen, where he'd been trawling through the texts exchanged between Anastasia and Lefsky.

'This last one, late on Boxing Day evening, from Lefsky to her, is the clincher,' Gillard said, pointing to the translation of the Russian.

> Он получит информацию сегодня вечером. Я бы не задержался слишком долго после этого. Увидимся в Москве. Спасибо за все xx.

> He's going to get the info tonite. I wouldn't hang around too long after. Tks for everything. J. xx.

'A conspiracy,' Townsend said.

'He was working for Moscow, but her? I'm still not sure.'

'What a nice girl,' Townsend said.

'Damaged, is the nicest thing we can say. Unloved, certainly.'

'Doesn't excuse what she did,' Townsend said.

'No, you're right, but her upbringing was the perfect one to create a psychopath.'

'We will be able to trace her in Moscow, Russia is a member of Interpol,' Townsend said.

Gillard smiled at the naïveté of his younger colleague. 'Good luck with that, Rob. She is connected to some very powerful people and will inherit some critically valuable mineral companies. And if you think she is a transactional person, then she is nothing compared to the powers that be at the Kremlin. Everything with them is a negotiation, a bargain to be made.'

—

Anastasia disappeared off the radar, as Gillard expected. But some things could be traced. On Sunday, with the help of Sophie Cawkwell, research intelligence officer Rob Townsend managed to retrieve every flight plan and video recording that had been produced on all of the drones that Sophie's TV company owned. Townsend wasn't interested in any of the dozens that were in the main database. He went straight to those that were marked deleted, recovering them using a police software tool developed to retrieve deleted images of abuse from paedophiles' computers. The video he showed to the assembled detectives in the Khazi turned out to be every bit as shocking.

'This, ladies and gentleman, is a drone's eye view of the crime in action,' Gillard announced, as Townsend began a big screen projection.

The screen began in black, framed by the gyroscope bearings and a clock along the bottom, which showed it was recorded from the first minute of Christmas morning. After a few seconds there began the sounds of fireworks and coloured light reflected into a dark room. The drone's light came on, showing it was under a table in a dimly lit room lined with bookshelves.

'That looks like one of the library meeting rooms,' Michelle Tsu said.

The characteristic buzz of the rotors could now be heard. The viewpoint rose slowly by a foot, and pivoted slightly, until an open door could be seen. In the distance was loud echoing conversation, several voices and laughter.

'This is amazing,' said Rainy. 'We are seeing and hearing from the murderer's perspective.'

The drone crept forward beyond the last of the table legs, and then gradually began to rise further. It headed for the door, which led out to the ground floor of the library. The lens went to wide-angle, which showed the great dark bulk of the fossil rock above.

The talking in Russian continued nearby and was then interrupted.

'This must be when they heard the noise,' Gillard said. 'They stopped talking because they'd heard the drone.'

'But they wouldn't have been alarmed,' Rainy said. 'Talin and Yelena would have thought it was all part of the show. They knew Sophie was making a documentary about the fossil.'

With a loud buzz, the drone rose rapidly. It soared above the fossil and continued climbing, giving the wide-angle lens a panoramic view below of the sixty-yard balcony, halfway along which three figures could be seen, close to each other, leaning on the rail and looking up towards the drone. Talin was on the left, Yelena in the middle and Volkov on the right.

'They seem friendly enough,' Rainy said. 'A bunch of pals leaning at the bar.'

'It certainly kiboshes the idea they were having an argument,' Hoskins said.

On the screen, Talin pointed right up at the drone, and whatever he shouted caused both Yelena and Volkov to step back from the balustrade.

'Aye, he spotted the wee gun,' Rainy said.

On their screen the lens switched to telephoto, and closed in. Red crosshairs appeared, jerking around as the drone was manoeuvred. The first shot, seemingly aimed at Yelena, came as a loud shock, and the screen jerked wildly.

Once the screen had stabilised Gillard pressed pause. 'I couldnae see where that went,' Rainy said.

'I suspect the operator had the same problem,' he replied. 'It does explain the wild shooting.' He resumed the video, and there were three more shots in quick succession. Talin could now be seen with his own gun in his hand. Volkov was ushering Yelena to the right, towards the end of the atrium where the panic room was, but she was shouting back, gripping the handrail and refusing to move. They were still all within five yards of each other.

Rainy had her hand over her mouth. 'Och, the poor wee hen doesnae want to leave her beloved Maxim.'

The drone's next shot was clearly a bull's-eye, because Talin staggered, and when the screen stabilised a huge red flower of blood bloomed in the centre of his dress shirt. He still managed to get off a couple of shots.

'Missed us,' Rainy said.

'Us?' Gillard queried, pausing the video.

'Sorry, sir. I'm getting a bit too involved.'

The next bit they watched in slow motion, Yelena had escaped Volkov's grip, and had squeezed past to reach Talin. He had staggered back, gun still pointing, but was gripping a bookcase behind for stability. Another flurry of shots from the drone emphasised a target they had already seen: the crosshairs were again on Yelena. The first one missed because she knelt down to attend to Talin, who had collapsed; the second hit Volkov, who had interposed himself between her and the balcony rail.

'Definitely trying to kill her,' Hoskins said.

'But not Volkov, seemingly,' Gillard observed.

The next moment, Volkov grabbed Yelena, plucking her from the ground even as she was holding out her arms and screaming for her beloved Maxim.

'Och, it breaks your heart,' Rainy whispered.

With bullets flying thick and fast, Volkov then ran as best he could, with Yelena in his arms, towards the panic room.

Gillard suddenly exclaimed: 'Ah, *that's* why there are none of her footprints in the blood on the balcony. Volkov carried her for a good thirty yards. It all makes sense now.'

'Anastasia's still trying to get her,' Michelle said, noting the crosshairs that jerkily followed Volkov's progress.

'Oh!' a collective gasp went up from the detectives as a shot aimed at Yelena's head hit Volkov and caused him to topple sideways into the bookcase. He managed to steady himself and stagger the last five yards towards the panic room. It was with seemingly superhuman strength that after taking another bullet, this time in the leg, he pulled open the door with his free hand. He placed his ex-wife delicately on the floor right by the open door.

Gillard hit pause: 'That's the mysterious bloody footprint, right there,' he said.

He resumed the video, and saw Yelena scramble into the panic room, just as three more shots came. Two of them hit Volkov, one in the back of the head. He managed to kick the door to the panic room closed, as he turned around to face the drone. Then, even his massive body twitched from another shot, and he fell backwards against the door.

'He was a hero,' Michelle whispered. 'I thought they hated each other.'

'It's not over yet,' Hoskins said. 'We haven't had Bryn Howell.'

In the thirty-second gap before the bodyguard's appearance, the drone buzzed back and forth, from Volkov's body to Talin and back again. The slam of the library door and the slap of ascending footsteps heralded the arrival of Bryn Howell. The drone quietened and set itself down gently on the surface of the fossil, like a miniaturised moon lander.

'Och, it's staging a wee ambush,' Rainy said.

Howell came to the top of the stairs, and stood with both arms straight out, holding a pistol. He called out 'Mr Volkov?' but got no reply. He must by then have seen the two bodies, because he let slip just one word: 'Shit.' Talin's body was just twenty yards away and that of his boss right at the other end of the library. Professional that he was, Howell looked for the killer. He turned ninety degrees, legs braced towards the balcony by the window. Then he leaned over the balcony and swept the downstairs area. At this point, the drone motors restarted and it jumped off the fossil and headed straight for Howell. Credit to him, he must have heard or seen because his swivel to target was rapid. But five quick shots from the drone found their mark, and he staggered backwards, discharging his own weapon just once before tumbling backwards down the stairs.

That shot caused the drone to rotate, and the engine note changed.

It stabilised, did a quick 180-degree sweep, then shot off at high speed towards the panic room end of the atrium. It hovered by the skylight control, tapped the button with the gun barrel, then ascended sharply, rising upwards and out of the open skylight. The camera caught the dazzling arc lights as the drone hugged the contours of the roof, and headed north, fast and low across the lake and towards the woods. At some point over the water there was another change of motor tone, and it lost altitude, dropping quickly into a watery darkness.

'Amazing,' said Carl Hoskins.

'But the shooting was manual, I take it?' Gillard asked.

'I think so,' Townsend said. 'It's the one thing she had no chance to practise. Recoil was obviously an issue.'

'I think you'd have to be a really good shot to hit the drone,' Hoskins said. 'It's no bigger than a human head, at least the vital bits are.'

'Aye, and it's bobbing and weaving like Ken Buchanan on six bottles of Irn Bru.'

Gillard's quizzical expression earned an explanation from her. 'Scotland's wee flyweight champion. He was my second cousin on my Auntie Myra's side. He won the world championship in 1971.'

'You're a woman of hidden depths,' Carl Hoskins said admiringly.

At that moment, Gillard got a text. He looked at it and announced, 'Oleg Volkov and Marcus Dolan have just been arrested after a car chase.' He stood up. 'They've been taken to Staines police station, so I'm off to interview them. Rainy, why don't you come with me?'

Now that he knew he wasn't in the frame for murder, Oleg Volkov confessed to the firearms offences, involving both the illegal AK47, which had fallen from the back of their truck, and the golden Kahr P380. Oleg admitted that he and Dolan had used an armed drone with the AK47 for target practice in Westgrave Woods but maintained they had never aimed the weapon at any person. Both insisted that the pickup trip to the stables was simply to remove incriminating evidence of the firearms offences. Gillard was inclined to believe them.

'You really think it was my sister who killed them?' Oleg asked.

'Aye,' said Rainy. 'She's skilled with a drone, had plenty of opportunity to practise, and hated her mother. She's also fled the country. If that's not a sign of guilt, I don't know what is.'

Gillard glared at his junior colleague for revealing so much of their thinking.

'I'm a little surprised,' Oleg said. 'I saw her on her balcony, the one next to mine, just as the fireworks were coming to a climax.'

'Aye, but she then went inside,' Rainy said. Gillard grasped her arm, to stop her saying any more.

'What is it you want to tell us, Oleg?' Gillard asked.

'I saw her in the corridor after the fireworks had finished. She was a bit drunk, and said she'd been sick.'

Gillard's eyes narrowed. 'Are you sure?'

'Yeah. I always assumed Jason was the killer.'

'Aye, but—'

Gillard was just in time to escort Rainy Macintosh into the corridor. 'You've got to put a sock in it, Rainy. Don't give out information.' He knew she was about to blurt out that Jason Lefsky was seen on video trying to get into the Volkov Library at the time the shooting was taking place. He clearly couldn't have been controlling a drone at the same time.

'Sorry, sir. But if Oleg is correct then Anastasia cannae be our shooter,' she said.

'That is a very big if.'

Further conversation was halted by a call on Gillard's mobile. It was Rob Townsend, in a state of considerable excitement.

'Sir, you are not going to believe this. I'm at Mount Browne with the electronic specialist team, and we've been taking all Dr Cawkwell's drones apart. They've been trying to link together the electronic flight plan created and adapted by her and Anastasia and the actual device that used it. Dr Cawkwell's drones were mostly standard commercial but we found a couple that had been built around a little computer called a Raspberry Pi. That means they can be controlled by a PlayStation console.'

'Sorry, Rob, I don't get where you're going with all this.'

'The long and short of it is, sir, that we assumed that Anastatisa's PlayStation was used to direct the drone. But it's not true. There is no trace of her PlayStation ID in any of the Raspberry Pi memory files copied to Dr Cawkwell's hard drive.'

'Maybe she had a different device.'

'No, we've found the PlayStation in question, in the evidence van. It had been there for a long time, but of course no one looked at it. Firstly because PlayStations are thought of as toys, and secondly because of where it came from.'

'You're saying it wasn't the PlayStation recovered from Anastasia's bedroom?'

'No,' said Townsend. 'The PlayStation and a load of other computer kit was found in a small bedroom on the second floor of the annexe, one thought barely relevant to the inquiry.'

'Whose room was that?'

'The cook, Tatiana. Her fingerprints are all over both devices.'

'Are you really telling me that Tatiana is our shooter?'

'It appears that way.'

Gillard's brow furrowed as he tried to get his head around this revelation. 'She flew the drone and murdered all three in the library?'

'That's what the electronic audit trail appears to show, sir.'

–

Gillard abandoned the rest of the interview and with Rainy in the passenger seat blue-lighted it back to West-grave Hall. As soon as they got on the road, he rang Carl Hoskins on the hands-free, and found him still in the Khazi.

'Carl, this is one occasion when instead of dragging you out of the kitchen I actually need you to go into there. Straightaway. Find out where Tatiana is, and stop her leaving until we get there. Just make some excuse.'

'Why? What's going on?'

'I'll tell you later.' He hung up.

'Och, Carl's going to be so upset, if she turns out to be the killer.'

'That's why I'm keeping him in the dark for now,' Gillard said.

Gillard arrived to find Tatiana bawling her eyes out in Hoskins' arms. 'It's been awful, I haven't been able to sleep. I knew you'd come for me. Such a terrible mistake, I'm so sorry.'

The portly constable hadn't quite managed to make sense of what she seemed to be confessing to.

'Nah. That's not possible, sir,' he said after hearing what Townsend had discovered.

'I'm afraid it is. And I'm going to ask her myself.' Gillard told Hoskins to stay outside while he and Rainy interviewed her.

—

As they re-entered the room, they saw the ample figure of Tatiana Chumak splayed over the kitchen table weeping, her head in her hands. She had a half full tumbler of what smelled like vodka in front of her, which Rainy quietly moved away as the two officers sat down.

When the cook showed no signs of sitting up, Gillard rested a hand on her arm and said: 'I'm going to ask you directly, Tatiana. Were you controlling the drone which shot Alexander Volkov, Maxim Talin and Bryn Howell?'

Tatiana nodded, still crying, her fist jammed in her mouth.

'Why, may I ask?'

'I could never forgive her.'

'But wasn't it over with Yelena?' Gillard asked. 'Volkov had taken you on, at a higher salary. Wasn't it all in the past?'

'No, not everything. She killed Ibrahim.'

'Sorry, who's he?'

'Ibrahim Kone worked with me in her kitchen in Paris, a lovely man who could sing such songs, with a smile that

360

lifted everyone's heart. She treated him like a dog, because he was black. When I was fired, so was he, but she twisted the knife for him. She reported him to the immigration authorities, said he was a thief, and he was deported back to Bamako.'

'Was he the man who died in prison?' Gillard remembered him from the divorce coverage.

'Yes. He was no thief, but in Bamako they beat him, every day.'

The story that poured from Tatiana's lips over the next hour made perfect sense. She showed Gillard all the letters she had received from Ibrahim, and wept freely. 'He said that the prison authorities knew he'd worked for a wealthy woman and would free him if he paid a hundred thousand euros. I had no money but went straight to Sasha and he said, "Of course, I will pay it for you. Your love must be free." There was no hesitation from him. But when we paid, we heard nothing. Sasha made enquiries for me and discovered Ibrahim had died after a beating a week earlier. His kidneys failed. He was the love of my life and he was gone for ever.' She began to sob again. 'Do you know what Bryn said to me when he heard?'

'Do tell,' Gillard said.

'He saw me crying and said, "Never mind. He probably only wanted you for a passport".'

'Och, he wasnae a diplomat, that's for sure,' Rainy said.

At the end of the interview, Gillard arranged for her to be taken to Farnborough police station and formally charged. The hard part was walking out of the room to tell Carl Hoskins.

Hoskins looked shocked. 'How did she learn how to fly the drone?' he asked.

'It helps that she was a qualified computer technician and was skilled with the Raspberry Pi. She wrote a navigation program for Anastasia on a drone borrowed from Dr Cawkwell, and went out to Westgrave Woods with her on numerous occasions to fly it. Tatiana then borrowed it to practise with on her own, then claimed it had fallen into the lake. Sophie apparently just wrote it off. Tatiana's own desktop computer history showed she had looked at the various videos on Oleg's Instagram account, and saw how to adapt drones to carry guns on them.'

'How did she get the gun, sir, or the keys to Oleg's Humvee?'

'That was easy, by her account. Seeing as she was running a constant room service both to the control room and Oleg's bedroom, she was able to access any of the keys, at least if she picked her moment. She also admitted that it was her that Mary Hill saw early on Boxing Day morning, rowing in the lake trying to find Oleg's golden gun. Mary described a broad figure with a ponytail, and we assumed it was Jason.'

'I suppose with enough clothing and a hat she might look male.' Hoskins looked crestfallen. 'But I can't really believe it.'

'Her original idea was to hide the recovered gun in Oleg's room. But he was still there when she first tried, so she managed to get it in his car instead. Her frequent appearances on the CCTV were never suspicious, as she always seemed to be carrying food about. That was her cover for placing the drone in the library's ground floor meeting room on the afternoon of the party. She had gone in to clear away the buffet she'd set out for Dr Cawkwell at lunch. The drone was, as we saw, placed under a big table, and stayed there until she activated it from her room at midnight.'

Hoskins shook his head. 'She mentioned Ibrahim to me, and showed me his photograph when I searched her room. I just thought they had simply broken up.'

'She said she'd planned her revenge months ago, as soon as Wolf told her Yelena was on the guest list.'

'She's a chef, why didn't she just poison her?'

'I asked that. But as she says, it's too obvious who might have done it, apart from the fact Yelena ate virtually nothing.'

'But Tatiana's such a kind woman,' Hoskins said.

'Perhaps, and she told me she nearly didn't go through with it. She finished her shift two hours before the fireworks and hit the bottle. It was only because she was drunk that she regained the nerve to go through with it. She'd copied the flight plan into the stolen drone days earlier.'

'She adored Volkov,' Hoskins said.

'You heard her say how she bitterly regrets killing him. She was aiming for Yelena, that's what she says. It makes sense, when Volkov got in the way she went for Talin, someone Yelena loved. And Bryn, who said such cruel things about her lover.'

'I noticed she'd been drinking a lot after the killings. I thought it was grief.'

'Well, it was grief. And guilt. She'd probably have confessed off her own bat eventually.'

Hoskins shook his head ruefully.

'She's going down for a long time, Carl. You know that.'

'Yeah, I know,' Hoskins said. 'I now realise she used me, to find out what was going on in the inquiry.'

'Really?'

'Yeah, she always brought me food when I was working, and probably got to see the whiteboards as well. I got too relaxed to bother covering them up every time.'

'She admits trying to break in to the Khazi, too,' Gillard said. 'Well, there's something for all of us to learn in this. You did a Simon Woodbridge, Carl. You got too close.'

Hoskins nodded. 'Yeah, I'll be keeping my distance in future.'

Epilogue

At her Old Bailey trial Tatiana Chumak pleaded guilty to two counts of murder and one of manslaughter for the shootings in the Volkov Library. She was sentenced to life, with deportation back to Ukraine at the end of the minimum twenty-five-year term. As she was taken down, she stared at Carl Hoskins, who was in the public gallery.

Mary Hill's terrorism trial followed a similar course. She made no plea of mitigation and was sentenced to life with a minimum tariff of twenty years, a verdict she took with a ramrod straight back and no discernible expression. She would be ninety-three on expected release. Husband Colin, blinking back tears, said he would stand by her. 'For better, for worse, that's the promise I made back in 1985 when I married Mary,' he told the *Daily Mail* in its front page exclusive. A book deal is hotly anticipated.

Marcus Dolan was jailed for six months for his attack on PC Butterfield. He and Oleg Volkov received five-year suspended sentences for their firearms offences, and were each fined five thousand pounds. Oleg laughed at the fine. He spent more than that on aftershave.

Westgrave Hall is up for sale, price on application. Oleg Volkov entertained a delegation from Steeple Risby who pleaded with him to donate the site to the National Trust, though he has yet to make up his mind. Dr Sophie Cawkwell, who reputedly inherited half a billion pounds from the Volkov will, has put in a bid to buy the library and turn it into a permanent natural history museum, open to the public. She disclosed in a TV interview that she had received over a thousand offers of marriage since news of her fiancé's murder, but has decided to re-marry Paul, her former husband. 'That will make for a stable home environment for little Sasha, who is due in April,' she said. A *Hello!* magazine deal for her story was signed within two days of that revelation.

PC Zoe Butterfield has been making regular visits to hospital to see Wolf. With enough willpower and physio-therapy, the Westgrave Hall security chief is likely to be able to walk again and has floated the idea of buying the Fox and Hounds pub in Steeple Risby with his pay-off from the Volkov organisation. Zoe is considering his offer of marriage.

A month after Anastasia's speedy escape to Moscow, Gillard got the expected letter from Interpol saying that his extradition request had been turned down by the Russian authorities. Moscow passed on copies of documents from Kazakhstan to show that she had been granted diplomatic immunity because of links to her maternal grandfather, the former finance minister.

–

It was three p.m. on New Year's Eve when Gillard made his last trip to Westgrave Hall. Charges had been preferred against the various suspects. The trials were many months in the future, but there were still checks to be made on behalf of the Crown Prosecution Service for any overlooked evidence. Gillard and DS Vikram Singh had thoroughly checked the evidence van, and Gillard had then given him permission to drive it away and go home. He then finished removing the final evidence bags and documentation which had been stored in the Khazi.

He was almost done when he got a call on his mobile from Haldane, the MI5 officer, offering what seemed like a belated apology.

'I'm terribly sorry we got under your feet during the Westgrave Hall murder inquiry. I couldn't tell you very much at the time, but as I think you may have gleaned from the press, we wanted to protect a very useful intelligence asset in Yelena Yalinsky.'

'Why did she ever agree to become an agent for you?'

'We had promised to retrieve for her certain personal tissue she had stored at a Swiss clinic.'

'Her chance to make a baby with Talin. You let her down, didn't you?'

'Unfortunately, someone got there before us. Still, by then we had been getting some prize intelligence for more than a year about the various officials in Moscow and elsewhere that she met. We taught her how to plant listening devices, and of course she could access places we'd never otherwise have a chance of reaching. We're still reaping the benefits.'

'Do you ever feel guilty for using people, Haldane?' Gillard asked.

'Emotions don't help get the job done.'

'Don't tell that to Anastasia,' Gillard said. 'She hated the idea that her mother may have had other children. Do you know where she is, by the way?'

'Yes, she's in Moscow. She hadn't been our principal concern until this morning, when we were alerted to a new and rather unfortunate development, which was my main reason for ringing you.'

'Yes?'

'It's about Simon Woodbridge, the former police constable.'

Haldane's tone was formal, almost reverential. Gillard feared he knew what the news would be.

'He was found dead in Liechtenstein yesterday, having apparently fallen from the fourth floor of a block of luxury flats. The Foreign Office is contacting his next of kin before we release it to the press.'

'That's very sad news,' Gillard said.

'You can't be surprised, surely.'

'I suppose not.' He thanked Haldane and hung up. Satisfied there was no overlooked evidence, he closed down his computer, and turned off the Khazi lights and the noisy fan. He walked out onto the steps, locked up the mobile incident room and then gazed up into the sky. White fluffy flakes of snow were now beginning to fall, blown by a keen wind from the east, perhaps all the way from Russia. He made his way across to his car, started the engine and cleared the windscreen. He reversed out of the parking space, drove down the majestic tree-lined drive and passed through and out of the gates of Westgrave Hall on his way back home.

He did not look in the mirror.

It was the last day of the year, one he would be glad to see the back of. He considered how much he was looking forward to seeing Sam for the New Year's Eve celebration, and to the two-week Caribbean holiday they had planned together afterwards.

As he turned onto the narrow lane, winding out of Steeple Risby, a flurry of snowflakes landed on the windscreen. One, caught on the wiper blade, trembled momentarily before vanishing without leaving a trace.

Acknowledgements

Please don't read this until after you have completed the novel, as there are spoilers.

The creation of The Bodies at Westgrave Hall relied heavily on embedding the plot within the real-life background of the deaths of Russian oligarchs in Britain. For a full and shocking account of all these unsolved killings I leaned on a 2017 BuzzFeed news article, still available online, by Heidi Blake and others: *From Russia with Blood*. For the wider arc of Kremlin politics I can recommend Catherine Belton's excellent and up-to-date history of *Putin's People* published earlier this year.

Westgrave Hall itself does not exist and neither does the village of Steeple Risby. I am as ever grateful to retired detective Kim Booth who guided me on the complexities of dealing with an enormous crime scene, and to Gail and Francis Dymoke for allowing me access to the Scrivelsby estate chapel, on which the chapel at Westgrave Hall is based. I am indebted to Andrew Griffiths, the managing director of Droneflight, for guiding me on the intricacies of these devices. Those who doubt that weapons can effectively be mounted on hobbyist drones can dissolve their scepticism with a quick check on YouTube. Eighteen-year-olds in the United States have already been arrested in possession of them. I'd like to thank the National Ballistics Intelligence Service for their help too, and Irena Lingard for checking Russian names and patronymics. Any mistakes remaining are my own.

Michael Bhaskar and the Canelo team as always were enthusiastic about the book. Miranda Ward did an excellent editing job. I would like to thank my readers circle, Tim Cary and Sara Wescott. Above all is my wife and first reader, Louise, to whom this book is dedicated.

CANELOCRIME

Do you love crime fiction and are always on the lookout
for brilliant authors?

Canelo Crime is home to some of the most exciting
novels around. Thousands of readers are already enjoying
our compulsive stories. Are you ready to find your new
favourite writer?

Find out more and sign up to our newsletter at
canelocrime.com